BIG BAD

LILY ANDERSON

HYPERION

LOS ANGELES

First Edition, September 2022
1 3 5 7 9 10 8 6 4 2
FAC-004510-22203
Printed in the United States of America

This book is set in Albertina/Monotype
Designed by Marci Senders

Library of Congress Cataloging-in-Publication Data
Names: Anderson, Lily, 1988– author.
Title: Big bad / by Lily Anderson.
Description: First edition. • Los Angeles ; New York : Hyperion Avenue, 2022.
• Summary: "Buffy the Vampire Slayer meets Suicide Squad in this dark,
rompy novel in which the show's most beloved villains must team together
to stop the Slayer from ending their world"—Provided by publisher.
Identifiers: LCCN 2021049149 • ISBN 9781368075466 (hardcover) •
ISBN 9781368075695 (ebook)
Subjects: LCGFT: Vampire fiction. • Novels.
Classification: LCC PS3601.N54429 B54 2022 • DDC 813/.6—dc23
LC record available at https://lccn.loc.gov/2021049149

Reinforced binding

Visit www.HyperionAvenueBooks.com

For Laura, my Watcher

"But someone could wish the whole world to be different, right? That's possible?"

"Sure, alternate realities. You could have, like, a world without shrimp. Or with, you know, nothing but shrimp. You could even make, like, a freaky world where Jonathan's, like, some kind of not-perfect mouth-breather, if that's what's blowing up your skirt these days. Just don't ask me to live there."

—*Buffy the Vampire Slayer*, "Superstar"

ONE

Jonathan

Demondale, California

1999

SINCE THE MAYOR had gotten rid of the sun, there was no reason to wait till nightfall to throw a party. Or a demon Ascension. Starting at noon meant that the Trio would have plenty of time to cast their final spell and watch the newest episode of *Doctor Who*. All before Andrew got the ten p.m. sleepies.

In the Docktown district, bass rattled the metal walls of an abandoned warehouse. Strobe lights pulsed their best impression of the *Tron* opening credits, cutting multicolored lines through the cloyingly scented fog-machine smoke.

Filming the proceedings for posterity was aspiring supervillain Jonathan Levinson. Armed with a handheld video camera, he did his best to capture the partygoers' swaying limbs. Dutch angles and quick pans helped obscure their oddly vacant expressions. The crowd wasn't the real focus of the video, anyway. Warren's transformation ritual was.

Jonathan had always been called "short for his age." Although, now that he was nineteen, it seemed like it was going to be a permanent affliction. He had to climb onto a folding chair to get an unobstructed view of the makeshift dais Warren was standing on. Through the zoomed-in camera lens and copious faux fog, you could barely tell that the dais was actually a stack of wooden pallets that Jonathan and Andrew had painted black and inexpertly nailed together. The heavy oak lectern Warren stood behind lent the scene necessary gravitas. Jonathan was glad that Warren had demanded that they use a real pulpit. Andrew had complained that stealing from a church felt wrong, but it wasn't like anyone was going to miss it. Since the congregation of the Eternal Night had arrived, all the human churches had been abandoned. There weren't many humans left in Demondale.

Chanting a stream of Latin, Warren was reading aloud from the last of the Books of Ascension. The five ancient tomes contained dark and complex magical rituals that could transform an ordinary human into a full-blooded demon. One of hell's most powerful. An Old One. More powerful than any of the human-tainted monsters that roamed the earth.

The Trio had spent the last month following the steps detailed in the first four Books of Ascension. Warren had paid tribute to the most powerful demons—some with treasure, some with his own blood. A giant pentagram had been burned into the grass in their backyard when their sacrificial goat had kicked over a candle. And yesterday, Warren had been made impervious to pain after a Book

Four spell involving some ancient Sumerian, a bowl full of tarantulas, and yet more candles. Jonathan and Andrew had a lot of fun testing out his invulnerability, smashing him with various household objects.

Today all those rituals would culminate in Warren's final transformation. Today Jonathan—and Andrew—would have the coolest, strongest best friend in the town formerly known as Sunnydale.

At this point in his Ascension, however, Warren was pretty much still just Warren, except with an elongated torso and a thickening exoskeleton. His gelled hair was still pointing up.

Static buzzed in Jonathan's headset just before Andrew's voice came through. "Breaker, breaker. We've got a stray bumping into the security table."

Climbing off the folding chair, Jonathan turned away from the camera, whispering into his own headset mic, "I thought you were supposed to be guarding the magic stuff."

"Um, no," Andrew said, tone sharp with annoyance. "I'm in charge of turning the pages for Warren and restocking the snacks table."

The partygoers threw their hands overhead as the song changed, jumping up and down to a *Mario Kart* theme remix. Shielding his face with the camera, Jonathan squeezed between their pogoing bodies.

"Who cares about the snacks table? The guests can't eat anything!"

"Okay, but you keep helping yourself to Chex mix whenever you pass the bowl," Andrew scoffed in his ear. "You think it just refills itself?"

"Someone move the damn robot! Now!" Warren's voice growled through the headset. Halfway through the ritual, his growl was significantly growlier than it had been the day before. Enough so that neither Jonathan nor Andrew reminded him that he'd forbidden the R word on the recording. The whole point of throwing an Ascension party was to make themselves look cool. Warren hadn't wanted the world to know that the three of them didn't have enough friends to fill a dance floor without building the crowd by hand. Now, it seemed, he was too far gone to care.

Ever since they had come together as Sunnydale High's inaugural Klingon language club, Warren Mears had been their de facto leader. He'd even named the group, shortening the nickname their peers had given them—the Trio of Losers—to the more streamlined *the Trio*. It was Warren who had first suggested that they look into villainy, inspired by Mayor Wilkins revealing that he was actually an immortal sorcerer with designs on creating Hell on Earth. After the Mayor blocked out the sun with a magical shade that created perpetual midnight, cracked open the Hellmouth hidden under Sunnydale High, and changed the WELCOME TO sign to say DEMONDALE, vampires and demons moved to town in droves. New businesses opened, catering to bloodsuckers and hell spawn.

It was a new era. An evil era. The age of good boys who played nice was over. The time for supervillains had arrived. And the Trio was uniquely positioned to be those supervillains.

Being some of the only humans left in Demondale had its upsides. The job market was hardly competitive—the sunshade scared most people off, clearing the way for Warren to get his dream internship at City Hall. And there was rarely a line at Starbucks because the majority of residents drank blood.

But since the Mayor had declared Demondale the world's first official colony of hell, it had become too clear to the would-be supervillains that they needed more power to stay alive. More and more demons were arriving by the day. Before the sunshade, the only people who got eaten were college kids whose parents never came to check on them. Or anyone stupid enough to walk alone down damp, dark alleys in the former cannery row. Now that the monsters didn't have to wait until sunset to prey on the weak, it was open season on humans.

Which was why Warren had bought the Books of Ascension off a pasty demon named Skyler for five thousand dollars printed off a counterfeiting machine Andrew had designed. Hopefully by the time the demon realized he'd been ripped off, Warren would be the embodiment of Shaak'garar, the primordial Old One whose name translated to something pretty close to "the Scorpion King."

Then Jonathan would finally be safe. No more constantly looking over his shoulder. No more worrying about getting murdered just for going to the grocery store. No more sleeping with a stake under his pillow. He would have real protection. Not just a tableful of magical objects to point and shoot at anyone looking for a quick meal.

Warren had been amassing the items on the security table since high school. Even before the Hellmouth had been officially opened, humans had needed help staying alive in Sunnydale. The artifacts were the Trio's first line of defense. There were weapons for warding off vampires—holy water, a crucifix, a crossbow that shot wooden stakes. There was a corkscrew knife called the Dagger of the Unkillable purported to, well, kill the unkillable. There was weird magical stuff the Trio only sort of understood, mostly purchased from the warlocks downtown—like the clay urn that was bigger on the inside and the Gandalf staff that always pointed itself west. And the pièce de résistance—a shrink-ray prototype Jonathan had made.

The guest disrupting the security table was a brunette girl with lifeless blue eyes. Andrew was pretty gifted with an airbrush, but even he couldn't paint realistic eyes. The robot stared vacantly into the middle distance as she repeatedly bumped into the table as though attempting to walk through it. Each thump made the Gandalf staff roll nearer and nearer to the edge of the table.

"Stop that," Jonathan told the girl, doing his best to shoo her without touching her. Knowing that the robots weren't technically alive didn't make approaching them any less terrifying. The party-bots couldn't talk, but were all the kind of pretty that made Jonathan feel puny and insecure. Warren had not taken his suggestion to create a line of practice girls, ones who were conversant and didn't look like models.

The robot thumped into the table again. The Gandalf staff clattered to the floor and rolled itself toward the west-facing door. Stupid useless prop.

"See what you did?" he scolded the robot. "What if that had been something breakable?"

With an impatient exhale, Jonathan set the video camera on the table next to the ugly clay urn and bent to scoop up the fallen staff. He used the blunt end to tap the robot, very lightly, on the leg.

"Just turn around," he said. "Please?"

Much like a real girl, the robot ignored him. She continued to walk into the table, every step making the artifacts jump again.

Replacing the staff, Jonathan heaved a sigh and reminded himself that the girl was nothing to be afraid of. She, like all the robots, was mostly made of salvaged Furby parts. She wasn't human. She wouldn't scream at him if he touched her with his clammy hands. She didn't have a withering stare or friends to make fun of him with.

He gingerly took her by the forearm.

A Klaxon sounded, replacing the music. The strobe lights' flashes changed to burning red.

Heart in his throat, Jonathan jolted away from the robot girl and cursed into his headset. "Not funny, guys!"

He expected to hear Warren and Andrew snickering in his ear, mocking him for being afraid of offending a robot—they were always teaming up against him; he knew it was because he was the shortest—but instead Andrew's voice came through in a shout.

"Perimeter breach! Perimeter breach! The side door is open!"

Jonathan's breath caught as he imagined any number of Demondale's evils crashing their party. Hungry vampires. Lizard monsters. Skyler the demon wanting the Books of Ascension back.

"It's fine, moron," Warren barked. Jonathan could see him behind the podium, face sweaty and strained as his new scorpion tail lifted above his head. "We practiced for this, remember?"

Practice had been taking turns aiming the bulky shrink ray at various things back at the house. Empty cereal boxes. Laundry piles. The least-prized of their action figures. There were bets on what would shrink or explode. The prototype was pretty much fifty-fifty on results. But either outcome would keep the party from being interrupted.

Hands over his ears to muffle the relentless drone of the Klaxon, Jonathan moved down the table toward the shrink ray. He struggled to hoist the weapon—which was shaped like a giant hair dryer with a glass bowl on the end—under his armpit. For an item created to make other things smaller, the ray gun itself was fairly heavy and hard to hold. The Trio hadn't managed to find a compact power source for it yet either. Jonathan had to unwind the long orange extension cord and search the wall for a power outlet. Having his back to the room, even for a moment, made his hands start to shake. It took him three tries to insert the plug into the socket.

The robots, following their party-protocol, continued to dance to the sounding alarm as Jonathan staggered among them, dragging the extension cord. Sweat prickled his forehead as he swished the shrink ray from side to side, searching for the intruder. Every brush of an arm or flick of synthetic hair made him jump, imagining his own death at the hands—or fangs—of something huge and evil. Vampires had to be invited over the threshold of private residences—but could they break into an abandoned warehouse as easily as the Trio had? Jonathan hated the idea of being bitten. Even if a vampire decided to turn you into one of them, the transformation could make you an unrepentant douche canoe. Like Andrew's older brother, Tucker, who, since becoming a vamp, refused to speak to anyone he'd known in his breathing life.

"Do you guys see anything?" Jonathan whispered into his headset.

"There!" Andrew said.

Jonathan strained to see Andrew across the warehouse. The fake fog swirled in the red strobe lights, literally clouding his view. "Where? I can't see where you're pointing!"

"Twelve o'clock! I mean, my twelve, your six!"

Turning around, Jonathan watched as someone—or something—cut through the crowd, knocking over robots. Even in piles on the dance floor, Warren's creations continued to sway and gyrate.

If the intruder turned out to be Andrew and Warren pulling another prank on him, Jonathan was going to be so pissed. Maybe not pissed enough to actually confront them, but he would definitely consider turning the shrink ray on their nearly completed LEGO

Death Star. That would show them. He was tired of being ganged up on. He was tired of being scared all the time.

Lugging the shrink ray, Jonathan hurried back the way he came. He apologized under his breath to the fallen party-bots as the trailing extension cord snaked over their bodies.

A blond girl in a white tank top was sitting on the security table. In one hand, she held the Gandalf staff. In the other was a jagged crystal Jonathan didn't recognize as part of the Trio's inventory. It looked like Kryptonite, glowing so strongly that it cast green light on the girl's fingertips. None of the robots had ever attempted to pick up any of the artifacts before. This was a bad time for them to start.

"Hey," he said, straining to keep hold of the shrink ray as he switched it from his right side to his left. "Put those down. They're important."

The blond girl cocked her head, looking at him shrewdly through narrowed green eyes.

"Oh," she said, tone flat with disdain. She twisted the Kryptonite crystal into the top of the Gandalf staff, fashioning together the gaudiest and most canon-clashing accessory Jonathan had ever seen. "You must be the nerd."

Jonathan blinked in surprise. Only the most advanced of Warren's robots had the ability to talk—programming them was wildly time-consuming. In building an entire crowd of party-bots, the Trio's main concern had been in creating a variety of heights and hair colors for believability on-screen.

"I didn't think we brought any of the T-1000s with us," Jonathan said into the headset.

"We didn't," Andrew whimpered.

"Shoot her!" Warren roared.

Jonathan pulled the trigger. A jet of blue-white light crackled out of the bowl of the shrink ray. The blond girl hopped down from the table and kicked, her leg coming up in an arc that knocked the gun—and Jonathan—aside. As Jonathan fell, the sizzle of shrinking light blasted through the crowd, exploding through party-bots. On the snacks table, the Chex mix erupted, raining down pretzels and rice cereal.

Before Jonathan could regain his balance, the shrink ray's light continued to burn, eating through the Books of Ascension, the stolen podium, and, finally, Warren. One moment Warren was speaking in Latin. The next, the blue-white light hit him square in the chest, lighting his new half-scorpion skeleton from within. He didn't have time to react before his body burst. Gore and goo splattered in every direction.

In the headset, Andrew screamed.

Horror turned Jonathan's blood to ice. The shrink ray fell out of his numb fingers and clattered to the ground. His brain immediately started running a series of calculations as to how the last two minutes could be undone—reversing the rotation of the earth to turn back time or getting access to a TARDIS or forcing himself to wake up from what was surely just a nightmare. Regardless of the how, what he knew for certain was that Warren couldn't stay dead. Jonathan—and Andrew—needed Warren. Without him, how would they take over the world? How would they walk the streets of Demondale uneaten? Who would kill the spiders that got into their lair?

Unbothered by the carnage, the blond girl scooped all the artifacts on the security table into the open mouth of an unzipped backpack. Andrew's backpack.

"Thanks for the party favors," she said. When she knocked the staff twice against the dance floor, a portal of swirling purple nothingness opened directly in front of her.

Jonathan heard his name being shouted through the headset. He glimpsed Andrew climbing up the dais, stepping awkwardly around the pile of yuck that had once been their friend.

When he turned back, the blond girl already had one foot inside the portal.

"Wait!" Jonathan called after her. Even though, if he thought about it, he didn't really want her to wait. He just wanted to know who she was and why she had appeared only to steal their magical objects and make him kill one of his only friends.

The girl looked over her shoulder at him. She gave a halfhearted shrug. "Later, nerds," she said. And then she leaped into the darkness. The portal swallowed her whole and closed up, leaving no trace of itself behind.

Jonathan stood, stunned. The blaring alarm sounded far away. As did the whirring gears of the party-bots struggling to dance on their backs, like so many fallen turtles. It was only fear that the blond girl could come back and karate-chop him to death that spurred him into action.

He ran up to the dais, dragging a weeping, blood-splattered Andrew away from the charred remains of the Books of Ascension.

"We need to get out of here," Jonathan said, holding down the headset button out of habit. "Turn off the alarm, grab the laptop, and let's go."

Andrew wiped his nose on the back of his wrist, glaring down at Jonathan. "Who made you the leader?"

Jonathan gulped, looking down at the floor of the dais. Teeth and bone shards mixed in a horrible white confetti. "We don't have a leader anymore. It's just the two of us. I don't want to stand here in a room covered in blood, do you?"

Andrew's jaw trembled, but he shook his head, crunching his way over to the computer set up behind the dais. After a few keystrokes, the alarm finally stopped. As did the dancing party-bots. Suddenly the warehouse was full of resounding silence. It just felt like an abandoned building again, although now it was an abandoned building that smelled like vampire bait.

Jonathan found Warren's messenger bag underneath the snacks table, untouched by any of the nearby mess. He stashed the video camera inside and, after a moment's hesitation, the shrink ray. Touching the murder weapon made him queasy, but he couldn't leave behind their only prototype. What if it fell into the wrong hands? What if they needed to shrink something within easy reach of a power outlet?

He met Andrew at the door, standing open after the blond girl's mysterious appearance. Outside was fully dark, of course, but Jonathan's watch said it was only quarter to one in the afternoon. Times like this, he missed the sun. Running through the pitch-dark of Docktown felt like jumping out of the frying pan and into the fire. Less than two hours ago, he, Andrew, and Warren had talked about leaving the warehouse under the protection of an Old One, all of them finally free of the feeling that they were prey in their hometown.

Now, not only did they not have an ancient demon to protect them, they didn't even have Warren.

Or, it turned out, the keys to their van.

"We can fix this," Andrew panted as they ran out of Docktown. "We can bring Warren back!"

"Back from the dead?" Jonathan asked. "We can't command-Z life!"

"*We* can't," Andrew said. "But I know someone who can. We just have to buy a Wish."

Who the heck was that? Jonathan wondered, picturing the blond girl disappearing through the portal. *And how did she know we're nerds?*

TWO
Anya

ANYA JENKINS SPANKED the side of the blender, coaxing a chunky purple smoothie into a tall plastic cup. She slapped a lid on top and called, "Kitten-kidney smoothie for..." She squinted at the black ink scrawl on the side. Human-Mike couldn't spell demon names for shit, even though they were largely phonetic. "Bwomreon?"

A male M'Fashnik demon in a gray hoodie sidled over to the counter. Lizardy in the face with cranial crests that gave the impression of swept-back hair, the demon pulled back his green lips in a pointy-toothed sneer. He said, "It's pronounced..." and then made a noise like a foghorn being run over by a semitruck. "Spelled just like it sounds. Idiot."

He grabbed the smoothie and strode out of the juicery.

"It's okay," said Human-Mike at the cash register. He wore the same Best Pressed Juicery uniform visor and apron as Anya, although his were both adorned with MANAGER ON DUTY flair pins. "He didn't even tip. Demons never do."

"That's because it's a stupid earth custom," Anya shot back, offended. She considered sticking both of Human-Mike's MOD pins into his eyes. Demon-Mike never spewed casual prejudice, not even against the puny human manager who shared his name. "In hell, everyone makes a living wage and doesn't have to beg for customers' change."

Not that Anya didn't enjoy getting money from customers. She liked money. Capitalism was one of humanity's better ideas. But she had to stick up for her demon brethren. Just because she looked human didn't mean that she identified as one.

Since Anya had moved topside, the few humans she encountered thought they could announce their antidemon bigotry to her. Sure, she'd been born human. But that was over a thousand years ago. Eleven and a half centuries as a vengeance demon put her more on the side of the monsters. Even if she herself was just a part-time demon now, six months into her sabbatical from Vengeance LLC.

Anya had always been a good vengeance demon. Great, even. She'd found a decent niche enacting the Wishes of heartbroken women. The phrase *Hell hath no fury like a woman scorned?* Anya was that fury, sent from Arashmaharr, the hell dimension where Vengeance's headquarters were located. For most of her long life, she'd only come to earth long enough to curse some cheating spouse. She'd cover them in weeping boils or ship them off to a brand-new pocket dimension full of endless torments. Then she'd head back to her condo in Arashmaharr and wait for her talisman to ring. It was a decent life. But it just didn't thrill her the way it had back in the early days.

Facing down the dawn of another millennium, Anya had found herself wondering whether or not she wanted to spend another thousand years doing the same job. Another thousand years of competing for raises against Halfrek, who was always granting Wishes that would end in chaos, wars, and apocalypses. The sort of pandemonium that the gods of Arashmaharr totally ate up. How could Anya compare with someone who refused to specialize in one type of Wish? No matter how often her boss assured her that she and Halfrek had different strengths, she knew that she was second best. Despite being centuries younger than Anya, Halfrek lived in the penthouse of Anya's condominium building and had an unobstructed view of Arashmaharr's famous lava falls. And she wasn't even there most of the time! Halfrek camped out on a job, living in different realities until she found the perfect Wisher. Anya didn't have that drive. Not anymore.

She had found herself tired of the office politics. And tired of the office. The new Vengeance LLC receptionist was fresh out of school and so ridiculously chatty. If Anya didn't know better, she would have assumed the girl was a vampire whose lungs were purely decorative. Anya couldn't even pop into the office to turn in a time sheet without getting stuck in an hour-long conversation about every change in the weather or rumors about interdemon feuds. If Anya had to hear one more story about Lloyd and Balash's prank war or how someone kept stealing Frex's lunch out of the break room, she would scream. Or send the receptionist to an empty pocket dimension where she couldn't bother anyone.

Instead, Anya had requested a sabbatical. She wasn't prepared to quit. She didn't know how to live without her powers. But she wanted time to try something new. Something human-ish.

Earth on the threshold of the twenty-first century was completely different than the world she had been born into. The mortality rate was much lower. Medicine was based on science rather than balancing humors. Bathing was encouraged. It was as good a time as any to experience the fullness of the human life she'd once abandoned, without having to actually live solely among humans. There were more possibilities for demons ever since Mayor Richard Wilkins had won his Sun Is Out, Sin Is In campaign.

At the entrance of town, just under the lip of the sunshade, there was a huge sign that read DEMONDALE: WELCOME TO THE HELLMOUTH. Seeing it made Anya realize that she'd never felt more at home. This was truly a town for her. Hell on Earth. The best of above and below. Pizza and demons. Evil and cable television. Money and things worth spending it on.

Eternal darkness suited her. Her human skin was prone to sunburn. And vampires were the best tippers at Best Pressed—not that she'd ever admit that in front of Human-Mike. Say what you wanted about the living dead, they had their own generational wealth and they were not stingy with it. Especially since the juicery had started offering nutritional boosts in their blood smoothies. Turns out most vamps were low on vitamin D.

But even with her pockets fat with tips, she was beginning to worry that she had traded one listless existence for another. She got up, counted her money, went to work, and came home. The same on earth as in hell.

Except on earth, with its oppressive gravity and linear time stream, she was susceptible to aging. She could practically feel her skin losing elasticity. She looked very nearly twenty now. Maybe it was time to throw in the towel and give the whole topside experiment up as an identity crisis. She could give her two weeks' notice, murder Human-Mike, and take the first portal back to Arashmaharr. Her condo was sublet for another six months, but she could probably sleep in her cubicle for a while and call it dedication. Or she could try to pull a Halfrek and go live on assignment.

The juicery's glass front door banged open. Two huddled, bloodied bodies tumbled inside. Human-Mike shrieked when he saw the bloody footprints on the pristine lobby floor and darted into the back room for a mop. It took a moment for Anya to recognize the blood-covered people. One was her off-duty coworker Andrew. The other was the littler of his two friends, the one whose hair went down instead of up.

"Ugh," Anya groaned, peering out the window toward the dark sky. "Is it raining blood already? The weatherman said it wouldn't hit until Friday, but I knew that good-for-nothing was lying again...."

"It's not rain." Andrew gasped for air as he slammed his reddened forearms on the handoff counter. Beneath the gore, he was looking particularly pale, even for Andrew, which was saying something. Normally the buggy-eyed human boy was as pale as the bleach streaks in his hair. Now he looked like he'd seen a ghost. Ghosts were still pretty rare, even in hell's first colony on earth. "Anya, we need your help."

Anya eyed him warily. "I'm not interested in picking up any more of your shifts, Andrew. You said you were going to be too busy to come in today and yet here you are, bleeding all over the place and flaunting your freedom."

"It's not—" The shorter boy choked down a breath. His bag clattered to the floor. "It's not our blood."

"That's why we need your help," Andrew told her. He clasped his hands into a pleading prayer position. "Jonathan and I need a Wish."

This caught Anya's attention. She hadn't done much vengeance magic since moving to California. She had the ability, but there weren't many spurned exes living in Demondale in need of revenge. Under the sunshade, if you wanted to get even with an ex, you just pointed the nearest hungry monster at them and then *bye-bye, bad boyfriend.*

So, on occasion, she'd grant a Wish outside of her usual purview. For a little extra cash. Or a lot of extra cash. Depending on how she was feeling and what kind of rube she was dealing with. She had bills to pay, and even with tips, working for the juicery wasn't terribly lucrative. Sometimes—mostly when she was stuck on shift with Human-Mike—she fantasized about getting a different job. Something that wouldn't require a uniform or smelling like animal blood all day. Something sexy. Like being a bank teller or an accountant. But it was hard to find a position when you couldn't promise how long you were planning on living on earth.

"What kind of Wish?" she asked. It was in her best interest to keep her vengeance skills spry. She couldn't waltz back into Vengeance LLC with rusty magic.

Andrew and Jonathan launched into a story about a demon Ascension gone awry—something about a girl and a warehouse and a misplaced blast of energy that had gone *kapow* instead of *kablooey.* Or maybe the other way around. Anya was only ever half-sure what Andrew was talking about. All of his pop-culture references were so irritatingly recent. And they seemingly always revolved around media set in outer space. Just once she'd like a nice ninth-century joke, something she could relate to. Like the increasing price of ale. Or the wonder of the rotary grindstone.

"And then the girl took the Kryptonite and the staff and went through this portal—" the shorter boy, Jonathan, was saying.

"So, you'd like me to what?" Anya interrupted, growing bored with the story. She hated when people turned a Wish into an excuse to recite their whole autobiography. She was interested in vengeance, not tedious backstory. "I could make it so she was never born. Or turn her into a dog? I used to do this great thing where I turned someone fully inside out but kept them alive. It's sort of like a full-body paper cut. Apparently, the wind on your spinal cord stings like the dickens."

"Ew!" Andrew recoiled from her. "No! That sounds awful. We don't want revenge on the girl. We don't even know her."

Confused, Anya said, "But you said it was her fault that the stink ray—"

"Shrink ray," Jonathan said.

"Does it matter if it didn't work?" Anya asked, brushing off the correction. "You said it was her fault that you ended up aiming it at your friend."

"Well, yeah," Andrew said. "But we just want Warren back."

"Okay," Anya said, in an unsure singsong. If it had been *her* friend who got exploded by some random blond, she would definitely want true vengeance, not a happily-ever-after pocket universe to live in. But, hey, maybe that was why she didn't have any friends. "Obviously, since this isn't my standard ex-boyfriend revenge deal, this will cost you."

"How much?" Jonathan asked at the same time Andrew said, "Anything!"

Anya smiled. She loved when negotiations were this easy. "Let's say a bucket of money." She inclined her head toward Human-Mike, who was shuffling out of the back room, balancing a WET FLOOR sign, a mop, and a bucket. "Hey, Mike, how much money do you think you could fit into that mop bucket?"

Human-Mike lifted the bill of his visor and scratched his forehead. "Well, this bucket holds about nine gallons of water, so—"

"Perfect," Anya said. She held her hand out to Andrew. "Nine gallons of money, please."

"Actually, gallons are a measurement of liquid," Jonathan said.

"Liquid assets are acceptable," Anya said.

"Here." Andrew retrieved the wallet from his back pocket and fished out a handful of cash and credit cards. Jonathan divested his wallet of its contents, too. Andrew slid the collection of currency across the counter. "Is this enough to start?"

"Looks good to me," Anya said. She slipped the wad into the pocket of her apron. Cracking her knuckles and stretching her neck from side to side, she warmed up for some old-fashioned Wish-granting. She even pulled her green Marnoxon amulet out of the collar of her shirt, even though it would work just as well covered up. She couldn't help but lean into the showmanship. She so rarely got to show off in her new life as a juicery crew member. When she'd left Arashmaharr, she hadn't considered how boring it would be to live a mostly non-magical existence. Grinding sheep hearts and chicken gizzards didn't have the same pizzazz as creating entirely new universes out of thin air. No wonder people thought she was just a boring old human.

"Now, I assume you're familiar with what we call the 'genie rules'?" she asked the boys.

"You can't make anyone fall in love with us?" Jonathan asked.

"What? Of course I could," Anya harrumphed, insulted at the thought. "I could make a goat fall in love with a tiger if I wanted to build an entire universe around it. No, the genie rules are: You have to say the words 'I wish' for it to count, and you can't wish for more Wishes. It's cheating. And it's cheap. You're paying per Wish."

"Got it," Andrew said, wringing his blood-drenched hands. He glanced sidelong at his friend. "Ready?"

Jonathan bit his lip and nodded.

Andrew took a deep breath, counting to three on his fingers before he and Jonathan said in unison, "I wish Warren wasn't dead."

Anya took a dramatic step backward, her palms spread wide as her skin shriveled into its demon form, revealing the red tendons of her demon face. "Wish grant—"

"Oh, hey, Anya, could you refill the bat-blood Cambro? We're getting low after the lunch rush," Human-Mike said, slopping his wet mop over the footprints in the entryway. The sudsy water turned pink as he wrung out the mop into the yellow bucket.

"Not now, Mike!" Anya said, her voice deepened to its most threatening demonic rumble. She blew out an annoyed sigh and tilted her head apologetically at Andrew and Jonathan. "Dang it. Now we have to start over. Would you guys mind wishing again?"

The two boys obliged, albeit with slightly less oomph than the first time.

"Wish granted," Anya intoned with all the gravitas she could muster while wearing an indoor visor. She thought about taking it off but didn't want to get yet another lecture from Human-Mike on maintaining a professional appearance behind the counter.

She waited for her amulet to glow, imbuing her with the full might of Arashmaharr. But it didn't happen. Searching inside herself for the feeling of power and connectedness that she usually felt in her demon form, Anya found nothing.

She still felt human. Just wrinkly and human. The worst of both worlds.

Her face heating up with an embarrassed flush, she cleared her throat and tried again. "Wish granted!"

And again, she felt nothing. No wellspring of unlimited creation. Not even a hiccup of power. Complex Wishes like bringing someone back from the dead meant creating a pocket dimension where the killing blow had never happened. Normally when Anya set out to create a new Wishverse, her magic became linked to the ever-expanding infinite schema of timelines and universes. She should have been able to sense all the other worlds created by vengeance demons. Worlds where losers were heroes, the dead lived, where only famous people worked in coffee shops and constantly fell in love with their customers.

She couldn't even sense the world without shrimp.

Something was definitely wrong.

Andrew shifted his weight uneasily from foot to foot while Jonathan skittered out of the way of Human-Mike's passive-aggressive mopping.

Anya gripped her amulet between her thumb and forefinger. It was cold to the touch and refused to glow, no matter how much she mentally begged it to connect her to its Creation magic.

"This almost never happens," she said, flinching a sheepish smile at the boys. "Unless the Powers That Be have a particular reason for not wanting someone to stay dead. Your friend wasn't politically important, was he?"

"He was an intern at City Hall," Andrew said.

"So, no," Jonathan said.

"He was really good at building robots," Andrew said. "Do you think that they want him to stay dead so he won't accidentally create Skynet?"

"I knew we shouldn't have called the party-bots T-800s!" Jonathan said, stamping his foot. Blood splattered out of his canvas sneakers. "Even as a joke, I knew we were tempting fate!"

"Oh, this is your friend who makes the femme-bots?" Anya said. She had a vague recollection of Andrew talking ad nauseam about the genius of his friend turning some old toy parts into automaton girlfriends. Anya had been fairly disgusted by the idea of women created only to "party" with Andrew's little gang and had stopped listening in favor of wondering if she could honor the vengeance Wish of a robot against its creator. She supposed if Warren stayed dead, she'd never get to find out. Heaving a sigh, she said, "This glitch is probably just a paperwork thing. I haven't been into the office since I moved to earth. Let me call my supervisor real quick."

Andrew turned around and started to call out to Human-Mike before Anya cut him off.

"No, God, not him. My real supervisor."

She pulled a second necklace out of her collar. This one had a much smaller jewel and had been given to her eleven hundred years ago during her brief human life. She curled her hand around the talisman and cried out, "Blessed be the name of D'Hoffryn!"

After a moment's pause, there was a crackle of indoor lightning that made Human-Mike spill his dirty mop water. Andrew and Jonathan yipped, jumping out of the way.

A deep voice boomed, "Behold D'Hoffryn, lord of Arashmaharr! He that turns the air to blood and rains death upon—*ahem*. A little help, if you please?"

Anya peered over the counter. Her longtime boss, D'Hoffryn, the master of all vengeance demons, had materialized as a disembodied blue head on the floor between Jonathan's feet. The boy's eyes bulged as he staggered backward.

"Get that thing off my floor!" Human-Mike cried, backing away from the soapy puddle he'd made.

"Andrew, pick him up," Anya said, flapping a hand at what was left of D'Hoffryn. "He's one of the Lower Beings of hell, for God's sake. Show some respect."

"He's pretty low right now," Jonathan said.

Andrew reached down, both of his hands shaking as he lifted D'Hoffryn's spiky blue head and set it on the handoff counter between him and Anya.

"Anyanka," D'Hoffryn said. Andrew's hands had left smears of dark blood on the Lower Being's cheeks. His goatlike beard brushed the counter as he spoke. "I'm glad you called. As you can see, there's been trouble in Arashmaharr."

"What happened to your body?" Anya asked with what could have been considered a shriek. D'Hoffryn was usually over six feet tall and sturdily built under a brown velvet robe he'd been wearing since the dawn of time. Seeing him without limbs was perturbing.

D'Hoffryn side-eyed Andrew and Jonathan. "Who are these mortals?"

"Coworkers," Anya said. "They're harmless."

"*Mostly* harmless," Andrew said under his breath. For some reason, this made him and Jonathan snicker.

D'Hoffryn glared at them for a moment before his gaze slid back to Anya. "My body was cleaved in twain."

"Cleaved?" Anya asked. "By whom? Or what?"

Anya didn't know of anyone who would dare attack one of the Lower Beings. Outranked in hell only by the primordial Old Ones, the Lower Beings had their own magic beyond what was granted to the vengeance demons by their connection to the Marnoxon gem. D'Hoffryn could teleport and fly and shoot fire out of his hands—when he had hands.

"Yesterday," D'Hoffryn said with a weary sigh, "a slayer gained entry into Arashmaharr—"

"Who left a talisman where a slayer could get to it?" Anya asked, aghast at the thought.

"Lloyd, we believe. He was found dead here in Demondale, his amulet missing," D'Hoffryn said. A chill ran up Anya's back as she pictured a fellow vengeance demon murdered in the town where she lived. Lloyd wasn't some soft-skinned former human, either. He'd been an Asphyx demon with shoulders sharp as pikes. "His talisman brought the slayer directly to the office. She was wielding an ax twice her size and slaughtered everyone that came between her and the Marnoxon gem. There are very few survivors. Only those of us with magic of our own are even able to leave the scene."

Horrified, Anya pictured the vast hallways of Vengeance LLC, terrorized by a mythical vampire hunter. She imagined the cubicles splattered with blood, her coworkers for the last millennium hacked to pieces. If Anya hadn't taken her sabbatical, she would have been one of them. Instead of blending smoothies, she would have been murdered by a slayer.

Had there been any survivors? Halfrek? Frex? Balash? The gods? The chatty receptionist?

Ugh. Anya wasn't sure she wanted to live in a universe where that girl lived but Lloyd didn't. Even with his penchant for pranks, Lloyd had been a good demon. He always brought everyone in the office topside souvenirs when he returned from a long mission. He used to leave earth coins on Anya's desk because he knew she collected money.

"Excuse me, sorry," Jonathan said. "What's a slayer?"

"The bogeyman for vampires. When they're bad, the Powers That Be send the slayer to stake them," Anya said distractedly. She had heard rumors of slayers before, but never actually seen one. Until this moment, she'd assumed it was just what vamps called any human strong enough to kill more than one of the undead. "Why would a slayer want the Marnoxon gem?"

The gem was the most precious item in Arashmaharr, if not in all of hell's many dimensions. Housed in the deepest bowels of Vengeance LLC, it was guarded at all times by no fewer than five armed demons. Anya herself had only glimpsed it on her very first walk-through of the office when D'Hoffryn had cut a sliver of it to make her amulet.

"What's a Marnoxon gem?" Andrew asked.

"And does it look like a piece of Kryptonite?" Jonathan asked.

"Is that another space reference?" Anya asked, annoyed.

"Technically," Andrew said, shoulders coming up to his ears. "Krypton is the planet Superman is from. Kryptonite is a green rock. I mean, it comes in a lot of colors, but the classic—"

D'Hoffryn cut him off. "The Marnoxon is a large green gem. A piece of Creation." He did his best to nod toward Anya, but accidentally slid himself toward the edge of the counter. Anya nudged him back to safety as he continued, "Anyanka wears a piece of it around her neck, as do all vengeance demons. It is what allows them to create and destroy as a Wish dictates. Without it, Vengeance LLC and all in its employ are powerless."

"Which means, without it, I can't bring your friend back to life," Anya told Andrew and Jonathan. Her head swam as she imagined being stuck on earth, completely powerless. No extra vengeance money. No superstrength. Would she age at an accelerated rate? Her immortality was directly tied to her contract with Vengeance LLC. Was that a wrinkle she felt forming on her forehead? No, she was being ridiculous. She could still transform into her demon self. She just didn't have any magic. "We need to get that gem back."

"So," Andrew said, wringing his bloody hands. "We need to find someone who knows how to stop a slayer?"

THE SLAYER

OUT OF THE spiraling dark falls the Slayer. The staff in her hand towers over her, the glow of the green gem illuminating the night. From one darkness to another. Of course.

If the whiny little British man she beat up at the magic store was right, then the staff can only point her toward the most malevolent places on earth. Something about the spell cast on it constantly searching for the closest pinnacle of evil. Which means that—combined with the magical portal-creating gem that she filched from Vengeance LLC—it should have no trouble taking her on a tour of hells on earth.

She takes a moment to close her eyes and wait for the new world to stop spinning. It's official. She hates portal travel. This ride was as vertigo-inducing as the one that first landed her in Demondale. Hopefully this doesn't mean she's jumped forward in time again. Demondale is a full two years ahead of where she started.

Although she'll take queasy-twirly portals and time-jumps over talismans to hell anytime. Even after she'd been trapped in Demondale, seeing the vengeance-demon dimension had been horrific. The moment she had landed outside of Vengeance LLC, she had learned there is a big difference between a colony of hell and an actual hell dimension. Demondale might be full of monsters, corruption, and unnatural nighttime, but it was still on earth.

Arashmaharr, on the other hand, was definitively *not* earth. It was somewhere with burning skies, sulfurous stink, and throngs of demons wearing business casual. Truly horrifying.

Opening her eyes, nothing jumps out at her as indisputably hellish. Unlike the world under the sunshade, this version of Sunnydale still has the ability to grow plants. The Slayer leans down and runs her hands through the grass, delighting in its prickly softness. In Demondale, most of the parks and lawns have been replaced with Astroturf. One of the many reasons she wants to destroy it.

But first, she needs to make sure her intel is correct. If this gem can really end Hell on Earth, then there's a chance she can send herself back. Inside the portal, she saw all the evil Sunnydales, dozens of entry points all leading to something rotten. One of them has to be the hellmouth she calls home.

After a month trapped in Demondale, this is the Slayer's first flicker of hope.

Once there are no dimensions more evil than her own Sunnydale, the green gem will have no choice but to point her back to *her* Sunnydale.

She just has to clear out any dimension with an open hellmouth and a Black Flame flag. The only thing she wants more than a way home is to bring an end to Hell on Earth.

Because if being stuck in Demondale has taught her anything, it's that hell doesn't belong on earth.

This first stop on her apocalypse tour doesn't look particularly bad. There are no demons parading down the street. The streetlamps shine down on parked cars that don't seem abandoned. Nothing screams *Hey, look, I'm evil*, except for the colonialist-glorifying Spanish-revival architecture of City Hall and the public library. But those are the same in her own Sunnydale.

She shifts the weight of the backpack she filled with the magical crap from the demon Ascension. Should she have just taken a stake and left the rest? She's not sure what most of these things do. She hopes that some of them will come in handy during her quest. And, if not, at least she has them and the nerd boys don't. Guys who would accidentally murder one another in the middle of the day while playing terrible techno *so* cannot be trusted with a giant corkscrew knife covered in runes.

Besides, she's left her ax behind in Arashmaharr, stuck in the skull of the last demon who'd been guarding the gem. She'd been totally hurting for weapons. And if a stake-shooting crossbow isn't her Chosen One birthright, then what is?

Walking past buildings that in Demondale are all Mayor Wilkins's campaign offices—here, a post office, a bank, and a bail bonds company—the magical staff jerks hard to the left, nearly knocking the Slayer out of her sneakers. She comes to a stop in front of a small innocuous building. The sign out front reads SMILEYDALE PUBLIC ACCESS. The Slayer frowns.

Smileydale. That's a new one. Definitely not what big tough demons would name a town.

The staff seems to vibrate with excitement, aiming the big green gem on the top toward the building's front door, like a dog begging to go for a walk. When the warlock in downtown Demondale had first told her about the magical dowsing rod, he had made it sound so much cooler than this overeager wooden stick. The Slayer had pictured something more sleek and subtle. Portable. Efficient. Fits in a pocket. Which, okay, might just be describing a stake. But why mess with a perfect weapon? This giant, cumbersome walking stick is hideous *and* bossy. Adding the Creation gem made it lethal but has not helped its appearance. Honestly, if she weren't already planning on ending every evil world the staff led her to, she'd have to unplug them from reality just so there'd be no witnesses to her holding such an ugly accessory.

She stole the Creation gem in hopes that it would be her direct ticket home. The first two vengeance demons she had interrogated in Demondale had used their glowing green amulets to teleport away from her before she could get any real information out of them. It was clear that the amulets were the source of their powers. Of the magic that had ruined the Slayer's life. In the month since she was ejected from her own reality, she has relentlessly hunted vengeance demons. For information. For revenge.

Unfortunately, vengeance demons can be from any humanoid or demonic species, all different shapes and sizes, united only by their awful Wish magic. Taking one of the amulets for herself only gave the Slayer enough power to portal to and from Vengeance LLC. She went in armed, cut her way to the Creation gem, and wished to teleport home. But once she'd jumped into the portal, it had spat her back into Demondale. The gem doesn't seem to be able to tell one Sunnydale from another.

So, here she is, knee-deep in plan B. Take the wizard staff that sniffs out hellmouths from the nerds, attach the gem, and blow up every reality that stands between her and home.

Providing that the British man hasn't lied to her. He's a little weasel. Just because he works with Giles doesn't make him trustworthy. It's not *her* Giles he knows—it's Demondale Giles. The real Giles wouldn't be caught dead going by something as casual and tawdry as a nickname.

After she slips inside the public-access building, the door closes behind her with a heavy *thunk*. The office is small and poorly lit. She's grateful for the light from the Creation gem; its internal glow is brighter than the yellowed fluorescents overhead.

No one sits behind the front desk. Brown dust crusts the buttons of the multiline phone and the keys of the computer keyboard. The Slayer isn't super proficient in technology—in her normal life back in the *real* Sunnydale, she leaves computer stuff to her friend Willow—but even she can tell that the computer isn't old. Just disused.

Moving deeper into the building, the Slayer tiptoes past more empty desks and unattended sound equipment. She squints to see through the beige blinds of the individual offices. The door to the break room stands open, revealing a refrigerator that's warm, its power cord curled neatly behind a water cooler with a full jug covered in cobwebs. Everything looks as though it's been abandoned for months.

But if it's abandoned, why was the front door unlocked? Anyone could walk in off the street and steal any of the computers.

So why are they all untouched?

At the end of the hallway, a single red light glows above a sign that reads ON AIR. Below it is a door that says SMILE TIME STUDIO. The staff knocks itself against the doorknob.

Slipping inside, the Slayer recoils as she's faced with burning-bright stage lights. As her eyes adjust, she can make out the shadows of TV cameras aimed at a set of eye-watering primary colors. It looks like a day-care toy chest blown up in size and scope. Giant alphabet blocks and massive teddy bears frame the set, but the TV cameras are all aimed at a fake tree house with puppets dancing in front of it, singing a song about the importance of building confidence.

"That's right, kids." A puppet with a shock of red hair sticking out through the snapback of a tiny baseball hat dances up to the TV camera, pressing his face close to the lens. "Get real close, that's it. Put your hands on the screen. We'll play patty-cake together."

Shimmering purple light flows out of the camera and into the red-haired puppet's hands. The puppet shudders and groans, a sound that is wholly disconcerting coming out of a children's entertainer.

The purple light crawls across the set, filling each of the other puppets, who continue to sing and dance. Word by word their song shifts from being about confidence to a series of Latin phrases the Slayer doesn't know.

What she does know is that nothing good is ever sung in Latin. It's some kind of magical spell, drawing the purple light out of the TV camera. Out of whoever is watching this puppet show.

Looking around the room, the Slayer realizes that there are no people here. Just like the offices in the front of the building. The director's chair is empty.

There are no cameramen.

There are no puppeteers.

"No way. Puppets?" the Slayer snorts, talking as much to the glowing green staff as to herself. Is it possible for a magical item to make a mistake?

She's fought a lot of evil in her time, but never anything made of felt. A ventriloquist's dummy once, but that was a misunderstanding. Still, she knows that puppets don't sing and dance on their own without some kind of magic and, honestly, anyone magically controlling puppets has got to be evil.

Next to what looks like McDonald's Grimace with a plastic trumpet for a mouth, a female puppet with daisies sewn into her pigtails stops dancing. Tiny furious eyebrows appear on her face, drawing together into a scowl.

"Who the hell are you?" she asks. Inside her mouth is a half circle of fabric someone cut to be a tongue. "This is a hot set, missy!"

"You're this dimension's Big Bads?" the Slayer asks the puppets, feeling more than a little ridiculous. It makes her think of being a kid, talking to Big Bird through the TV like he could hear her.

"You bet your ass, sweetie," says the puppet in the hat. He shoves himself away from the TV camera, leaving the purple light to float freely around the room. "What are you gonna do about it?"

"I guess I'm going to Fraggle Rock your ass," the Slayer says lightly. She's not bragging, just stating a fact. She takes a step forward, and the staff lurches away from the leader puppet's red hair and toward the cameras. In front of the director's chair, there is a small monitor. At first glance, it seems to be turned off. Until the Slayer notices the movement of a black flame dancing behind the glass. What was it that the spiky-shouldered vengeance demon had called it? Hell's

Own Herald. The Black Flame flag. The mark of an evil province. The Slayer allows herself a small, self-satisfied smile. "Actually, I'm going to end you and everything you've ever known."

That's a bit of a brag, she has to admit.

The red-haired puppet boy launches himself at her, his tiny woolen fists pummeling her face while the pigtailed one kicks repeatedly at her shins. It feels like being hit over and over again with a Nerf bat—not painful as much as distracting. And annoying.

The other puppets stop singing their Latin curse to join the attack. A brown dog who looks like a drowned version of Rolf the Muppet climbs her backpack, pulling at her ponytail. She rips it down and uses its body to smash the pigtailed one off her leg. Kicking the Grimace-thing in the chest sends the purple puppet crashing backward into the ABC blocks. It tootles its mouth horn in distress. The red-haired one in the hat—obviously the leader—raises his fists, bouncing on his floppy little legs.

"Come on, Blondie, put up your dukes," he taunts.

"I don't think so, Sugar Ray Lamb Chop," the Slayer says.

With an irritated swipe of the staff, she launches him across the room and runs toward the TV full of black flame.

With the staff loaded over her shoulder, she flashes back to gym classes where she'd been forced to play softball and chokes up her grip. Swinging as hard as she can, she smashes the green gem into the TV monitor, spraying glass all over the floor. For a second, she can smell the rotten-egg stink of hell as the black flame surges out of the screen. Then the Creation gem makes contact with the fire.

The force of it ricochets up her arm, sending tremors through her bones. She imagines her body bursting apart like the scorpion boy at the Demondale rave. Would it be worth dying to kill a bunch of puppets? Then, all at once, the pain disappears and white lightning shoots through the studio. Everything it touches crumbles. The magical purple light flows back into the TV camera. The bricks rattle out of the walls. The tree house set and its oversize toys turn to sawdust. The puppets unravel at the seams. Their voices, still cursing the Slayer, are the last to go.

"Nothing can stop Hell on Earth," the spiky vengeance demon had finally told her after she made it clear she wouldn't let him go without getting what she needed. "Except scrubbing it from the timeline. Extinguish the Black Flame."

"And how do I do that?" the Slayer had asked, twisting a knife in his chest until yellow blood oozed between his craggy teeth. "Can I just huff and puff and blow the damn thing out?"

"Creation gem," he'd burbled, his hand clutching helplessly at the green amulet he wore. "Pure Creation meeting pure evil. Oblivion."

At first, she'd thought that he'd been talking nonsense. Or referring to his own impending death. Until she went to buy an ax from that rat-faced warlock and he told her that pure evil existed in every Hell on Earth in the form of a flag made of black hellfire. And that he knew where to find a staff that could point her directly to that fiery black flag. All she had to do was rough up some nerds.

All around her, the world unmakes itself. The Slayer, victorious, laughs as she conjures a portal and leaps inside. The Creation gem is the key. And the Black Flame flag is the lock.

She really can end the world.

All the worlds.

THREE
Jonathan

"ARE YOU CRAZY?" Jonathan asked in a loud whisper. Digging his heels in, he grabbed the nearest NO PARKING sign and did his best to hide behind it. "You want us to go to the Bronze? That's a vamp club!"

From the outside, the Bronze looked like any other converted factory space. Two stories of corrugated steel walls and a flat roof. Before the Mayor's sunshade had gone up, the cool kids at Sunnydale High had flocked to the all-ages club to drink cappuccinos and see local bands play. Jonathan had never even been brave enough to set foot inside the club then. He never developed a taste for coffee, and loud music made his ears hurt.

But now the Bronze was infamous for having blood on tap.

Human blood, every type. The building would be crawling with vampires. Setting foot inside was just asking to get bit.

Anya put her hands on her hips. "No, it's *the* vamp club. Why do you think I told you to shower and wear turtlenecks?"

Jonathan glanced down at his and Andrew's matching outfits. The black turtlenecks were from the Halloween the Trio had all accidentally worn the same Steve Jobs costume. Andrew was even wearing the lensless wire-frame glasses. He insisted that they completed the ensemble.

"We need information about a vampire slayer," Anya continued, at an exasperated clip. "Obviously, we need to talk to vampires."

Andrew tugged on the collar of his turtleneck, gazing at the front entrance with undisguised interest. "Come on, Jonathan. It could be cool inside."

"Of course *you* think so," Jonathan hissed. "You'd love to get turned into a bloodsucker."

Andrew's obsession with vampires had started after his brother Tucker got fangs. Undead Tucker cut contact with his living relatives—Andrew and their aunt Sandy. Shortly after, Aunt Sandy sold their house and left, following the mass exodus of nonevil suburbanites from Demondale. Jonathan's own parents left when Mayor Wilkins had won his reelection. Living in a town with an immortal sorcerer mayor had been bad enough.

"Watch the vampire slurs. They have excellent hearing," Anya said. "Plus, it's just plain rude. Now, are you coming or not?"

"Do you know what happens to humans who hang around with vampires?" Jonathan asked. He hugged his NO PARKING signpost a little tighter, his heart hammering against the steel. "They get eaten! Murdered! Killed to death!"

"Hey," Andrew said, reaching out and lightly setting a hand on Jonathan's shoulder. "Sometimes they get turned into the undead."

Jonathan tore out of Andrew's grasp. "I don't want to be undead!"

Anya twisted her arms in a shrug. "Vampires don't eat vengeance demons. They say our blood is unpleasantly astringent. Like clove oil."

"Was that supposed to be comforting?" Jonathan asked. He wasn't sure he liked Andrew's coworker. Even the manager with the aggressive mop would have been a better companion.

"You didn't wish for comfort," Anya said. "If you want your friend back, we have to go in there and find out about the slayer. Just act like you belong and lead with money. Everyone likes money. Vampires take bribes like anybody else. Did you get more cash?"

"Yes," Jonathan said. He patted Warren's messenger bag, bloated with freshly printed bills. Back at the lair, the counterfeiting machine had churned out bribe money while they changed out of their blood-soaked clothes. Jonathan prayed that none of the vampires would notice the code hidden inside the serial numbers. Warren had loved signing his crimes.

"Great," Anya said, her face brightening in a wide smile. "Hopefully the promise of cash will distract them from your human veal bodies."

Jonathan reluctantly let go of the NO PARKING sign, shuffling behind Anya and Andrew toward the Bronze's single illuminated sign. Seated on a tall stool, the bouncer was a thick-necked demon with skin the color and texture of pumice.

"ID," the bouncer grunted.

Jonathan's hands fumbled through his wallet and pulled out his driver's license. It quivered in his hand as he held it up for the demon, who, in return, slapped a pale blue UNDERAGE wristband on him. Andrew got one to match.

"ID," the bouncer said to Anya.

The girl's face transformed, just as it had back at Best Pressed. Her eyebrows disappeared and her eyes sank back into dark hollows. Skin shriveled, veins popping, she looked like she'd been flayed alive, leaving only her musculature behind.

The moment the bouncer put the red AGE VERIFIED wristband on her, her face popped back to normal. Rosy-cheeked and smiling, she pushed past Andrew and Jonathan into the club.

"I was born before the invention of the printing press," she explained. "So I don't have a birth certificate. I can't convince the DMV to give me a license without one. Outside of Demondale, I can't vote or drink, but as long as I'm in town, my demonic form gets me in wherever I need to go."

"Cool," Andrew breathed.

"Is it?" Jonathan asked. He wasn't convinced that teaming up with a known demon was a safe bet. What if she got her powers back and decided to enact vengeance on them? Or if she didn't get her powers back and left them for dead?

Inside, the Bronze smelled like a handful of pennies clenched in a clammy fist. Sweat and iron. It had once been a metalwork factory and none of the owners in the time since had bothered to rid it of that aesthetic. It was dim and industrial, with a foreman's balcony that overlooked the bar and dance floor. Even in the late afternoon, it was fairly crowded with the glamorous undead and the Hot Topic goths who followed them around.

Back when the sun still rose over this side of Santa Barbara County, no vampire would ever have hung around in public with their feeding face on. Their bumpy permanent snarls used to be private, only seen by those they preyed upon. But now all around the Bronze were patrons of ostensibly all ages whose exposed fangs and yellow eyes announced them as undead. Most of them drank from tall glasses. Others lured human lookie-loos into shadowy corners.

Anya strode across the club. Andrew eagerly followed her, openly gaping at his surroundings and whispering to Jonathan over his shoulder.

"Look," Andrew said, pointing at the pool tables crowded with monsters. "They play games, just like us!"

Jonathan was sure he was going to die here. Fangs in his neck. Throat torn out. Blood drained. No one would even know he was dead because surely Andrew would die too and Warren was already gone. His parents would comfort each other, saying that they'd told Jonathan that only humans with a death wish would stay in Demondale.

Jonathan didn't have a death wish. He just wanted somewhere to belong. The only place he'd ever fit was with Warren and Andrew. He'd do anything not to lose that. Even if it meant risking his life in a vampire club.

On the stage against the far wall, the goth-rock house band was playing. The logo on the drum kit announced them as Drusilla and the Dollies. The lead singer—Drusilla, presumably—danced trancelike, her face mostly concealed by a curtain of long dark hair. Black-and-white-striped stockings peeked out from under her corseted red dress. Seated behind her was a loose-skinned demon whose pale batwing ears sagged beneath a bowler hat. As the demon in the bowler hat drew his bow over an electric cello, the singer whispered luridly into the microphone, *"Kiss me, kill me till I bleed."*

The crowd pressed against the stage and burst into anticipatory applause. One—a chaos demon from the look of their gooey antlers—passed the singer a single red rose, which she used to blow kisses into the crowd.

The bartender, a bleached-blond man with a face that was 90 percent cheekbones, rolled his eyes, seemingly disgusted by the proceedings onstage. Anya pushed Andrew and Jonathan toward him.

"Can I get you a pint of plasma?" the barman offered Anya in a thick Cockney accent. He narrowed his eyes at Andrew's and Jonathan's wristbands. "Or a glass of milk?"

"Do you have chocolate—" Andrew began to ask.

Anya cut him off. "Actually, we're looking for information. You're a vampire, aren't you?"

The barman glared at her in annoyance. He took a moment to lick his teeth, letting his canines change into fangs and back again. "What do you think, love?"

Jonathan had never been so close to a set of fangs before. Just seeing them made him feel light-headed and anxious. On jelly legs, he took a step away from the bar and bumped directly into a passing Fyarl demon in a waiter's apron. Foot-soldier demons that usually worked for vampires or even scarier monsters, Fyarls were a common sight in Demondale. They all had curved black horns and sharp knobs for shoulders. They were extraordinarily strong. Jonathan had once seen one throw people out of its way just to make it to the front of a line at the bank.

The waiter Fyarl growled down at Jonathan, gesturing to the serving tray it had balanced on one hand. A basket of cheese fries sat beside a bowl overflowing with live cockroaches. Jonathan didn't speak Fyarl—to him it just sounded like grunts and roars—but he apologized a few times for good measure, hoping the demon could at least sense his contrition. It seemed to work. The Fyarl trudged away toward the patrons at the pool tables.

Anya set her forearms on the bar and leaned forward, catching the barman's full attention. "We need to know about the slayer."

"Is that right?" the barman drawled. He picked up a pint glass and buffed it with a towel that was more bloodstain than not. "Well, I've slain a few slayers in my time. What do you want to know about them? And how much is that information worth to you?"

Anya turned around, raising her brows significantly at Andrew and Jonathan and not very subtly tilting her head toward the vampire bartender. Jonathan opened the messenger bag and withdrew a handful of twenty-dollar bills before taking out the video camera. He fast-forwarded the playback to the moment the blond girl interrupted the Ascension.

"This girl interrupted our, um, party earlier," he said. He set the camera on the bar, pressed play, and stepped back again, this time checking behind himself first.

The barman watched the video camera's display placidly. Even when the girl busted out her kick-ass ninja fighting moves, round-housing the shrink ray in the split second before Jonathan could shoot her, the blond vampire just yawned, scratching at his chin with black-painted fingernails.

When the girl in the video vanished inside the portal, Jonathan reached out and turned off the playback.

Anya's nose wrinkled in distaste. "She's a lot younger than I expected. She barely looks old enough to wish vengeance on a cheating ex."

"You know," the barman said, blue eyes fixed on Jonathan the way a spider might watch a fly, "just because she kicked your ass doesn't make her the slayer."

"The slayer?" rumbled a second bartender, striding up behind the first. This one was taller and broader, his dark brown hair pulled into a short ponytail at the nape of his neck. He spoke in a far less discernible accent, something that might once have been Irish but now landed firmly in the mid-Atlantic.

"Ah, Angelus," the blond barman said, beckoning to the other vampire. "These kids think they've found a slayer."

Andrew looked at Jonathan with eyes so wide they were in danger of popping out and bouncing on the bar. Few people in Demondale did not know the name *Angelus*. The owner of the Bronze and one of the most powerful vampires in town—second only to the leader of the Church of the Eternal Night—Angelus had been one of the first undead to announce himself after the town went dark. He'd staked his claim—no pun intended—to the Bronze by killing the last owner and using his blood to fill the town's first plasma kegs. Even now, the Bronze was the only restaurant in town that sold human blood. Everywhere else served varieties of animal. No one asked where Angelus got enough blood to keep his kegs full of A, B, and O. No one dared.

Jonathan wondered how far running would get him before Angelus ripped out his throat. His eyes slid over the walls, searching for an electrical socket he could plug the shrink ray into. Shooting might be the only way he got out of this vamp nest alive.

Angelus gave a derisive snort. "There hasn't been a slayer on the West Coast since the Gold Rush. The latest girl is in Boston, I heard, with some milksop Watcher with two last names. If she's smart, she'll stay there. What could one slayer do against an entire town of vamps and demons?" He cocked his head and leered down at Anya. "It's not you, is it?"

"Me? I'm eleven hundred years old. But thank you." Blushing, Anya held up her red wristband. "No, my boss, D'Hoffryn of Arashmaharr, was attacked by the slayer. She slaughtered basically everybody at Vengeance LLC, stole the Marnoxon gem, and then made this one"—she hooked a thumb at Jonathan—"kill his friend on camera so she could steal a bunch of magical artifacts and run off through a portal."

Angelus shook his head. "If she's not killing vampires, she's not the slayer. Of everywhere in town she could have burst in and picked a fight, she chose a party with you all? A slayer would be in the cemetery, at the least, killing off the newly risen. Better yet, she'd come try her luck with us. Between myself, Spike here, and Drusilla, we've got some of the most famous slayer killers in history under one roof."

That sounded to Jonathan like reason enough for the slayer to never ever set foot inside the Bronze, but he didn't say so. He was too busy trying to figure out how he could make a portal gun that would immediately eject him from situations this dangerous.

Andrew cleared his throat and held up an index finger. "There is . . . one more thing. Warren was in the middle of Ascending into a demon. Maybe she wanted to stop the second coming of Shaak'garar?"

"The Scorpion King?" Angelus scoffed. "All of the insectoid Old Ones eventually go mad from the leakage of their own venom sacs. He's better off dead."

"Hey! That's our friend you're talking about!" Jonathan said, anger overtaking sense. Warren wasn't better off dead. He was the only reason that Andrew and Jonathan had survived in Demondale this long. "He didn't deserve to die!"

Angelus frowned, confused. "Didn't you kill him?"

"The slayer made me!" Jonathan said, his voice coming off as whiny even to his own ears.

Anya slid herself onto the closest stool, propping her elbows on the bar and squinting at the draft taps.

"Can I get a pint of Black Frost?" she asked Spike, the blond bartender. "Go ahead and start me a tab."

"Sure thing," Spike said. He retrieved a fresh glass from under the counter, flipping it in the air and catching it under the tap. "You want a bloomin' onion with that? Best thing on the menu. And they're half price through happy hour."

"Oh, that does sound good," Anya said. She wet her lips in apparent relish and slapped a couple of bills down on the bar. "*Half price.* I'll take one. I'll be here for a while. You know how long it takes for vengeance demons to get drunk."

"That I do," Spike said, inclining his head to her as he gathered the cash. "I'll keep the drinks coming, then, shall I?"

"Please," Anya said. "I've got a pocketful of cash just waiting to become a hangover."

"What?" Andrew asked, his face pinched. "You aren't giving up on searching for the slayer already? Just like that?"

"Like this," Anya said. She accepted the ice-cold cup of quitting from Spike and raised it in cheers to Jonathan and Andrew.

"But what about Warren?" Jonathan asked, helplessly.

"You killed him." Anya shrugged, licking away her beer foam mustache.

"By accident!" Jonathan yelled. Panic tightened his chest. He couldn't just sit back and eat happy-hour snacks. The only reason he'd agreed to brave the inside of this godforsaken club was so that they could get the gem back from the slayer and get Warren back from the dead. If Anya gave up, then all hope was lost.

This never would have happened to Warren. He would have known exactly what to say to make the vampires believe him and to make Anya agree to keep searching for answers. Jonathan struggled to imagine how Warren would respond to this situation. He would have been effortlessly authoritative, cool, and threatening. Like Magneto.

"We paid you!" Jonathan said, prodding Anya in the shoulder. "You promised us a Wish, and you promised your supervisor you'd look for the gem."

"And I looked," Anya said, exasperated. Her beer glass clinked against the bar. White froth sloshed over the rim. "We followed our lead, boys. I'm done playing detective. As long as that little girl has the Marnoxon gem, I have no magic. That means no portal-hopping, no telekinesis, no Wish-granting. I'm basically as useless as you two. Except prettier. And with the good wristband. All I can do is wait and see if the slayer makes any more trouble in Demondale. But if I were her, I would cruise into a pocket dimension where slayers are queen shit of the universe and stay there."

Onstage, the music was cut off by a bloodcurdling wail. Thrashing in the fabric of her own skirt, the vampire singer fell to the floor. The microphone landed with a thud beside her, amplifying her horrified, helpless keening. Rose petals shredded to mulch in her hands. Screams rent the air as her face flickered between vampire and human guises, both contorted into masks of abject despair.

In an instant, Spike was jumping over the bar. One of his leather motorcycle boots kicked over Anya's beer moments before he shoved past Jonathan and Andrew. Audience members flew against the walls as Spike bum-rushed the stage screaming "Dru!"

"Time," the vampire girl shrieked between sobs. "Time *is dying!*"

"Don't mind Drusilla," Angelus told Anya. He shook out a towel and mopped up her spilled beer. "Just one of her fits. That's the trouble with having an insane clairvoyant in the house band. It's my own fault."

"Did you know she was insane when you hired her?" Andrew asked. Jonathan fought the urge to clamp his hand over his friend's mouth. If Andrew could tamp down his undead curiosity for a minute, the vampire girl's freak-out would have been the perfect cover for the two of them to sneak out of the Bronze unnoticed. But Andrew couldn't help himself. Vampires were his current chief obsession, taking the top slot from *Legend of Zelda* and the Star Wars expanded universe. He just couldn't shut up about them when the opportunity presented itself. No matter how dangerous that opportunity might be.

"Of course I knew," Angelus said. He blinked rapidly, seemingly perplexed by the question. "I'm the one who tortured the sense out of her."

Jonathan felt faint. He dug his fingernails into his palms, doing his best to stay alert. If he lost consciousness, there was no way he'd live long enough to leave the club.

Angelus glanced over at Anya. "Can I pour you another Black Frost?"

"Please," Anya said with an easy smile, as though vampires confessed to torturing each other every day. Maybe they did. Jonathan knew that plenty of vamps were regular customers at Best Pressed

Juicery. Andrew was always coming home with stories of customers who paid in ancient coins or who were so recently turned that they still had the fang marks on their necks.

Under the stage lights, Drusilla shrieked and clawed at her face until red rivulets wept down her forehead and cheeks.

"Stop her!" Drusilla screamed, staring up, unseeing, at the ceiling, even as Spike made it onstage and scooped her up. She pitched in his arms, wailing, "Stop the slayer!"

His brow creased in a pained furrow, Angelus released the beer tap, leaving Anya's fresh pint half-filled. There was no sign of his mocking smile now. His eyes were hard and appraising as his gaze traveled evenly over Jonathan and Andrew.

"You better come with me."

The band's name—Drusilla and the Dollies—made a lot more sense after Angelus ushered Jonathan, Andrew, and Anya backstage into the singer's dressing room. The walls were thick with dolls. Porcelain dolls so old that their skin was cracked and flaking. Barbies plucked bald. Baby dolls missing eyes. So many of them it was hard to see the shelves they were seated on.

Jonathan's shoulders crept toward his ears. He had the overwhelming urge to pull his turtleneck over his face and run screaming in the other direction. Especially when he spotted Drusilla babbling on a red velvet fainting couch, her face continuing to flicker between human and vampire.

Spike knelt on the floor beside her, holding out a glass of blood. A pink Krazy Straw bobbed up and down in the gore.

"Relax," he murmured, stroking the singer's bumpy forehead as she cried out again. He nudged the Krazy Straw against the corner of her mouth. "Drink your juice, pet. It'll pass."

Jonathan had never seen a vampire show overt tenderness before. He looked down at his shoes, embarrassed to witness such a private moment.

Angelus obviously felt no such embarrassment. He strode into the dressing room, his shadow falling over Spike's face.

"We don't want the vision to pass, Spike," the larger vampire rumbled. "It could be important."

Spike's eyes blazed at his employer, the gentle lover transformed into a menacing beast of prey in a blink. "Look at her, you massive-foreheaded git. She's in anguish. And not the kind she enjoys." He peered around Angelus at the group assembled in the door. "So, thank you for the snacks. You can leave the boys and take the girl back to the bar. Can't you smell a vengeance demon when you meet one?"

"If I put it in my batter, it will make my batter bitter!" Drusilla howled in a Cockney accent even thicker than her boyfriend's. She slapped the Krazy Straw away from her face. "The bitter blood spills secrets, the slayer laps them up. Bitter batter secret keeper."

Jonathan's courage bottomed out. He spun on his heel, barreling into Anya, who forced him back into the room. It felt like being thrown into the lion's cage at the zoo. Except with a million times more creepy dolls.

"They're not snacks," Angelus told Spike, gesturing at the door without looking back. "You think it's a coincidence that these blood bags came in talking about the slayer and then Dru gets a vision of her? We need to know what she's seeing." He bent down, drawing

Jonathan's gaze to a miniature fainting couch. It was the same color and shape as the one Drusilla lay upon. A single porcelain doll was seated there. This doll, nicer than any on the walls, wore a dark pink silk dress trimmed with lace. Her blond hair was curled in the same style as Drusilla's. Disconcertingly, her painted mouth was gagged with a red silk ribbon. Angelus handled the doll with great care, lifting it off the tiny chaise and holding it out to Drusilla. "Here you go, Dru. Why don't you tell Miss Edith what you see? What's coming?"

Jonathan held his breath, terrified at the idea of the doll coming to life, choking against her restraining ribbon. But Miss Edith only stared, inanimate.

Drusilla didn't seem to notice that the doll was inert. Gripping Miss Edith's arms, she drew the doll's nose close to her own, transfixed by her painted eyes.

"Don't you see, Miss Edith? The slayer is coming. And going," Drusilla said, speaking softer for the doll's ears. Her features flickered again and she set Miss Edith's forehead against her own, rubbing the smooth porcelain against her vampire bumpiness. "She's everywhere. Torturing demons and men for information. I can hear their screams echoing through time. There's such exquisite rage in her, such hopelessness. So far from home and still running. She's got a sack of toys like Father Christmas, but there will only be coal for presents. She means to unmake us, unravel our stitches. She'll make it so we never are and never were."

Jonathan didn't like the sound of any of this. Being unmade sounded painful. He and Andrew exchanged a worried glance.

"Oh, you wicked dolly," Drusilla said, giving Miss Edith a firm shake before plucking the ribbon off the doll's face. It fluttered onto the floor next to Spike's knee. "You knew, didn't you? This is punishment for Mummy telling you to keep quiet. You'll be pleased as punch to watch us all die, won't you? But we'll see who's laughing when the slayer comes calling. You won't exist either, my dear. We'll all be squelched and swallowed by the great nothing."

Angelus lifted the red ribbon, twining it between his pale fingers like a garrote. "What's that about the great nothing? A new big, bad fellow in town?"

"Oh no," Drusilla said, her head lolling toward Spike. Clamping down on the Krazy Straw, she sucked greedily. Pulling back to smack her lips, she sent a dreamy smile around the room. "There won't be a town left when the slayer is done with us. She means to kill everyone in Demondale."

With a wince, Spike turned to face Jonathan, Andrew, and Anya.

"So, uh." He sucked his teeth. "What kind of magical item did you say the slayer stole from you?"

THE SLAYER

THE PORTAL DUMPS her onto a residential street she doesn't recognize. Small houses and more chain-link than picket fences. She assumes she must be on the edge of the Docktown district. If there is a Docktown in this Hell on Earth.

Leaves cover the ground, choking the gutters in crispy orange and brown. Jack-o'-lanterns crowd porch steps. There's a chill in the air.

Autumn.

The Slayer had nearly forgotten seasons. Without the sun, Demondale was always a temperate midnight, rarely warmer than sixty-five degrees. The first week after she was sent there, the Slayer couldn't sleep a wink. She had been obsessed with waiting for the sun to rise. The morning hours would tick by—six, seven, eight o'clock—and the sky wouldn't fade. The first Demondale vamp she slayed attacked her at ten-thirty in the morning. Ten-thirty! Vampires weren't meant to walk around during brunch hours.

Not that the Slayer had been enjoying any brunches in Demondale. She has taken to robbing vamps before dusting them, just so she can buy fast food and tickets for the one bus with a route out of town. She would never feel safe enough under the sunshade to sleep there. In the month since she fell through her first portal, she's only slept in broad daylight, on the bus or in the stiff-backed armchairs of the Santa Barbara Public Library. She'd slink back into Demondale when it was time to hunt. For information. For vampires. For vengeance demons.

If she ever gets home, she worries that she'll never get used to sleeping in the dark again.

Here, in this new dimension, the sun is out. It isn't warm, but it's bright. Looking up and seeing blue sky rather than the matte-black disk of the sunshade is a relief. Even though there must be something evil enough to lure the magical staff here, the Slayer feels herself relax. How bad could anything be in broad daylight?

Daydreaming about a cardigan left behind in her closet, she wishes she had a change of clothes. Maybe if she sneaks over to Revello Drive, there will be a closet of similar clothes and similar smells and a similar mom to tuck her hair behind her ears and tell her everything is fine. . . .

But no. The staff has a singular purpose. Inside a portal, when the gem shows her the fork in the road leading to any Hell on Earth of her choosing, the staff is pliant. But once she makes her choice and leaps into a new world, it grows heavy and sluggish in her hands if she dares turn it in any direction other than the one it wants, like a compass with an attitude problem. She can follow it, or she can leave it behind, abandoning her mission.

The staff wouldn't have brought her to this dimension if it weren't evil. Who's to say that Mom in this reality wouldn't also be evil? That the clothes in her other self's closet wouldn't be off-brand, ill-fitting, or—God forbid—unstylish? Better to follow the plan and destroy it all. Once there's nothing left to distract the staff's evil sensor, the gem will have to ship her home. All she has to do is carve out the path for herself, one extinguished Black Flame at a time.

It's either fight or live in Hell on Earth. Fighting is what she was born to do.

A black cat runs past her on silent paws, setting off a parked car to flash its lights without an alarm. Behind a short chain-link fence, a Rottweiler opens and closes its jaws in the pantomime of a bark. Where there should be noise, there is only silence. A silence that presses hard into the Slayer's ears, blocking out everything but the sound of her own pulse. It's as though there's a finger on the lips of the whole neighborhood, a breath held while listening for approaching footsteps.

Welcome to Silentdale, she thinks, and a chill runs up her spine.

She's all too happy to follow the staff's urging and leave the sidewalk for the center of the street. There are no cars driving here, although she's unsure if she would be able to hear their engines even if there were. The thought makes her paranoid. She looks repeatedly behind herself. Checking for jump scares.

Nervously moving forward, the Slayer whistles to keep herself company. She's relieved at her own noise. The whistle is startlingly loud, echoing tunelessly through the empty neighborhood. But it's better than the oppressive hush, so she keeps going, swishing the wizard staff in time. The movement helps push her forward, keeping her going even as a prickle in the back of her mind tells her that there's something very wrong here.

Duh. Of course something's wrong. Otherwise the staff wouldn't have dropped her here.

At the end of the street, she finally sees another person. A girl with long braids and brown skin runs at full speed, eyes wide and hands waving.

Run! the girl mouths. *They're coming!*

The Slayer stops walking, reaching out to the girl. "Who's coming?" she asks. She wishes she knew sign language. Speaking out loud feels so rude, like shouting at someone who can't speak English.

The girl mouths something else, gesturing first at her mouth and then at her chest. The Slayer repeats the gesture, hoping to discern its meaning. But, after a glance over her shoulder, the other girl is off and running again. Leaving the Slayer alone in the middle of the street, shivering, as an icy wind picks up the dead leaves in the gutter.

When she turns back, the Slayer finds the answer to her question.

Three loping figures, shaped like humans but hunched over in the postures of men in gorilla suits, elbows and knees akimbo. Their faces are bandaged like half-dressed mummies. Buckle-covered white coats are tight against their chests, but are so long in the arms that they flop against the asphalt. Only as they caper closer does the Slayer recognize the coats for what they are. Straitjackets. The dragging arms are meant to be fastened in the back, to hold their wearers prone.

Behind the straitjacketed figures are four besuited creatures that must be demons. Smiling horrible smiles on faces frozen and cadaverous. Whiter than even the palest vampire. So upright, with ramrod posture that reads as aristocratic rather than hellish. Their black suits are tailored to their tall, skeletal bodies. They float down the street. Actually float, like Thanksgiving Day balloons with shiny leather shoes six inches from the ground, casting shadows beneath.

The one in the center holds a sharp metal scalpel. The tallest has his long-fingered hands wrapped around a small wooden box. The other two twirl their hands, as though each is spinning a cat's cradle with invisible thread.

The Slayer is rooted to the spot watching these demons approach. She rarely feels the urge to retreat, but seeing sunlight reflecting off an ordinary surgical scalpel makes her want to run screaming in the other direction. Monsters have come at her with plenty of weapons in the past—swords and clubs and claws. But doctors' instruments? The implied precision is spine-chilling.

Without warning, the straightjacketed cronies surge toward the Slayer. Their footsteps make no noise, even as they gallop on their knuckles. The three of them surround her, bodies bouncing and spinning like people forever hyping themselves up to break-dance but never actually getting down to business.

She doesn't hear the whoosh of air that would normally precede a punch landing in her kidney, but pain detonates in her side, surprising her into dropping the staff. It spins itself on the ground, pointing toward the floating demons, as though there could be any doubt that they were the epitome of evil in this dimension. The cronies are just a distraction.

Someone pulls hard on the backpack full of magical artifacts, yanking the Slayer backward. She throws the point of her elbow. It bashes into a bandaged face that makes no sound of protest in response. An arm wraps around her throat and presses down hard against her esophagus. The straitjacket canvas is musty and rough. The Slayer gasps for air. Spit bubbles at the corners of her mouth.

She rears back, reverse-head-butting the crony. Its grip loosens just enough for her to get a gulp of air. Her hand fastens on the restraining arm and she flips the crony over her shoulder. Keeping hold of the end of the overlong jacket arm, she yanks it toward the next-closest crony, who swipes at her in a clumsy punch. She ducks, quickly buckling the arm that tried to choke her to its friend's back.

Running between the cronies, she grabs at all the arms that reach for her, tugging and buckling, until she's lashed them all together. The three cronies can now only spin each other in furious circles, no matter how hard they pull. A daisy chain of straitjackets.

With the cronies distracted, the Slayer scoops the staff up off the ground, chest heaving as she tries to catch her breath. When she looks up, she can see the empty-handed smiling demons giving her a silent golf clap. It feels unnecessarily sarcastic.

The tallest demon lifts the lid of the wooden box. The Slayer can't see inside it, but she can smell the sulfurous stench even before the Black Flame flag comes dancing up.

"Aw, you brought me a gift?" she asks.

Still smiling, the hideous Gentlemen recoil at the sound of her voice.

"What? You don't talk, so nobody else can?" she asks. "You're the kings of Silentdale?"

They shake their heads as though trying to dislodge her words from their ears. The tallest one drops the box of black flame. It falls to the ground inaudibly, even as the lid breaks and a beet-red human heart rolls out onto the street. Black flames rise out of the heart's untethered aorta.

The Gentlemen scurry around the loose heart and its growing black flame, creating a wall between it and the Slayer. She mirrors their toothy grins, feeling sharklike as she runs at them. The blunt end of the staff may not have the portability or pointiness of a stake, but, jabbed into the gut of whatever these silent demons are, it manages to knock them down. Throwing the staff around takes the Slayer back to a simpler time. Before demons and vampires. Before she was the Chosen One. Once upon a time, in a reality far away, she was a Los Angeles cheerleader in charge of spinning a battle flag on the sidelines of a football game.

Whistling again, she cracks a demon in the side of the head and the reverberations make its arms shake. The scalpel falls to the ground. The Slayer kicks it aside, clearing her path to the heart spilling over with black flame.

Raising the green-gem staff over her head, she belts out, "Go! Fight! Win!" and splatters the heart into the asphalt.

Around her, white skulls explode into yellow pus. The jack-o'-lanterns on the nearest porch shrivel in on themselves and the houses collapse into piles of drywall. The cronies all fall down like they've hit the end of ring-around-the-rosy and crumble to dust. The hazy sunlight fills with motes of the decaying dimension. In the distance, a car alarm blares, breaking the silence.

The cold wind picks up again, making the Slayer shiver. She conjures another portal, hoping that her next stop will be a warmer colony of hell.

FOUR

Anya

THE UNDEAD WALKED surprisingly fast.

Angelus, Spike the bartender, and Drusilla the mad clairvoyant moved with determination, like three people on a mission. Which, Anya supposed, they were.

There was a mega-apocalypse to thwart.

She didn't know much about slayers, but she was pretty sure they were supposed to stop the end of the world. Not cause it. Angelus seemed pretty sure that Drusilla's vision was a legitimate threat, not the ravings of a madwoman talking to a doll. Or, at least, not *just* ravings. He'd left the Bronze in the care of the cello-playing loose-skinned demon and the Fyarl waiters, and demanded that

Andrew and Jonathan take him to the store where the stolen staff had come from.

All of a sudden Anya's mission to track down the Marnoxon gem had become a mission to save the world. She might not have been sure about wanting to stay on earth past New Year's Eve, but that didn't mean she wanted it destroyed by some Chosen One teeny-bopper. Especially since, without her magic, Anya wouldn't be able to seek shelter in a pocket dimension.

As they passed under the faux-gas-lamp streetlights that lined downtown, Drusilla seemed to recover from her psychic attack. She had left her dolls back at the Bronze, but her arms were draped around Spike's shoulders, holding him with the same reckless affection that she'd shown Miss Edith.

"Nasty slayer," she said with a pout. "She ruined my encore. My poor babies will never get to hear the end of my song."

"You play the same set every day, ducks," Spike said, combing his painted nails through Drusilla's dark brown hair, having zero effect on her sausage-link curls. "The stage-door Johnnies can come back tomorrow."

"But who knows what I will be tomorrow?" Drusilla mused. Her tongue laved one of Spike's sharp cheekbones; then she rubbed her lips together, contemplating the taste. "Live performance exists only in the fleeting present. It is created in the moment and murdered by replication. Much like love."

Spike's face dropped into an expression that reminded Anya of a kicked dog. He flipped up the collar of his long coat, hiding his wounded expression inside the leather. Drusilla didn't seem to notice, taking the shift in movement as an excuse to skip ahead, dancing in the shadows between streetlights.

Angelus slowed his pace just enough to fall into step beside Anya, who studied the hard line of his jaw. Were there ugly vampires? Did the average-looking get invited to eternal life? This one, Anya had to admit, was more handsome than she would have expected of Demondale's notorious club owner. A big Cro-Magnon forehead. Hard brown eyes. The latent intensity of a jungle cat.

It was a pity about the little ponytail.

Vampires so often clung to outdated styles. Hence Spike's punk-rock peroxide dye job and his and Angelus's thick leather coats despite Demondale's mild climate. Anya had never quite figured out why the undead had such a penchant for leather. It made them all so squeaky and cow-scented. Hardly the sort of thing that struck fear into the hearts of the innocent—or so she assumed. Her body had a beating heart, but certainly not an innocent one.

Angelus pointed his large forehead toward the sulking Spike and prancing Drusilla.

His mouth pulled to one side in a smirk. "They've been together for over a hundred years," he told Anya, sotto voce. The low rumble of his voice made the hair on the back of her neck stand up, not unpleasantly. "A century of dating puts a strain on even the most obsessive relationship."

"You'd know something about that, old man," Spike said, without turning around. With a swipe of his boot, he kicked an empty Doublemeat Palace cup off the sidewalk. The Styrofoam floated gently into the gutter. Spike swore under his breath, throwing a dark look over his shoulder at Angelus. "At least my sire stuck by me, instead of running off and marrying Daddy. How many kids do you reckon the vicar and his wife have got now?"

"That's enough, Spike," Angelus warned.

"Holy shit!" Jonathan cried, darting behind Andrew and pointing across the street. "It's a land shark!"

The demon in question did look like a shark. At least, on top. A gunmetal-gray fin protruded from the top of a shark's head, complete with flat black eyes and teeth that made the vampires' look like kittens'. From the neck down, he had a humanoid body clothed in a shiny maroon suit.

"Nah, he's a *loan* shark," Spike said. "That's Bro'os. He's got a pay-advance office over on Third Street. Good guy. But God help you if you don't pay him back on time."

Anya fixed the human boys with a glower she hoped communicated her displeasure with them. "If you scream at the sight of every demon you encounter, how do you survive in this town?"

"We don't usually walk places," Jonathan said in a sheepish mumble. "We just misplaced the keys to our van."

"They were in Warren's pocket when he exploded," Andrew said.

"Sure, and no demon is strong enough to open a tin can on wheels," Angelus said sarcastically. With an irritated flick of his little ponytail, he extended a grabby hand to Andrew. "Let me see that manifest again, boy."

"Right, sure," Andrew said, jumping to squeeze himself between Anya and Angelus. He flipped open the flap of the ugly green messenger bag slung across his chest and rummaged around inside for a crumpled piece of notebook paper. It was slightly damp in one corner. Andrew gave it a shake, a vain attempt to either smooth out the wrinkles or air out the sour smell it had acquired from being on the damp bar back at the Bronze.

Walking on her toes to see over Andrew's shoulder, Anya read the handwritten list. Andrew and Jonathan's dead friend had inventoried all the artifacts needed on hand for his demon Ascension. Now it was a list of the slayer's arsenal.

"Okay," Angelus said with a heavy sigh. "We've established that the slayer has the unlisted green gem—"

"The Kryptonite," Andrew said, panting to keep up with Angelus's long stride.

"The Marnoxon," Anya corrected.

"Attached to the Gandalf staff." Angelus paused, tilting his head ponderously. "I don't know this demon Gandalf. Is he an Old One?"

"He's a wizard," Andrew said.

"From *Lord of the Rings*," Jonathan piped up, lagging nearly half a block behind the rest of them. Anya couldn't tell if it was his fear of the vampires or the length of his legs holding him back.

"There's also the Dagger of the Unkillable." Angelus continued reading, as though no one had spoken. "That's mostly a threat to gods and Lower Beings. I've never heard of this Urn of Fernda—"

"It's bigger on the inside," Andrew said. "Like a TARDIS."

Angelus looked at the human boy, frowning. "A what?"

"A TARDIS. *Time And Relative Dimension In Space*," Andrew said. When Angelus showed no sign of recognition, Andrew cleared his throat. "Spike, you're, um, English. You must know *Doctor Who*."

"Haven't needed a sawbones since Victoria was queen, mate," Spike said.

Andrew's shoulders slumped. "It's a TV show," he said faintly. "They show it on PBS."

"When in doubt, he's talking about space." Anya sighed, shaking her head at Angelus. "Imaginary space."

"Ah," Angelus said, swatting the idea away with the back of his hand as his focus settled on the list again. "The magic bone and the pan pipes don't seem like they'll be much of a threat. Neither does the Ram's Horn horn . . ." A cruel smile played at the corner of his mouth as he lifted his eyes from the page and looked at Andrew. "Now, what were you two going to do with a stake-throwing crossbow, a crucifix, and a"—he double-checked the list—"Super Soaker full of holy water? Sounds like a vamp-killing kit to me."

Andrew put up both his hands and backed away until he was nearly level with Jonathan. "They were purely for self-defense, I swear!"

"Naughty, naughty boys and their naughty, naughty toys," Drusilla tutted. Red skirt streaming behind her, she hopped into the gutter and rushed toward the human boys. Pale fingers encircled Jonathan's wrist and turned him toward the vampire woman. "What's a vampire ever done to you?"

"N-n-nothing!" Jonathan jabbered. "Andrew's telling the truth. Warren bought the kit for self-defense! We never even learned how to load the crossbow!"

Even though she understood it was the nature of vampires to murder humans indiscriminately, Anya found herself overcome with the unusual urge to protect Andrew and Jonathan. First of all, if they died, she would be the fourth wheel on her own mission to recapture the Marnoxon gem—the only member of the party who'd missed out on a century's worth of bonding. The vampires would assuredly have topside references and inside jokes she didn't get.

But secondly, Andrew and Jonathan were the only ones who could ID the slayer. The grainy video-camera footage wasn't good enough for Anya to be sure she'd recognize the blond girl on the street. It would be so embarrassing to attack just any old teenage girl with a backpack full of magical paraphernalia.

Besides, she kind of liked Andrew—as a coworker at least. He was one of the few humans who had never said anything antidemon to her.

"These two couldn't stake you even if they tried," she said, blowing a raspberry of disdain. "Look at their noodly little arms. They don't have the upper-body strength to kill anybody."

Drusilla extended her index finger and traced down one of Jonathan's cheeks with the sharp side of one fingernail. "Oh, what a tasty little jam tart you are," she purred.

The boy tumbled into a metal trash can.

"Leave him be, Dru," Spike said. "We need him to tell the warlocks what he knows."

"Surely not both of them," Drusilla said, eyeing Andrew next. She reached out and looped her finger in his turtleneck. Andrew's shoulders squirmed as though something were slithering up his spine.

"Spike's right," Angelus said. A wrinkle between his eyebrows betrayed how little he enjoyed that particular statement. "Leave them alive for now. There will be plenty of time to play once we've found the slayer."

"What a horrible tease," Drusilla said, folding her arms across her chest and tromping through the gutter. The heels of her boots stabbed at every piece of litter she passed over, each clanging footfall announcing her displeasure. "Water, water everywhere and not a drop of blood."

"If you needed a snack, there was plenty of blood back at the Bronze," Spike told her.

"You know it tastes better when the fear is fresh," Dru said. She gnashed her teeth at Jonathan. When he flinched, she threw her head back with a throaty giggle.

"Look!" Andrew announced. He hurried forward, pointing at the sky. For a moment, Anya expected to see a bigger threat overhead—blood rain or giant murder bees or a falter in the sunshade spell—but instead she was faced with a drab gray awning that read RIPPER AND RAYNE'S METAPHYSICAL BOUTIQUE. "This is the place."

"Hey, we know you!" Anya said. She elbowed Andrew in the side and pointed to the man behind the counter. "Look, it's Medium Green Drink with Extra Honey and Bee Pollen!"

No one at Best Pressed remembered any of the regulars by name, only by the fussiness of their orders. The last time Medium Green Drink had sent back his juice, demanding more kale, he hadn't been sporting the black eye currently swelling the left side of his face.

"My name is Ethan Rayne." The painful-looking bruise didn't stop the reedy British man from looking down his nose at the assembled party, despite them being the only customers in the store. "As it says on the sign, I am one of the proprietors of Ripper and Rayne's Metaphysical Boutique. How may I help you?"

While thin on customers, the Metaphysical Boutique was packed with magical artifacts and spell ingredients, most of which even seemed to be authentic. Towering dark wood bookcases were crowded with relics. Human skulls carved into candle holders and gnarled monkey paws were prominently displayed on a table with a 10 PERCENT OFF sign. Unlike the other downtown shops, which tended toward the bright, cheery paint jobs of the world before the sunshade, Ripper and Rayne's walls were a dour shade of charcoal. Like a particularly sad tweed coat.

There were cobwebs in the corners of the ceiling and dust on the apothecary jars, as though the boutique had always been there. Anya doubted that the Sunnydale before would have had much use for a magic shop selling Sobekian blood stones or Orbs of Thesulah. It was entirely possible that the warlocks aged the place through magic, decorating it in grime to give the appearance of history. Warlocks were tricky that way. Anya had once wrought vengeance against one who magicked wrinkles and white hair onto himself to pretend to be his own father and escape his wife. Anya cursed him to stay the age he pretended to be, inflicting upon him all the bodily ailments of the geriatric—backache, gout, incontinence, impotence, debilitating nostalgia. The human body was a treasure trove of self-inflicted punishments.

"You two were here last week, weren't you?" Rayne asked, narrowing his eyes suspiciously at the human boys. "Looking for some very specific spell ingredients. Kandarian fangs and a jar of infernal sands. Your friend claimed to have the Books of Ascension. Has he reconsidered selling them?"

"Oh, the Books of Ascension," Andrew said, his shoulders sagging. "They sort of, um—"

"Blew up," Jonathan finished for him.

"As did their friend," Anya said.

"Ah, well," Rayne said, his face relaxing into something like relief. "Demon Ascension is a sensitive business. It can easily overwhelm a magical novice. You're keeping"—his eyes flickered toward the vampires lurking near the door—"*hardier* company these days. Feel free to take a look around, my friends. There's nothing on the premises that could cause you harm." He reached back, tapping a framed paper with an official-looking golden seal in the shape of a snake spitting fire. "We've been certified for vampire safety by the Church of the Eternal Night themselves. Won't even eat garlic for lunch except on days off."

"Then you must be delicious," Drusilla said, floating down the stairs toward a display of tarot cards.

"We need some information on the boys' magical arsenal," Spike said flatly.

"Right," Andrew said. "Warren bought a lot of stuff from here, but we were never sure what all of it did. And now that he's gone he can't tell us." With a gulp, he glanced back at Angelus and cautiously held out his hand. The beefy vampire slapped the crumpled list into his waiting palm. Andrew flattened the page on the top of the glass counter. "We were hoping you could fill us in on the official names and combat stats of these."

"Quite the list," Rayne said, examining the contents without deigning to touch the paper. He squinted through his bruised eye. "Ah, you are the owners of the Ram's Horn horn. Have you found much use for calling forth all the livestock of hell?"

"Not yet," Andrew said defensively.

"Well," Rayne said with a flick of his eyebrows. "Tracking down all of these would take quite a bit of time. Sure, the Urn of Fernda is well known for being adamantine—"

"Like Wolverine's claws?" Jonathan asked, his face scrunched. "But it's made out of clay, not metal."

"Adamantine, not Adamantium!" Andrew said, whacking his friend with the back of his hand. "It means unbreakable."

"So . . . like Wolverine's claws," Jonathan said slowly. "But clay?"

Rayne didn't look up from the list. "These unknown items would be much harder to parse. For instance, who's to say whether this 'medieval knight's gauntlet' is the Glove of Myhnegon, which shoots lightning, or the Gauntlet of Hellfire or even just a spare bit of armor your friend found on a shelf? I'd need to go through our sales records and cross-reference to our inventory, which, of course, we keep by hand—"

"What needs cross-referencing, Ethan?"

A second British man with short, graying hair ducked out of the back room, holding a steaming mug that Anya could only assume was tea. She hadn't lived on earth for long, but Anya did find it odd that there were this many English accents in one room in California. Between the warlocks, Spike, and his wild-eyed prophetess Drusilla, you could chart all London by cadence alone.

"Back from your break so soon?" Ethan asked the taller man, his eyes bulging in a way Anya recognized as trying to silence someone without words. Her coworkers often made that face when they wanted her to stop talking. It was so much less effective than just telling someone to shut up. Demon-Mike had tried to tell her that human manners wouldn't allow for that kind of frankness. He hadn't been able to explain *why*.

The taller man didn't seem to notice Rayne's silencing face. He lifted his green mug in greeting and introduced himself as "Ripper Giles, co-owner of the Metaphysical Boutique. What is it you need cross-referenced? I know these inventory books like the back of my hand. I wrote them myself."

"We need to find out about some magical items," Andrew said, tapping the list with his index finger. "Especially this staff."

"I've got this handled, Ripper," Rayne stressed. "Go back to your cuppa."

"You know, I'm beginning to see why that slayer popped you in the face," Ripper said, frowning at his associate as he neared the hand-written list. "Not that I questioned it much before. I've said for years that you have a very punchable face—"

"The slayer?" Angelus asked, marching down the steps in the entryway. "She was here?"

"Yesterday," Ripper said. He set down his mug and ran a hand through his hair. "She was searching for the Dowsing Rod of Vem. When she found that we no longer had the item in our possession, she got violent."

Anya's eyebrows went up. A dowsing rod could certainly be something stafflike. Angelus shot her a significant look that said that he was thinking the same thing. Or, at least, Anya assumed that's what the look meant. She got momentarily lost in those soulless brown eyes, imagining how it would feel to rub her warm body against his cold one.

"There's no proof she was the slayer. Just a girl with a powerful right hook. She could have been anyone," Rayne said, shaking Anya out of her reverie.

Right. Interrogation, she thought. *The impending dissolving of the universe. No time to get distracted by hunky corpses.*

"Is there any chance that this Rod of Vem could be confused with Gandalf the Gray's staff?" Andrew asked. "The one with the flat top, not the curved one with the Elven runes—"

"Don't waste their time," Jonathan told his friend in a harsh whisper, lurking near a shelf with a large sign that warned not to speak Latin in front of the books. "The curved one is obviously Gandalf the White's staff—"

"You'll need to be more specific," Ripper said. "Was it birch wood or olive?"

"Olive? I think?" said Andrew. "You sold it to our friend Warren, like, two years ago—"

"And the slayer stole it from them earlier today," Anya interrupted, cutting to the heart of the matter. Really, these humans would dance around the point for hours if they could, talking indirectly until they'd aged themselves into obsolescence. "Resulting in the death of the guy who bought it from you. I wonder who told her where to go looking for it? You did say you knew about the demon Ascension?"

She raised her eyebrows significantly at Rayne and his recently punched face.

Rayne lifted his hands and backed into the Church of the Eternal Night certification on the wall. Sweat beaded on his temples. "Hold on a minute! I don't like what you're implying."

"That you got your ass kicked by the slayer and told her exactly where to find a treasure trove of weapons?" Spike asked.

"Look," Rayne said, his voice quivering with desperation. "The slayer came in, demanding to know how to track down something that could be considered pure evil. She tortured me for information! I had to tell her who had the dowsing rod! She would have torn me limb from limb!"

His eyes darted from person to demon, searching for a friendly face. Even his associate stepped away from him, taking a quiet sip of his tea.

"Traditionally," Ripper said in a flat tone, "the slayer is a young woman able to blend in with her teen peers."

"Well, this one was huge," Rayne lied easily. "Hulking! Six feet if she was an inch, fourteen stone of pure muscle—"

Anya folded her arms. "She's a five-foot-four hottie with the body and blond highlights of a pop star. We've all seen the tape."

"I can see her," said Drusilla, tracing the air and twirling dreamily around a table of chalices and small cauldrons. "Jumping into other people's gardens and stamping on the roses. She won't stop until every flower is dead."

"If she's just killing flowers, then we have no problem here," Rayne said quickly.

"Drusilla is being poetical," Angelus said. "She's insane."

"She's prognosticating is what she's doing," Spike said. Wrapping a possessive arm around Drusilla's corseted waist, he stopped her twirling and clutched her tight to his side. "My girl sees the future. Or, rather, the lack of future coming our way. The slayer is up to something big enough to disrupt her visions. So tell us what you know, or we'll have to bleed it out of you."

"It's been ages since I had a taste of home," Drusilla crooned, eyeing Rayne and licking her lips.

"'Into every generation a slayer is born: one girl in all the world, a Chosen One,'" Ripper intoned, his voice softening into the musicality of recitation. "'She alone will wield the strength and skill to fight the vampires, demons, and the forces of darkness; to stop the spread of their evil and the swell of their number. She is the slayer.'"

Suspicion bloomed in Anya's chest. She wasn't convinced that they should trust either of these warlocks. Letting the vampires eat them was sounding more and more appealing.

"You seem to know an awful lot about her," she said to Ripper. "Are we sure she didn't kick the crap out of you too?"

Ripper gave a weary shake of his head. "I was on my lunch break when the girl came looking for information. I didn't even see her. But I grew up hearing the legend of the slayer."

"What about the Gandalf staff—I mean, the dowsing-rod thing?" Jonathan asked. "Why did the slayer want it so badly? All it ever did for us was roll off tables and try to point itself toward the coast."

Ripper came out from behind the counter and pulled a moldy leather book off the closest shelf. With a few expert flicks through the pages, he held up an illustration of what looked to Anya like a regular old walking staff. A long tree branch with a flat top and some curvy stick bits at the top.

"The Dowsing Rod of Vem," Ripper said, tapping the picture with his index finger. "Otherwise known as the Sycophant's Staff. It points the wielder toward the closest source of most potent evil."

Angelus popped the collar of his heavy leather jacket, lips drawn down in a smug smile. "Then why didn't it bring her to me?" he asked.

"Us," Spike amended. He inclined his head to Ripper and Rayne. "You're looking at what's left of the Whirlwind."

"The Whirlwind?" Andrew asked. "Are you guys in a band? That's so cool. If you ever need a different sound, I play panpipes and the ocarina and—"

"Basically any instrument you can play in *Legend of Zelda*," Jonathan finished for him.

"Nuh-uh!" Andrew said. He gave a self-conscious shrug toward Angelus. "I never learned how to play a harp."

"We are *not* a band," Angelus said.

"We're a family," Drusilla said.

Spike flashed a predatory smile at the human boys. "The most bloodthirsty vampire family to ever cross the Atlantic."

"Oh, how I miss Grandmummy," Drusilla sighed. She pulled free of Spike's grasp, clasping her hands and swooning toward

Angelus like a child begging for candy. "Can't we ever go bring her flowers?"

"I'd rather sunbathe than set foot in that bastard's mausoleum," Angelus growled.

This was exactly the kind of exclusionary history that Anya had wanted to avoid. The vampires didn't seem to care that no one but them could understand this undead doublespeak. It was just like when a group of Anya's vengeance coworkers had gone on vacation together, then spent the next hundred years making jokes about the screaming frogs of Acheron Cove.

"So what if," Anya asked Ripper and Rayne, "the slayer got ahold of this Dowsing Rod of Vem *and* the infinite reality-hopping power of the Marnoxon gem, for example. Would that be a coincidence or, like, real bad news?"

"The Marnoxon gem?" Ripper repeated. He set the leather book on the counter and leaned back. "The bit of Creation that vengeance demons use to grant Wishes?"

"No duh!" Anya threw up her hands. "The slayer went a'murdering in Arashmaharr and stole it. She's got it screwed into the top of that staff—very tacky if you ask me—and has been using it to portal-jump...."

Both warlocks paled. A feat for two pasty-faced Brits. Ripper reached into his back pocket and retrieved a pack of cigarettes. Fishing one out with his teeth, he lit it, surely contaminating the books and relics sitting out in the open air. Drusilla danced in the trails of smoke.

"If what you're saying is true," Ripper said, exhaling a long poisonous breath, "then we are facing something far worse than just a

76

thieving slayer. If that girl is following the lead of the dowsing rod, it will take her to Demondale's Black Flame flag."

"Demondale has its own flag?" Jonathan asked. "Where? City Hall?"

"It's not a literal flag to be run up a pole and saluted," Rayne said with a sneer. "It's Hell's Own Herald, the burning heart of evil hidden in plain sight. A touch of hellfire that marks this town as a colony of hell."

"If the slayer so much as taps the Black Flame with the Marnoxon gem," Ripper said, squeezing his eyes shut, as though blocking the image from his mind, "they'll eradicate each other. And everything else."

"Right, an apocalypse," Spike said with a snort. "So what? This is Demondale, mate. Every day is the End of Days for you humans."

"An apocalypse! Ha!" Ripper laughed mirthlessly. When he spoke again, his voice was a rough whisper. "An apocalypse can be thwarted or survived. What we are looking at is unmitigated erasure."

"Tabula rasa," said Rayne gravely.

"The total bloody destruction of the entire universe we exist in—from planet to atom—erased from the fabric of reality. As though it never happened," Ripper concluded. He took another long drag from his cigarette, not seeming to notice as ash rained into his tea. "Not even the roaches will remain."

"The end of existence?" Anya spluttered. Images of her life whirled through her mind—her apartment on earth, her clothes, her new coin-sorter. She hadn't even had a chance to count the cash in her pocket. "But—but I live here! I finally have a hair color that suits me!"

Drusilla yowled, covering her face with shaking hands. "All gone, all gone. 'My worldly rest hath gone; with a scream as it passed on.'"

"Your clairvoyant is right," Ripper said, looking at Spike and Angelus. "You lot might as well go see the sunrise and turn yourselves to dust because if the slayer sets her mind to it, she could extinguish any reality where hell exists on earth. Including ours."

In a blur of leather and ponytail, Angelus charged behind the counter. He gripped Rayne by his silk collar and lifted him bodily off the ground.

"You did this," Angelus roared in the smaller man's face. "You doomed us!"

"I—I just told her where to find the staff," Rayne choked. The heels of his shoes scrabbled against the wall. "She wanted to find the Black Flame flag and I thought, 'Why not?' I told her that she could steal the dowsing rod during the current owner's Ascension ceremony—it's not in the slayer's purview to murder teen boys, even ones meddling in dark magic. No harm, no foul!"

"No harm?" Angelus bellowed, giving Rayne a firm shake. "What did you think would happen when she found the Black Flame flag?"

"I figured the staff would lead her straight to the guardian of the flame and that would be the end of her. When she was dead, the boys could even get their staff back, if they wanted to," Rayne said, talking at a rapid pace as though trying to expel all the words before he ran out of air. "I didn't know she was searching for the Creation gem! Perhaps she already had it. Or already knew how to get it! She only asked me about dark magic. 'Pure evil,' she said. She needed to find pure evil. I'm a warlock, not a demonologist! I wouldn't know how to get ahold of the Marnoxon if I wanted to. I had nothing to do with her fight with the vengeance demons!"

Anya considered the slayer's rampage through Vengeance LLC. Picturing her coworkers cleaved to bits made her equally sick and hungry for revenge. It had been eons since she had considered taking vengeance on her own behalf.

"Did she leave here with a big-ass ax?" she asked Rayne.

Rayne's shoes stopped struggling. "Oh, well. I suppose she did leave with a Pylean Crebbil, but it was up as decoration over the bathrooms. I never assumed she would use it to—"

Ripper pinched the bridge of his nose. "Oh, Ethan, you absolute prat."

Angelus's fangs struck Rayne's neck. The man didn't even have time to cry out. One moment, his feet helplessly doubled their kicking. The next, his eyes were empty, and his body was limp. There wasn't even a slurping sound.

Did all vampires eat so quietly or was Angelus a particularly dainty killer?

Angelus dropped Rayne's body unceremoniously to the ground and wiped his mouth with the back of his hand. "Spike, Dru, come on. We've got a slayer to hunt."

"Wait!" Anya said. She knew that the vampires didn't really need her help, but she definitely needed theirs. At any moment, the sky could come crashing down, a torrent of obliteration snuffing out everything in its path. Including her, entirely human without the magic that marked her as a demon, powerless to escape. It was torture, knowing that she couldn't just hide in a nonhellish universe until the slayer was done with her killing spree.

She had to get back the Marnoxon gem. It was either that or die—and she was *not* interested in death.

"We don't even know where the slayer is going!" she said. She peered over at Ripper, who looked as pale as his dead associate. "You sold the dowsing rod. Where is it pointing?"

"The only place it can point is a colony of hell. At the Black Flame flag," Ripper said stiffly. He seemed determined not to look down at Rayne's corpse.

"And where is that?" Angelus asked.

"How the hell should I know?" Ripper huffed.

"Why don't you give us an educated guess, mate?" Spike said. The threat in his voice was clear.

Ripper tossed down his cigarette and ground it under his shoe, smearing desiccated brown leaf bits across the floor. "The City Council appoints a powerful demon to act as the guardian of the flame," he said. "To prevent something like *this* from happening. But if you want to know where to go, you'll need to rough up someone higher in the food chain. I have no idea where the Mayor would want his flag planted."

"The Mayor?" Andrew echoed. He nudged Jonathan, who flinched, his gaze stuck on the dead Rayne. "We have an in at the Mayor's office."

"We used to," Jonathan said. He dug in the front pocket of his backpack and retrieved a City Hall ID tag. The photo on the front was of a smug-looking boy whose dark hair was gelled into points. Underneath the word INTERN was the name Warren Mears.

THE SLAYER

THE SLAYER HAS never been to a winery before. Technically she's only a junior in high school. The wizard staff leads her to a hillside lined with grapes hung on wooden trellises, acres of fruit strung up like scarecrows. She gets all the way to the cavernous tasting room at the top of the hill before being attacked by a horde of evil monks.

Finally, a fight worthy of her training.

Wine barrels line the walls, stacked three high and stamped with the words SHADOWDALE VINEYARDS. At the far end of the room, above an eight-foot-long bar with a concrete top and empty stools waiting for tasters thirsty for evil wine, there is a metal seal of a goat head. Out of its horns, the Black Flame flag burns smokeless fire.

She's never seen the Black Flame split into two before either. Does that make this Shadowdale doubly evil? Probably. After all, what kind of place has evil monks?

At least, she assumes they are monks. Their faces are demonic but they're all dressed like Robin Hood's badger friend—in thick brown robes cinched at the waist with rope belts that make it all too easy to grab and spin them. They fight en masse, an endless wave of punches and kicks for the Slayer to anticipate and counter.

Ramming the end of the staff into the nearest monk's solar plexus for leverage, she backflips, landing kicks on two more assailants before she lands. Arm block. Rotational wrist lock. Spinning back-fist. A leg aims for her knee and she sweeps it, sending a brown robe crashing to the floor. Hands clamor for the staff, pulling it even as she holds firm. Duck and swipe. Elbow strike. She smashes the bottom of the staff into whatever foot or leg is nearest—whac-a-mole-ing demons away from her. If she can make it to the wine barrels, she can climb to the top and dash around the room, hit the Black Flame flag, and be on her way. But she's kind of enjoying the workout.

The Slayer throws a demon over her shoulder, slamming its body into two more. When she looks up, the breath leaves her lungs as fast as if she'd been sucker-punched.

Her mother cuts through the crowd. The monks that the Slayer hasn't trounced fall back, their shouts and grunts silenced to a more monklike quiet.

Joyce Summers has liquid-brown eyes and soft blond curls. She wears a white cashmere cardigan and linen pants. In the darkness of the tasting room, she looks like an angel.

She holds her hand out to the Slayer.

"Mom," the Slayer says on a sigh.

"Buffy," Joyce says, her voice like music. "I've missed you so much."

"I've missed you too," the Slayer says. She steps forward, wanting to wrap her arms around her mother, to stop running long enough to drown in a hug full of that perfect Mom smell: basil and gardenias and sunlight and hairspray and the powdery perfume of Mother's Day gifts gone by.

But Joyce takes a step back, her palm still extended.

"Buffy," her mom says again. "Give me the staff. The Marnoxon gem is too dangerous for a teenager to wield."

The Slayer's heart sinks. She keeps her grip on the staff firm, holding it across her body like a shield. Her body stiffens, remembering its former defensive posture.

"My mom doesn't know anything about magical objects," she says, edging backward. "If it's not an indigenous fertility mask, she's not interested."

"Excuse me for taking an interest in your life. As the mother of the Slayer, I've had to learn more about the occult," the creature that looks like her mother says in a decent impression of Joyce's exasperated laugh.

"You're not my mom," the Slayer says, bending her knees and preparing for an attack. She doesn't know if it'll come dead-on or from behind, where the monks lie dormant, but she knows now that she walked directly into a trap. Shame at her own stupidity makes her antsy to punch something. "My mom has no idea what a Slayer is. Much less that I am one."

"You never imagined that I'd find out?" the Joyce impersonator says. "You thought you could keep it a secret from me forever? While you go out every night and come home bloodstained? While you use the Marnoxon gem to slide from reality to reality, wreaking havoc?"

"Well, now I know you're not my mom," the Slayer says, wetting her lips. "Even if she did know about the supernatural, she definitely doesn't know about portal travel. I didn't even find out there was more than one dimension until I got thrown out of mine."

"Well, maybe if you'd told her there was a way out of this world," the fake Joyce says, a vicious smile pulling up the corners of her mouth, "she'd still be alive."

Without warning, without sparkly light or magical preamble, the Slayer's mother transforms into a girl, younger than the Slayer. In a fuchsia Limited Too T-shirt and a cocked hip posture that screams middle school, the girl flicks her long brown hair over one shoulder.

"Who are you?" the Slayer asks.

"Oh, like you don't recognize your own sister?" the girl says, crossing her arms over her chest. "Real funny, Buffy. Ha-ha."

The Slayer gives an apologetic wince of nonrecognition. "Sorry, whatever you are. I can see you're trying real hard to get under my skin, but I don't have a sister. I mean, look at yourself. Could you look any less like me? Brown hair? Blue eyes? And you're at least three inches taller than me."

"You really think you're pulling off a natural blond? Give me a break." The fake sister snorts. "I'm your sister. Dawn. Dawnie? Little bit? I steal your clothes and read your diary and follow you around when you do Slayer stuff. You rescued me from a gang of dancing demon bears? And an evil ventriloquist dummy? Come on, Buffy! You know me!"

"I really don't. The dummy rings a bell, but you? Not so much," the Slayer says. "Maybe this dimension's Slayer has a sister, but that's so not my backstory. I'm an only child. Practically prototypical. Spoiled rotten, custody battle, trouble with authority. You've got me all wrong."

"I'm not wrong!" the girl shrieks. In her rage, she begins to swell. Inflating like a tweenage bouncy castle, her willowy limbs fill the empty space at the center of the tasting room. Six feet tall. Then seven. Eight.

The Slayer climbs atop the nearest stack of barrels to avoid being squashed. Her route to the goat-head seal isn't as clear as it had been before she tried to hug some evil shapeshifter pretending to be her mother. Live and learn.

"Give me the gem, Slayer," the giant "sister" roars, bending down so that her enormous face is within spitting distance. If she starts to fi-fie-fo-fum, the Slayer is going to have to pull off some drastic maneuvers to keep from being eaten. "You're not worthy of carrying it!"

"Just take the L—Dawn, was it?"

"I am the First Evil," roars the entity. "Beyond sin, beyond death—"

"Beyond boring, beyond help," the Slayer says as she takes off running down the line of barrels, which are, unfortunately, not as stable as she would have hoped. They roll and tumble out from beneath her, cracking against the ground like a particularly difficult *Donkey Kong* level. A tidal wave of wine splashes against the concrete floor. Somehow, the giant girl's jeans remain unstained.

"Careful!" the Slayer warns the giant. "If you're really my *little* sister, then there's no way you're old enough to drink that!"

The giant lets out another ear-piercing rage-screech. The monks swarm again, their robes rustling as they crowd toward the Slayer. She jumps off the last remaining wine barrel and onto the back of the closest monk, using the clamoring mass of them as stepping-stones to the bar top.

The goat-head seal watches impassively as the Slayer takes a running leap and slam-dunks the green gem into both prongs of the Black Flame. As the vineyard tumbles into nonexistence, the giant girl in the center of the tasting room shifts between shapes, wearing the faces of dozens of strangers before bursting into floaty pink mist.

"I told you that you weren't my sister," the Slayer says, shaking her head. "Summers women are all distinctly corporeal."

"You cannot kill me, Slayer," the pink mist says. "I am a concept that you will carry with you wherever you go, the very nature of evil itself—"

"I might carry the concept of you, but *you*-you? You're a goner."

With a flick of the staff, the Slayer lets herself fall backward into the purple light of the Creation gem's portal.

FIVE
Jonathan

THE DOWNTOWN STREETLAMPS made the white limestone of City Hall glow the way the moon used to. Back when the moon was visible. The sunshade spell blocked out all light in the sky, even the stars. Jonathan, who had grown up with a telescope in his room, assuming that one day he'd be tall enough to become an astronaut, missed being able to chart the constellations.

He also missed Warren. In the hours since he and Andrew had left the botched Ascension, Jonathan felt like he'd become completely invisible. He was pretty sure that Anya the vengeance demon hadn't learned his name yet. And the vampires only looked at him when they were thinking about killing him. Undead-obsessed Andrew was thrilled to have three vamps to pepper with questions. He hadn't even noticed that Jonathan was lagging behind the group.

If Warren were there, he would have seen the way Jonathan strained under the weight of the shrink ray in his messenger bag. Even if it was just to make fun of him for being the slowest member of the group, he would have noticed.

"Hey, do you guys know Tucker the Merciless?" Andrew asked the bloodsuckers as the group climbed the stairs leading to City Hall. "He's a vampire. About my height, dark hair. Beautiful singing voice."

Spike's upper lip curled. "Sorry, mate. No self-respecting vampire would call himself Tucker. No matter how mercilessly he was tucking himself—or anyone else."

"Oh, well. He might have changed it by now. I always thought that if I were a vampire, I'd change my name to something cooler. Like Cyrus. Cyrus the Virus." Andrew's shoulders came up to his ears until he was hunched, vulturelike, into his own chest. "But Tucker's my brother. He got turned right after the sunshade went up."

Jonathan rolled his eyes, the same way that he and Warren used to whenever Andrew started telling Tucker stories. Andrew was full of Tucker stories. Even before Tucker had become a vampire, there had been a dozen stories about him for any prompt.

Tucker, who was the best Dungeon Master since Gary Gygax himself.

Tucker, who spoke multiple languages, including Klingon and Elvish.

Tucker, who summoned demons to Sunnydale before it was trendy.

Jonathan wasn't surprised at all that Tucker had cut contact with Andrew once he'd been turned. Nothing would ruin the mystique of the undead like an overeager little brother.

"Freshly turned, huh?" Angelus asked. "He's probably one of those goofballs in a pirate shirt and a fake accent, quoting Anne Rice. This town's full of amateurs. Do you know who sired him?"

"He, um, volunteered," Andrew said. "At the Church of the Eternal Night? I couldn't go because I was still in school—I mean, there still were schools then—but I think it was the Master—"

Letting out a growl closer to that of a lion than a man, Angelus gripped Andrew by the turtleneck. When the vampire's face transformed, Jonathan was hyperaware of the threat of violence in the glint of his fangs. His mind kept replaying the moment Angelus killed Ethan Rayne, the viper strike of those teeth that had torn the life out of Rayne's body. It had happened in a blink. If Angelus decided to kill Andrew, Jonathan would be powerless to do anything but dive out of the way of the blood splatter.

"Don't *ever* speak that name in front of me!" Angelus warned, yellow eyes flashing.

"I'm sorry!" Andrew's teeth chattered in fear. "You asked!"

"Come on," Anya said with a bored-sounding groan. "City Hall closes at five. We don't want to have to come back tomorrow. There might not *be* a tomorrow, remember?"

Angelus released Andrew and stormed the rest of the way up the stairs, the other monsters in tow. Flushed, Andrew fell back, reluctantly trudging beside Jonathan once again.

"It's no use sucking up to them," Jonathan muttered to Andrew. He knew that the vampires could hear him even when he whispered, but he didn't care. "They're not going to turn you."

"I was just making conversation." Andrew sulked, avoiding eye contact. "Do you think it's racist to assume that all vampires know each other?"

"Probably," Jonathan said. He had found that it was safer to err on the side of not offending people. Especially people who wanted to eat him. "But that's not why they'll never turn you. Nerds don't get eternal life."

Andrew shot him a look of scorn and said, "Tucker did," before taking the rest of the stairs two at a time, just to prove that he could.

And Jonathan couldn't.

If Andrew did succeed in his quest to become a vampire, what would happen to Jonathan? How would he survive in Demondale without either of his friends? He had only stayed under the sunshade so that he could be part of the Trio. He could have moved to Orange with his parents and gone to college for computer science. He could have moved through the world, alone and anonymous. A nothing student who would graduate into a nothing employee. Maybe some-day a nothing middle manager with a business card that no one ever took. Doomed to forever water his parents' plants while they went on cruises without him.

If Warren didn't come back from the dead soon, Andrew would expose his neck to any vamp willing to turn him. Or lie about turning him long enough to drain him.

If the slayer found the Black Flame flag, there wouldn't be a world to live in. So, at least Jonathan would be dead before he was officially friendless.

Was it pathetic to find comfort in the impending apocalypse? Probably. But he did it anyway.

By the time he caught up to the group, they were inside City Hall's echoing lobby, gathered around a secretary's desk.

"I'm sorry," the secretary said. He appeared to be fully human, in a button-down shirt and a black vest that made him look like the concierge of a fancy hotel. "But without an appointment, I'm afraid I cannot allow you an audience with the Mayor. He's very busy and in the middle of an election—"

"This is a matter of life and death!" Anya said, slamming her hands down on the secretary's desk. "The apocalypse is coming!"

"You think you're the first group to come in with news of an apocalypse?" the secretary asked stoically. "The Mayor is well informed on the threats posed to his city."

"Listen here, you poncey little git," Spike said, letting his face transform into a fanged snarl. "We need to find the Black Flame flag right *now*—"

The secretary yawned and opened a desk drawer without looking. He held up a wooden crucifix the size of a ruler. Spike, Drusilla, and Angelus all let out leonine roars and flew back from the desk as though hit with a force field. Jonathan was deeply impressed. He wished he'd saved the crucifix from the security table before the slayer had stolen it.

"What a waste of time," Angelus huffed. "Let's get out of here. We'll find the flag without the Mayor's help."

Jonathan felt a tug of smug satisfaction as he retrieved Warren's badge from the heavy messenger bag. He approached the secretary's desk in open defiance of the crucifix, feeling unusually powerful. He slid the badge over to the secretary.

"One of the Mayor's handpicked interns was murdered," he said. "By the legendary vampire slayer. I think he'll want to know about it."

The secretary's jaw worked as he considered this information. "One moment, please," he said and picked up the phone on his desk, murmuring the information into the receiver. He replaced the handset. "He'll see you. But you'll need these to gain entry."

Out of another desk drawer, he retrieved a fistful of metal and scattered it across the surface of his desk.

"What the hell is that?" Anya asked. "Enchanted tokens? Anti-violence shields?"

Jonathan cautiously reached out and flipped over one of the aluminum pieces. The other side was high-gloss red, white, and blue with the words BRING HELL TO SACRAMENTO in a bold font.

"Campaign buttons," he informed the group.

"I hope you're all voters," the secretary said.

Spike and Angelus looked mutinous as they affixed the buttons to their leather coats. Drusilla gave an experimental lick to the needle-sharp pinback before attaching it to the front of her corset. Andrew had to help Anya place hers, after explaining that people generally didn't wear pins in the center of their chests.

"Why not?" she asked. "Isn't that where it would get the most notice?"

Jonathan didn't know how someone so old could be so clueless. If he'd been alive for eleven hundred years, he definitely wouldn't need *Andrew's* help in being stylish. The guy had a velvet cape in the back of his closet. He said it was for Halloween, but Jonathan knew that was a lie.

Once everyone was decked out in election swag, the secretary motioned them toward the door at the end of the hall, which stood open and waiting for them.

"Well, howdy, compadres! Aren't you a fun-looking bunch?" Mayor Richard Wilkins said, welcoming the group into his office. He was fair-haired, presenting as a middle-aged white man despite being a known immortal sorcerer. Jonathan had only seen him in person once. On New Year's Day, the Mayor had publicly cast the spell that had blotted out the sun and opened the Hellmouth lurking under Sunnydale High. The Mayor made the complex dark magic look effortless, never breaking a sweat even as the last of the magic-deniers in town had screamed in terror. Warren had applied for his City Hall internship the very next day, telling Jonathan and Andrew that the future was going to be in openly evil politicians.

"Please, make yourselves comfortable," the Mayor said, gesturing to the two chairs in front of his expansive desk.

Andrew helped himself to one of the chairs. Spike and Angelus stationed themselves on either side of the door like bodyguards. Anya sat on the floor, her legs crisscross-applesauce, which Jonathan found unbelievably embarrassing. He slunk into the remaining chair—because someone had to—and hugged the messenger bag in his lap like a security blanket. He would rather disappear altogether than be associated with this bizarre collection of demons. Especially when Drusilla started singing to the picture frames on the wall.

The Mayor was unperturbed by the odd behavior of the demons. In deference to the lack of seating for everyone present, he sat on the edge of his desk, between his nameplate and a display of expensive-looking pens.

"I hope all of you are planning to rock the vote in the upcoming gubernatorial election. I want to bring the sense of community and citizenship we've seen here under the sunshade to all of California," he said, punching the air with an avuncular wink. "Now, what can I do you for? My man up front said you all had some less-than-stellar news for me."

He seemed to be asking Jonathan directly, his ageless stare affixing Jonathan to the chair he had so grudgingly taken. Jonathan broke out into a cold sweat, feeling like he'd been called on without raising his hand. Had the secretary in the vest communicated to the Mayor that it was Jonathan who had shown Warren's badge to get them in?

"Mayor Wilkins," Jonathan said. Movement in the corner of his eye distracted him and he turned in time to see Drusilla creeping behind him. She planted her nose firmly on the top of his head. Her deep inhale ruffled his hair. Jonathan swatted wildly at her, wriggling in his chair but unable to escape. "*Stop that!* Mister Mayor, it's about your intern, Warren Mears—"

"He's dead. And it gets worse," Anya said, hijacking the Mayor's focus. "There's a slayer on the loose, and we're pretty sure she wants to end existence."

The group launched into the story of the slayer and the description of the superpowered weapon she'd crafted for herself. No matter how many details of impending doom they added and underlined, the Mayor's face remained set in an implacable smile.

"With the Marnoxon gem, she can erase any reality with a Black Flame flag just by tapping the gem against the flame," Anya said.

"And her magical dowsing rod will lead her directly to the flag," Spike added.

"Tinker, tailor, soldier, slayer," Drusilla sang in what might have been agreement, running her nails through Andrew's hair. "Lady, baby, eat her spleen."

"She could end reality!" Andrew said, cringing away from the vampire woman's hand. "Like smashing all the servers in the Matrix, but worse, because there's no real world to wake up to!"

"And we could all die at any moment!" Jonathan concluded. "Unless we find the Black Flame flag and stop her."

"Now, this is what I love about this town." The Mayor beamed, opening his arms to gesture at the assembled party. "Vampires and humans and"—his smile strained a bit as he examined Anya—"miscellaneous demons coming together for the common good. You all got concerned enough about one little slayer to band together? Gosh, that just makes my day. I'd love for you to share your story with our media team. It could sway a lot of the undecideds on this whole hell-expansion plan."

"All due respect, sir," Angelus said, somehow not managing to sound very respectful at all. "I think that the impending end of existence should take precedence over speaking to your media team."

"Well, on that point we will just have to agree to disagree, Mister Angelus," the Mayor said, shutting down the hulking vampire without so much as a flinch. From the scowl on Angelus's face, it was clear he was unused to being disagreed with, but he didn't dare argue. Jonathan had never seen a more impressive display of power in his life. It was amazing. Like Lex Luthor telling Superman to shut up. What would it be like to wield that kind of power?

As the clock on the wall struck exactly five o'clock, Mayor Wilkins loosened the knot in his tie, winding the silk through his hands. He folded it into a neat square and set it behind him on the desk.

"I appreciate you bringing this information to me. I hear your concern, and I value your insights. However, I have the utmost faith in the guardians of the Black Flame appointed by the City Council. We don't just give Hell's Own Herald to any old demon, you know. It's very safe. With old friends of yours, if I'm not mistaken." He nodded to Spike and Angelus. "Although I suppose I can't say I'm surprised you didn't know. I don't keep in touch with any of the women who broke my heart either. Of course, all the women who broke my heart are long dead now." His eyes twinkled with so much mischief that Jonathan couldn't tell if he was referring to his centuries-long life or his ability to make women who wronged him disappear. Either option was unpleasant. "I won't say that I'm not touched by you all coming together, however. Very touched. Seeing the undead and the powerless join forces for the greater good is what this town is all about. If you'd like to see for yourself just how safe the Black Flame flag is, I'd be happy to send you with my best girl to check on it. Just for everyone's peace of mind. How does that sound?"

Even as no one jumped to accept the offer, the Mayor picked up his desk phone and pressed one of the autodial buttons.

"Yes, Jeff, would you send in the security officer? I've got a field trip for her. Thank you."

In a matter of moments, the door crashed open. Spike had to leap out of the way to avoid being splattered against the wall.

"There she is!" the Mayor said, his smile widening. Jonathan wasn't sure where his cheeks had found the extra real estate.

In a black bustier catsuit that no one with a need to breathe could pull off, a vampire girl walked in, her face already transformed and ready to fight. Below a curtain of bright red hair, her yellow eyes swept the room.

Shock made Jonathan's jaw drop. He knew this girl. Or, at least, he had known her. When she had been a living, breathing nerd, just like him. The teacher's assistant in the Sunnydale High computer lab and valedictorian with early admission to any college of her choice, she'd been part of the last SHS senior class, granted a diploma by technicality when the opening of the Hellmouth blew up the school. Instead of an extended education, it seemed she'd found extended life.

"Oh my God. Willow Rosenberg?" Andrew gasped.

The vampire girl let out a catlike hiss. "Willow Rosenberg is dead. It's just Willow now."

"Vampires love a mononym," Anya observed to no one in particular. "Look at how well it's worked for Madonna. She's a thousand if she's a day."

"This here is my right-hand gal, Willow," the Mayor said, beaming at the furious redhead. "She'll accompany you to see the Master and his missus so you can see for yourself just how safe we are. And if on the way back you decide to chat with our public relations team about your experience today, just tell Jeff at the front desk."

"The Master." Angelus grimaced as Drusilla jumped up and down, clapping and crying, "Family reunion! Family reunion!"

"Come on," barked the vampire Willow. "Let's get a move on."

"Just a moment, Will," the Mayor said. "I need a private moment with the human boys."

Willow gave a nod of acknowledgment, pushing Spike and Angelus out into the hall. She looked Drusilla up and down and gave an approving flick of her eyebrows. "Nice dress."

"Thank you," Drusilla said, swishing her skirt back and forth so that her striped tights showed. "It's dyed with the blood of virgins."

Willow reached out, rubbing the fabric between her thumb and forefinger, maintaining intense eye contact with Dru. "Ingenious," she purred.

Anya started to leave, but Andrew caught her hand, holding her still as the door swung closed. Jonathan resisted the urge to smack Andrew's hand away. There was no reason for the demon girl to hang back with them. Her only connection to Warren was in failing to bring him back to life.

The Mayor's bright smile dimmed to its lowest wattage, the closest thing to a frown he seemed to be able to conjure.

"I couldn't let you boys go without saying how sorry I am to hear about Warren's passing," he said, clasping his hands. "I can't say I was never tempted to Ascend myself. But it's a risky business changing from one species to another. He'll be very missed around this old place. Never had such reliable IT. What a waste." He reached into his desk and pulled out a long white box of See's chocolates. He extended it to Jonathan. "Take this with my deepest condolences. And don't forget to vote in November."

THE SLAYER

THE SLAYER FINDS herself at the base of the stairs leading to Sunnydale High. Or whatever they call it in this dimension.

Her school. Go Razorbacks.

Not that she's been to school in—who knows how long? Time doesn't add up right switching between realities. She doesn't even know if she's technically still sixteen. How long has it been since she landed in Demondale? How many weeks did she spend stealing lunch money from vampires and torturing vengeance demons? How many days did she sleep on the bus? How long has it been since she got wished away?

She's starting to worry that she wouldn't recognize home even if she tripped and fell into it. Her memories of where she came from have started to go hazy, like a good dream that feels real until the details suddenly evaporate and never come back.

Still, this school looks right. Back in Demondale, Sunnydale High was razed to the ground by the opening of the Hellmouth. This main building seems intact. Two stories under a red tile roof. Stone pillars framing the front door. Concrete benches and tall shaggy pine trees. The front lawn where she studied with friends. When she had friends.

Even without the staff's pushing, she feels herself drawn inside.

It must be after school. The hallways are empty. Her footsteps echo on the waxed linoleum as she passes closed lockers. She can't help but pause in front of locker number 309 and try her combination on the lock. It doesn't open.

It's not her world. Just another reflection.

The staff nudges her deeper inside the bowels of the school, past unfamiliar graffiti and classrooms with teacher names she's never seen before.

The door to the library is closed, but the lights are on, so somebody must be home. Nudging open the door, she slips inside, breathing in the scent of neglected books and the lemon Pledgeiness of the polished wooden railings. For a single moment, she can close her eyes and believe she's back home, that Giles will turn around, ancient book in hand, and reprimand her for being late to today's training. And Willow and Xander could rush in, inviting her out to do something decidedly un-slayery. Like going to see the new coolest band at the Bronze. Or sitting on the couch to marathon movies and scarf snacks. And they'll have the same argument they always have about whether licorice should even count as candy when there's such candier candy to be had.

Instead, she hears a whoosh of air and opens her eyes to find a giant snake springing at her, baring the teeth of its five identical human heads.

"Buffy Summers," the snake heads hiss in unison. Each of them has big ears and a ring of hair receding from a bald skull that gleams in the overhead light. "At lasssst."

The Slayer's jaw drops. This is what she gets for thinking she was beyond surprises. She's seen some wack demons in her time—giant bugs and zombies and, once, a possessed desktop computer that only spoke in binary code—but this . . . This is a first.

"Principal Snyder," she says, taking in the sight. The last time she faced a giant snake demon was in her own reality, when she stopped the Master from opening the Hellmouth and its guardian popped out. That snake had definitely not had the face of the Sunnydale High principal. She tilts her head to examine the creature's singular body coiled around the octagonal center of the library. Its tail loops over the tables and chairs meant for studying. "You look good as Hellmouth spawn. Scales really work for you much better than a little suit and tie."

"I knew you would come here, Slayer," the Snyder snake heads say, bobbing up and down on their green scaly necks. "You're a pathological delinquent. You can't resist breaking the rules. Trespassing after hours, carrying an obviously stolen weapon, out of dress code. I don't know whether I would enjoy killing you or expelling you more. Thankfully I have the power to do both."

The Slayer glances down at herself. Sure, this tank top and jeans isn't the most stylish outfit she owns. If she'd had more warning that she was going to get punted out of her reality, she might have chosen a more versatile ensemble. Or, at least, sneakers that didn't show dirt so easily. The dust of at least three collapsed dimensions has turned her shoelaces a dingy gray.

"Out of dress code?" she asks.

"No religious artifacts are permitted on school grounds," the Snyder snake says. "But you knew that, didn't you, Slayer?"

The Slayer's hand reaches up, finding the silver crucifix around her neck. She's so used to its weight; she barely registers it anymore.

"Wow, someone took the separation of church and state way literally," she says, walking slowly around Snyder, keeping close to the bookshelves as she follows the staff's lead past the circulation desk and toward the audiovisual cage. She's relieved to see the Black Flame flag flickering out of a wall sconce inside. "So, I guess you've finally figured out that there are vampires in your town, huh? I gotta tell you, that would make my life so much easier back home. The Principal Snyder in my reality is, like, wholly in denial." She keeps the Black Flame flag in her peripheral vision as she slides around an empty circulation cart. "It makes sense that once you found out about evil, you decided to join up with it. Did you even want to protect the Hellmouth, or were you just hooked by the idea of being taller? It must have killed you to be so much shorter than most of the student body."

The snake's tail smashes a table lamp and topples a chair as it slithers forward, positioning itself for an attack. Stealth has never been Snyder's forte. The Slayer once saw the principal in her own Sunnydale get his tie stuck in his office door.

"You talk too much, Slayer," the snake heads hiss. "What? Are you too afraid to fight me, your mortal enemy? Me, your worst nightmare."

Without warning, one of the snake heads lunges for her. The Slayer flips out of the way and comes up swinging the staff. It cracks into the nearest principal face, knocking his jaw sideways. The other four heads roar in sympathetic pain, pressing themselves against the injured face to push its chin back into place.

"You think you're my worst nightmare?" The Slayer hiccups a laugh. "I've fought puppets more threatening than you, Snyder."

As the heads rise, preparing for another strike, the Slayer somersaults inside the A/V cage, closing the door behind her with the heel of her sneaker.

"I mean, come on," she says. "You can't even give me detention here. I'm totally interdimensional. The Sunnydale I'm from is just hell-adjacent, not a hell colony."

"*For now*," the Snyder heads warn. The five of them smoosh their huge foreheads against the cage, doing what Snyders do best, making threats with very little follow-through. "If you're here, Summers, then who is protecting *your* world?"

Buffy opens her mouth, willing a retort to find its way to her lips. But, inside, she feels the gnawing worry that's followed her from dimension to dimension begin to grow. What if she was cast out of her dimension so that something evil could take over Sunnydale, the *real* Sunnydale, without her interference? Every moment she's away, she's leaving the people she loves at risk. What if she finds her way back and her home is just as broken and evil as the worlds the green gem has brought her to?

What if she erases every Hell on Earth that has ever existed and the gem *still* won't show her the path home? How long will she have to run through realities, searching for answers?

Ten beady little eyes watch her with interest, the Snyder snake pleased with getting the last word. The Slayer lets him have it. The eradicating light let out by the Creation gem meeting the Black Flame is comeback enough.

SIX
Anya

BY THE TIME Anya, Andrew, and Jonathan made it down the steps of City Hall, the vampires were already halfway down the street. The group cast no reflection as they passed the giant picture windows of the Sunnydale Public Library.

"Hey! Wait up!" Andrew called, jogging to catch up.

Anya decided against telling him that getting his blood racing was a very dangerous way to win the vampires' attention. She didn't want to give the vamps any ideas. If the human boys died before she got her powers back, she'd never make any more money off them. There was no way she was going to devote an entire day to saving the world with no cash reward at the end.

What would be the point in living in this world without money?

Overhead, an owl flew in concentric circles. Owls were the only birds left under the sunshade. All the songbirds had migrated into Santa Barbara, craving sunlight. Instead of chirping, the trees in Demondale were full of screeches and squeaks. At least there were plenty of moths and crickets for the owls and bats to eat. The bug population loved the dark.

The owl dove for something that Anya's eyes couldn't make out. Unlike most demons, she didn't have very good night vision. It was one of many things about her body that hadn't upgraded with her vengeance powers. The majority of D'Hoffryn's employees didn't have to worry about obnoxious human limitations like skin that bruised or eyes that couldn't see the fourth dimension. Other human-born vengeance demons like Halfrek countered this by working harder than any natural-born demon, constantly trying to prove that their limitations were a gift. Halfrek could infiltrate humans and trick them into wishing whatever she wanted.

Anya wasn't sure that being human was anything more than a curse. She would have loved to have multidimensional vision like Frex or stony skin like Lloyd.

Not that it had saved any of them from the wrath of the slayer. She had killed them all. Slaughtered them in their cubicles. Even if Anya lived long enough to go back to Arashmaharr, it would be changed. Empty.

"Why do you have these humans following you around? Are they your servants?" Willow, the red-haired vampire, asked Drusilla as Anya, Andrew, and Jonathan rejoined the group.

"We're not servants!" Andrew said, his cheeks pink and shining from his brief sprint. "Willow, you know us! We were all on the academic decathlon together! We won state when you aced the globalization super quiz!"

"We went to the same synagogue," Jonathan added. "I was at your bat mitzvah. I gave you a copy of *Elder Scrolls: Arena* on CD-ROM, and your mom got mad because the cover had a girl in a leather bikini. Remember? She called me an 'agent of the patriarchy'? Your mom. Not the girl in the bikini."

"Knowing who you are is exactly *why* I'm confused, Jonathan," Willow said flatly, throwing a yellow-eyed glare over her shoulder. Anya noticed that the Mayor's guard vamp had yet to relax her face into something human-passing. Was it a political statement of some kind? Or did Willow just prefer herself bumpy and ready to fight? "Dorks don't generally get invited on reconnaissance missions."

That was a good point. Too good, actually. Anya couldn't have this new vampire talking the others out of letting Andrew and Jonathan tag along. Not only were they her ticket to a payday, but they had already proven to be quite useful. The group never would have made it past the officious little man at City Hall's front desk without Jonathan's intervention. Anya knew perfectly well that there were still places under the sunshade where people were prejudiced against demons. Too many times she'd caught Human-Mike upgrading the juices of human-passing customers free of charge—in some bizarre sign of mortal solidarity. Keeping Andrew and Jonathan nearby could be their ticket into places the vampires wouldn't be invited into. She only looked human. Andrew and Jonathan spoke fluent mortal.

"Hey!" Anya shouted at Willow. "These dorks are the ones who tracked down the slayer to begin with! Shouldn't that have been *your* job?"

"That's right!" Jonathan said, his teeth full of chocolate and caramel from the Mayor's box of condolence candy. "We have every right to help protect reality!"

Willow ignored them, turning back to Drusilla. "They could be snacks."

Drusilla considered the boys, her usually vacant blue eyes sharpening to an uncanny focus. She drummed her sharp fingernails on the curve of her jaw. "They do smell deliciously of fear. And chocolate."

"There could be just moments left on earth, and you want your last meal to be these two?" Anya raised her voice to get the vampire girls to focus on her and her nontasty demon blood. She recalled Spike sniffing her vengeance demon–ness back at the Bronze. Did she smell bad to vampires or just inedible? She didn't like the idea of being stinky. Particularly not when standing within sniffing distance of Angelus. "They're barely a chicken nugget compared to most humans. Hardly a meal."

"And certainly not enough to go around," Spike said. "It would take both of them to slake my thirst."

"There were plenty of humans waiting to be bitten at home," Drusilla said, waving a dismissive hand, her interest now solely with Willow. "Now, where have you been waggling your tail, Little Robin Redbreast? I would remember if you had flown into our nest before."

"Oh, I was sired last year," Willow said, bashfully lowering her lashes. "Just before the sunshade went up."

"No!" Drusilla clutched the other girl's leather-clad forearm. She lifted Willow's hand to her face and sniffed her wrist. "I never would have guessed you were such a baby. You're already so strong, so powerful."

Spike looked scalded by Dru's dismissal and fell into sulky step with Angelus.

"You know, there's this new thing called polyamory," Angelus said to him. "Where you don't have to get jealous every time your girlfriend falls in love with someone else."

"Sod off," Spike grumbled.

"Of course," Angelus continued, throwing a wink back at Anya, as though annoying Spike were a private joke between the two of them. Her heart cramped in her chest. Before she could decide whether or not to wink back—were winks reciprocal?—Angelus was talking to Spike again. "There is this old thing called *breaking up with your girlfriend who keeps falling in love with everyone but you.*"

"She's not falling in love," Spike grunted as Drusilla tripped over a crack in the sidewalk and fell into Willow's arms. "It's been ages since she made a friend. All those stage-door Johnnies don't count. Disgusting chaos demons and weak humans courting death."

The group started to trudge uphill, leaving the lights of downtown behind. Was part of the vampire physiology an immunity to aching feet? It certainly wasn't a skill vengeance demons had. Normally, Anya would use her powers to teleport where she needed to go. Before today, she'd never realized how dependent she was on the Marnoxon gem's magic. She was beginning to realize why humans were forever sitting in traffic. If she had to be powerless for longer than a day, she would definitely have to learn how to operate a car. At least then she could travel and sit at the same time. What could be more human than that?

"Excuse me, Willow the security officer?" she asked, shouting over Spike's and Angelus's irritated mutters. "Where exactly are we going?"

"To see the Black Flame flag," Willow said without glancing back. "At the Church of the Eternal Night."

On either side of Anya, Andrew and Jonathan took on the greenish pallor of mortal illness. Anya hoped that they'd keep their bile in their stomachs and off her shoes. She told them as much as she plucked the box of candy from their hands and took an almond cluster for herself. Hopefully protein would help fuel her fragile human feet.

For most of Sunnydale's history, the Church of the Eternal Night's headquarters had been the site of a Catholic church. Sprouting castle-like out of a neighborhood of banks and hair salons, it had the same red tile roof and white stucco façade as all the other important buildings in town. Two bell towers chimed on the hour. The marquee listed times for meetings and services. From far away, it would be easy to mistake it for a human house of worship.

Until you got close enough to see the stained-glass images of blood overflowing from bent necks and dripping down hands pressed in prayer. Demon labor had torn off all the iconography painful to vampires, every crucifix replaced with the new church's symbol of a coiled snake breathing fire.

Walking up the palm-tree-lined path to the front entrance, Anya could smell the magic keeping the trees alive. It gave them a sort of plasticky scent that reminded her of the fake Christmas tree the new receptionist had erected in the Vengeance LLC break room.

"At what point does a church become nonlethal to a vampire?"

Andrew asked as Willow threw open one of the heavy wooden doors leading inside. "I thought Catholic stuff was toxic to you guys. Crucifixes, holy water—"

"Missing your self-defense kit?" Spike asked him.

Willow gestured to the huge circular stained glass above the front entrance. It depicted a hand shooting out from a mound of grave dirt, underneath a white crescent moon. "The old bishop deconsecrated the building at the Mayor's request. But it was *desecrated* when the Master spilled that bishop's blood in the baptismal font." She and Drusilla cackled together as though this was the punch line to the funniest joke ever told. Seeing no one else enjoying themselves, Willow explained further, "Just to be safe, they replaced all the floors that could have been tainted with holy water. It's perfectly safe. It has to be. It's a vampire church."

"Vampire church," Angelus scoffed, slowing to a stop outside the open door. "I've never heard such an oxymoron. It's a cult of the arrogance of one egomaniac."

Anya sidled up beside him, close enough that she brushed his leather sleeve. His head snapped toward her. Was she imagining the way his gaze softened when he looked at her? Or wishing for it? She was unused to wishing for herself.

"All cults are feeding farms for egomaniacs," she said.

"That's true. But this one has a literal feeding farm on the premises," Angelus said.

He reached over, his cool fingers curling under her chin while his thumb brushed at the corner of her mouth. A shiver ran through her as she watched him lick the side of his thumb.

"Chocolate," he explained with a smile.

Anya's lips parted. She felt suddenly very human, helpless, and hunted. Only it wasn't as distasteful as she would have assumed. It was sort of exciting. Like being a teenager again.

Over her long, long life, Anya had done her fair share of dating. Mortal men, trolls, demons with mostly compatible genitals. But she hadn't gone out with anyone in Demondale. The only creature she'd even been tempted by since moving topside was Demon-Mike—but Best Pressed had something called a "fraternization policy" that had extinguished that daydream.

It had been years since she'd dallied with a vampire. There wasn't much mixing between vamps and vengeance demons. Vampires could inflict their own vengeance just fine.

But something about Angelus made her tingle. Like her, he was a demon cursed to wear his human skinsuit around. He participated in human society while also preying upon it. And he was so delectably unpredictable, both man and beast. A business owner and a murderer.

She wondered if he could absorb body heat, even if he couldn't generate it.

"Are you flirting with me?" she asked him, regaining her sense. "Or are you just snacky?"

"Can't it be both?" Angelus's lips twitched into a satisfied smirk as he started to stroll toward the church door. "Better keep your boys close if you don't want them drained and dished out for Sunday supper."

"It's Tuesday. And they aren't *my* boys—" Anya tried to explain, but Andrew and Jonathan cut her off by latching themselves on to her arms like barnacles.

She shook them off. "What did I tell you about looking like veal? Be normal, for God's sake," she said.

The inside of the vampire church was vast and ornate. The terra-cotta floors shone, as did the rows and rows of mahogany pews. Fallen angels with taloned hands looked down from the ceiling's many frescoes, their black bat wings rendered in horrible veiny life-likeness. Behind them, a silver full moon was painted above verdant hills, eclipsing all but the yellow glow of the sun's rays, a hint of the light behind the false dark.

Drusilla plunged both of her hands into the blood-filled baptismal font. She took a deep drink out of her overflowing palms, loudly smacking her lips.

"Do you know, I was very nearly a nun," Drusilla told Willow as blood dripped down her chin and chest. "Until my daddy Angelus found me and tortured me for weeks."

"You were tortured?" Willow asked, face open with fascination. "You're so lucky."

"I know," Drusilla said wistfully. "Nothing's ever been as good since."

At the far end of the room, the pulpit stood taller than anything else. And behind it was a wall of painted black flames licking up at the words *To do aught good never will be our task, But ever to do ill our sole delight.*

Jonathan read the inscription aloud, his face scrunched in confusion. "What is that?" he asked Anya and Andrew. "Is it from the vampire bible?"

"There's no such thing as a vampire bible," Angelus said, crossly. "It's probably just a quote from Baldy Redlips himself. He's exactly the kind of narcissist who would paint his own words on the wall."

"What?" Spike exclaimed, appalled. "That's *Paradise Lost*, you uncultured swine. Did you never read a book when you were alive, Angelus?"

Angelus puffed up his chest and schooled his face to look indifferent. "At least I didn't waste my life praying to turn into Lord Byron and doting on my mother!"

"Hey, you leave my mother out of this!" Spike yelled, shoving Angelus into the nearest pew. "You know how hard it was for me to kill her!"

"Praise darkness!" a pert voice cried out behind them. "The prodigals are returned home."

In an archway leading to some shadowy back room was a small blond vampire woman. She wore a powder-blue skirt suit with matching heels. Not that anyone could focus on her clothes when her transformed vampire face was so heaped in makeup. Anya had never seen yellow vampire eyes adorned with false eyelashes before, much less complemented with hot-pink spots of blush and matching lipstick. The overall effect was more disturbing than any of the imagery stained onto the windows.

Drusilla dashed down the aisle, crying out, "Grandmother!"

She towered over the blond vampire woman but didn't let that stop her from stooping for a hug.

"Hello, Darla," Angelus said. His shoulders were so stiff, Anya wouldn't have been surprised to find a dozen knives in his spine.

"Welcome to my home, darlings. I've been waiting for you to visit for ages," Darla, the vampire being crushed in Drusilla's hug, said. Freeing an arm from the embrace, she gestured to the room. "What do you think?"

"It's bright," Spike said. "I haven't been in a church since they were lit with candles."

"William, the last time you were in a church, lightbulbs hadn't been invented." Darla giggled. She peered around his shoulder at Anya and the nerd boys. "Aww, did you bring us an offering for the blood farm? How thoughtful!"

Anya stepped in front of Andrew and Jonathan. "Sorry, no, not offering these. They're key members of stopping the apocalypse."

"They're here to see the Black Flame," Willow said. "Someone had a nightmare about the slayer."

"It was dreadful, Grandmother," Drusilla said, nuzzling Darla's shoulder and smearing blood all over the smaller woman's suit in the process. "That horrible slayer won't stop until she's plucked every thorn out of the bush. Who wants a world with no thorns? How will the flowers defend themselves?"

"She's Drusilla's grandma?" Jonathan asked Andrew in a loud whisper. "Is it just me or do they look nothing alike?"

"I think they're blood relatives," Andrew whispered back. "I mean, vampire blood. Family through bites."

"Darla is my sire," Angelus said darkly. "I sired Drusilla. She sired Spike."

"Are you sure there isn't a vampire bible?" Andrew asked. "Because this sounds exactly like the part in Genesis that's all begats."

"Wait a minute! *She* sired *you*?" Anya asked, pointing from Darla to Angelus. "But she doesn't have an accent! All of you have accents!"

Darla let out a sparkling laugh that made her fake eyelashes bobble. "We've been in America for a hundred years. I let myself assimilate."

"Is that why you got kicked out of the band?" Anya asked her.

"She didn't get kicked out," Angelus rumbled, glowering at Darla. "She left. To sire hundreds of strangers and pollute our bloodline. Seems like every newborn vamp in town is my sibling."

Darla's sunny smile disappeared. "I left to bring about the advent of the vampiric era. To bring our people into dominance! I know you love your little nightclub, but feeding the masses isn't the same as *creating* them."

Angelus stared up at the ceiling. "Ugh, you sound just like him now."

"Just like whom, Angelus?" asked a new voice. A hidden door opened behind the pulpit. Out slid the oldest vampire Anya had ever seen. There was almost nothing human in his face. The usual transformed vampire snarl was compounded by wrinkles of age. Around his mouth and the tip of his nose was a permanent ring of blood-tinged skin. His ears were as pointed as his long fingernails. Light bounced off his hairless pate. His eyes were burning red.

"Speak of the devil and he shall slide out of a trapdoor," Spike muttered. "Good to see that the Church hasn't lost its flair for the theatrical."

Anya felt Andrew and Jonathan inching closer to her again. This time, she let them, feeling equally uneasy. The Master was legendary—in that he was so old that that he was practically a living myth. A vampire so powerful that no one knew his real name. It was said that he was so ancient that he had been created within the first two generations of vampires, closer to an Old One than a human. Even Drusilla cowered at the sight of him, backing away from Darla and behind Willow.

"Master, darling," Darla said, her perky face reinvigorated as the Master descended the steps toward her. "Did we wake you?'

"The old coot still sleeps during the day?" Angelus snorted, and elbowed Spike in the ribs, gesturing with his thumb in the universal sign for *get a load of this guy*. Anya wasn't sure if she was impressed by his fearlessness or worried that he was going to get them all slaughtered. The Master was more than strong enough to kill everyone in the room without breaking a sweat. If vampires could sweat.

"I received a call from the Mayor that I am supposed to show you Hell's Own Herald," said the Master. He spoke with a mild lisp, the words fighting to get around his huge fangs. "Although why such a ragtag group should be given a private viewing of a significant relic is beyond even *my* comprehension."

"Yeah, well, you're just the flag's guardian, not the decision maker, aren't you?" Angelus scowled.

"Angelus, if you can't be nice—" Darla warned.

"No, let the boy speak his mind. He's entitled to his hurt feelings," the Master said. He lifted Darla's chin with his sharp nails as though she were an apple he was considering biting into. "After all, he lost the greatest jewel in creation."

"Actually, the Marnoxon gem was being guarded by some grappler demons when the slayer broke into Arashmaharr," Anya said.

Darla glared at her, which seemed to be difficult under the weight of her fake lashes. "He was referring to *me*. Before the Master and I got married, Angelus and I were . . . involved. For a century or two."

Scandalized, Anya gaped at Angelus. "You dated your vampire mom?"

"It's very common," Angelus said defensively. He thrust an accusatory finger at Darla and the Master. "What *isn't* common is for your sire to sneak out of the family crypt and then return, married and the leader of a brand-new cult!"

Darla splayed a defensive hand on her chest. "I invited you to join the Church! You declined!"

"You invited me as a *friend* to come live with your *husband*!"

"Which I thought was very magnanimous!"

"Bored now," Willow said with an exaggerated yawn. "Domestic squabbles are so not how I want to spend my eternity. Can we see the flag so we can all go back to our afterlives?"

"Gladly," Darla huffed. She looped her arm through the Master's, her eyes never leaving Angelus. "Lead the way, hubby."

The Master gripped Darla's arm tight, his wrinkled head held high as he marched back up the church aisle and the steps to the pulpit. Behind him, the group formed a reluctant processional: Willow and Drusilla with Spike close at their heels; Anya, Andrew, and Jonathan clustered together; then Angelus, who waited so long to follow that Anya worried he might just leave and go back to the Bronze.

"Are we allowed to just announce when we're bored with people talking?" Anya asked Andrew, tipping her head to indicate Willow. "Because when I did that at work, Human-Mike threatened to write me up for bad customer service."

"I think it's an undead perk," Andrew told her. "They can just kill anyone who takes offense."

Anya sighed as a dizzying pang of yearning hit her. "If I had my magic, I could send each of you to your own pocket dimension, where your clothes tried to eat you and food turned to ashes in your mouth." Seeing Andrew's and Jonathan's horror-stricken faces, she added, "Not that I would! You haven't done anything to earn my vengeance. You shared your chocolate and promised me more money. I just miss knowing that I *could*. You don't understand how hard it is to be powerless. You've never been anything else."

The door hidden in the wall led to a rickety wooden staircase descending into inky blackness. In the dark, Anya's imagination taunted her with visions of what could be lurking beyond her perception. Quicksand. A giant swinging blade that sliced and diced anyone the Master found annoying. Disgusting fluffy bunnies with their razor-sharp teeth and long flopsy ears, just waiting to spring at her with their all-too-powerful back legs . . .

Ahead, hinges creaked. Picturing the bunny cages being opened, Anya screamed. Which made Andrew scream. Which then made Jonathan scream. Drusilla joined in, possibly just for fun.

At the bottom of the stairs, Darla and the Master paused inside an open doorway leading to a well-lit room. They looked questioningly up the stairs at Anya, who struggled to swallow and said, "Sorry. I thought I heard bunnies."

Darla shook her head in disgust, which Anya took as a sign of anti-Leporidae solidarity.

"Bunnies?" Angelus asked softly as they continued the rest of the way down the stairs. His voice made the hair on the back of her neck stand up. He moved so soundlessly in the dark, it was easy to forget that he was behind her. He must have been such an effective predator. "Is that what strikes fear into the hearts of vengeance demons?"

"I don't know about all vengeance demons," Anya said. "But this one, yes."

"You mean like Peter Cottontail and the Easter Bunny?" Angelus said. Even without seeing him, she could hear the mocking smile in his tone. "Cute little herbivores who couldn't hurt a fly?"

"Obviously *you've* never seen *Watership Down*," Jonathan said with an impressive amount of venom for a boy chock-full of chocolate and fear. "That cartoon gave me nightmares for years. I'm with Anya. Bunnies are gross."

"Thank you, Jonathan!" Anya said, feeling, for the first time, a small amount of warmth for the human and not just for his money. She set a hand on his shoulder. "If you want, when I have my powers back, I could send you to a dimension where there are no bunnies."

"Oh, um, that's nice of you to offer," Jonathan said, squirming at her touch. "But I think I'd still rather just have Warren back."

"Right, of course," Anya said. She took her hand back. "You're living with the gnawing guilt of murdering your best friend. I get it."

They passed through the door at the bottom of the stairs and entered an antechamber. The stone walls were damp, a reminder that they were underground. An oddly ornate chandelier hung from the ceiling, illuminating the humans that decorated the walls like living statues.

At least, Anya assumed they were alive. Their skin was missing the vibrance of life; all of them had taken on a flat grayish hue. But their chests rose and fell, and their closed eyes twitched as though they were dreaming. Dressed in matching black sack robes that did nothing for anyone's figure, the seemingly sleeping people stood on marble pedestals. Plastic tubes jutted out from their wrists and behind their knees, collecting blood and depositing it somewhere inside the pedestals.

"This is the blood farm," Darla said, motioning at the gray people with the same dispassion that Anya expressed when she showed customers the flash-frozen pastries in the glass display case at Best Pressed. "These gracious volunteers are filling up the font upstairs, as well as the meal kits we send home each week after services."

"You don't teach your parishioners to hunt?" Spike asked, touching the nearest blood-filled tube with a black-painted nail.

"Of course they don't," Angelus said, lurking in the doorway. "This keeps their flock dependent on them."

"They're our children, Angelus," Darla said with an insulted gasp. "We feed and care for them as any loving parents would."

"Funny," Angelus said. "I recall being taught to track and kill when I was a fledgling. Don't you remember, Darla? The two of us stalking through Galway, pouncing on any fool who stumbled into the dark—"

"That was a different time," the Master said, flapping a long-fingered hand dismissively. "In the age of the sunshade, there's no reason for us to rely on the stupidity of humans for food. No need to wait for invitations into their homes or to lure them down dark alleys. Since our presence was made known to them, the humans come to us. All these people walked willingly through our doors, wanting to service us."

"In exchange for eternal life, right?" Andrew asked. His gaze remained stuck on the closest gray person, a woman whose hair, stark white at the roots, grew darker as you moved to the brown tips. "This is the first step before they get turned?"

"Yes, of course," Darla said, quickly. "We have a very strict first-in, first-out policy. Once a new volunteer arrives to take their place, each of these lovelies will be granted the bite that saves."

"However long that takes," Angelus muttered.

Darla and the Master ushered the group through the next set of double doors. Here was a much larger room, lit exclusively by candelabras and held up with columns made of the same rough stone as the antechamber. Burial niches pitted the walls like a dresser missing its drawers. Anya had only been inside a catacomb once before. In the eighteenth century, she had trapped a Wisher's husband in a crypt full of chattering skeletons to punish him for asking his wife if she'd put on weight.

These catacombs had been transformed into a bedroom. A massive bed heaped in black silk sheets and fur blankets stood at the center of the room. The far wall was dominated by a gold-framed portrait of Darla and the Master in an alarmingly detailed nude embrace. The Master rendered in oil paint had more abs than Anya had ever seen on a person. Whether that was one of the benefits of immortality or simply artistic license was unclear.

An arm hung limp out of the niche closest to Willow, who craned her neck to get a closer look inside.

"Uh-uh," Darla said, shaking a finger at the security officer. "Let him rest. He's new."

Anya looked up at the many rectangular holes that overlooked the single bed. "Your children sleep in here? With you?"

"Yes, we're firm believers in co-sleeping with our newborns," Darla said. "At least until they can find a home of their own. Not everyone dies with good credit—and the cemeteries are positively packed these days."

Drusilla crawled inside a low niche, lying flat on her back and wiggling into the darkness.

"Is that black mold I smell?" She sounded muffled and far away. Just how deep were the niches? "Oh, Grandmother, I could sleep away an age in here."

Angelus skirted the room, refusing to look directly at the gigantic mattress. He stopped short at the oil painting. Beneath the gold frame stood a stone coffin, lidless and full of dancing black flame. Anya wasn't sure how she hadn't noticed it before—and then found herself, once again, distracted by the Master's portrait and its beefy pecs.

"You keep the flag of hell in a casket underground?" Angelus asked the Master. He prodded the corner of the stone coffin with the toe of his shoe. "Not exactly flying it proudly, eh? Worried you couldn't protect it up where anyone could find it?"

"This is a place of utmost distinction," the Master hissed. Salivary foam gathered at the corners of his mouth. "That sarcophagus was my home for centuries. It alone protected me from the sun and those who sought to kill me. Within its stone walls, my beloved Darla and I sailed away from the shores of the Virginia Colony and her wasted mortal life. Belowdecks on a state-of-the-art pinnacle ship, my love and I lay entwined for months—"

"We get it. You bone," Spike groaned in disgust.

"That sarcophagus was my salvation," the Master continued. "To imbue it with Hell's Own Herald is the highest honor."

"I thought it was a flag," Jonathan said. He knelt in front of the flaming coffin, fingertips extended and wiggling toward the fire. "It's not even hot."

The Master folded his arms over his chest and gave an ambivalent little shrug. "They are the embers of eternal darkness. They radiate neither light nor heat, but if your hand were to so much as graze the flames, you would immediately die, your soul forfeited to damnation."

Jonathan jerked his hand away and bolted backward, knocking into the nearest candelabra. He yelped in pain as candle wax dripped onto the top of his head. Anya pulled him up, placing him next to Andrew, where she could keep an eye on both of them.

"There is no room in Demondale as safe as this one," Darla said. "The pulpit door opens only for the undead, and there's an alarm spell on the blood farm that would let us know if anyone was trying to enter our bedroom unescorted. And on the rare occasion that the Master and I weren't here to keep watch over the Black Flame flag, our bedroom is always guarded by our children sleeping in the walls."

"So you see, everything is perfectly safe. You may return to the Mayor and tell him you have been assured," said the Master. "Here endeth the lesson."

"I think the lesson is just starting." Standing in the doorway was a teenage girl, holding a crossbow in one hand and a wizard staff in the other. The light of the Marnoxon gem cast emerald shadows on her blond hair. The slayer smiled. "You left the door upstairs open."

SEVEN
Jonathan

PANIC SWEAT PRICKLED down Jonathan's back. The slayer was less than twenty feet away from the stone sarcophagus. If Ripper and Rayne were right, then all she had to do was throw the Marnoxon gem into the black flames and this reality would cease to be.

Someone had to stop her.

Someone had to get the Gandalf staff.

Shying backward as the vampires all started growling at the intruder, Jonathan whispered to Andrew, "Do you see an electrical outlet anywhere? If we hit her with the shrink ray, we could definitely get the gem and get out of here."

"If they had electricity down here, why would there be all these candles?" Andrew asked.

"I thought they were just for ambience," Jonathan said. Casting around, he noticed that all the candelabras seemed to be more practical than romantic. The walls were too full of grave holes to have any room for electrical wiring. "What about in the blood farm? Those draining tubes have to be powered by something."

"Probably gravity," Anya said, inviting herself into the conversation. "They just have to pull the blood out. How hard can that be?"

"Even if you could find a power source, I don't think we should use the shrink ray on the slayer. What if you blow up the staff?" Andrew asked, panic making his voice squeak.

"Then I wouldn't be able to get my powers back," Anya said.

"And we won't be able to save Warren!" Andrew added.

"What if saving the world is more important than saving Warren?" Jonathan asked, surprising even himself. Until this moment, he had thought that he couldn't want anything more than to undo the moment of Warren's untimely explosion. But, being this close to the elimination of the universe, he realized that he was pretty attached to being alive. There was no time for wishes and what-ifs here. Death was at the door, ready to take all of them, to unmake the world.

Andrew did not seem to agree. He looked even more offended than he had the day that Jonathan had proclaimed his preference for *Deep Space Nine* over *The Next Generation*.

"Slayer," the Master hissed, his hands curving into claws at his sides. "You dare enter my private quarters? I will anoint my altar with your blood and feed your entrails to my nurslings!"

"Oh my God!" the slayer said, her face alight with recognition. The crossbow swung toward the Master. "Fruit Punch Mouth, you old so-and-so! I, like, just killed you back home! I mean, not just-just because I've been stuck in this hell for who knows how long, but . . .

Wow." She slid the Gandalf staff into the straps of the bulging blue backpack she wore—Andrew's backpack—and fanned her eyes with her newly free hand. "Sorry, I am getting super nostalgic here. By any chance did we do the whole *I may be dead, but I'm still pretty* thing in this dimension already? Because, I've gotta say, it's one of my better comebacks, and I'd hate to waste it."

"Ha!" Angelus barked a laugh. "Fruit Punch Mouth. That's a good one. I need to remember that for later."

The slayer whirled toward him. The crossbow went limp as her eyes rounded.

"Angel!" she exclaimed.

The vampire's brow furrowed. "A little familiar of you, Slayer. The name's Angelus."

The crossbow was aimed squarely at his chest again. "I hate this dimension," the slayer said. Her nose crinkled. "And your ponytail. Yuck."

The Master flew at the slayer, his feet leaving the ground and his hands outstretched. There was a whoosh of air as the crossbow fired. The shot wooden stake met the Master halfway, plunging into his heart. With a screeching discordant squall, he erupted into dust.

"Huh," the slayer said, cocking her head to watch the dust flurry onto the floor. "The last time I did that, he left a skeleton. I guess he's less special here."

Darla fell to her knees in the sooty puddle her husband had left behind. Her howl of despair echoed throughout the catacombs.

"My children!" she shrieked. Her French-manicured nails reached toward the holes in the wall. "Awake and protect your home! Your father is dead, and your mother is under attack! Kill the slayer!"

Arms and legs unfolded from the burial niches. Bodies fell out of the walls as newborn vampires of all shapes and sizes answered Darla's call. Although their faces were transformed into vampire bumpiness and their eyes were the yellow of predators, they lacked the menace of the other monsters in the room. Maybe it was their distinctly human clothing. Jonathan suddenly understood why the people in the blood farm had to wear those robes. There was something about a Bubba Gump Shrimp Company T-shirt that just didn't scream *creature of the night*.

Even so, at Darla's command, the newborns threw themselves at the slayer with all the intensity of starving carnivores.

Facing down a throng of vampires, the slayer just smiled.

It was the most terrifying thing Jonathan had ever seen. Even more than the first time the murder bees had landed in Demondale or the day it rained flesh-eating slime or the moment Angelus had killed Rayne without warning. People knew to be afraid of those things.

The slayer didn't seem to be afraid at all. She was excited to fight her way to the Black Flame flag. Like she knew something they didn't.

A hand pulled hard at Jonathan's sleeve. He held in a scream, afraid that a fledgling had gotten turned around by the smell of his distractingly human blood. But he found Anya painfully gripping his arm.

"Are you trying to die?" she asked. "Because I could leave you to it."

"What? No!" he said.

"Good," Anya said. She pulled him behind the giant bed's ornate headboard. Andrew had already taken cover and scooted over to make room for Jonathan and Anya. The vengeance demon was much stronger than she looked. Even after she let go, Jonathan could feel her fingers bruising the crook of his elbow. He tried to ignore the pain, squeezing the messenger bag close to his chest as he surreptitiously scanned the floor for a power outlet. Or, at the very least, avoided looking at the soul-sucking flames in front of him and the huge naked painting on the wall.

"The slayer still has our artifacts," Andrew said, over the sounds of fighting on the other side of the headboard. From his pocket, he withdrew a small knife. Its wooden handle was emblazoned with the Eagle Scout logo on one side and Tucker Wells's name on the other. Despite wanting to do everything Tucker did, Andrew himself hadn't made it past Webelos because he'd been too scared to camp overnight away from home. He unfolded the knife with a snap, the three-inch blade reflecting the dark hellfire in front of them. "We just need to get the backpack away from her."

Jonathan scrubbed his hands over his face in disbelief. "Yeah, that sounds exactly like something *we* could do. Fight a legendary vampire hunter for a bag full of weapons. You want to do any other superhuman feats while we're at it? Send the slayer to the Phantom Zone? Wield Mjolnir? Ask Cordelia Chase to prom?"

"Sunnydale High doesn't exist anymore!" Andrew yelped.

"I was being sarcastic, moron!" Jonathan sneered back.

"Don't call me moron!" Andrew said, his knife dangerously close to Jonathan's nose. "That was Warren's nickname for me, not yours!"

Anya frowned. "Moron isn't a nickname, Andrew. It's an insult. He was insulting you. Right, Jonathan?"

Jonathan blinked in surprise at being addressed. "Right."

Anya looked pleased to have been proven right. "See, Andrew? Now, we need to get the gem and get out of here!"

Jonathan leaned around the headboard. The slayer's fight with the newborns was in full swing. Dust littered the floor. Darla was still screaming, even as Drusilla tried to pull her to her feet. Angelus and Spike had the exit blocked—not that the slayer seemed interested in turning tail. She had abandoned the crossbow and was duel-wielding stakes, flinging herself from fledgling to fledgling. The newborn vampires fought in a clumsy mass, more menacing as a throng than individually. Jonathan thought about how Darla and the Master hadn't taught any of them to hunt. Hand-to-hand combat might have been more integral to being undead than they'd assumed. The fledglings could only slow the slayer down so much, throwing their bodies in her way and making bumbling attempts to hit her. She dusted them as fast as they approached.

Willow stood just outside the fray, watching for an opening like she was trying to calculate the right moment to hop under a jump rope.

"Willow!" Jonathan whispered, hoping the vampire's sensitive hearing would save him the trouble of yelling. When she didn't respond, he tried again, slightly louder. "Psst! Hey, Willow!"

"What?" she snarled, spinning around. Her harsh yellow eyes pinned him to the spot, reminding him that this wasn't the shy, good-natured girl who had helped him code a *Stargate SG-1* fan page. This was one of many creatures that could kill him as easily as draining a juice box.

Once activated, Jonathan's fight-or-flight instinct always chose *flight*. Reflexively, he wrenched himself back behind the bed. As he rested against the headboard, his heartbeat slammed in his temples and he had to choke down the urge to throw up.

Andrew crawled forward so that his head stuck out the side of the bed.

"Willow!" he said in a loud whisper, motioning with the tip of his knife. "Get the backpack!"

Anya popped out beside him. "And the green gem! Really just the gem would be fine!"

"I'm a little busy here, unhelpful mortals," Willow said.

Jonathan took a deep breath and peered around the headboard. "We wouldn't ask you if it wasn't *very important!*" he stressed.

"And I'm not mortal," Anya said. She tossed her hair so that the ends whipped across Andrew's face. "I'm a demon too. Just not the punching, kicking kind."

Willow glowered as though she wanted to keep arguing with them but had suddenly remembered that doing so was beneath her.

A streak of black leather cut through the remaining newborn vamps. Willow cast aside those that didn't automatically move out of her way. The high heel of one of her boots kicked a stake out of the slayer's right hand. The slayer reached out to stab with her left, but Willow grabbed her by the backpack straps and threw her down—a move Jonathan was all too familiar with. As someone who had been a full foot shorter than his bullies for most of his life, he'd been flipped over by the backpack, the legs, and the elastic of his underwear more times than he could count.

The slayer landed flat on her back, the air escaping her lungs in a pained "Oof!" The Gandalf staff rolled just out of her reach. She didn't seem to notice. She was staring up at the red-haired vampire who had attacked her.

"Will?" she asked, breathless.

Sensing an opening, a fledgling in a Hawaiian-print shirt and cargo shorts flung himself at the slayer. Willow tossed him into the nearest candelabra, not bothering to look even as he burst into flames and ran screaming out of the room. Spike and Angelus moved out of the way to let him burn in the antechamber.

Backpack now in hand, Willow loomed over the slayer and cocked her head. "You know me?"

"Of course I do! You're my best friend," the slayer said. Crunching her legs into her abdomen, she did a kip-up and brushed off her pants. "Your favorite food is gingerbread cookies, but you hate when they're shaped like people because then you feel bad for eating them. You're scared of horses. You love math and computers! You've had a crush on Xander Harris since kindergarten!"

Willow's face contorted in disgust. "You do not know me."

Willow threw the backpack. It sailed through the air, punching the painted Darla in the face before falling to the ground beside the stone coffin. When Willow bent down to snatch the Gandalf staff from the floor, the slayer grabbed her by the shoulders and cracked her knee into the vampire's nose. As Willow reeled, the slayer recovered the staff and one of her stakes from the ground.

Drusilla bounded toward the slayer, wrapping her hands in the slayer's blond hair. Dru's fangs gleamed in the candlelight, poised to strike the girl's neck. The slayer bashed her skull against Drusilla's. Spinning around with the staff, she struck Dru's chin with the Marnoxon gem, sending her flying against the wall.

Spike cracked his neck from side to side, bouncing on the toes of his motorcycle boots. "Ready to dance, Slayer?" he asked.

"Sure," she said. "But I should warn you: I like to lead."

She gripped him by the wrist and twirled him hard. There was a popping sound, and Spike hissed in pain. When he got his arm out of the slayer's hold, his leather jacket didn't look right. His formerly square shoulders now had a slope, his hand hanging lower on one side than the other.

Behind the headboard, Jonathan ripped open the blue backpack, relieved to find all the items he'd packed for the Ascension's security table. Except for the crossbow, which was languishing wherever the slayer had dropped it. Probably for the best. Jonathan wasn't entirely sure he could shoot the girl with a stake, even if it would stop her from setting off the apocalypse. She was so obviously human—albeit a human with an advanced black belt and the power to destroy existence. There were only so many murders Jonathan could have on his conscience.

"It's all here," he told Andrew. "Now what do we do with it?"

Andrew's knee started to bounce against the floor. Warren had hated that nervous tic. When Andrew got anxious during board games at the lair and his leg shook, Warren would threaten to make Andrew roll his dice in another room. The knee bounce had never bothered Jonathan before—but right now it felt like an earthquake that could alert the many threats in the room to their location.

"There has to be something we could use to stop the slayer," Andrew said, peering into the bag while his knee continued to flop against the ground. "We could blow the Ram's Horn horn and flood this place with evil livestock!"

"That sounds more like us getting trampled by poisonous sheep than us saving the world," Anya protested. Seething, she folded her knees to her chest. "I can't believe Willow didn't get us the gem. I was very clear that the gem was the only thing that mattered. If I had my magic, I could wish all of us to a beach resort where they'd take my demon face as ID."

"Then why don't you go fight the slayer for it?" Jonathan asked.

"And get stabbed when no one could even wish me back to health?" she asked. "No way."

Out of the backpack, Jonathan gingerly withdrew the clay Urn of Fernda. It was shaped like a potbellied teardrop with curved handles on either side of its neck. The top was plugged with a ceramic screaming-faced stopper. Biting his lower lip, he looked from the urn to the fire-filled coffin.

"If the flag can burn in a sarcophagus, it should be able to live in this Adamantium jar, right?" he asked Andrew.

"You want to steal the flag of hell?" Andrew exclaimed.

"We can return it after the slayer leaves!" Jonathan said. "But if the vamps can't beat her, we have to do *something* to stop her from putting the gem into the black flames!"

He thought about how many bullies had played keep-away with his stuff over the years. Lunch boxes, homework assignments, his gym clothes. They all made it look so easy. Just snatched things out from under Jonathan's nose and held them where he couldn't reach.

He might not have had the height to keep the flag away from the slayer, but he had something none of his bullies had ever had. Subtlety. He wouldn't rub the slayer's nose in the missing black fire, making her jump and beg like a dog to get it back. He could just steal it and slip away.

Digging his nails under the screaming stopper, he eased it out carefully. He let out a sigh of relief when he found that the slayer hadn't filled it with anything since she'd stolen it from the security table. At the bottom of the jar, much farther down than should have been possible, was a single Ninja Turtle action figure. A Raphael, Warren's favorite. Jonathan considered trying to shake it loose, but seeing the slayer kick Angelus in the side of the head changed his mind. They were running out of time.

Rocking onto his knees, he crawled toward the sarcophagus, making it only an inch before Andrew grabbed at his foot, whisper-screaming, "Didn't you hear the Master? If you touch the flame, you'll immediately lose your soul!"

Jonathan paused, momentarily frozen by this very good point. He glanced at Anya with a wince. "Um. Do vengeance demons have souls?"

"Well, that's rude," Anya said, sucking in an insulted breath. "Just because I don't emote exactly like a human and have lived most of my life exacting reprisal justice against wrongdoers, you think I don't have a *soul*?"

"Wait, does that mean you do?" Andrew asked.

Anya shrugged. "Maybe? They don't make us give them up to grant Wishes, and I never officially died, so I think I've just got, like, a really vintagey one."

Rummaging inside the blue backpack again, Jonathan found the giant metal glove and withdrew it. "Rayne said that this gauntlet could be something that shot lightning or hellfire. Maybe it can withstand the black flame?"

"Like a giant oven mitt," Anya said with a nod of approval.

"Except made of metal," Andrew said. His nervous knee redoubled its bouncing. "Which conducts heat."

"Then it's a good thing the fire isn't hot," Jonathan said.

Staring down at the gauntlet, he could see his face reflected in the silver. Shiny with sweat, hair mussed. He didn't look like someone who could save the world. He looked like someone who hid during climactic battles and waited to die. If he was being honest with himself, he'd been a coward his entire life. His earliest memory was hiding inside a toy chest at his third birthday party while all the kids his parents had invited played pin the tail on the donkey without him. For nineteen years, he had hidden. First alone. Then behind protectors like Warren.

There was nowhere left to hide.

Jonathan didn't deserve to live in a world he wouldn't fight to save.

He stuck his hand into the gauntlet and flexed his fingers. Nothing magical happened, unless you counted the glove not immediately falling off as magic. Which wasn't entirely out of the question. Jonathan had small hands, but the gauntlet fit comfortably. Did the armor have some kind of one-size-fits-all spell on it? Or maybe the gauntlet really was just an ordinary historical remnant and had once belonged to a diminutive knight. People had been shorter in the past. Jonathan had often fantasized about going back to a time when his height would be closer to average.

Using his metal-clad index finger, he scooped up one of the handles of the urn and crept toward the sarcophagus. Praying the gauntlet provided enough protection from the cursed fire, he closed his eyes, thrust his hand into the coffin, and scooped. It didn't feel like anything except dragging a clay jug through the empty air. His stomach sank.

Then he heard Anya and Andrew gasp. Opening his eyes again, he joined them. The sarcophagus was empty. The inside of the urn was pitch-black and shimmery. The hellfire blocked his view of the Ninja Turtle at the bottom of the pot.

Shock made him light-headed. He had to fight to keep hold of the urn.

It had worked. His plan actually worked. *His* plan, no one else's.

"Quick," he said, shaking the urn at Andrew. "Close it!"

Andrew smashed the stopper into place. The three of them sat staring at the urn. Anya reached out and poked the side. She seemed satisfied with the result.

"Time to run," she told Jonathan and Andrew. "Ready?"

After pocketing his knife, Andrew slid on the backpack and tightened the straps so that it rode up near the nape of his neck. Jonathan lobbed the messenger bag at him.

"What am I? A pack mule?" Andrew whined.

"Would you rather carry Hell's Own Herald?" Jonathan snapped.

Andrew slung the messenger bag's strap across his chest, grumbling under his breath about feeling off-balance.

Crouching, Anya sneaked around the headboard and motioned for the boys to follow her. The three of them slunk forward. Piles of candles were burning on the floor. The silk and furs on the bed were gray with the dust of burst fledglings.

The slayer and Angelus were bo-staff-fighting, using the Gandalf staff and an empty candelabra respectively.

"Seriously, Angel," the slayer was saying as the olive staff and the metal body of the candelabra clacked together from side to side. "Not having your soul I can forgive. You're a vampire. But that rat tail is a crime. You look like an exotic-pet guy. Do you have an iguana on a leash somewhere in your crypt? Or a ferret? I know you definitely don't have any hair product because you are looking *frizzy*."

"I told you to use some of my gel," Spike said, holding his dislocated arm in a corner.

"Shut up, Spike," Angelus grunted.

"Yeah, there's such a thing as too much hair product, Billy Idol," the slayer said.

Angelus reared back, aiming for the slayer's head as he brought the candelabra down hard. She blocked him, holding the Gandalf staff in two hands. With a flick, she wrenched the candelabra out of his grasp. It flew overhead and clipped Drusilla in the collarbone. Rotating herself one hundred and eighty degrees, the slayer came up and kicked the disarmed Angelus square in the chest.

None of them noticed as Jonathan, Andrew, and Anya went scurrying out of the room.

The blood farm was hazy with greasy gray smoke. The flaming fledgling had fallen into a heap in the corner of the antechamber. His hair and Hawaiian shirt had burned away, leaving only his flesh to feed the fire. His skin had crisped and charred like cheap bacon. Bits of muscle and bone peeked out in patches as he continued to roll against the wall, trying in vain to put himself out. The smoke had an aroma that both reminded Jonathan of barbecue and made him nauseous.

Dry-heaving, he plugged his nose with his free hand. He was almost through the door to the staircase when he saw Andrew stop in the middle of the room to wrestle out of the many bag straps. He flailed as Anya tried to get him to keep moving.

"We need to save them!" Andrew said, ripping open the blue backpack. Withdrawing the neon-green Super Soaker, he pumped the piston rapidly and shot a stream of holy water onto the smoldering door.

"We're already in middle of our heroic deed!" Jonathan said, shaking the Urn of Fernda. Somewhere in its depths, the Raphael action figure rattled.

Andrew didn't turn away from the sleeping people. Timidly plucking at their plastic tubing, he swallowed thickly. "They'll die down here!"

"They died the second they volunteered to be planted in a blood farm!" Anya said, exasperated.

Andrew's face fell. "They just wanted to live forever," he said.

Anya successfully knocked the Super Soaker out of his hands. The plastic gun clattered to the floor. "And we are trying to live *today!*" she said. "Let's go!"

Andrew looked to Jonathan, imploring. Jonathan wanted to turn away, to run up the stairs and out of the church—not looking back until he was safe at home. Maybe safe *and* under the covers of his bed. But he knew what Andrew's silence meant. They couldn't leave human beings here to die. Once, Andrew's brother, Tucker, had come to the Church of the Eternal Night, seeking immortality. And if Warren hadn't stopped him, Andrew would have turned himself over to the Master and Darla too. If the Wells boys were stuck in this blood farm, Jonathan wouldn't have second-guessed freeing them.

Passing the urn full of fire into Anya's arms, Jonathan dug into the blue backpack and fished out the corkscrew dagger with his metal-clad hand. Andrew unfolded his Eagle Scout knife. Together, the two of them hurried around the antechamber, slashing the blood tubes connecting the black-robed people to their pedestals. It was disgusting work. Sticky red plasma gushed onto the stone floor. Jonathan was sure that the vampires in the next room could smell the wasted feast in here.

The first person Jonathan cut loose appeared to be the oldest person in the blood farm. Her wispy white hair was as colorless as her wrinkled face. She stepped down from the pedestal, black robe trailing in her own blood as it pooled out of the severed tubes dangling from her arms and legs.

"Today's the day," the woman rasped, her joy dampened by a voice in dire need of water. "I have earned my eternity!"

"Uh-oh," Jonathan said. He hadn't considered that the people in the blood farm wouldn't immediately see the vampire consumed in flames and assume something was amiss. Random death was probably a common occurrence at the Church of the Eternal Night.

Andrew paused halfway through sawing the tubes of a young man whose eyelids had started to flutter.

"Um, excuse me, ma'am?" Andrew said, waving his blood-drenched knife in the air and trying to get the freed woman's attention. "It isn't safe in here."

Without looking at either Jonathan or Andrew, the old woman gripped Anya's forearms, the Urn of Fernda pressed between them. Gazing at the vengeance demon with reverence, she croaked, "I have waited so long. And it's finally my time! I surrender my life to you, my savior. My sire."

Anya goggled at the woman pawing at her. "The church is on fire, you mortal idiot! Run!"

"Why doesn't she think *we're* her saviors?" Andrew asked Jonathan.

"Vampires probably don't do their own dirty work," Jonathan said, cringing as blood from a cut tube glugged across his shoes. It felt like his socks were full of molasses—which actually would have been far less gross. "Or gag at the sight of this much blood."

"Turn me! Save me!" the woman pleaded, scratching at Anya's forearms. "Please, it's my time! I've waited. I've given of myself. I've earned the bite that saves!"

"I'm not a vampire," Anya snapped, successfully pulling out of the woman's grasp. "Get your demons straight, lady."

"You're not..."

The woman gawked at Anya. Then, for the first time, she took in the rest of the burning antechamber. The Super Soaker on the floor. The growing puddle of gore spreading from one wall to the other. The other groggy pedestal people staggering toward the stairs.

The woman's face contorted into a mask of hideous rage. She launched herself at Anya again, this time with her nails aimed at the vengeance demon's eyes. "Intruders! Thieves! This was my chance! My one chance!"

"Anya!" Jonathan dropped the hand he was holding, accidentally letting the pedestal person he'd been helping down tumble to the floor. He tried to pull the furious woman by the shoulders, but she wouldn't budge. She rained blows down on Anya's face and shoulders while the vengeance demon tried to fight her off using the clay urn.

"Stand back," Andrew warned. Jonathan jumped the moment before the messenger bag came swinging. Inside the canvas, the ray gun's bulk smacked into the old woman's skull. The force of it pitched her through the door, sending her into the Master's bedroom. Terror that Darla would tear him limb from limb for freeing her prisoners made Jonathan even more eager to leave.

The rest of the blood-farm people had awakened too disoriented to fight. Most saw the growing fire and ran out of the room without waiting for an explanation.

"Let's get out of here," Jonathan said, one foot already on the bottom stair. The smoke had begun to sting his eyes.

The three of them tumbled up the stairs, their footfalls loud. The smoke followed them, burning Jonathan's throat as he made his way through the darkness. Falling into the bright light and clean air of the cathedral, he let out a breath of relief, then coughed gray sludge onto the altar. He felt a pang of guilt. It was probably sacrilegious to spit up in a church. It certainly wouldn't have flown in a synagogue. Not that there were any vampire synagogues.

The church was empty, the escaped pedestal people having already vacated the premises. It was eerily quiet, even though Jonathan knew that, below them, the vampires' fight against the slayer was still raging.

"You guys saved me," Anya gasped as she limped down the steps into the aisle. "You chose me. Over another human."

"You're human-ish," Jonathan said.

"Not that I feel good about leaving that old woman behind," Andrew said, weighed down with the two bags full of weapons and money. "But she was hurting you. We had to do something."

"You *didn't* have to do something," Anya said. "You could have just used my death as a distraction so you could run away. That's probably what *I* would have done."

"Well, you're on our team, and teammates help each other out," Jonathan said weakly. Looking back at his life, he couldn't pinpoint another moment when he'd done anything remotely self-sacrificing for another person. The realization made him feel very small. He cleared his throat. "We should get the flag to the Mayor. He can keep it safer than us. Maybe the City Council has another demon who can protect it. An understudy guardian."

"Then you can hold on to this," Anya said, shoving the urn at him and claiming the corkscrew dagger in one fluid motion. "From here on out, I want to be armed. Without my powers, I can't even kick an old lady's ass. How do you guys deal with being so weak all the time?"

"You get used to it," Andrew said with a shrug. "Or you get really into engineering so you can create overpowered weapons to even the playing field. You should have seen the perspective manipulator

Jonathan made in high school. It was so cool. Before it melted Connor whatshisname's eyeballs."

"Eyeball-melting sounds more useful than perspective manipulation," Anya said.

"That's what Warren said too!" Andrew said. "But Jonathan scrapped the project."

"It was really messy," Jonathan said, guiltily remembering the moment one of Sunnydale High's most popular kids had stolen his prototype sunglasses and stuck them on his own face. For a moment, Connor had appeared as tall as an NBA player. Before his eyes turned to sludge and dribbled out of his skull. "It was before everyone in town knew about magic, so I don't think Connor ever got his sight restored. And the perspective spell could only ever make me like an inch and a half taller. Barely worth it."

Staggering up the aisle, Jonathan tripped over a lost blood tube. The urn fell. His heart leaped into his throat as he dove to catch it. Sure, Ripper and Rayne had said that it was unbreakable, but what if the hellfire made it more fragile? What if the Black Flame flag was infecting his soul through the thin walls of the clay? What if the Ninja Turtle was melting?

"The sooner we give this to the Mayor, the better," he said with a sigh.

"Maybe one of you could pay for a taxi." Anya panted, staggering down the aisle. "Or hijack a car. I'm not picky. I'm just tired of walking. I worked today, and you know that Human-Mike thinks that if you have time to lean, you have time to clean."

"Both Mikes say that," Andrew said. "I think all managers might."

"Not so fast."

At the top of the aisle, the slayer held the Super Soaker in two hands, the Gandalf staff tucked awkwardly under her armpit. She pumped the bloodstained piston twice, her finger on the plastic trigger as she inched forward.

"You know what's in here?" she asked.

"Uh, yeah. Holy water," Jonathan said. "I'm the one who filled it."

"I helped," Andrew interjected, readjusting his bag straps. "I held the funnel."

"You stole it from us today," Jonathan said to the slayer.

"Oh my God, was that *today*?" the slayer asked. The Super Soaker momentarily sagged in her arms. In the overhead light, she looked suddenly exhausted. Shaking out her hair, she recovered herself and took aim again. "Fine, so you can touch holy water. If you're human, what are you doing hanging out with the worst of the worst? Are you, like, servants? Or familiars? There's a word for it, hold on. It's on the tip of my tongue. Robards? Reynards...?"

"Renfields," Andrew answered pleasantly. "Renfield was Dracula's human helper. Only in the movies, though. In the book he mostly just ate bugs in a sanitarium in a pretty offensive portrayal of mental illness."

"We aren't Renfields," Jonathan said. He gestured to himself with the urn. "I'm Jonathan. This is Andrew and Anya. We're, uh, mostly human."

"Then why are you in a vampire church?" the slayer asked. Waving the Super Soaker's nozzle, she gestured at the floor-to-ceiling windows illustrated with stained-glass nightmares. Although compared to the oil painting in the Master's bedroom, the gory pictures in the glass weren't all that bad. She narrowed her eyes. "I know you aren't blood sacrifices. You aren't dressed the part."

"Those hideous black sacks?" Anya asked. "No, thanks."

"Then why are you protecting the Black Flame flag?" the slayer asked.

Jonathan tightened his grasp on the urn. "Because you want to use it to end the world."

"Yeah," Anya said. "And as people who live in the world, we take offense."

The slayer goggled at them. "You live in *the* worst world. Ever. Trust me, I've been exploring the others." Snorting, she gave a cheeky shrug. "I say exploring, but I mean exploding."

"You mean like how you exploded Warren?" Jonathan asked.

"Who, the guy at your robot party trying to turn himself into a demon?" The slayer curled her lip. "Pretty sure *you* blew him up. I mean, I guess if he'd succeeded in Ascending, I probably would have had to kill him. Part of the whole Chosen One thing is stopping the Old Ones from taking over the world."

"Are you even from this dimension?" Anya asked, stepping forward like a guard dog. Her index finger twirled in the air, tracing the slayer's shape. "You've got *tourist* written all over you. Taking things that don't belong to you. Recognizing people you don't know. Getting mad at the rules that have always been. Are you still the Chosen One if *this* world didn't choose you?"

The slayer's nostrils flared, her eyes hard. "This is a world that shouldn't exist. All I want is to see Demondale destroyed."

"Well, we aren't going to give you the flag," Jonathan said. "Good luck bringing about the apocalypse without it."

Spike and Angelus tumbled out from beneath the *Paradise Lost* quote, leather squeaking as they fought to be the first out of the door.

"The bloody stairs are on fire!" Spike shouted. "Let's get the hell out of this place!"

The slayer spun around, aiming the Super Soaker at him. "No one leaves until I get the flag. Take another step and I'll burn your eyes out."

Willow and Drusilla came out of the door next. Willow had her arm around Drusilla's shoulders. Drusilla had her skirt pulled up to her knees, her face buried in the dirty hem as she sobbed.

"Grandmother, Grandmother," Drusilla wailed, burying her head in Willow's shoulder. "Our poor Angelus, an orphan."

"I'm not dead, Drusilla. I'm right here," Darla said, appearing in the doorway. Her face and suit were grimy with vamp dust. One of her false eyelashes was missing, making her blinks lopsided. She pointed a dirty finger down the aisle. "It's the slayer who should be crying. I'm going to tear your throat out, bitch."

"Yikes." Anya sucked in a wince. "I know you're from another time and she's trying to end existence, but do we have to use misogynistic language? Just saying. It's a bad look all around."

Darla bounded down the pulpit steps. The slayer fired the Super Soaker. Jonathan could hear the crackle of the holy water burning Darla's flesh. Angelus called her name and Drusilla screamed, but Darla didn't slow down. Even as white smoke rose from her face.

With a shriek, the blond vampire slammed into the slayer. The momentum sent both of them careening through the nearest window. The stained-glass illustration of a snake breathing black fire shattered as the collision of blond bodies hurtled through, then plummeted toward the ground. Jonathan ran to the hole in the wall just in time to see Darla fall to dust, leaving behind a single stake and the Super Soaker clattering between the palm trees.

And a black portal closing behind the slayer.

THE SLAYER

HUMANS HANGING AROUND with Demondale's baddies? Protecting the Black Flame flag? The Slayer can't believe it. It doesn't make any sense. Any human with a brain moved out of Demondale when the sky went dark—but these bozos not only stayed, but are siding with the vampires? And they aren't even Ren-thingies! What could they possibly be getting out of an alliance with soulless creatures that see them as chatty smoothies?

At the crossroads within the portal, she glances at the light radiating out of the green gem and addresses it directly.

"Is there an evil dimension where I could find more information on those humans?" she asks the gem. "Jonathan, Andrew, and Anya. Any of them? All of them?"

The potential portals lined up in front of her shrink down to one. Easier than expected. It gives the Slayer pause. She's never made a direct request before.

"Could you just give me the portal home?"

The gem doesn't answer, but the offered portal doesn't change. She takes this as a no.

"My bad for asking. Thanks anyway."

Falling out of the portal, she lands facing the ocean.

Clear blue waves break against the shore below. The air is misty with salty spray, and the sun is warm on her skin. Distracted as she is by her basking, it takes the Slayer a minute to realize that she's in an empty parking lot.

Underfoot, she sees the easily recognizable International Symbol of Accessibility. A white stick figure in a wheelchair, but the background is painted orange rather than blue. She considers this odd, then remembers the girl at the vampire church telling her that being mad at things being the way they are is a clear sign that she's an interdimensional tourist. Maybe this is a world where orange is considered friendlier than blue. Or easier to spot. She can be open to change. Call her Flexible Thinking Girl.

The staff tugs at her arm, forcing her to turn away from the ocean and face the brutalist concrete building behind her. It looks like some sort of future jail, the kind in the over-the-top action movies Xander likes, with cells made out of ice blocks or animated purple lines that are supposed to be electricity.

But the sign across the front reads: THE JONATHAN LEVINSON PRESIDENTIAL LIBRARY AND MUSEUM.

There's even a bronze statue on an unusually tall base of the brown-haired boy the Slayer has just seen wearing a metal glove and carrying a jar full of evil. The statue depicts him dressed in a tuxedo. And giving finger guns.

"No way." She laughs. "They'll really let anyone be president these days."

The front door is locked. The hours posted in a digital display built into the glass inform her that the library is open Sunday through Friday from nine to six. And closed on Saturdays.

The Slayer frowns at the gem. "You couldn't have brought me through on a day when it was open?"

The gem is unapologetic.

Climbing the jutting concrete walls is a breeze, reminding the Slayer of scaling the vertical staircase at Chuck E. Cheese. Minus the padding and the diaper smell. Up on the second story, she forces open a window and shimmies through, relieved not to hear the sound of an alarm.

She jumps down into what must be the museum part of the building. Overhead pin lights illuminate individual displays loaded down with text on the white walls. Each one includes a life-size Jonathan mannequin. Here's Doctor Jonathan with his stethoscope and a description of how he cured restless-leg syndrome. And there's Jonathan dressed like a founding father and receiving the Pulitzer Prize for writing a rap musical. Here's Jonathan posed with his Teen Choice Award surfboard. Jonathan and a set of his eight-book series of super-best-selling novels, A Song of Sleet and Embers, then another display of him starring in the TV show based on the series.

"This guy has more jobs than Barbie," the Slayer says, passing by Jonathan in military fatigues, credited with ending all wars in the year 2040. The number gives the Slayer pause. For a second, it seems like a joke. The mid-twenty-first century? Someone get her a hoverboard and self-lacing sneakers, stat. She glances up at the gem. Demondale is a year or two ahead of her own timeline, the world under the sunshade mere months away from the new millennium. But could the portal really drop her off this far in the future?

She hasn't checked a calendar in every evil reality she's demolished. Maybe those demon puppets were from the year 3000. How would she know? The idea makes her a little woozy.

In the darkness—somewhere beyond Jonathan the panda whisperer and Jonathan breaking the world-record score for something called *Guitar Hero*—there's movement. Heavy footfalls reverberate against the floor.

The Slayer ducks into a display of Jonathan's film career. In front of a giant TV screen playing a clip package of movie trailers and Academy Award speeches, there's a line of Jonathans dressed in his most famous costumes. Jonathan in a floor-length leather coat and wraparound Ray-Bans. Jonathan in a fedora and khakis with a whip clutched in his plastic hand. Jonathan in shiny green pants that look like mermaid scales and a nubby orange shirt, holding a gold trident. The Slayer wrestles the trident away from him, pleased to find that— although it's light—it's actually made of metal.

The approaching footsteps grow louder. The Slayer, picturing Secret Service agents with drawn guns, is relieved to find a square-headed monster in shiny military boots. People have to be reasoned with. Monsters she can fight.

Throwing the trident javelin-style, she spears the monster through the arm, pinning him to the back of the closest Jonathan mannequin. Grabbing hold of the end of the trident, the Slayer throws her body weight into the pole, pushing until she hears the monster's arm crunch.

The monster doesn't flinch. Jiggling his shoulder and jabbing the trident's tines, he tests his mobility. Finding himself stuck, he looks down at the Slayer, curious.

"You are trespassing on government property," he says. His voice is a resonant monotone, a mechanical impression of a baritone. The pin lights refract off the metal plate molded to one side of his skull. "And this trident is on loan from the Smithsonian. You shall incur a fine for damaging it."

The Slayer steps out of kicking distance and picks up her staff again. It pulls at her arm, ready to continue its quest for the Black Flame flag. But she can't stop staring at the security bot. There's something repulsively compelling about him. It reminds her of living in Los Angeles and seeing people walking around with healing plastic surgery scars. Bruised, puffy, sutured.

"I should have guessed that the future museum would have a robot guard," she says.

"I am no robot," the robot says. He tips his boxy head in a stiff bow. "My name is Adam. I am a bio-mechanical demonoid. The first of my kind. Although no longer the last."

"Yeah, your body has a real first-draft vibe," the Slayer says, gesturing to the metal stitches holding the two halves of his torso together. Shirtless in camo pants, the monster is a bit camo-colored himself. White human skin blending with Wicked Witch of the West green and patches of silver plating. The Slayer grimaces, squinting at the metal port built into his chest. "Is that a *floppy-disk* drive?! Bro, how old are you?"

"I am not your brother," Adam says, the humanoid side of his face scrunched in confusion. "In my estimation, it is you who has stepped out of time. The false highlights dyed into your hair are an inch wider than is currently fashionable. The stitching on your pants belies an industrial sewing machine used by mass manufacturers reliant on overseas slave labor that Jonathan himself outlawed. And your shoes are in remarkable shape for a brand that has not existed in over twenty-five years."

The Slayer blinks, too impressed to be insulted. Well, almost. She can't help but smooth her hair. "Wow, I haven't been so skillfully insulted since my first day at Sunnydale High. Is Cordelia Chase still alive? Because she could learn a thing or two from you."

Adam's eyes—one brown, one red—search the empty air, seeing beyond the Slayer and the museum. "I have no knowledge of a Cordelia Chase. I could search the vital records, if you would like to inquire further about her death?"

The Slayer wonders if he's got a Terminator view-screen thing in his head, one that sizes up his opponents' weaknesses. Or if it's just a regular search engine connected to the internet.

"Nope, I'm good," the Slayer says. Even in the future, in another dimension, the prospect of hearing about her classmates' deaths makes her stomach churn. She thinks back to Demondale and having to fight the vamped-out Willow, unable to bring herself to plunge a stake into her friend's heart. More than anything, she longs to be back where she started, keeping the real Sunnydale safe. It's what she was chosen to do. But the staff and the green gem can only drag her from terrible place to terrible place. "Anyway, you're right. I'm a time-traveler on whatever's the opposite of an excellent adventure.

I'm just here to find out what makes this Jonathan guy tick. I met him in the past, but we didn't get a chance to chat. You must know a lot about him, patrolling these exhibits all day. Does he have any hidden talents? Obvious weaknesses? Known enemies?"

"Jonathan is beloved in this world," Adam says. He turns his head to the nearest display case, admiring the Jonathan mannequin dressed in Klingon armor. "A movie star, humanitarian, and president unlike any before him."

"Are you sure? He kinda sounds like Reagan," the Slayer says, sticking her tongue out. "Was he a pay-or-play Republican too?"

"President Jonathan Levinson is beyond political parties. He won as an independent."

"Oh," the Slayer says, eyebrows rising in surprise. "So he sold his soul?"

"To the great Shaak'garar. The Scorpion King. The Old One granted him this world as his own, a dimension built in honor of Jonathan's greatness." He sweeps a green palm around at the many Jonathans on display. The Slayer remains unimpressed. Somehow, she just doesn't think that making a Star Trek–Star Wars crossover film series should fall under the category "greatness." It's niche at best. Masturbatory at worst.

"Here, he was allowed to flourish," Adam continues. "To mold unity and foster peace."

"And bring about Hell on Earth?" the Slayer interrupts. "Because, unless I took a wrong turn at portal junction, there's gotta be a Black Flame flag in here somewhere. Which is not exactly my definition of utopia."

Adam flexes his free arm. His fingernails are pointed, brown, and thick. Imagining how gnarly his toenails must be makes the Slayer want to gag. Out of his wrist, a long sharp bone stake slides out. Talk about a keratin surplus.

"Hell's Own Herald is sensitive compartmented information," he says. "You do not possess the security clearance required to know of its being."

"But didn't *you* break some kind of security protocol by even mentioning it?" she asks, scanning the visible displays for any sign of black fire. The staff in her hand trembles, prodding her back toward the movie Jonathans and Adam. "I was guessing. You confirmed it. If I had to bet which of us was going to be in more trouble, I'd put my money on you."

"Gambling is illegal outside of licensed Levinson Casinos!" Adam says.

"Probably not as illegal as spilling top secret information to a time-traveling civilian, though. Do they have robot prison? Oh, sorry. Is playing security guard at the fake president museum already a punishment?"

The Slayer sweeps the green gem through the air like a metal detector. She's relieved when the staff flinches away from Adam. If the black flame had been on his person, she would either have to pull out his battery pack or figure out how to use a floppy disk. Neither would be pretty.

She turns her back on him, the staff pulsing as she creeps through the exhibit.

"You will never find the Black Flame flag," Adam says. Both of his green hands are wrapped around the trident in his shoulder as he tries to rock it out of his skin. "It is invisible to human eyes, hidden in plain sight—"

The green gem knocks against the giant screen, thudding against the image of Jonathan crying, *"You like me, you really like me!"* while clutching an Oscar statue. Even his acceptance speeches are plagiarized. What a ridiculous world this is.

Good thing she's going to end it.

With a sharp jab, the wooden end of the staff splinters the screen. Expecting the crunch of glass, the Slayer is confused when the staff tears through the screen like fabric. The Black Flame thrusts out of the rip in the screen like Porky Pig at the end of a Looney Tunes cartoon.

"I spy with my human eye." She looks back at Adam and grins. "Hey, RoboCop, have you ever read any Mary Shelley? I'm guessing you didn't have to pass sophomore English to get this job."

"I have the ability to download any work of literature ever written. I am connected to the high-speed wireless network provided by the library. It is ... gratis."

"Go ahead and download *Frankenstein*. I'll wait."

Adam's skull whirs as his circuits exert themselves.

"The Modern Prometheus," he says. He rapidly scans the air left to right for a full minute, seeing something beyond the Slayer's perception. His circuits stop humming. A single tear runs out of his demon eye, down his green skin, splashes onto the metal plate on his chest, and sizzles.

"Oh," he says.

Satisfied, the Slayer stabs the gem into the Black Flame flag and watches as the Jonathan Levinson Museum burns.

EIGHT

Anya

SMOKE BILLOWED FROM the Church of the Eternal Night's broken stained-glass window, stinking of burning shellac. The pews must have finally caught fire. The magicked grass in the courtyard beside the burning church pricked at Anya as she sat down. She tipped her head back to watch the sooty plumes disappear into the dark sky. The view was much better from outside, away from the threat of imminent death.

"Well," she said to the group, gingerly touching the shallow claw marks the old woman had made above her eyebrow. "That was exciting."

"Infuriating," Angelus said, kicking the nearest palm tree. Above him, the fronds quivered noisily. "I can't believe she got away!"

Anya inched her left hand away from the Super Soaker left behind on the grass alongside a pile of ashes topped with a single fake eyelash. "Oh. Right. Sorry about your vampire-mom ex-girlfriend."

"Not Darla," Angelus said, his gaze working hard to avoid looking at the ash pile that had once been his lover-mother. "The slayer! It was thirty to one in there and she still managed to escape with barely a scratch!"

"*I* did scratch her," Drusilla said. She had stretched out on Willow's leather-clad lap, writhing against the grass like a gothic Victorian cat. She licked the side of her hand before reaching up and offering a taste to Willow. "That slayer's a tawny port."

Spike flopped his loose arm in recrimination at the vampire girls. "Excuse me," he said loudly. "I'm standing right here!"

Willow gave him a slow blink, Drusilla's hand still cupped to her mouth. "All gone," she said. The pink tip of her tongue flicked across Drusilla's palm. "Unless you want to see if there's any slayer blood left inside."

"I don't mean the blood, I mean—ARGH!" He yowled as Angelus gripped his shoulder and shoved him hard into the nearest palm tree, cramming his arm back into its socket. The arm made a crunch almost exactly like a rat being run through the Best Pressed juicer.

Angelus let go and shook his head. "What'd I tell you, man? Respect yourself."

"How can I when we've been trounced by a little girl?" Spike growled. He adjusted his leather coat so that it once again sat square on his shoulders.

"At least you all made it out alive," Andrew said. "Or, you know, still undead. That's worth celebrating, isn't it?"

"We got our asses handed to us by the slayer, so no, I don't want to sit around and sing 'Kumbaya,'" Spike said. He scuffed his heel in the grass, which refused to budge no matter how hard he kicked it. "What I want is a bloody rematch. I want to tear her head from her adorable little body."

Angelus gave a contemplative nod, pacing between palm trees. "She is cute for a slayer. The last one I faced was back when we were in Rome. She was all teeth and gums."

Drusilla closed her eyes, lost in a reverie. "Oh yes," she moaned. "Long Gums. She was yummy. AB negative in the wild. You don't find that every day."

"This one talks a lot of nonsense," Angelus said. He stroked the end of his ponytail without seeming to realize it. "But she's cute."

"Ugh, she's a child, you creep," Willow spat at Angelus, her hands combing through Drusilla's fight-mussed ringlets. "What are you? Two hundred years old? Three?"

"Two fifty," Angelus sniffed. "Ish."

Spike let out a laugh, punching the taller vampire in the arm. "Try two seventy-two, you old git. I was at your last birthday party. And the hundred and fifty before that. Blimey, I need new friends."

"Wait, how old is the slayer?" Anya asked, looking to Andrew and Jonathan for help. "Like eight years old? Ten? I'm not great at human ages. You all decay so quickly."

"She's a teenager," Andrew said, glancing up from the backpack open in front of him. "She looks like one of the popular girls from our high school. You know, when we went to high school. Before it blew up."

Willow's lip curled in apparent distaste. "Exactly. There's no way she's a legal adult. She smelled like naturally occurring collagen."

"You smelled her collagen? Who's being creepy now?" Angelus

sneered. He turned his outrage on Jonathan and Andrew, who were noisily sorting through their bags, taking inventory of what they had recovered from the slayer. "And where were you during the fight? The slayer isn't supposed to kill humans. You could have distracted her!"

"I'm only kind of human," Anya reminded him. She batted her natural not-glued-on eyelashes, doing her best to look attractive and available, despite the ache in her face from where the bloodless woman had battered her. "And I'm four times your age."

"Why'd you all tag along if not to help?" Spike asked the humans. "You came all this way just to hide like the Little bloody Rascals and sneak out when the fight got too intense?"

"We also stopped the slayer from ending the world." Jonathan lifted the clay urn, his right hand still covered in the dented metal gauntlet. "By stealing the Black Flame flag."

Spike's eyebrows flew up. "Oh, did you? Well done."

Drusilla crawled off Willow's lap and slunk across the grass on all fours. Jonathan froze in fear as she pressed her ear under one of the urn's handles and cooed, "I can hear the fire singing inside. Like carrion crows having their feathers pulled."

"So less like singing and more like screaming?" Anya asked.

"She really can't tell the difference," Angelus lamented. One of his hands came up and rubbed his forehead, the same way Human-Mike's did when Anya asked too many questions. Could vampires get stress headaches?

"So, it's really in there?" Willow asked. "Good work, dorks. I'm almost glad I haven't killed you yet."

"Um, thanks?" Andrew said.

Jonathan shifted uneasily as Drusilla began scream-singing along with what only she could hear inside the urn. "Could we move this jar full of damnation somewhere safe? Somewhere the slayer can't immediately portal back to? And maybe somewhere less on fire?"

Anya considered the urn, remembering how the black flames had twisted together and oozed out of the sarcophagus. Like it was making a choice to leave. It wasn't just unpredictable for fire—it was unpredictable for something earthly. Since it was a threat to anything with a soul and a will to stay alive, they couldn't just pour it out anywhere. And she got the feeling that it wouldn't sit wherever they left it.

"Where do you store half the ingredients to end the world?" she asked aloud.

"The City Council has a backup plan on file," Willow said. "But the Mayor isn't going to like it."

"Now, I don't mind telling you that I am put out by this turn of events," the Mayor said, climbing out of his town car and dusting off his slacks. He'd put his tie back on since Anya and the others had last seen him. "And there will be H-E-double-hockey-sticks to pay if we don't get this taken care of ASAP."

"He spells a lot when he's mad," Willow murmured to the group.

On a jagged cliff overlooking the foamy breakers of the inky black ocean, Anya could see the edge of the sunshade miles out from shore. The distant sky was rainbow-sherbet pink and orange as the sun sank into the water. It was hard to look away from. Anya hadn't seen a sunset since she'd left Arashmaharr.

She sensed Angelus moving to stand beside her and admire the faraway sky. However long it had been since Anya had seen the sun, it had certainly been longer for the vampire. At least in her capacity as a vengeance demon, she'd happened upon some daylight in the last three hundred years. Angelus was drinking in the sight like he'd been dying of thirst. It made him look oddly human. Clinging to the fleeting present was the ultimate mortal vice.

"Weird to think we used to see this every day, huh?" Anya said.

"I knew the shade had to have an end," he said, too enthralled to look away. "But I never thought it would be so . . ." At a loss for words, Angelus simply shook his head and wiped a hand over his forehead, as though checking to make sure he wasn't in danger of bursting into flames.

"Her Holiness pays dearly for the view," the Mayor said, his obliging tone edged in impatience. "But the sun sets here every day, Mister Angelus. So, if you wouldn't mind."

Turning away from the ocean, Anya examined the humongous house of worship. Gaudier than the Church of the Eternal Night and propped up on white stone columns, the circular temple had no walls. It lured guests in from the parking lot with gauzy curtains, invitingly swollen with the sea breeze.

Anya didn't trust it. She folded her arms over her chest and hung back as the rest of the group moved forward.

"Are there any nondenominational places to fly this flag?" she asked aloud. "Or does the City Council see some connection between organized religion and Hell on Earth?"

"Hey now, I don't appreciate that sort of blasphemous tittle-tattle, young lady," the Mayor said with cruel eyes and a smile. Anya found his expressions even harder to parse than the average human's. Probably because of the sorcerer thing. Sorcerers were just extra-fancy warlocks. Slippery flimflammers that would do anything for the smallest increase in power. If she had been in possession of her magic, she would have snapped her fingers and sent the Mayor to an alternate reality where there was a sorcerer more powerful than him around. Just one. She bet he would tear himself in half rather than be second best. The idea cheered her. Another thing to look forward to when they finally got the Marnoxon gem away from the slayer.

"I only look young. I'm the oldest demon here," Anya said tightly. There wasn't a doubt in her mind that she'd been exacting vengeance since long before the Mayor had sold his soul. Before he'd even had a soul to sell. "And do we *all* need to go in? The new protector of the Black Flame flag isn't going to want to talk to a bunch of random demons—plus Andrew and Jonathan—are they?"

"If I know her, she'll prefer an audience," the Mayor said ambiguously. Flapping his hands in the air, he ushered the group onward. "No more dillydallying. Everybody inside. The temple is public property, so no invitation needed for our vampiric friends."

Anya's legs protested climbing the stairs, but she held in her pained groans, mostly so that she wouldn't get lumped in with Andrew's whining. The bags strapped to his back were dragging his shoulders into humps. Jonathan didn't appear to be breathing at all as he labored over every single step, keeping the jar full of hellfire perfectly level in his hands.

Anya frowned over at him. "I thought the warlock said the urn was unbreakable?"

Beads of flop sweat ran down Jonathan's forehead and into his eyes. He blinked hard. "With my luck, I'd find a way to break it right before we got it somewhere safe," he said. Lowering his voice to a nervous quiver, he added, "I don't want to give the vampires any reason to kill me."

"What if we kill you for being such a nerd?" Willow asked, swiveling her head to glare down the steps at him. "Hurry up! She's vicious when she's been kept waiting."

"Who is *she*?" Andrew asked Anya in a whisper.

Anya didn't like having to admit that she didn't know.

Unlike the other new buildings under the sunshade, the temple didn't smell like magic. Not common magic, anyway. Whatever had built this was more powerful than anything Anya had ever seen.

Gold glittered from every surface: The floors. The ceiling. The vases and the bouquets of roses contained within.

Anya felt as though she'd plunged into a pile of riches. She liked the feeling. A lot. Possibly too much.

"You're drooling," Angelus whispered to her.

She quickly wiped her chin with the back of her wrist. "It's my dream house," she said, agog.

A throne stood at the center of the room, ten feet high on a gilt base. From the ground, Anya could only make out a pair of shapely purple legs dangling over one ornate arm.

Adjusting the knot in his tie, the Mayor whispered sharply for everyone to kneel. Willow obliged immediately, the leather legs of her catsuit screeching at the strain. Anya looked to Angelus, considering rebelling against this degrading posture. He shot her a shrug as he lowered himself to the floor and pulled Spike down beside him. As Anya's knees reluctantly bent, a trumpet blared, scaring her the rest of the way to the ground.

The temple was suddenly teeming with dancers carrying batons sprouting white silk. The silks whipped and floated through the air as the dancers cantered soundlessly across the shiny floor. One of the curtain walls pushed outward, revealing a choir singing an exaltation in perfect harmony.

"Glory to Glory," the choir sang as the dancers squiggled their ribbons through the air. Anya could see the giant legs swinging down. The purple calves were nearly as tall as one of the columns holding up the ceiling. "Glorificus the luminous. Glorificus the sublime. Glorificus superior!"

As the choir powered through its last note and the ribbon dancers sashayed to the sides of the room, a red carpet manifested out of thin air, bisecting the room with the throne as the focal point.

Two bare feet touched down at the base of the throne and strode the red carpet toward the group of vampires, demons, and human boys. Jonathan fumbled the urn, and Andrew reached out to catch it. Anya found herself a bit stunned. The legs belonged to a colossal naked purple woman with ice-white curls and pearlescent eyes. More shocking was the way the woman seemed to shrink with every step, strutting herself all the way down to human size. Tall-human size. Anya was pretty sure that if they'd been standing, the woman still would have towered over everyone. Except maybe Angelus.

The Mayor coughed, looking down at the red carpet with even more determination than Jonathan, which Anya considered a feat. "Now, Glory," he stammered. "You know how I feel about speaking to you in this state."

Plum-colored lips split into a black-toothed grin, and the nude woman reached down and patted the Mayor on the top of the head. "Aww, Richie. I forgot what a prude you are. Here." As she whirled around, her skin turned a pale human pink and her curls became as golden as the floor. A toga made of the same gossamer fabric as the walls and the dance ribbons wound around her nakedness.

Her human disguise came complete with bright red lipstick and kohl-rimmed blue eyes. "Better?"

"You're too kind, Magnificent One," the Mayor said, dragging his eyes up to her face. "You know I'm an old man. My ticker can't handle your radiance without a bit of a filter. The full force of your godlike beauty might just do what many before have tried and put me straight in the ground."

Glory waggled her index finger in front of the Mayor's nose. "Not god*like*, Richie. Actually divine."

Oh, Anya thought. *A goddess.* That made more sense. Hell dimensions were lousy with extra gods. Arashmaharr worshipped Niandeer, the goddess of wrath, and Twerfon, the god of cubicles. Anya wasn't surprised that a goddess had found her way to Hell on Earth. Just like any demon or vampire looking for a safe place to live full of cheap food and upward mobility, an evil goddess in search of gullible followers could do a lot worse than Demondale.

"Of course," the Mayor said, holding up his hands in surrender. "And, may I just say, your effulgence was utterly wasted underground."

Spike made a face, his chin tucked back against his neck. Anya couldn't tell if he was uncomfortable or irritated. It was, she supposed, possible to feel both in tandem.

"It's true," Glory said, tossing her newly yellow hair over her shoulder. "My curls love the sea air. Although I could do without the screaming white birds. The more I pull them out of the sky, the more take their place."

"Ah, that explains the missing seagulls," the Mayor said to himself. He looked back at Glory, simpering. "Not that they're needed. They're only good for defecating on tourists and eating garbage."

"And we have demons for that." Glory laughed for a moment

before pausing to bark at the ribbon dancers. "Ha-ha!" she prompted, and the dancers burst into terrified laughter.

Anya felt her enjoyment of the goddess start to wane. Watching the Mayor feel both literally and figuratively small was satisfying, but not enough to cancel out casual demon prejudice. Most demons wouldn't be caught dead eating garbage. Except for Muckers, but everybody knew they only ate trash for sexual gratification.

"Now, who are these ruffians tracking dirt into my temple?" Glory asked, taking notice of the kowtowing group.

The Mayor sat on his heels, his jittery hands fussing with his tie once again. "I come bearing new devotees to your divinity. And a gift!" He shoved Jonathan forward.

Jonathan tottered out of the line of supplicants, his knees scraping against the red carpet. It seemed difficult for the boy to scoot, bow, and keep his grasp on the urn all at once. He settled for just lifting the urn over his head and staring at the goddess's bare feet.

Glory raised the Urn of Fernda, staring directly into the screaming-faced stopper. "An old pot with an ugly plug?" she asked. She lifted the urn to her ear and screwed up her face in disgust. "That constantly screams? Why not just bring me a pile of pestilent seabirds to shit on the floor?"

With a careless toss, she pitched the urn back to Jonathan, who dove on top of it as though it were a live grenade.

"Now, your brilliance," the Mayor said tremulously. "That's not just any urn. That's Hell's Own—"

"Enough, Richie," Glory said, reaching down and pinching his lips shut between her thumb and forefinger. "If you have to explain your gift, then it's not good enough! Let me examine what else you've brought me."

Releasing the Mayor's face, the goddess waded through the group, toes splayed against the floor.

"So many vampires," she noted. "It's been my experience that a vampire only worships blood. These stink of it. Like a bunch of iron pills dressed in dead cow." Bending down, she tapped on the top of Drusilla's head. Drusilla's eyes crossed as she tried to look at Glory's hand. "And someone scrambled this one's sense like an egg."

Angelus raised a hand. "Guilty," he said.

With a titter, Glory turned and booped Angelus on the nose. "You are cute for a bloodsucker," she proclaimed. Then she saw Spike and wiggled the tip of his nose. "Cuter." As she drew Andrew's face up by the chin, the goddess's teeth flashed in a devilish smile. "Cutest! Hello there. Finally a gift with some life in it."

Andrew floundered in Glory's grasp, unsure as to where to look or how tall to sit. Words fell out of his mouth in a slurry. "Oh, I don't— I'm not—I mean I do have life, but I'm really not comfortable.... Hello, your, um, goddess-ness."

Glory's ghastly smile only increased in the face of Andrew's fear. "Try something that ends in -ence," she instructed, stroking the sides of his stammering mouth. "Like magnificence. Prominence. Iridescence." Her lips puckered, blowing the susurrations at him.

"Of course, your, uh, opalescence?" Andrew's face burned crimson, his embarrassment so clear that even Anya could read it. "But I feel like you should know—that is, I should probably tell you ..." His eyes darted from side to side, like he was trying to shoo everyone else away with only the power of his discomfort. He gulped, the lump in his neck bobbing like a buoy in a storm. "I'm gay."

Glory crouched, putting her face level with his. "And I feel like you should know that I wouldn't mind keeping you around to clean

167

out the ribbon dancers' toilets. But I would never ever *ever* in the life-time of hell itself let any human born on this miserable rock touch me. *I* am a goddess and *you* are a bug. With cute hair."

Her fingers inched toward his temples, pressing down hard until white light appeared and her nails began to sink impossibly into his skull. Andrew cried out in pain, wild-eyed as he attempted to see what the goddess was doing to him. The white light grew brighter and Andrew's screams intensified.

"Hey!" Anya shot to her feet. Fury made her skin tighten as her demon form burst to the surface. If she'd been in possession of her magic, she would have blasted the goddess out to sea with a wave of her hand. Being powerless, she pulled the Dagger of the Unkillable out of her pocket and pointed it at Glory. "Stop hurting him! He's a weak little mortal who can't defend himself! It was hard for him to disclose his sexuality to you! For reasons I don't fully understand!"

"The regressive mores of a heteronormative society," Willow muttered behind her.

Anya nodded at the red-haired vampire in thanks, then turned back to Glory. "And you are being cruel for no reason! We came all the way up this very steep hill to bring you the Black Flame flag so you could help protect this dimension from being destroyed! So, if you don't want to help, fine. But that means we have to go fight the slayer ourselves! Again!"

The white light disappeared as the goddess withdrew her finger-tips from Andrew's head. Andrew fell forward, gasping for air as Glory narrowed her eyes at Anya. Colors roiled in the whites like an oil slick, making them difficult to look at directly.

"Did you say the slayer? You can't mean the vampire slayer?" Glory asked. Her red lips pulled away from her teeth as she swung her head toward the Mayor. "Ew, Richie! This is the emergency you wanted to speak to me about? This is plebeian! A fire in the anthill. Boo-hoo. Life goes on."

The Mayor cautiously rose to his feet, keeping his shoulders hunched in frightened deference. "It won't, though, your eminence. According to our intel, the slayer means to wipe out this whole plane of existence. Top to bottom. Which means all of us." He motioned at everyone on the nondivine side of the carpet. "And all of your worshippers, dancers, singers, temple guards, and hairdressers will cease to be. And you, I'm afraid, will go straight back to Aftarex. With your sisters. Always fighting over who's the strongest, who's the prettiest."

"I'm the strongest and the prettiest!" Glory shouted, her voice taking on an impressive reverb effect. "And I will never go back to that horrid little dimension! Do you know they made me share a castle with those gorgons?"

"A fate worse than death, I'm sure," the Mayor said, somehow managing to keep the sarcasm out of his tone. Another tricksy sorcerer ruse. There was no doubt in Anya's mind that a man who had sold his soul for immortality feared death more than anyone else in the room. "But the vengeance girl is right. We do have this jug full of Hell's Own Herald in need of protection." He held his hand out to Jonathan, who mistook the gesture and set his own hand in the Mayor's palm before realizing that what the Mayor actually wanted was the urn. He handed it over with a wince. The Mayor, holding the jar by the tiny handles, gave it a delicate shake so that it very lightly rattled. "If the slayer gets her greedy little mitts on this, then it's good-bye world. Good-bye, temple. Good-bye, newly repaved parking lot funded graciously by the taxpayers."

Glory rested the crook of her index finger against her chin. "I thought there was no money in the budget for my parking lot?"

"That was back when we thought that the world was going to keep on turning without your gracious assistance."

"How very foolish of you," the goddess said. She snatched the urn out of the Mayor's grasp and peered at the screaming stopper again, considering it more agreeably than before. "And all I have to do is keep this out of the slayer's hands?"

"If she so much as looks at it, squash her like the roach she is."

"I suppose I could do that," the goddess said with an imperious flick of her thin eyebrows. She glared down at the assembled party. "This is where you say, 'Thank you, Glorificus.' And give it some flair. Your presence wearies me."

"Thank you, Glorificus!" everyone said in unison. Behind one of the gauze curtains, the choir joined in, making the gratitude sing.

Dismissed, the group descended the temple steps. In the distance, the sun had finally sunk, leaving no difference between the sunshade and the night sky.

Andrew set his hand on Anya's elbow. "Thanks. For standing up for me back there. I don't think anyone else would have yelled at a goddess for me."

"No problem." She shrugged, sliding the Dagger of the Unkillable into her belt loop. "Teammates help each other out, right?"

"Right." Andrew grinned.

"What did it feel like to have her fingers in your head?" Jonathan asked.

Andrew scrunched his face in thought for a moment. "Like a brain freeze mixed with all the existential dread in the universe."

"Is that bad?" Anya asked. "Vengeance demons don't get brain freezes. Or ear infections. Something about the job makes us immune."

The Mayor mopped his brow with the end of his tie and shook his head, incredulous. "Great work today, gang! Now we can all go home and get some rest. Oh, except you, Willow. I'd appreciate if you keep an eye on the temple, just until Glory gets the flag settled. If the slayer shows up, you know what to do."

"Take the Marnoxon gem from her," Anya urged emphatically, hoping that this time it would actually stick in the redhead's brain.

"Yeah, sure," the Mayor said, his voice flat with disinterest. "But first, kill her. I don't want any more campaign meetings interrupted by her shenanigans, understood?"

"Yes, sir," Willow said, frozen in place on the temple steps while the Mayor jogged toward his waiting town car.

His chauffeur, a lizard demon with crocodile-like coloring, opened the back passenger-side door and doffed his black flat cap, exposing his tan cranial ridges. Once the Mayor's feet were safely tucked inside the car, the chauffeur closed the door and climbed into the driver's seat.

As the engine roared to life, the tinted back window opened. The Mayor stuck his head out, grinning. "Don't forget to stop by City Hall and describe your experience of working together as a diverse group of monsters and mortals to Jeff!" he called. "And make sure you're registered to vote!"

"Ugh," Willow said, letting her face fall into a scowl as the town car peeled out of the parking lot. "I hate Jeff."

"A ridiculous name," Drusilla said. She lifted her foot to take another step but misplaced her boot, sliding down a stair. Her head flopped back. Her eyes rolled back.

Willow reached out, catching the other girl with an arm around the shoulders. She pulled her close, pushing the hair out of Drusilla's face. "Dru? Are you okay? You're even paler than normal."

"Bugger off, Red. She's having a bloody vision," Spike said, stepping close to Drusilla's other side. The backs of his knuckles stroked her cheek. "What do you see, pet? Is that trumped-up aubergine going to renege on our deal?"

"A chopper to chop off your head, chip-chop, chip-chop," Drusilla whimpered. She pawed at the empty air, eyes hollow and unseeing. "There she is. The slayer. She's here, back with us. I can see her, clear as crystal. Searching, but not for the black fire. She won't heed the call of her wand, no matter how clearly it shows her the path. She's surrounded by toys. But not a store. Games, but not for children. So many trifles and trinkets, and yet all the dolls are hard, unfriendly, unbending. No, no Miss Edith would not like these. All oil and gas calcified into little boys. So many toy boys. And chairs full of . . . beans?"

"Oh my God," Andrew gasped. He clutched Jonathan's gauntlet-covered arm. "She's in our house."

The Slayer

JUNK EVERYWHERE.

An unfinished gray orb made of LEGOs sits on the kitchen table, surrounded by tiny spaceships and even tinier figurines in white helmets. Towers of board-game boxes line the walls. How many versions of Risk and Settlers of Catan can there be? Apparently enough to clutter an entire room.

If the Slayer didn't know any better, she would think that she'd broken into a ten-year-old's fort rather than a modest-size house near the charred husk of Sunnydale High. As far as she could tell when the portal deposited her in the driveway, most of the other houses in the neighborhood have been abandoned. Is that because of the whole eternal darkness, Hell on Earth thing? Or does no one want to live near Jonathan, Andrew, and their dead friend? Either option would make sense. The Trio's lair has a distinct, unpleasant smell. Like drug-store cologne, industrial-strength glue, and inedible cafeteria pizza. The worst thing would be finding the source of the smell all coming from the same place.

There's no couch in the living room. Three king-size beanbag chairs are arranged around a big-screen TV. Stacks of movies and video games cover the floor. There are more Star Trek films here than she knew existed and piles and piles of Monty Python's Flying Circus DVDs. The walls are blank except for a mounted longsword with a purple hilt and a matching steel-plated shield with a coat of arms on it, which features a red bird and a pyramid of three yellow triangles.

In the garage, a souped-up Xerox machine nearly the same height as the Slayer is making a racket, its inner gears chugging and wheezing as it spits sheet after sheet of green paper onto a conveyer belt. The pages are rolled through an automated paper cutter with a machete-like blade. The sliced paper flutters to the top of a small mound of newly minted twenty-dollar bills. The Slayer picks one up. Except for being still warm from the printer, the bill has the look and weight of real money. She drops it back onto the money pile. Demondale won't last long enough for her to need it.

A dry-erase board is propped against the garage door. One half of it is dedicated to what was obviously a list of names for the robots she'd encountered at the Trio's Ascension rave—*party-bots, femmebots, girl-borgs, cy–long legs.* The other half of the board is a complicated blueprint that looks not unlike the big plastic gun that Jonathan used to blow up his friend. It is labeled FREEZE RAY. On the ground below is the realization of the drawing, a blue plastic hair-dryer–looking thing plugged into a long extension cord.

This could be useful, she thinks, unplugging the plastic weapon and stepping back inside the house.

The green-gem staff pulls at her arm, trying to make her leave. The staff only wants to destroy. It isn't interested in *reasons*. But the Slayer has to know *why* these humans aligned themselves with the undeniably evil mission statement of Demondale. In her time stuck in this awful dimension, she has seen humans subjugated to the monsters. Taking jobs that put them in harm's way. Walking the streets draped in religious artifacts that don't protect them at all from the demons and hellspawn that roam the streets. Attacked in what would be broad daylight if the Mayor hadn't banished the sun from within city limits. Why would these human boys fight alongside the vampires who live to feed on them? If they wanted to become vamps themselves, it would be much easier to give themselves over to the Master at the Church of the Eternal Night.

Or it would have been. Before the Slayer dusted him.

The Jonathan she studied in the last reality seemed totally obsessed with molding the world into his particular brand of utopia. Although, after seeing the museum display about it, she wasn't sure how playing both Aquaman and Superman was particularly helpful to humanity. But the museum display had recounted the feat with the same amount of admiration as the exhibit on Jonathan creating world peace. Was it only the selling of his soul that made him altruistic?

The Slayer sets the staff down. "I'll be back soon," she promises it.

Padding down the hall away from the living room, she finds three closed bedroom doors. *How very Goldilocks*, she thinks, smashing open the first one. The room on the other side is tidy except for a desk pushed under the window. A disembodied arm and slender leg in two different skin tones sit atop a heap of nuts and bolts.

Throwing an arm over her nose, the Slayer approaches cautiously, sure that she's found the least stealthy murderer in the world—until she sees the hardware sticking out of the top of the loose limbs.

"Right. Robot parts," she says, hesitantly lowering her arm. She remembers the glassy-eyed girls dancing at the nerd boys' warehouse party and their loud mechanical joints. "Less creepy, but not *not* creepy."

Without the bossy staff in hand, she's officially talking to herself.

On top of a dresser full of button-down shirts with huge collars, the Slayer finds an old Sunnydale High student ID card. The boy in the photo is the same one she saw Jonathan shoot with blue lightning. The card identifies him as Warren Mears. Glancing around his room—the bikini babes poster on his wall, a photo of himself shaking hands with the Mayor, and a framed letter of recommendation calling him an "upstanding young gentleman" signed *Principal Regis Snyder*—the Slayer knows everything she needs to about this guy.

"You seem like a real douchebag, Warren," she tells the ID, and moves on to the next room. She has no business with the dead. Unless, of course, they rise again.

Andrew's bedroom—identifiable by the sign on the door that reads ANDREW'S BEDROOM—seems to be where the majority of the cologne smell is coming from. His dresser is overflowing with aerosol cans—hairspray, deodorant, body sprays, compressed air. This guy doesn't care about the ozone layer *at all*.

Scanning his bookcase, the Slayer finds a photo of Andrew posed with a slightly taller, slightly more handsome brown-haired boy whose name pops into the Slayer's head unprompted. Tucker Wells. In her Sunnydale, Tucker is a year ahead of her at school. She's had detention with him a few times when Snyder's caught her doing Slayer business that can't be explained. She remembers Tucker as the sort of shy, awkward type who's always muttering to himself under his breath and filling his notebooks with serial-killer scrawl.

And it would appear that Andrew is his brother.

Where is Tucker in Demondale? Did he survive the wreckage of the Hellmouth opening? Did he join the mass exodus of normal people leaving town? Or…

Behind the photo of the brothers is a line of books about vampires. Ranging from highly realistic—*Der Vampyr* by Kaspar Hershberger, a Giles favorite—to the mostly apocryphal—*Dracula, Interview with the Vampire, Bunnicula*. The Slayer continues her search around Andrew's room. Now that she knows to look for it, she finds vampire stuff everywhere. Not repellents—there's no crucifixes or bulbs of dried garlic in sight. But she does find a newspaper clipping announcing the Bronze's grand reopening as a vampire club—owned by Angelus, of all people. Even though there is a large color picture of him, unsmiling behind the bar in his best leather jacket, the article spends a number of inches describing "the demon with an angel's face." She tries to reconcile the vampire with a soul she knows in her world with this evil entrepreneur who replaced the Bronze's espresso machines with blood on tap. The Angel she knows can at least appreciate a decent cappuccino. Not that he prefers it to blood, but he certainly wouldn't deprive Sunnydale of its best coffee. This Angelus guy is truly a monster.

Andrew seems to disagree. The drawers of his desk are stuffed with flyers for the Bronze, detailing its *half price for succubi* drink special and performances from Drusilla and the Dollies. He even has a menu with all the human food highlighted. At least, she assumes it's human food. She's not entirely sure how one would make gravy fries into something evil. Maybe the gravy is blood? Is gravy not normally blood? What even is gravy?

Oddly, the evil Angelus-owned Bronze serves the same deep-fried blooming onion as the Bronze in her Sunnydale. The more things change, the more they stay the same.

Pushing aside Andrew's Bronze research, she finds a bundle of glossy pamphlets for the Church of the Eternal Night advertising its infuriating "bite that saves" crusade. The Slayer hates thinking of how many souls have been lost to the Master and Darla. If she'd known how easy it would be to break into the church, she would have slayed them weeks ago.

Of all of Demondale's evils, the existence of the Church of the Eternal Night was what had convinced her that this dimension was beyond redemption.

Her first week in Hell on Earth, she had been so focused on finding out how to leave that she hadn't noticed the sheer number of newly turned vampires that were walking around. She'd attributed the vampire-crowded streets to the security provided by the sunshade.

Then she'd roughed up a teenage vampire, doomed to stay forever squeaky-voiced and pimply. No vampire in their right mind would go around turning kids. It ruined the allure of the undead. Normally, vamps were as picky and beauty-obsessed as the editors of *Vogue*. But the puberty-stricken vamp told her that he'd been turned by the Church.

It was turn and die or die and be dead, he told her. *I'd rather die and get to keep living.*

The Slayer had pitied him enough that it had been hard to stake him. Until he'd tried to bite her.

The Church of the Eternal Night didn't care who they turned. The Master and Darla preached about an era of vampiric supremacy, a world full of the undead. They rewarded people for bringing in new "volunteers" to be drained and turned.

The only way to stop the monsters was to unplug the entire dimension.

After finding more advertisements for Demondale businesses that cater solely to vampires—Second Life Gym, Blood Bath salon and spa, Dr. Curtis Constantine, DDS, a dentist specializing in fangs—and a black velvet cloak hanging in the back of the closet, she decides to move on from Andrew's room. His motivation seems clear enough to her. Just another Demondale human toying with the idea of dying to survive.

On to Jonathan's room.

It isn't much of a surprise that Jonathan's room is the smallest. The snug walls are lit by the soft blue glow of a large aquarium full of plastic plants. Despite the size of the tank, its sole occupant is a fish about the length of the Slayer's thumb. It dives between the tank's fake foliage, flipping crimson-red fins that look like amaryllis petals.

A Rube Goldberg machine wraps around the base of the ceiling like tacky crown molding. Hot Wheels tracks, neon-colored gerbil tubes, a pulley system rigged with dental floss, two of those clackety ball things people keep on their desks, plastic cups and ladders the Slayer recognizes as pieces of the game Mousetrap, an analog alarm clock, and a jar full of marbles, poised to set the whole thing off just above the bedside table.

She releases a marble, watching it shoot around the ceiling, spinning fast and clattering like a pinball until it finally runs into a switch on top of the fish tank that releases exactly five food pellets that the fish gratefully slurps up.

Okay. So, *this* Jonathan has a lot of time on his hands and cares about keeping his fish alive. That doesn't automatically make him a good person. And it doesn't explain why he's protecting the Black Flame flag. Or where he's keeping it.

She tears through this room more aggressively than she had the other two. She throws the clothes out of his dresser, shocked that any one human being could own so many oversize striped T-shirts. She pulls up the mattress, which, upon glimpsing the teenage-boy detritus beneath, she immediately regrets. This is why she wasn't chosen to fight humans. Slaying vampires never puts her face-to-face with anyone's porn collection.

Throwing the pillows and blankets onto the bed, she feels a square lump inside the duvet. Praying not to find any more X-rated magazines, she tears open the blanket cover and fishes out a notebook.

Inside, she finds cramped handwriting and undated journal entries. The first page reads:

Mom and Dad sold the house today. The buyer never came to take a tour, and they sent a proxy to deal with all the inspections and paperwork, so Andrew is convinced that a vampire bought it. I guess a vampire might want a house with a sunken living room and wood paneling if they were turned during the 70s and miss it.

Warren's mom said that I can come stay with them if I don't want to move to Orange with my parents. Warren will even give up his gaming room for me. He says the garage will have more space for his computer, anyway.

I think I'm going to do it. I don't want to drop out of school just because the Mayor wants to block out the sun. When Mister Burns on The Simpsons installed the Sun Blocker, it led to one of the best two-part episodes in the show's history. I mean, everyone remembers Who Shot Mr. Burns?! I bet this whole eternal-darkness thing is just a campaign stunt. Warren says the Mayor has his eye on becoming president someday, and everyone will remember the guy who took the sun out of Sunnydale, no matter how long it lasts.

Flipping ahead, the Slayer reads another passage.

It's been eight days since Mrs. Mears disappeared. There are too many missing-person cases here for the police to stay on top of. They say that after the first forty-eight hours, we should just assume that she got bit. Warren has already filed the paperwork to put the house in his name. He keeps saying, "She knew the risk of staying here." But I don't know if she did. I don't know if any of us realized how different things would be living on an open hellmouth. Sunnydale was always a weird place to live. Things happened that we couldn't explain. Like the time that the SHS swim team all grew gills and flippers and Principal Snyder said it was a side effect of black market steroids. Or the number of people who went missing every year. And those hyena people. But knowing for sure that there are monsters out there, waiting to kill all of us . . . it's worse. It's so much worse.

Horrified, the Slayer skips to the middle of the journal.

Warren says that we're sitting ducks without some powers. Andrew sees this as an excuse to go get himself some fangs, obviously, and Warren is looking into rumors of a transformation spell that turns a human into a super demon or something. I think staying human could be something we use to our advantage. We should use what we know from comics and rule this town! Or, at least, be equals with the vampires and demons and magic users. The best supervillains are just really smart humans. Lex Luthor. Doctor Octopus. Ozymandias.

I keep trying to convince Warren that if he'd stop obsessing over building the perfect robot girl, we could come up with some killer tech. He says that if I want to play with phasers, I should make one myself. Since the schools all closed when they couldn't find anyone brave enough to teach in Demondale, I guess I have time to learn some advanced mechanical engineering.

The Slayer shuts the journal, unsettled. In searching for proof that these boys had some nefarious purpose, all she's done is found exactly what happens around an unprotected hellmouth. If this reality had a Slayer to defend it from the nasties and the baddies, then helpless people like Jonathan wouldn't have to spend their lives trapped in a town that literally wants to kill them.

Giles always harps on the importance of the Slayer's mission. She has been chosen to stop the spread of evil and the swell of its numbers. And Demondale hasn't had someone to do that. So innocent dorks are out here dreaming of building sci-fi weapons just so they can stay alive for another day. If she'd only gotten here sooner. Or if when she'd first landed, she'd focused on the town's biggest bads—the Master, the Mayor, Angelus. Would it have made a difference? Could she have saved this world?

But no—it was already too late for Demondale when she got here. The Hellmouth is open. There are more demons here than any one person could ever hope to slay. The only option left is the nuclear one. It's time to wipe Demondale off the map.

NINE
Jonathan

THE METAPHYSICAL BOUTIQUE had been ransacked. Open books sat on every surface, covering the displays, stacked on the floor. Books inside other books. Some upside down, their spines broken.

Behind the counter, Ripper stood alone with a book in each hand, his focus darting between the two.

"We're closed," he announced as the bell over the door chimed. "For the end of the world."

"We're here," Angelus said, leaping over the books sandbagging the stairs. His coat flapped behind him like Batman's cape. "To stop the end of the world."

"Oh. You again." If Ripper noticed that the group had shrunk since the last time they'd visited, he didn't show it. Drusilla had stayed with Willow to guard the Black Flame flag at Glory's temple. "Did you stop the slayer?"

"We, um, delayed her?" Jonathan said. Inching through the room, he did his best not to step on any of the books. It reminded him of playing hot lava alone in his childhood home, trying not to step anywhere his parents could see him. "We have reason to believe that she's now hunting us."

Knowing that the slayer had singled out him and Andrew made Jonathan anxious. Even more anxious than he'd felt waiting for the world to end. The entire walk from the temple back downtown, he'd been convinced that the slayer would appear out of thin air and attack them again. Angelus said that the slayer wasn't supposed to hurt humans, but from what Jonathan could tell, she wasn't supposed to destroy entire dimensions either. Maybe someone reversed her moral alignment with some tar-riddled Kryptonite like in *Superman III*?

Ripper's left eyebrow lifted in judgment, making Jonathan worried that he'd said his *Superman III* theory aloud.

"Why would she hunt *you*?" Ripper asked. "Your deaths will have no effect on the end of reality, will they?"

"They will for us!" Andrew said. He tiptoed over to a table to rescue a wilted leather tome perched atop a crystal ball. "And haven't you ever heard of a bookmark?"

"Yeah," Anya said, picking up a book opened to an illustration of a scythe embedded in a rock. She snapped the book shut. "This has to be bad for your inventory."

"If we are still facing down imminent destruction, then I was right and there is no time to waste on quitter sticks," Ripper said, setting the books in his hands down on the counter. "Unlike you American children, I had an *actual* public school education. I can handle reading more than one book at once."

"Hey, Andrew and I went to public school," Jonathan said.

Andrew nodded as he dropped both the backpack and messenger bag to the floor. "My mom wanted to send me to Christian Brothers High but then she died, and my aunt couldn't afford the tuition for me and my brother—"

"He's not talking about your high school. In England, public school is privatized, and private school is for the public," Spike said with a grunt, speaking for the first time since they left Drusilla at the temple. Leaning against an empty bookcase, he gave Ripper an unfriendly once-over. "This one's an Eton nob if I've ever seen one. I bet that rough accent is a fake, too. Never been south of the Thames, have you?"

Ripper's blue eyes showed outrage, but his face remained placid. "And you, William the Bloody, are said to have been such a mama's boy that you couldn't bear to be parted with her long enough to attend a proper boarding school." At Spike's look of shock, Ripper let out a self-satisfied chuckle. "It wasn't Eton. It was the Watchers Academy. Then Oxford."

"You're a Watcher and you didn't mention it before?" Angelus asked sharply.

Anya folded her arms defensively across her chest. "Don't you have to go door to door and tell all your neighbors that you're a nasty peeper?"

"Not that kind of watcher, you silly bint," Ripper groaned, staring up at the boutique's gray ceiling. "A slayer's Watcher. Mentors in charge of the slayer's training in the history and practice of vampire hunting. But I'm not one. I got the education and then got out of the family business. It wasn't for me. I chose another path."

"Magic," Spike snorted. "I'm sure your mum and dad were chuffed."

"Look, Mister Ripper," Jonathan said before the Brits could start throwing esoteric references at each other again. "We need help stopping the slayer."

"Permanently stopping her," Spike said, tromping across several of the open books on the floor as he made his way over to the farthest display case. The spines cracked apart with an awful sound. "Do you have any weapons in here?"

"I've spent all day searching for the right weapon for this fight," Ripper said, flinging an arm at the many open books. "A spell, a sigil, something! There's nothing on earth that can overpower the Marnoxon gem. It can't be summoned, located, or destroyed. So long as the slayer wields it, she's basically invincible."

"Then we'll have to cut off the arm that's wielding it," Angelus said. "Slayer or not, she's just a little girl. Any long-range weapon could slow her down. She's hunting the humans, so we're going to hunt her right back. We've got the bait on our side."

"Ah, so it isn't actual concern for these two humans that motivates you," Ripper said.

"They got us in to see the Mayor and stole the Black Flame out from under the slayer," Angelus said, considering Jonathan and Andrew. "They're okay. For blood bags."

"High praise," Ripper said sarcastically.

Shock made Jonathan light-headed. The biggest and baddest vampire in Demondale thought he and Andrew were okay? And had given them credit for their help? He could have just as easily pretended that they had only tagged along all day. That's what Warren would have done. No matter how much time and energy Jonathan put into the development of new weapons, Warren was the one who had final say on naming rights. Warren filed the patents. Warren fired the first test shot.

How could it be that Angelus was better at treating Jonathan and Andrew as equals than their own best friend had been?

Glass shattered as Spike punched his way into the case and retrieved a broadsword. "This should do the trick," he said. "Oi, Angelus, there's a chain mace in here. You want it?"

"A mace?" Angelus cried, joyfully trampling the books on the floor as he bounded to Spike's side. "All right! I haven't killed anyone with a mace in decades!"

Ripper glared at Jonathan and Andrew. "That'll be five hundred dollars for the flail and the sword. And a thousand for the broken case."

"We're gearing up to save the world!" Jonathan protested, gripping the edge of the counter that stood between him and Ripper. "Can't you cut us a break? Or at least a discount? If we don't all die today, we'll bring the weapons back to you!"

"We could trade some of the stuff we already bought from you," Andrew offered. He swung the blue backpack off his shoulder and ripped open the zipper. "Do you want a horn that can call upon the livestock of hell? Poisonous sheep on command!"

"You gits have earned none of my goodwill," Ripper said. "The last time you were here, you murdered my business partner!"

"*We* didn't!" Jonathan protested. He did his best to covertly point at Angelus, who was swinging his new chain mace around. "We can't control that guy. He's almost three hundred years old!"

"He's here with you," Ripper said, unmoved. "And I won't let you borrow so much as a pencil from my inventory. This is my life's work here. I'd rather die with it than give it away to Ethan's killers."

"Fine, *Smaug*," Andrew jeered at the older man. "Sit on your treasure pile while the world ends! We don't need your help!"

"That's not true," Anya said, inserting herself into the conversation. She clapped the book she was holding down onto the counter. Its title was in Latin. Had Anya actually been able to read it or was she playacting to look busy? She did claim to be over a thousand years old. When had Latin died as a language?

"We absolutely need your help," Anya told Ripper. "Well, your stuff. But we're willing to pay for it." She looked expectantly at Jonathan and Andrew. "What are you waiting for? Hand him money. Lots of it. Money always changes people's minds. It's the best thing about it. Other than being exchangeable for goods. And the smell of it. And how safe it makes you feel when you have, like, a lot of it."

Jonathan reluctantly retrieved the messenger bag, He handed the last of their money over to Ripper, who rubbed one of the twenties over a craggy pink crystal next to the cash register. As the bill passed over it, the crystal glowed orange as though filled with an inner fire.

"Are you taking the piss?" Ripper asked sharply. The bill crunched into a ball in his fist. "You think I'm going to fall for this again?"

Jonathan shied away from the counter, hugging the shrink ray inside the messenger bag like it could save him. He cleared his throat, finding it suddenly very dry.

"Fall for what?" he asked.

"I told your tall friend that I wouldn't take any more of this counterfeit shit," Ripper said, pitching the crumpled bill onto the floor and

189

picking up another from the stack. "He's still got his name written in binary here. W. Mears. What a twat."

"You read binary?" Andrew said, impressed. "That's so cool."

Ripper threw the money off the counter so that it rained down the front of Jonathan's shirt and onto the blood-encrusted toes of his sneakers. Jonathan stooped to shovel the cash back into the messenger bag, his face and ears burning with embarrassment. Stupid Warren. Always signing his crimes. Always assuming he was the smartest person in the world. The counterfeit machine wasn't even his. It was Andrew's. Andrew had done all the programming and building. Warren had just insisted on changing the serial numbers.

"Look, I'm sorry," Jonathan said to Ripper. "All we've got is fake money. I don't have a job, and Andrew blew his last paycheck on these hyper-realistic fang dentures—"

"Dude!" Andrew whispered, tugging on the neck of his own turtleneck like it was suddenly too tight. "Shut up! Those are a secret!"

A faint scream made Jonathan turn around. Anya clutched at her heart, the blood draining from her face. Terrified that she was about to go into cardiac arrest, Jonathan started to reach for her. She staggered away from him and shrieked, "Fake money?!" before digging through her pockets and pulling out the money they'd paid her for their Wish. Tears of betrayal glazed her eyes. "What did I ever do to deserve fake money?"

"I mean, we were paying you to get a Wish you couldn't grant," Jonathan said, knowing this was a weak rejoinder. The sight of the vengeance demon's tears made him want to shrivel up and disappear. He hadn't realized that Anya had any feelings to hurt.

"I helped you! Protected you! Defended you!" Anya spluttered at Jonathan and Andrew as she dumped all the counterfeit cash onto the floor. It fluttered down to cover a line of open books. "I thought we were a team! I thought we were—well, not friends precisely—but something more than neighbors you have to wave at and less than people who share an intimate knowledge of one another's personal histories."

"No, what you're describing is friends," Spike told Anya, crunching his way across the store, the broadsword slung over his shoulder. "Not particularly close friends."

"That!" Anya said, jabbing a finger at Spike but continuing to glare daggers at Jonathan and Andrew. "I thought we were not particularly close friends! But you were just conning me! Cheating me like filthy, stinking warlocks!"

"Excuse me," Ripper said stiffly. "I'm a warlock."

"You have a crystal that smells lies and ruins friendships," Anya retorted.

"Anya, enough," Angelus said, his voice firm but not unkind. The mace in his hand swung jauntily by his side as he came up beside her and set a hand on her shoulder. "There will be time to fight about money after the slayer is dead. Hell, if we live another day, I'll kill the boys for you myself."

Anya scowled at the larger vampire, looking like a petulant child. "You'll just eat them," she said, shaking off his hand. She fixed Jonathan with another withering stare. "When I have my magic back, I can make them truly suffer."

"Great, so we all have things to look forward to," Andrew said weakly.

Jonathan's blood ran cold. He couldn't even guess what Anya would deem acceptable punishment for him and Andrew. She had spent an entire millennium inflicting vengeance for other people.

How much worse would her vengeance be when she was acting on her own behalf? Would she feed them to Hellhounds? Skin them alive? Force them into a *Groundhog Day* scenario of eternal torment?

Angelus lifted his weapon by the handle so that the sharp metal ball jingled on its chain next to his face as he addressed Ripper. "Spike and I will be taking the mace and the sword on a little field trip. Our clairvoyant got a picture of the slayer back in town, so we're going to go take her down. I'll front the bill for the weapons. Just send an invoice over to the Bronze, will you?"

Hatred plain on his face, Ripper gritted his teeth. "I suppose if I were to turn you down, the coroner would need to make a second trip here today."

"Let's not find out." Angelus grinned. "Why don't you just hop on team Save the World? You did your best with your books. Let us take care of the rest."

"Whatever gets you out of my shop," Ripper said, holding the vampire's gaze.

"About that," Spike said. "We're leaving the living with you."

"I don't think so," Ripper scoffed. "Take your forging Renfields with you!"

"We're not Renfields," Andrew corrected, holding his index finger in the air.

"And how are you going to get into our house without an invitation?" Jonathan asked Angelus.

"Do you want us to kill the slayer loose in your house?" the vampire asked.

"Yes! But—"

"Then issue the invite before we make you," Spike said.

Jonathan gulped. "You're invited into our house to kill the slayer."

"But don't look through our stuff!" Andrew added.

Angelus reached out and knocked a glass orb off the nearest shelf. It fell to the floor, cracking like an egg. "Why don't you all stay and help Ripper put his shop back together. It's a mess in here."

"Don't leave me with these lying humans!" Anya begged, rushing after Angelus and Spike as they climbed the stairs toward the boutique's front door. "Give me a sword! I'm totally stabby! I can help out! If I could just get my hands on the Marnoxon gem, I could undo this whole day!"

Angelus cupped her cheek in his palm. "Why don't you and Ripper finish tracking down the names and prices on all the magical garbage Andrew's been lugging around in that backpack? Maybe some of it is worth something."

Anya glanced back at Ripper. "How much would you pay for the Dagger of the Unkillable and two bald-faced liars?"

THE SLAYER

AS THE SLAYER makes her way out of Jonathan's room, she hears a persistent knocking. Padding silently on the balls of her feet, she creeps around the corner. . . .

Where she finds the staff rolling itself against the front door, making the green gem passive-aggressively thump against the exit.

"Yeah, yeah," she says, scooping up the outraged dowsing rod, "I know. Find the hell flag. Make the world go boom. You have such a one-track mind."

Yanking open the front door reveals two men in leather jackets standing on the front porch.

No. Not men. Vampires.

Armed vampires.

Tightening her grip on the dowsing rod, the Slayer considers running. With more of the other Hells on Earth destroyed, it's easier to find her way back to Demondale. Its evil seems to draw the staff like no other dimension. She tries to calculate the likelihood of the vamps chasing her through a portal. Seems high. Besides, running from them won't reveal the location of Jonathan and the Black Flame flag.

"We meet again, Slayer," Angelus says with a fanged grin.

In the Slayer's dimension, Angel has a softer, sweeter face. More unassuming, less arrogant. This Angel, Angelus, is sort of fratty. If she didn't know he was older than the sport itself, she would have assumed he was a football player. He's got a quarterback's bluster.

The blond one, on the other hand, she doesn't know. He must not have landed in her Sunnydale yet. Unless her Angel has a Cockney sidekick hiding somewhere. He's handsome. In an undead, pasty-faced, evil sort of way. Almost heroin chic, which is trendy in her dimension, but must be years out-of-date in Demondale. Not that vampires stay up-to-date on trends.

"Angelus," the Slayer says by way of greeting. She scrunches her face at the bleached-blond vampire with the sucked-in cheekbones. "And, um, you."

The longsword in the blond vampire's hand droops toward the porch. "What the hell? You know his name and not mine? It's Spike."

"Right, Spike," the Slayer says. She shifts her weight to her right leg, preparing for the impending brawl. "I had a boyfriend in LA named *Pike* who was also a sort of sharp-faced punk, so it's kind of confusing. Unless this is another alternate-universe doppelgänger thing. I mean, after leather-and-lace Willow, anything is possible. Oliver Pike, is that you? You have to tell me, otherwise it's entrapment—"

Spike charges before she can ask if he, like her ex, drives a motorcycle. The Slayer leaps back into the house, hoping that the invitation barrier will bounce the vamps back onto the front lawn.

It doesn't.

Spike and Angelus bolt over the threshold, fangs flashing and weapons flying.

They've been invited in. Of course they have. The Slayer has seen Andrew's room. The fanboy probably gave them a handwritten invitation. Now he can say that he's had real live undead in his house.

She throws the dowsing rod over her head, blocking Spike's sword before it can chop her skull in half. Using their locked weapons, she pushes Spike into the opposing wall. Angelus takes this as an opening, whipping his flail at her. The Slayer dodges to one side. Drywall explodes as the metal ball smashes an inch from her shoulder. A flurry of white dust fills the entryway, disorienting the three fighters. Gritty bits of plaster sting the Slayer's eyes. Blinking rapidly strobes her vision.

Spike, wiping dust out of his cranial folds.

Angelus, spinning the flail at his side with increasing speed, gearing up for another strike.

There's a notch cut in the center of the dowsing rod. How much damage can it take before it stops working? She can't risk it.

Darting into the kitchen, she casts around for something else she can use as a weapon. The overflowing trash can is plastic. The Batman-bust cookie jar is useless—and empty. On the stove, there's a nonstick skillet ringed in crispy yellow egg bits. Gag. But there's a wooden spoon balanced on the rim. That'll work.

As the vampires burst into the kitchen, the Slayer grabs the spoon and breaks it over her knee. Leaving the green gem and staff under the watchful eye of the ceramic Batman, she grips her two makeshift stakes.

Spike is first through the door, hefting his sword in both hands. The lapels of his coat fall to the side as he rears back, exposing his tight black T-shirt. The Slayer aims for his left pec and stabs half the broken wooden spoon at him. He throws an arm up to block it. The wood splinters against the sleeve of his jacket, not even leaving a mark against the leather. Grinning at her, he opens his mouth—to say something overconfident and Britishy, she's sure. A swift kick in the sternum silences him. And sends him sailing into the LEGO orb on the table and over the side.

"Bloody hell!" he shouts, thrashing to his feet. "Do you know how much landing on a LEGO Death Star hurts?"

"I don't even know what a Death Star is," the Slayer says.

Avoiding a wallop from Angelus's flail, she drops to the floor and covers her head as magnets rain down from the newly smashed fridge.

"What? They don't have Star Wars in your dimension?" Angelus asks.

"No, they do," the Slayer says. "It's just for dorks. Now, where did Jonathan hide the Black Flame flag?"

"Why would we tell you that?" Spike asks, dusting plastic bricks from his coat. "When we could just kill you?"

"The Master failed to kill me *twice*." The Slayer laughs. "You think you have a shot?"

"First of all, we've got weapons," Angelus says. "And all you've got is a dirty spoon."

He's got a point.

Dodging another blow from the flail, she runs into the living room. From the wall, she tears down the decorative sword and shield. Hefting the shield, she realizes too late that it's as featherlight as a disposable pie pan. The sword is only slightly better—it's made of decent metal but butter-knife blunt. Too late to back out now.

"Come on, Slayer," Angelus says over the whoosh of his flail slicing through the air. "You're forestalling the inevitable. Put down your toy sword and give in. We'll give you a quick death. After some light torture."

"How generous of you," the Slayer says. "Especially since I killed your sire. Have you had time to grieve Vampy Faye Bakker yet?"

The flail zooms toward her face, metal spikes twinkling in the overhead lighting. Stabbing through one of the chain loops, the Slayer flicks the tip of the sword and flings the weapon out of Angelus's grip. The metal ball and its handle sail through the air and splinter the sliding-glass back door.

Spike hurtles forward, his sword aimed for the Slayer. She discus-throws the metal-plated shield. One corner smashes into Spike's temple, staggering him.

The Slayer dives behind Angelus, pressing the toy sword against his throat. Even with her super Slayer strength, she can't quite make the dull blade cut through his skin. This is going to be the longest decapitation of all time.

"What's the matter, Slayer?" Angelus taunts. His hands wrap around her wrists, trying to force the blade away. She has to dig her knee into his back to keep him still. "You've got a boyfriend back home that looks like me too?"

"Not exactly," she says, voice strained. Even if she kills him, there's no way she'll survive the gloating if she tells this guy about her will-they-or-won't-they with Angel. "The you back home is way less of a try-hard. He doesn't need this whole threatening-torture thing. He's more of the strong, silent type. Maybe because he has a soul."

"A vampire with a soul?" Spike laughs. "Oh my God, how lame is that? Is he all 'Boo-hoo, poor me, I've got to eat people to stay alive, but I wish I could be a vegetarian'?"

"Yeah, basically," the Slayer says.

"Ha!" Spike guffaws. "I wish I could see that. Namby-pamby Angelus with a conscience."

"Tell me where Jonathan hid the Black Flame flag and maybe I'll bring you to the real Sunnydale," the Slayer bluffs, doing her best to sound coquettish. "There's no sunshade, which means there's still plenty of people to eat. You must be so hungry in a demon-only town. My Sunnydale has babies. Coeds. Whatever kind of human Happy Meal floats your fangy boat."

"Oh yeah?" Spike says, matching her smokiness. He sucks one of his elongated canines, his yellow eyes blazing. "Tell me more about these Happy Meals."

"Spike," Angelus grunts. "Can't you see she's trying to cut my damn head off?"

"Yeah, yeah, but it's bloody slow going," Spike says.

"She's sixteen years old," Angelus says.

"Hey!" the Slayer says. She hitches the sword tighter against his neck. "How did you know that? I'm way mature for my age. I could totally pass for twenty."

Angelus struggles to glare at her without turning his head. "You smell like Teen Spirit. And collagen."

Spike snorts, scraping the tip of his sword in the carpet. "Didn't stop you in another dimension, old man."

"I am not responsible for anything some ensouled vegetarian does with my face," Angelus grumbles.

One of Spike's heavy boots stamps on the Slayer's toes. Sucking in a pained gasp, she loosens her grip enough for Angelus to get free. He reels around, both of his big white hands reaching up for her throat.

"Let's see how you like it," Angelus snarls. "Pretty sure you're the only person in the room who needs to breathe."

The Slayer's knee slams into his groin. As he roars, she kicks his knees out from under him, shoving him down into the carpet with the dull tip of the toy sword.

"Pretty sure I'm the only *person* in the room, period," she snaps.

Sharp, stinging pain erupts in her skull as she's pulled back. Flinging around, she sees Spike's hand buried deep in her hair.

"Hair pulling?" she asks, more offended than hurt. "Really?"

He cocks his head at her. "You expect a fair fight from a vampire? Now hold still, Happy Meal."

Sensing the impending viper-strike of his fangs, the Slayer jams the purple hilt of the toy sword between her neck and Spike's mouth. Choking on the pommel forces him to let go of the Slayer's hair. Released, she backhands him into a tower of board games. Ten different Monopoly boxes fall on him. Plastic hotels and pewter Scottie dogs clatter like hail.

Either these dudes don't know where the Black Flame flag is or they aren't going to give up the information she needs. One or the other she could probably handle, but both at once is total chaos. Before either can lunge for her again, she speeds back into the kitchen, retrieving the green gem and staff from the counter.

"Who needs informants when I have you?" she says fondly. The dowsing rod, in response, vibrates westward.

Dashing into the front hallway again, she retrieves the freeze ray from behind the open door and tucks it under her arm. It's tempting to shoot it at the vamps, but she didn't look closely enough at the schematics to know exactly how it works. It needs to be plugged into an electrical socket. What if it needs to heat up—or cool down—before it can be fired? It would be so embarrassing to get bitten to death because she was trying to use a supervillain weapon that looks like a giant hair dryer. She'll portal somewhere else to try it out.

"Not so fast, Slayer," Angelus says. He staggers into the hallway, Spike close behind. "I'm gonna need that gem."

Spike smacks him in the arm. "So you can gift it to the vengeance girl? I knew I smelled something going on between you two. She's so your type. Ancient, petite, all the subtlety of a Fyarl with its horns on fire. Might as well call her Darla 2.0."

The Slayer freezes. Before, she might have been content to leave these vamps here, beaten but still walking. But fury makes her brain go fuzzy.

"You partnered with a vengeance demon?" she asks through gritted teeth.

"*Partnered with* is a bit of a stretch," Angelus says. "She's a new acquaintance. She came into the Bronze today to alert us about your plan—"

As he speaks, he rubs at the back of his neck. The motion is so painfully familiar to the Slayer. It's so Angel, *her* Angel, all bashful and unsure. If he had the ability, he'd be blushing.

Over a vengeance demon.

The Slayer's pulse pounds in her ears. Hatred and jealousy twist inside her, so knotted together that she can't pry them apart to reason with either. She knows this isn't her Angel. This isn't her reality. This isn't a man she'd even want to rub his neck over her.

And yet.

She bangs the staff into the ground, telling the gem, "Somewhere sunny!"

Obliging, a portal opens. The narrow entry hallway is flooded with natural light, illuminating the drywall-dusted floor. Exposed skin smoking, the vampires fall back, snarling.

The Slayer dives into the portal, pausing for one last glimpse of Angelus's ponytail catching fire before she disappears into a new dimension.

TEN
Anya

"I'M NOT GOING to let you rip me off here, warlock," Anya said. "There is no way this is worth less than a hundred and fifty."

"I paid fifty quid for that back in London," Ripper said.

"And I am saying that I want at least triple that. In American dollars," Anya said, shaking the Ram's Horn horn by the bend in the mouthpiece. "It's a seller's market here, Ripper! Do you know how many Demondale idiots would pay top dollar to command hell's livestock? Not just creeps and losers either. Think of the money they could earn on evil sheep alone. Evil wool for evil scarves. Evil lanolin. Evil mutton!"

"You've made your point," Ripper said. He was smoking inside again, tapping ash into a teacup. "If the world doesn't end, I'll be sure to market this horn as an evil shepherd starter kit."

"Are you being sarcastic? Or were you not listening?" Anya asked, using the horn to sweep the smoke away from her face. "One blow on this baby would give you an entire evil farm! Just add barn! Evil cows, evil sheep, evil horses. You buy this from me for one-fifty, and you could turn it around for at least four hundred dollars. And I'll expect a thank-you card when you do. Now, back to this Dagger of the Unkillable."

"No! We already agreed on two hundred for the dagger," Ripper said with a groan. He scrubbed a hand down his jaw. "For God's sake, woman, have pity. Our very reality could come tumbling down around us at any moment. I don't want to die in the midst of trying to prove to you that the Dagger of the Unkillable was forged in the nineteenth century to stop the rising of the demon Yoldar."

Anya set the Ram's Horn horn on the top of the stack of magical objects littering the glass counter beside the cash register, and retrieved the corkscrew dagger. She held it up to the light so that the runes carved into the blade sparkled. In Old Norse—which, when Anya had learned it, had been just regular Norse—the runes read *die, die, die.*

Or *elk, elk, elk* depending on which way the blade was aiming.

"You're right," she said, leveling the blade at Ripper's nose. "It would be very sad if you died in the middle of being so wrong about a piece of your own inventory. Because, as I have tried to explain to you, I saw a knife exactly like this one in Constantinople in the *thirteenth* century while I was there getting vengeance on a man with a secret family. Before your ancestors were even a glimmer in the universe's eye. Which means that this piece has at least a five-hundred-dollar trade-in value."

"Goddamn it!" Ripper swore, snuffing his cigarette in the bottom of his teacup. Turning from the knife in his face, he called over his shoulder, "Oi! You lot! Track down a copy of *Dram's Encyclopedia* and bring it here!"

Andrew and Jonathan popped out from behind a bookcase, armed with a broom and a feather duster respectively. Despite Ripper's disinterest in owning humans—something about a constitutional violation—the boys had volunteered to clean up Angelus and Spike's mess. Anya had been doing her best not to pay attention to them as they bustled around the store. Their continued existence tainted the otherwise pleasurable act of haggling.

It had been centuries since Anya experienced betrayal firsthand. It was something she saw happen to other people: To her Wishers. To Best Pressed customers when Human-Mike forgot to order enough yak urine or miniature vanilla scones. She was having a hard time reconciling the feeling in herself. How had she let herself get tricked by two humans? They didn't even have the magic of warlocks! Just pretend money and the temerity to defraud a lonely demon.

Anya's knuckles went white against the handle of the Dagger of the Unkillable. Before this morning, her life in Demondale had been a well-established routine of work and home, void of the obnoxious gossip and one-upmanship of Vengeance LLC. She earned money, ate the newest food creations that earth had to offer, read catalogs and magazines filled with pictures of human women of her general size and shape. It was exactly the life that had been advertised to her.

So why had she felt so much more alive today?

Was it just the threat of death giving her a new zest for life on earth? Or was it the prolonged socialization? If there was supposed to be more to life than just upselling customers, then why hadn't anyone told her so earlier? Maybe then she wouldn't have wasted a day keeping two human swindlers alive, thinking they were becoming friends.

After some shuffling and searching the various books still strewn around the store, Andrew deposited a massive blue tome onto the glass counter next to the Ram's Horn horn.

"Is this the right book, Mister Ripper?" Andrew asked. "The spine is pretty faded, and you had it sitting open, which is really bad for the binding."

"This is it, thanks," Ripper said, dragging the encyclopedia across the glass. It had a gold-stamped Art Nouveau cover of swirling vines and a human skull. The pages released a sweet mustiness as Ripper slapped through them. "Every magical object worth knowing about is in here, so long as it was discovered before 1904. Ah! Here!" He stabbed a finger into the book. "The Dagger of the Unkillable was forged in..." His lips pressed into an unfriendly line.

Anya leaned over the counter, peering into the encyclopedia upside down. "Constantinople!" she announced victoriously. "I knew it! You never forget a dagger once you've seen it shoved up the rear of a primordial Old One. So much goo came out of it. Like, an entire river of unrecognizable goo."

Ripper pushed the book away like it had wronged him. "Yes, yes, fine. You're right. But it does say that it was then *recovered* to fight Yoldar."

"And, Anya," Andrew said, leaning on his push broom. "You should know that Constantinople is called Istanbul now."

"What?" she squawked, turning to Ripper for confirmation. "Why? Since when?"

"Can't say," Jonathan said, his cheeks bulging as he held back a laugh.

"People just liked it better that way," Andrew said with a snicker.

The two of them dissolved into giggles. The sight of their mirth made Anya furious. Never had she missed her magic more. If her connection to the Marnoxon gem had been intact, she would have sent them both to thirteenth-century Constantinople to face the wrath of Renjej the Gooey One.

"Oh, um, Mister Ripper," Jonathan said, suddenly sobering. He clutched his feather duster to his chest. Streaks of spiderweb clung to his sweater. "All the glass is cleaned up, and if you tell us where to put the books, we can sort them out. It's just that, um—"

"What?" the warlock interrupted. "Spit it out!"

"Do you think we could order something in for dinner?" Jonathan squeaked. "We've sort of been on the run all day, and I guess Angelus ate when he, um, killed your friend, but the rest of us have only had some chocolate."

Anya wanted to disagree, to starve the traitors who had filled her pockets with lies and her heart with false friendship. But her treacherous human frailty gave her away. Her stomach gurgle was louder than Rayne's death rattle.

Cursing the hospitality of vampires, Ripper ordered a pizza and paid the delivery guy in counterfeit bills. He put the change in the register. Anya craned to see inside the till and was horrified when she could see the black plastic where ten- and twenty-dollar bills should be.

"Ripper, did you not make a single sale today?" She gasped.

"It was a bad day for business," Ripper said tersely, slamming the drawer shut and locking it with a small silver key. "My partner was murdered, and the store was ransacked by vampires."

"Right, of course," Anya said. "But you were open before and after those incidents. Have you considered a paint job? It's not like this place is drawing in the walking traffic. It looks like a tax office."

"It does not!" Ripper said, affronted. "You take that back!"

"The walls are gray! I've seen offices in hell with more cheer. And you could use a catchier name."

"It's a shop full of one-of-a-kind supernatural artifacts. What do you want me to call it? 'Uncle Ripper's Magic Box'?"

Anya tapped her chin. "That's not bad. It doesn't make me want to fall asleep halfway through like 'Ripper and Rayne's Metaphysical Boutique.' What about just 'Uncle Ripper's'? That's got some mystique to it. People might come in just to see what you sell."

Ripper peeled back the lid of the pizza box, letting a cloud of steam escape. "Absolutely not. Shut up and eat."

"Fine," Anya said, drawing a floppy slice out of the box. "Mushrooms and onions oozed off the sides. "Don't listen to me. What do I know about capitalism? I've only been studying it since its inception."

Anya took her dinner and *Dram's Encyclopedia* to the end of the counter, where she could mostly avoid having to look at Andrew and Jonathan. Paging through the book, she checked for random artifacts she'd come across throughout her long life. The Orbs of Nezzla'Khan were presumably still being guarded by the giant, roachlike Nezzla demons. The Gem of Amara, which let vampires walk in the sun, had been lost since the tenth century—when hundreds of vamps had killed each other to claim it.

"Hey, Mister Ripper," Andrew said between noisy bites of pizza.

He and Jonathan were seated next to each other on the steps at the front of the store. "You're British."

"Well spotted, Andrew." Ripper sighed. "What next? You want to discuss the wetness of water?"

"I was just wondering if you want to watch the new *Doctor Who*? I mean, if you have a cable package that gets BBC America—"

"I don't have a TV in the shop," Ripper said. "And even if I did, I wouldn't use it to watch a kid's show. *Who* hasn't been worth watching since Tom Baker left."

"Whoa, whoa, whoa," Andrew said with a sputter of incredulity. "You lost me at not having a TV, but then this Peter Davison slander?"

"Oh, please. Next you're going to tell me that *The Phantom Menace* was good," Ripper said with a frown.

"It has its merits!" Jonathan exclaimed.

Andrew quietly cringed in disagreement.

Ripper fished out another cigarette from his pack with his teeth. He lit it and shot a stream of smoke straight into the air like a whale clearing its blowhole. "Restarting a franchise twenty years later is for new audiences and the die-hard fans. They pick the bones of the original like vultures."

"Nuh-uh!" Andrew said. "It's about building something new out of the old clay!"

Ripper pointed the burning tip of his cigarette at Andrew. "Leave the clay of my childhood alone, mate."

Understanding nothing of what was being said made Anya bristle. She hated feeling left out. Almost as much as she hated being included.

"This would be the perfect time for the slayer to portal in and kill us," she said. She tugged a long stretch of melted cheese with her front teeth before noticing the resounding silence coming from the three men. "What? I'm not saying I *want* her to come kill us now. But any predator knows that its prey is at its weakest when eating. Or sleeping." She crinkled her nose at Jonathan and Andrew. "I guess you two are pretty weak whenever."

"Now we have to be afraid of eating too?" Jonathan asked Andrew.

"Eating is always dangerous for humans," Anya said. "There's the high risk of choking, poisoning, diabetic shock, adult-onset allergies resulting in anaphylaxis—"

The bell over the door chimed. Flinching in fear, Jonathan dropped his pizza cheese-side down on the floor.

Angelus and Spike stormed back into the Metaphysical Boutique with flaky red faces and hands. If Anya didn't know better, she would have said that they both looked sunburned. And Angelus had gotten a haircut.

"Is it done? Did you kill her?" Ripper asked, his cigarette bouncing at the corner of his mouth.

"Where's my gem?" Anya cut in. She dropped the encyclopedia onto the counter. "I swear, you vamps refuse to listen! This whole endeavor is pointless if I don't get my magic back!"

"Except that the world won't end?" Andrew said.

"Who wants to live in this world with zero magical ability?" Anya snapped at him.

"She got away," Angelus said, marching down the stairs. He paused to rake his hands through his hair, lingering in the space where his ponytail wasn't. "Spike was so busy flirting with her—"

"Hey! Don't blame me for trying to lure her into a false sense of security," Spike said, squashing Jonathan's fallen slice of pizza as he jumped over the stairs. He hurled the longsword he'd been carrying on top of the nearest table, sending neatly stacked decks of tarot cards falling to the ground. "Especially since you've been making goo-goo eyes at the vengeance demon all day!"

Angelus flung a hand at Anya. "She's not trying to erase our dimension!"

Caught off guard by the sudden spotlight, Anya felt a blush climb her neck. She tucked her hair behind her ears. "I don't erase dimensions. I only make new ones. When I have my magic." She coughed twice to catch Angelus's attention and asked, "Are goo-goo eyes good?"

He rolled his eyes and nodded.

"Oh. Good," she said, her flush creeping up to her cheeks. "And have I been giving them back?"

"Yes," said Spike, Andrew, Jonathan, and Ripper.

Angelus flicked his eyebrows at her, his mouth a sly smirk.

Anya turned back to *Dram's Encyclopedia*, willing her skin to stop burning. Maybe reading about the Demon Lance of Ezeria would calm her loins. The Demon Lance was cursed to turn its victims into jelly after it impaled them. Nothing sexy about that.

"The slayer still has the staff and the gem," Spike said, kicking the leg of the nearest display table. "We're bloody doomed."

Andrew held his hands up. "Please don't break anything! We just got everything back to normal!"

"Who gives a shit about how tidy this shop is?" Spike asked. "That dowsing-whatever-the-slayer's-carrying will take her straight to Glory's temple. The fate of the world depends on a giant purple goddess protecting the Black Flame flag rather than staring at herself in a mirror all day."

"Drusilla and Willow could still defeat the slayer," Jonathan said, sneaking over to the pizza box to help himself to the last skinny slice. "That was the Mayor's plan, right?"

"What does the Mayor know?" Angelus sniffed. "Drusilla's insane, as likely to sing the slayer a little song as she is to fight her. And Willow's a fledgling. She's had her fangs for less than a year. Who's to say she even knows how to use them? If real true-blue evil like me and Spike couldn't kill the slayer, why would they be able to?"

"Should we send more vampires to help them?" Andrew asked. "The slayer had a harder time back at the church when there were all those newbie vamps throwing themselves at her."

"You want to exhaust her by overwhelming her with pawns?" Ripper asked. "Not a strong chess player, are you?"

Pawns, Anya thought. The words itched in her mind, drawing her focus away from all other thoughts. *Overwhelmed by pawns.*

Scanning the tiny font in *Dram's Encyclopedia*, she found the paragraph on the Dowsing Rod of Vem.

Ensorcelled in Rome in the Year of the Six Emperors, 238 AD, by the warlock Publius Vementer, the Dowsing Rod of Vem (also known as the Sycophant's Staff) was created in an attempt to predict usurpers to the throne. Crafted from the branch of the cursed olive tree atop ancient Rome's sealed hellmouth and spelled with divination magic, the dowsing rod leads its wielder to the most potent concentration of evil within the boundary of a single city or populous area. Vementer devised the staff as a means of protection during a time of profound political instability but was killed shortly after the staff brought him not to the newly appointed emperors, Pupienus and Balbinus, but to the leader of the mutinous Praetorian Guard, who killed the warlock on sight.

"What if we could overwhelm the slayer?" Anya asked. Holding *Dram's Encyclopedia* aloft, she said, "It says in here that the Dowsing Rod of Vem will point itself at the closest *concentration* of evil. Not the most evil entity. And the slayer has to trust the dowsing rod to guide her to the Black Flame flag, especially since we moved it."

Her gaze traveled over the assembled party. Andrew was dabbing the top of his pizza with a napkin and offering Jonathan his mushrooms. Spike was trying to bum a cigarette off Ripper, who was absently patting at his pockets, pretending he couldn't feel the lump of the pack rolled into his shirt sleeve. Angelus blinked at Anya with more confusion than goo-goo.

She threw her hands up. "Do I have to spell everything out for you?"

"Yes," Jonathan said. "Your logic always requires spelling out, Anya."

Heaving an exasperated breath, she held up the encyclopedia for a visual reference. She tapped on the woodcut drawing.

"The slayer doesn't have her own magic, right? She's just a teenage girl with superstrength and some very powerful magical artifacts," she said, speaking slowly and bobbing her head a lot like she was trying to communicate with a group of dogs. "The Marnoxon gem makes portals and the dowsing rod tells her where to go, leading her from Black Flame flag to Black Flame flag. Because Hell's Own Herald is concentrated evil. So, what if we could pack enough evil pawns into one place? With enough corruption and depravity *concentrated* in one area, it's possible we could trick the dowsing rod. And the slayer. She'd portal right to us."

"And we want that . . . why?" Andrew asked.

"So we could break her neck and take back the gem I have been trying to get my hands on all freaking day!" Anya cried. "And, you know, save the world."

"How would we get all that evil into one place?" Jonathan asked.

"It's Demondale," Anya snorted. "You can't throw a stone without hitting something that wants to kill or maim you back. The whole point of this place is that it's a safe space for evil. We just have to convince evil to congregate."

"We'd need somewhere defensible," Andrew said uncertainly. "Somewhere we have the upper hand."

Jonathan jumped to his feet. "That's it! It's not a chess game! It's Risk! We need to find an easy-to-hold continent and fill it with as many troops as we can."

"I usually go for Australia," Andrew said. "It's hard for anyone to gang up on you there."

"Yes, Australia is perfect!" Jonathan said, snapping his greasy fingers. "In the middle of the ocean. That makes the borders easy to protect. We need the Demondale equivalent of a free-floating continent."

"There's only one door in here," Spike suggested, pointing at the entrance. "And plenty of weapons lying about."

"Too small," Anya said. "We could fit ten or twenty demons in here, maybe. We need at least a hundred if we want to try to trick the dowsing rod. We're trying to match the evil of an actual slice of hell here."

"How are we supposed to convince a bunch of demons to show up to one place?" Andrew asked. "Won't they want payment for risking their lives? I guess we could go print off some more twenties."

"Keep your phony lucre," Anya said bitterly. "Demons deserve better than your lies, especially if they're agreeing to fight. We should offer them something everyone likes—"

"Pizza?" Andrew guessed.

Anya's nose crinkled in bewilderment. "No, I was going to say alcohol. Haven't you ever heard of rum rations? Get your soldiers drunk enough to keep warm and stay loose for the indiscriminate murder of strangers in the name of God and country. And if you add lemon, it staves off scurvy. But I guess food is good too. Probably cheaper to buy in bulk."

"Okay," Jonathan said, chewing on his thumbnail. "We need somewhere defensible. Somewhere that can fit a lot of people—I mean, demons—with room to fight. And somewhere that has food and drinks..."

Slowly, everyone in the room turned to look at Angelus. The vampire fidgeted under the weight of the expectant silence, touching the space where his ponytail had once been.

"What?" he asked with a disbelieving laugh. "You want to turn my club into the battleground of Armageddon?"

Ripper's mouth unraveled a slow smile. "Come on, Angelus. Do it for team Save the World."

ELEVEN
Jonathan

MIDNIGHT AT THE BRONZE: *Fight the slayer, drink for free!*

Using all the ink in the Metaphysical Boutique's creaky printer was Ripper's last charitable act before pushing everyone outside and locking the door behind them. Standing at the glass door, he held up two fingers in a reverse peace sign that Spike informed them was not actually a peace sign. Even the Brit's middle finger had an accent.

"There has to be a magical way to recruit an army," Andrew said, looking down at the flyers in his hand. "Like a mass summoning spell. Or a bat signal."

Jonathan watched Anya and Angelus walking alone down the street. The two of them were going to prep the Bronze for the impending battle. Neither showed any sign of worry that they were sending the two most likely to die—and Spike—to do the dirty work. Who sent humans to conscript demons?

Jonathan hugged his own stack of flyers to his chest and sighed. "This is definitely punishment for giving her fake money," he said. "Which isn't fair. It's not like we meant to hurt her feelings."

"Come off it," Spike said with a snort. He was nursing the cigarette he'd taken from Ripper on the way out the door. The ember blazed menacingly orange in the darkness. "You schemed and you failed. It's not like you tripped and fell into printing your own money. What did you think would happen when someone found out it was fake? Own it. You're humans living in Hell on Earth. You've got to have a bit of the baddie in you to want to stay here."

Jonathan shuffled his feet. Like Warren and Andrew, he had grown up idolizing the genius supervillains in the comic books he read. He had always liked the idea of defeating his enemies by using the one thing he had that they didn't: his wits.

But he hadn't meant to defeat Anya. She wasn't an enemy. At least, she hadn't been before she'd found out that they'd given her counter-feit money. Now it seemed more likely that she'd be their adversary than their friend.

The idea made Jonathan deeply sorry. The vengeance demon was certainly tactless. And unpredictable. But she was an unusually good strategist. She'd spent all day saving Jonathan and Andrew from all sorts of dangers. And yet, Jonathan had been too ashamed to even apologize for paying her with forged bills.

She was right to send them into the night unarmed.

"You two are on foot, yeah?" Spike asked, idly scratching the scorched skin on his knuckles. "There weren't any cars parked at your place when Angelus and I went by."

"Our van is stuck in Docktown," Jonathan said. "The keys exploded with our friend Warren. If everything goes well, I guess we'll have to call a locksmith. Or learn how to hot-wire it."

"I bet the warlock could get it running again," Spike said, pitching the end of his cigarette at the door of the Metaphysical Boutique. The filter bounced off the glass and fell to the pavement, still smoldering. "Not that he's in the mood to do any more favors tonight. You two can take your papers around downtown. Hit the restaurants and neighborhoods. I'll take my bike out to the edge of the sunshade, check out the graveyards and other demonic hidey-holes."

"You ride a motorcycle?" Andrew asked, breathless with interest. "What kind? Roadster? Cruiser? Sport?"

Spike cocked an eyebrow. "You ride?"

Andrew shrank back, shoulders going self-consciously concave. "No, but I've always wanted to. Balance isn't really my strong suit. I've got this inner-ear condition. Do you think that would go away if I were a vampire? I know that the bite that saves can heal, like, cancer and stuff, but I've seen vamps who have to wear glasses and I wonder if my Ménière's disease is more like an astigmatism. It's not fatal, just sort of annoying."

Ignoring this, Spike gave Jonathan an upward nod, the kind that cool guys used to give each other in the halls at school. Jonathan had never been on the receiving end of one before. He accidentally shook his head in return.

"If you live through recruitment, I'll see you on the front lines," Spike said. "Beers on me if we make it to the other side."

"We're underage," Jonathan blurted out. Cursing himself, he tried to stand taller and did his best to imbue his voice with some resonance. "But we'll, uh, definitely take you up on those beers. Brewskis. Cold ones."

"But since we can't get into bars, would you take the flyers into anywhere that's twenty-one and over?" Andrew asked. "We definitely want some tough biker demons on our side. Cheers!"

Spike's upper lip curled in irritation. Without another word, he strode off into the darkness.

"Cheers?" Jonathan asked Andrew.

Andrew tipped up his chin imperiously, starting to walk in the opposite direction of Spike. "It's how British people say thank you."

"They speak English. I'm pretty sure they say *thank you*," Jonathan said. "And why were you asking him about your ear condition? Do you really still want to become a vampire? After everything we've seen today?"

"What do you mean?" Andrew asked. His strides doubled, forcing Jonathan to scramble to keep up.

"We watched Angelus murder Rayne right in front of us!" Jonathan said. "We freed all of those people in the blood farm! We watched the slayer dust, like, fifty fledglings! None of those things changed your mind?"

Andrew bristled. "I haven't made up my mind. It's not like I asked anyone to turn me. I was just asking questions."

Jonathan wasn't convinced. This whole year, Andrew had had one foot in the grave. Every video game, comic book, novel, or movie Andrew brought into the house was about the undead. When he thought no one was looking, he fished vampire advertisements out of the trash and kept them in his room. He'd even spoiled the Trio's Dungeon & Dragons campaign by insisting on changing his character into a vampire, so now all of the party's adventures had to happen at night and their elf cleric was suddenly a lawful-evil bloodsucker.

"I don't understand," Jonathan said faintly, "why you'd rather be one of them instead of one of us."

"Us?" Andrew scoffed, throwing a sour look at their reflections in the darkened windows of an abandoned Hallmark store. Demons weren't big on greeting cards. "Weak human dorks?"

"No!" Jonathan protested, waving a hand between them. "Us! The Trio! I mean, I guess we're a duo now, but... You know. Friends. Best friends. The last humans in Demondale."

Andrew frowned. "We could still be friends even if I did turn into a vampire."

Jonathan came to an abrupt stop. His pulse was loud in his ears, sounding a confrontation warning. This was the moment when he was supposed to back down. This was when cowardice won out and he smooshed his feelings down to where no one else would ever have to notice them. It had always been his job to be small and agreeable and unnoticed.

He was sick of it.

"You mean like how you and Tucker are still friends?" he asked the back of Andrew's head.

Andrew spun around, jaw hanging open. "That's not fair!"

"Isn't it?" Jonathan spat. "Tucker bailed on you the second he got fangs. Who's to say you wouldn't do the same thing to me? We're not family. We don't have Warren to keep us together anymore."

"Is that what you think of me? That I would just abandon you?"

"Isn't that what people do when they get 'the bite that saves'?" He held up the most sarcastic air quotes he could muster without spilling his stack of flyers. "They pretend they were never human. Tucker. Willow Rosenberg. Do you think Spike's mom called him *Spike*?"

"Maybe!" Andrew said, annoyance making him supercilious. "Why are we even fighting about this? We could die any minute!"

"Well, I don't want to die without talking about the important stuff! So just admit it! Without Warren around, there's no reason for you to hang out with me. You don't need me. You don't trust me. You didn't even tell me you were gay!"

Jonathan said it before he could stop himself. The thought had plagued him since they were kneeling back at the temple at the foot of a literal goddess from hell. After a childhood of pity invites and getting picked last for everything, Jonathan thought he had finally found a true friend in Andrew. They'd been part of Klingon club and the academic decathlon team—along with Warren, of course. Warren had been Andrew's obvious favorite, but Jonathan assumed that he was a decent runner-up. A second-place best friend.

"I didn't want it to be the only thing you saw when you looked at me," Andrew said, avoiding Jonathan's eye. "I already had less of a role in the group. Warren was the leader. You're the inventor. I didn't want to just be your gay friend. If you'd even keep me as your friend."

Confusion scrambled Jonathan's brain. Sure, there was no arguing that Warren had been in charge, but Jonathan never thought of himself as the inventor of the group. Andrew was the one who had the computer-programming skills to create the counterfeiting machine.

"What are you talking about?" he asked, stepping closer to Andrew, trying to catch his averted gaze. "Why would I stop being your friend?"

Andrew's eyebrows drew together. "Why would I stop being your friend if I was a vampire?"

"Because!" Jonathan cried. The word echoing down the dark street, magnifying Jonathan's exasperation. "If you could have any other friend, why would you need me? I'm some short idiot you met in high school. A high school that doesn't even exist anymore! And I don't want to be a vampire. Or Ascend into a demon. And I'm not gay. So how can I compete with people who are more like you than I am?"

Andrew finally looked up at him, the ghost of a smile flickering across his face. "You're still a lot like me, Jonathan, even if you are straight. I mean, we're dressed identically."

Jonathan touched his turtleneck. "For safety."

"And you're the only other person I know who likes old British sitcoms," Andrew continued. "Who else is gonna watch *Fawlty Towers* and *Are You Being Served?* with me?"

"You could meet a vampire who loves farce," Jonathan grumbled. The more his pique faded, the more ridiculous he felt for picking the argument.

Falling into silence, he and Andrew resumed their trek through the heart of downtown. A cool breeze flapped the edges of the flyers they pinned to the lampposts and trees. Overhead, jacaranda flowers fluttered but didn't fall. Jonathan had spent his entire life dreading the annual appearance of the blue-violet flowers. Every spring, when downtown would become carpeted in petals, Jonathan's eyes would itch and swell shut. He'd sneeze hard enough to propel himself backward, leading to years of Sneezy Dwarf jokes. But now whatever spell kept the trees blooming all year round also protected Jonathan from their allergens. He could even stick his nose directly into a trumpet flower and inhale its soft perfume without getting sick. To him, it was the most magical magic in Demondale.

"I'm sorry I never told you," Andrew said suddenly. "About me."

"I'm sorry I never asked," Jonathan said, retreating from the jacaranda tree. "Did you want me to ask?"

"Not really," Andrew said, smoothing a scrap of Scotch tape against a plywood board nailed over the windows of a shuttered Christian Science reading room. "Then you might ask why I never date guys."

"Oh," Jonathan said. "Have you? Dated guys, I mean."

Andrew laughed over his shoulder. "Jonathan, we've known each other for four years. We live together! How would I hide having an entire love life from you? Don't you think you would have noticed if I liked anyone?"

Continuing up the street, Jonathan pressed his lips together, his mental gears grinding while he considered this.

Because he *had* noticed. There was only one person Andrew had ever liked. The only person who had been able to convince him not to run off after Tucker and get turned into a vampire by the Church of the Eternal Night. The only person he ever even talked about other than Tucker. Jonathan felt so stupid that he hadn't noticed it sooner.

"You like Warren," he blurted.

"What? No!" Andrew stumbled over a crack in the sidewalk. With a wince, he barely lifted his shoulders in a defeated shrug. "Okay, well, yeah, I do. I did. Now he's dead, and there's a chance that we could die at any second too. But—"

"But he was awful to you!" Jonathan interrupted. "He called you names and made fun of you! He hid your Boba Fett action figure in the toilet tank!"

"You liked him too," Andrew shot back.

"Not like that!" Jonathan said.

Andrew rolled his eyes. Jonathan felt guilty for being so defensive. How many times had he said something unconsciously homophobic in front of Andrew? Even implying that it would be bad to have someone think he was gay, even for just a second, probably made his friend feel less safe with him.

"You liked him enough to live with him," Andrew said, his tone even. "To follow him around. Take orders from him! Why would you do that if you thought he was so bad?"

"I don't know!" Jonathan exclaimed. And he didn't. He'd never had to think about it before. He'd been fourteen when Warren had taken him under his wing, protecting him from bullies and telling him that he could use his brain to get the revenge his body wasn't capable of exacting. Warren had shown him how to sneak into the Sunnydale High digital gradebook and flunk the guys who had tortured him since kindergarten. Even before the Mayor had proclaimed himself a liaison between hell and earth, Warren had brought Jonathan to the Metaphysical Boutique and shown him that magic was real. They'd gone in on a cursed pendant together. They used it against Percy West, who had trapped Jonathan in a locker with all of the basketball team's used jockstraps. After he'd worn the pendant, Percy's skin erupted in lime-green pustules that burst on the hour like horrible, stinking geysers all over his body. He'd transferred schools afterward.

It was the first time Jonathan had ever felt any kind of power. And he'd loved it. Thinking of it now made him hate himself.

"I think maybe I was afraid of not taking orders," he admitted to Andrew. "If nothing was my idea, then it was never my fault if it went wrong."

"And maybe liking a guy who was never going to like me back meant that I never had to wonder if someone *could* like me back," Andrew said.

For years, Jonathan had assumed that Warren had led them into being more themselves. That he'd brought out the potential in them. Instead Jonathan and Andrew had just been hiding behind Warren's viciousness.

"Wow, we're both pretty messed up, huh?" Jonathan said, his throat tight with shame. "Maybe it's a good thing that the slayer is going to erase us from existence."

"I hope she doesn't," Andrew said gently. "I hope you have a chance to find a new best friend. Someone better than Warren. It's not like Anya is going to let us bring him back now."

All day, Jonathan had fought the idea of Warren being gone for good. As he considered it now, it didn't hurt as much as he expected. The world would be different without Warren, but maybe it wouldn't be worse off.

"And I hope you find a guy who really likes you. Who's nice. And doesn't call you a moron," he told Andrew. "Anya's right. It's not a nickname. It's just plain mean."

Andrew's mouth quirked into a sheepish smile. "Warren was mean a lot, wasn't he?"

"Yeah," Jonathan said. "It's weird that I didn't really notice until we started hanging out with demons."

Downtown was shockingly busy. Even with the permanent midnight the sunshade provided, the population of Demondale was still more active after nine p.m. Creatures of the night poured out of every building, filling the patios and thronging the streets. Jonathan hadn't seen this big a crowd since the day the Mayor cursed the sky. Then again, at this time on a normal day, Jonathan would normally be locked safe inside the lair. In pajamas. Possibly with a mug of cocoa.

As he heard the hoots and grunts of demons having a good time, Jonathan's first instinct was to turn and run. Clenching the flyers in his hand, he took a steadying breath. Running would only guarantee the slayer's victory. He had to move forward, no matter how much he would prefer to go home and lock the door.

It wasn't like home would be any safer. The slayer had already been there and could return whenever she wanted. As long as she had the vengeance demons' gem and the dowsing rod, she was unpredictable. And possibly unstoppable.

The first group of demons they came across were seated at the picnic tables in front of the Doublemeat Palace, a formerly family-friendly restaurant. Jonathan had spent more than a few of his childhood birthdays here, climbing alone through the plastic tubes and getting sick on the spiral slide. Since no one would ever bring kids to Demondale, the owners had turned the indoor playground into a small blood-sport arena. The ball pit had been cleared out and turned into a space for demonic cage matches. Losers went up on the chalkboard menu as the next special burger.

Andrew smoothed the gelled point of his hair and squared his shoulders before stopping at the edge of a picnic table. He set a flyer down next to a frosty pint too yellow to be beer. Jonathan hoped it was apple juice, but knew from the Best Pressed menu that vampires were the only demons picky about the bodily fluids they'd consume. Jonathan didn't recognize the species of the demons at the picnic

table. They were large with neckless heads balanced on shiny bodies topographic with varicose veins. They reminded Jonathan of the
X-Men villain Juggernaut. With the needle-sharp teeth of a snake.

"Hello there, my fine fellows," Andrew said, addressing the
crowded table.

"Human child," rumbled one of the Juggernauts. They sounded
like a garbage disposal full of forks. "You want to be our next burger?
Sign up inside."

"Oh, no thank you," Andrew said politely. "I'm here to invite you
to save the world."

The demon nearest Jonathan had burger juice streaming out of
their lipless mouth. According to the menu in the window, right now
everyone was apparently enjoying a taste of "Skyler." The menu also
warned that Skyler burgers weren't safe for anyone with an allergy
to Manasseri demons. Or dairy.

Was it wrong to want to believe that the burgers were made of the
same Skyler that Warren had bought the Books of Ascension from?
Jonathan wouldn't mind not having to worry that the albino demon
was going to reappear, demanding either five thousand real dollars
or the exploded books back.

"Demondale is under attack," Andrew continued, seemingly
unfazed by the lidless stares of the Juggernauts. "There's a vampire
slayer on the loose. To stop her, we need strong fighters. Like you
guys."

At the next picnic table, a spiky-haired woman stood up. Yellow
vampire eyes stood out starkly against her brown skin. In a flash, she
had a hand fisted around the collar of Andrew's turtleneck and was
yanking him backward.

"Is this some kind of joke?" asked the vampire. A drop of red shone on the tip of one of her fangs. Jonathan prayed it was ketchup. "The whole reason I left Boston was because the slayer was there. That and Red Sox fans. Intolerable."

"It's not a joke, I swear," Andrew stammered. "The slayer is here."

"She burned down the Church of the Eternal Night," Jonathan said. Willing himself not to flinch, he held a flyer out to the vampire woman, hoping to distract her from Andrew's exposed neck. "Angelus, the owner of the Bronze, is promising free drinks for anyone who shows up to fight her."

The spiky-haired vampire released Andrew to snatch the flyer. "Angelus is putting his weight behind this, huh? That sounds legitimate. I never liked the Church much—call me old-school, but people should be turned in alleys, not on an altar—but Demondale's no place for a slayer. This is supposed to be our safe haven."

A decent-size crowd amassed around them. Demons poked their heads out of the restaurant and wandered over from the frozen yogurt place next door.

"What's the slayer like?" someone asked.

"Blond?" Jonathan answered uncertainly.

"As an angel," Andrew said. "Like goodness incarnate."

"And she carries a wizard staff that can sniff out evil," Jonathan said.

"Topped with the powerful Marnoxon gem," Andrew added, flourishing a hand for emphasis. "Stolen from the vengeance demons she slaughtered when she broke into hell."

The demons hissed and jeered at this. Jonathan wasn't sure he'd ever had so many beings listening to him at the same time. It was intoxicating. Was this how the cheerleaders had felt at Sunnydale High pep rallies? Or how the Mayor felt all the time?

"She's trained in karate," Jonathan told the crowd. "Or tae kwon do."

"Kicks like a mule!" Andrew said. "Or a Power Ranger!"

"She shot the Master with a crossbow and tackled his wife through a stained-glass window."

"She murdered a whole nest of fledglings!"

"Poor babies!" cried the spiky-haired vampire woman.

"How do we know this isn't a setup?" asked one of the Juggernauts sitting close behind Jonathan. "Why would Angelus have two puny humans do his bidding?"

"There's not a lot for Renfields to do in Demondale," Andrew lied blithely.

"Yeah," Jonathan agreed. "We pick up his dry cleaning and amass his army. So, tell your friends!"

"And your enemies!" Andrew said.

"Tell everyone!" Jonathan beamed. "Be at the Bronze tonight at midnight! To kill the slayer!"

"Kill the slayer!" the crowd roared.

Flyers rained down on the crowd. Jonathan and Andrew extricated themselves from the frothing demons and slipped around the corner to find the next group.

"You're a much better storyteller than me," Jonathan told Andrew.

"I just filled in the details," Andrew said dismissively. "Like when we do puzzles at home. You're the best at finding the border. I fill in the rest."

"The rest is the important part."

Andrew shook his head. "It's all important, Jonathan."

Jonathan grinned, feeling electrified. When was the last time that he'd contributed anything important? Had he ever? He'd never stood so close to so many demons without fearing for his own life. Being part of the crowd instead of standing outside it was amazing. Why had he spent so long hiding from the town he lived in? Why had it taken the threat of a mega-apocalypse to get him out of the house?

"Hey, man," he said, clapping Andrew on the shoulder. "I already have a friend better than Warren. It's you."

"Oh." Andrew's face flushed. "Thanks. That means a lot to me. You're better than Warren too. We make a pretty good duo."

"We do." Jonathan bit his lip, remembering the slithering shame that had been chasing him for the last hour. "But we were better as a trio."

"But you just said—"

"Not with Warren," he said quickly. "With *Anya*. She was the first one to believe us about the slayer, and she kept the vamps from eating us. We'd be dead ten times over without her. I think we really screwed up by hurting her feelings."

Andrew's face fell. "We should do something nice for her before the world ends. I mean, the only things I know for sure that she likes are money and vengeance. How can we gift those to her without letting her torture us?"

"I think she's going to torture us no matter what."

"Wait. I have an idea," Andrew said. Pulling Jonathan by the sleeve, he led him across the street, toward the neon BEST PRESSED JUICERY sign lighting up the end of the block. "I need to go talk to my boss."

TWELVE

Anya

ANGELUS COMPLAINED ABOUT the battle plan the entire walk from Uncle Ripper's Magic Box. Anya had never heard a vampire whine so much. Well, maybe that one time she'd been called to punish a vampire who had turned himself a new girlfriend without breaking up with the old one first. Anya had cast him into a world with only shrimp. Shrimp were a terrible food source for the undead. Very little blood. And zero hemoglobin, so eventually the vampire starved for lack of protein and oxygen. But it took ages.

Angelus was lucky Anya didn't have the power to send him to Shrimp World. And that losing his ponytail in his fight with the slayer had increased his attractiveness.

As he scowled at their single remaining flyer, Angelus's face stayed stuck in vampire bumps.

"It's too late to change it," Anya told him.

The flyer crumpled in his fist as he turned his peevish yellow eyes on her. "Shouldn't people be fighting for the glory of battle? To keep the slayer from destroying our reality? Do I really need to give them free drinks?"

"Look, I don't like the idea of profit loss either"—Anya clapped a hand on his shoulder and schooled her face into something she hoped was reassuring—"but you did fail to kill the slayer twice now, so maybe it's time to admit that we need to recruit some help. Besides, if you wait to serve the drinks until after the battle, then one: Everyone's sober for the fight. And two: Fewer people to comp. Did you see how many newborn vamps the slayer dusted back in the Master's bedroom? She's a killing machine."

Angelus huffed, his face smoothing out and fangs retracting. Anya chose to see this as a confirmation that she was right. She would have liked to hear it out loud for once, but she took what she could get.

"I guess, if the slayer doesn't show up, we could always tell the crowd that Andrew and Jonathan are slayers," Angelus grumbled. "Pay them back for giving you fake money."

Anya disliked the way this made her insides seize up. It was an unfamiliar, troublesome feeling. Like her organs had turned to bricks.

"No, I wouldn't like to see them torn apart by an angry mob," she said. "If they aren't already being torn apart by an angry mob."

Taking advantage of the eyebrows he only had when he wasn't fully vamped out, Angelus looked surprised. "You don't want vengeance?"

"I exact my own vengeance," she told him.

She was pretty sure that she should have been worried about Jonathan and Andrew being sent to recruit their army. It was a dangerous mission for two humans. All day, she had guarded the boys, only to send them to shepherd Demondale's nastiest creatures.

If they wanted my protection, they should have thought twice about giving me that mendacious money, she thought. In violating her trust, they had freed her of the burden of responsibility. Only having to look out for herself again was good.

Not that she felt good. But just because she didn't feel it didn't mean she didn't know it wasn't true. Feelings were the misfirings of her ridiculous human meat suit. Logic was logic.

It would have been nice to stop feeling the impulse to check if they were safe.

Seeing the giant steel box of the Bronze rise into the foreground was a relief. She could use a cold drink before her next attempt at saving the world.

At the Bronze's front door, the bouncer let Anya and Angelus pass without comment. Glancing down at her wrist, Anya found that she was still wearing a red wristband. It had been hours, not days, since she had brought Andrew and Jonathan to the vampire club.

Inside, it seemed that nothing had changed since Drusilla had foretold the slayer's arrival that afternoon. The barstools were occupied. Wellex demons crowded around the pool tables using their polelike limbs as cue sticks. Fyarl-demon waiters carried platters of food to tall tables. The musical stage was empty, but hidden speakers screeched what had to be Drusilla and the Dollies' greatest hits. The dance floor was congested with gyrating chaos demons. Antler goo flew across the club as they danced.

It was all disconcertingly normal.

Behind the bar, a loose-skinned demon's whole body swished with the effort of mixing something in a cocktail shaker.

"Hey, boss," the loose-skinned demon said to Angelus as he and Anya approached. "You take care of that slayer problem?"

"Not yet, Clem," Angelus said. He slid the wrinkled flyer across the bar. "We're gonna open the doors a bit tonight. See if we can't smoke the girl out. Things might get kind of hairy. I understand if you want to head out before the rumble starts. But your tentacle trick might come in handy here."

"It's not a trick," Clem the loose-skinned demon said with a frown. "It's a defense mechanism. I wouldn't call your dependence on violence to express your feelings a trick."

Angelus let out one of his big-cat rumbles. Anya stepped in front of him before he could take his fangs out again.

"Be nice to him," Anya warned Clem in a loud whisper. "He watched his mother-lover die today."

"Someone finally dusted Darla?" Clem asked. His batwing ears wagged, scandalized, as he leaned toward Angelus. "Do you want to talk about it? You don't understand how absolutely delectable grief can be. And the grief of a man scorned…"

Clem greedily jiggled his fingers in the air. Loose-skinned demons consumed feelings as their main form of sustenance. Working in a bar must have been a perfect spot to absorb passing emotions.

Curling his lip contemptuously at his employee, Angelus said, "If you stay and fight, I'll give you time and a half."

Clem raised his hand to his forehead in a military-style salute. "You got it, boss."

Angelus glanced down at Anya. "Are you armed?"

"Um, no?" Anya said, patting her pockets despite knowing full well that they were empty, aside from the money she'd made selling Andrew's magical items. "I sold my knife. Should I go steal it back from Ripper? I could pick the lock on his front door. Or smash the windows with a brick."

Angelus shook his head, the corner of his mouth nearly smiling. "That's okay. You can borrow something from my arsenal. Come on."

Anya followed him—past the tall bar tables full of demons splitting appetizer sampler plates and dart boards where vampires tried to hit the bull's-eye on a photo of Count Chocula. Upstairs on the overseer's balcony, vampires with their bumpy faces on entwined themselves around willing humans. Whether the vamps were drinking from the humans or canoodling with them, Anya couldn't tell. The activities had a lot of overlap.

At the back of the balcony was a single door, painted black to blend in with the wall. Angelus set an equally dark key into the lock and stepped aside.

"Please come in," he said, ushering Anya past him.

"I'm not a vampire," she reminded him. "I don't need a formal invitation."

Angelus gave an untroubled shrug. "It's polite."

"Human manners," she said with a snort.

Walking past him, Anya was amazed to find herself standing in a room about the same size as the lobby of Best Pressed Juicery. An ornate wooden desk faced the door with a leather chair already pulled out for guests. A Tiffany lamp with an acid-green glass shade provided low light.

The floor was tinted-black glass, like the windows on the Mayor's car. Through the darkness, Anya could see most of the demons playing pool and some of the dance floor. She stepped across it carefully, unable to stop herself from imagining falling through.

"I assure you, the glass is very sturdy," Angelus said. He hopped up and down to prove it, making Anya wince.

"In my human life, I saw a child fall through a frozen pond," she said, reaching out for the leather chair like a lifeline. When it was within her grasp, she threw herself into the seat with a sigh. "The memory of the ground opening and swallowing him whole has never left me, even after all this time. Isn't that ridiculous?"

"Not that ridiculous. It sounds like a memorable sight," Angelus said. With another small dark key, he unlocked a steamer trunk pressed against the wall. The lid was inlaid with daggers and knives of all sizes and shapes. "What's your weapon of choice? I've got a bunch of swords here. Cutlasses, scimitars. A gladius if you're feeling old-school."

"I was born in a year that only had three digits. I'm always old-school," Anya said. Sitting higher in her seat, she peered into the trunk, seeing only a mass of razor-sharp silver staring back at her. "Do you have anything Viking-ish in there? Like a swordstaff? Or maybe a skeggøx?"

Angelus looked up from stuffing daggers in his boots. "A what?"

Anya furrowed her brow, working out the translation from Old Norse to English. "A beard ax? It's like a regular chopping ax but with a nifty little curve behind the blade for your hand. So you can punch the ax into your enemies. The last time I really had to protect myself without magic, I was still human. And I was mostly protecting myself from the idiot Vikings I was dating."

"Did you date a lot of Vikings?"

"More than one. Less than a longship."

Blinking rapidly, Angelus turned back to the trunk. "I should have an ax or two. I don't know if they'll be authentically Viking. I never spent much time in Scandinavia. Once I left Ireland I went south for warmer climates, you know."

The weapons bumped and clattered together as Angelus dug through them, continually pausing to set aside pieces that he seemed to like for himself. A longsword engraved with Celtic knots. Daggers with leather-wrapped hilts. A small war hammer.

"Here," he said, proudly withdrawing an ax and holding it overhead.

The blade caught the green light from the Tiffany lamp, giving it an otherworldly glow. Anya accepted it gladly. It was much lighter than the axes she had wielded in her human life. Metalworking had come a long way in the last eleven hundred years. The silver edge was less than an eyelash thick and wickedly sharp. She imagined hacking the Marnoxon gem off the top of the slayer's dowsing rod, letting the magic refill her veins.

Angelus settled himself in the chair on the other side of the desk and stretched his long legs on top of the weapons trunk.

"Now," he said. "How about a drink?"

"I thought you'd never ask," Anya said.

Out of a drawer, he retrieved an amber-colored bottle and two cut-crystal glasses. "Whiskey okay?" he asked.

"I've never tried it," Anya admitted. "I usually order beer. There's been beer as long as I've been alive. Almost everywhere I've been had a drinkable ale that wouldn't make you go blind."

Liquor glugged out of the bottle and into the glasses. Anya noted that the vampire poured an equal amount in each. She appreciated not being condescended to. The fumes wafting out of the cups were less appealing. The smell reminded her of the poison they poured down the wheatgrass-clogged drains at Best Pressed.

Angelus lifted his drink to her. "Sláinte!"

"Back at'cha," she said.

Their glasses clinked. The single sip she took disinfected her esophagus and bleached her stomach lining. One of her eyes squeezed shut. Upon exhaling, Anya found her breath to be pure ethanol.

Angelus drank most of his whiskey in a single gulp. It must have been easy to build up a tolerance when most of what he consumed was blood. At least whiskey was a thin beverage. Blood was like iron-filled syrup.

Angelus leaned back, swirling his whiskey cup in lazy circles just beneath his jaw. Anya wondered if the drink made an interesting sound that close to his ear. She tried it but heard nothing but sloshing.

"So, you don't consider yourself human?" he asked.

"Do you?" Anya inspected the inside of the cup for a moment before hazarding another sip. The whiskey already in her had started to heat up, sending warmth through her limbs. "I haven't been human a lot longer than you."

"True." His head bobbed as he ruminated on this. "But you don't have the same limitations as a vampire. You have a reflection. You can see the sun—or could, if you went someplace where they had the sun." He paused to examine the whiskey in his glass. The drink had made his indiscernible accent more pronounced. There was a musicality in his voice that hadn't been there before. "A vampire surrenders their humanity to the bite. The man I was before, in Galway, he's gone. But you—you get to walk in both worlds. You're a human and a demon."

"I left my name behind too," she admitted. "In Sweden, I was Aud."

"I mean, you're still odd, Anya. You're a thousand years old."

"No, my name. It was Aud." She spelled it for him.

"Oh. Huh," he said. His fingers drummed on the side of his glass for a moment before he said, "I was Liam. Before."

"Isn't Liam short for William?"

"It is. But my da . . ." He paused, clearing his throat. With some effort, he forced his vowels flat, Americanized. "My father was called William. As his junior, everyone called me Liam."

"Wasn't Spike also called William?" She took another sip of her drink, hoping to aim the liquid directly at the back of her throat and skip further numbing of her tongue. It felt a bit like drowning. Coughing, she continued. "William the Bloody, that's what Ripper called him. Is that why you both use nicknames? You couldn't decide who got to be *the* William?"

Angelus chuckled and swung his feet onto the floor so that he could lean forward. "You know, I never thought about it. Darla started calling me Angelus a hundred years before Dru ever sired Spike." He drained his glass again. "Drusilla kept her human name. She might be the only vampire who ever did."

"Drusilla doesn't seem like she does anything like a regular human or vampire."

Angelus gazed down at the see-through floor. Around the pool table, the Wellex demons were using their stick limbs to fence with each other. A Fyarl-demon waiter was breaking up the fight. Looking back at Anya, the vampire cocked his head. Anya resisted the urge to fluff her hair.

"You still have a soul," he observed. "A human soul."

"How can you tell?" she asked. She looked down at her arms like there was some visible seam tethering her soul to her body. "Does it show? Does it *smell*?"

"No, you smell like vengeance-demon blood. Like something food-adjacent. You know the white stuff inside an orange peel?" His face scrunched up, in thought rather than vampire bumps. "Pith! That's the word."

"I smell pithy?" Anya asked, not liking the sound of it.

"All vengeance demons do, no matter their species," Angelus said, waving off the idea. "They don't all have the glow. You look *alive*. I know you're old—"

"I prefer to think of myself as timeless, thank you."

"But your soul remains untouched. It's a feat."

Anya snuggled deeper into the leather chair. A low buzz of intoxication had taken up residence in the base of her skull, like a hive of lazy bees.

"I traded my life to D'Hoffryn when I dedicated myself to vengeance. The Marnoxon gem gives me my powers, but D'Hoffryn gave me my immortality." She held on to the pendant around her neck, rubbing her thumb over the green stone. Disconnected from its source, the stone was quiet and lifeless. She missed the thrum of power that usually coursed through it. "I should have been in Arashmaharr when the slayer showed up. I should have fought her there. Before she got to the gem. I could have stopped her."

Anya peered through the window in the floor again. The quarreling Wellex demons had been cleared away from the pool table. A group of humanoids had taken their place. They were all dressed in so much silk and velvet that Anya couldn't tell if they were vampires or humans in vampire costumes. Alive or undead, they didn't look strong enough to take on the slayer. They'd be dust stuck on the green billiard felt before they could finish fluffing their cravats.

Without her magic, would Anya fare any better?

"What if no one shows up to fight tonight?" she asked, still watching the maybe-vampires chalk their pool cues.

"Then we die," Angelus said.

"It's been a long time coming," she said, biting her lip. The buzzing bees of inebriation didn't make it any less embarrassing to have irritating human emotions. Like fear and shame. Looking into his fathomless black eyes, she confessed, "And I'm still not ready."

"No one ever is," he said. It wasn't quite an intimate, soul-baring revelation. But, then again, Angelus didn't have a soul. And he hadn't disagreed with her, which was maybe as much of an admission as he could manage. He was only 272. Still young and pretty.

"To the end of the world," she said, raising her drink again. "Or saving it. Whichever comes first."

"Sláinte."

In unison, they drained their glasses.

THIRTEEN
Anya

BY ELEVEN-THIRTY, the first floor of the Bronze was packed far beyond the fire code's maximum capacity. Discarded *Fight the slayer* flyers carpeted the floor.

They had requested the worst of the worst and that was exactly who had shown up.

Twirling her borrowed ax, Anya walked down the stairs on unsteady legs. She recognized a group of baby eaters swapping recipes with Jarvlen flesh eaters. A cluster of shrieking bone bats was making a racket near the bathrooms. The dance floor was at a standstill. The chaos demons pressed against the stage to make room for an encroaching gelatinous blob. What appeared to be the entire

Miquot Clan was shoving one another trying to be closest to the bar. Yellow-and-orange-striped elbows flew as the reptilian demons fought to yell their drink orders. The crystalline spikes on top of the Miquots' heads blocked Anya's view of Clem, but she could hear him begging everyone to put their knives away.

Anya's whiskey buzz was quickly evaporating. As she pushed her way through the crowd, the gravity of the situation was starting to weigh on her. How many more demons had to show up before the slayer arrived, raring for another fight? The flyer might have said midnight, but it wasn't like the slayer was going to get the invitation. She'd portal in whenever she wanted.

Anya closed her eyes and held her head firmly over her shoulders. She took in a deep breath, aware of how much of the club smelled like chaos-demon mucus and the vampires' leather. It was a reassuring odor. It smelled both hellish and earthen. A little bit of both. Like her.

"You okay?" Angelus had stopped walking too, watching her in obvious concern.

"Fine," she said.

He squinted as if he didn't believe her. "If you need to throw up, I can move the shrieking bone bats out of the way of the bathroom. They're more annoying than they are dangerous."

"I'm fine," she said again. "I have a strong stomach, Angelus. I ate lunch in the Vengeance LLC cafeteria practically every day for a millennium. I've had grimmer things in my gullet than your Irish liquor."

He smiled. "If you say so."

"Angelus, you son of a bitch!" called an approaching vampire in a black Stetson hat and beat-up brown coat. His face was vamped out, so Anya couldn't tell whether or not he was being friendly until

Angelus reached out for an aggressive handshake. The impact of it rang out like a slap.

"Lyle Gorch," Angelus said. "It's been ages. I thought you'd gone back to Texas."

"I'm Tector," said the vampire. His frown made his fangs stick out the sides of his mouth.

A mustachioed vampire stepped beside him, dressed identically except for the color of his hat. "*I'm* Lyle," he said, mustache wriggling.

"Didn't I say it's been a long time?" Angelus said, shaking Lyle's hand with far less enthusiasm than he'd shaken Tector's. "What brings you boys to Demondale?"

"What brings a bull to breeding season?" asked Lyle. He lifted the dingy white Stetson from his head and crowed over the noise of the club, "The heat, brother!"

"Welcome to the fire, Gorch Clan," Angelus said with a forced smile. Turning on his heel, he murmured to Anya, "If those block-heads don't die in the fight, I'll dust them myself. Can't have trash like that here. Last time they were here, they tried turning a pasture of cows on the outskirts of town."

"Anya!"

Jonathan and Andrew were bounding across the club, flinching when any one demon got too close. Andrew's turtleneck had been stretched out so that it flopped down, exposing a peekaboo glance of his neck skin. Something—or someone—had tousled Jonathan's hair so that it stood almost as tall as his friend's—without the miasma of stinking hair products Andrew used.

For a moment, Anya was relieved. Until she remembered that they weren't actually her friends. Their safety wasn't her problem.

So why was she so happy to see that they were still alive?

"You survived your flyering excursion," she said haughtily. "Congratulations."

"People were really receptive to the idea of fighting the slayer," Jonathan said. "And the free drinks."

Andrew nodded, trying in vain to pull his sagging collar over his neck. "There were some miscommunications in that area," he said. He gave up on righting the turtleneck, simply holding it in place as he spoke closer to Anya's ear. "I know you're still mad about the whole counterfeit thing, and we want to make it up to you. If you'll come outside—"

"I'm not going anywhere, Andrew," she said sharply, pushing him away from her. "I have to make sure that the Marnoxon gem goes back to its rightful place in Arashmaharr. What you and Jonathan do is none of my business. Literally. I'm not being paid to deal with you. If you want to talk to me, you can wait until we're scheduled together at Best Pressed."

Andrew's mouth opened as though he wanted to say something, but nothing came out.

For reasons beyond Anya's comprehension, Angelus took pity on the humans.

"Maybe the two of you should take cover," he said. "Hide until this whole thing is over. Things could get messy."

"No way," Jonathan said. Puffing his chest against the restraining strap of the messenger bag he still carried, he declared, "Demondale is our home! We were born here, and we'll die here if we have to!"

Andrew broke in, index finger raised. "Actually, I was born in Ventura. I moved to Sunnydale when my parents died."

"The slayer attacked us first!" Jonathan continued, stomping his foot for emphasis. The sound was mostly lost in the noise of the club. "She's the reason Warren's dead. She drew first blood! And I have been a coward for too long. Letting other people lead. Letting other people make my decisions. But the slayer has terrorized us for long enough! We owe it to ourselves and our community to see this through to the end. This is our town, not hers. It's up to us to send her packing! Right? Who's with me!"

He punched the sky with his eyes closed. It took him a couple of seconds to notice the lack of response.

"Sure, whatever," Angelus said. "Suit yourselves, blood bags. It's your funeral."

"The important thing is that we get the gem," Anya said, punctuating each word with a slash of her ax. "No one gets a free drink until the Marnoxon gem is secured. The apocalypse isn't thwarted if a piece of Creation ends up in the hands of a baby eater. Or a chaos demon. God only knows what kind of disgusting mucus-covered world they'd wish for."

Pushing his way through the throng, Spike marched toward Angelus, his face stormy.

"Jesus, who invited the Gorch idiots?" he asked.

"We don't need their skills, just their capacity for evil," Angelus said.

"This whole thing feels like a reunion no one asked for," Spike spat. He rolled back his shoulders and straightened the lines of his coat, as though expecting someone to take a picture of him. "It'd better bloody work. We'll never be able to get the ooze residue off the dance floor. Did you see the size of that Glairy bloke?"

"How can you tell it's a male?" Andrew asked, craning his neck for a view of the blob swelling near the stage.

"Female Glairys secrete corrosive ooze," Spike said, scratching the scalded skin on his hands. "If it weren't male, there'd be a hole in the floor from here to hell."

"Like a Xenomorph," Andrew said. "Cool."

"Cool, but not necessarily evil," Angelus said, scanning the room. "We've got plenty of amateur demons waiting on free drinks, but I'm not seeing enough true malevolence to make this plan work."

"The genital renders aren't bad enough for you?" Anya asked, gesturing to the line of miniature demons leaning against the far wall, digging trenches in the floor as they sharpened their scythe-shaped claws against the concrete.

"Amateurs," Angelus said with a sniff. "We need some fresh-outta-hell bastards. Give me a Bezoar or one of the Deathwok Clan. Someone not afraid to really get their hands dirty."

From across the room, Anya caught sight of a familiar pair of horns sticking out above the crowd. Demon-Mike was wearing his Best Pressed uniform, the cotton visor balanced awkwardly between his giant ribbed horns. His mottled red-and-black face split into a bright-eyed grin when he spotted Anya. He rushed toward her and Andrew, beaming.

"Other Mike said you had to rush out earlier, Anyanka," he said. He had a bone-rattlingly deep voice, more resonant than that of any human. Except possibly Barry White. "He didn't say it was to stop the apocalypse."

"Ugh, that is so like him," Anya said with a scoff.

"I'm so glad you told me about this get-together, Andrew," Demon-Mike said, patting the human boy on the back with one of his pot-lid-size hands. Andrew stumbled from the impact. "I wouldn't want to miss helping my community stand up to this slayer bully. And I get to fight alongside my favorite crewmates. What a—"

Abruptly, Demon-Mike's convivial demeanor shifted into stony silence. With his rocklike skin, he pulled off stony particularly well. Anya followed his gaze to Angelus, who was equally expressionless.

"Hello, Beast," Angelus said, taking a step backward so he could speak to Demon-Mike without having to tilt his chin. "Never thought I'd see you in my club."

"Beast?" Anya asked, looking between the two males, perplexed. "Is that a nickname, or are you being mean? I learned today that the two aren't always mutually exclusive." She peered around Demon-Mike's shoulder at Andrew. "Right, moron?"

"Right," Andrew squeaked.

"Hello, Angelus," Demon-Mike said, his tone missing its usual rosiness.

"Stop staring at each other and tell me what the hell is going on!" Anya demanded. There wasn't time to waste on men's cagey feelings. "Or did you forget about our impending doom?"

"The Beast and I have a history," Angelus said stiffly.

The two demons continued to stare at one another. Anya looked to Spike for answers, but he shook his head, as lost as she was.

Demon-Mike cleared his throat. It sounded like pebbles being ground to dust. "I may have asked him to kill some Prussian priestesses for me," he admitted.

Angelus let out a humorless laugh. "May have? You did everything but force my hand!"

"I craved an alliance with you!" Demon-Mike said. One of his huge index fingers shoved into Angelus's shoulder. Angelus stepped to the bigger demon, his hands curled into fists.

"And those Svear girls still kicked the shit out of me!"

"They sent *me* back to hell! And you could have stopped them!"

Demon-Mike bellowed. His mouth snapped shut, and his eyes closed behind calcified lids. Holding up his huge, craggy hands in surrender, he spoke again in a softer tone. "I'm sorry, Angelus. Prussia was a long time ago. I came to Demondale for a new beginning. New century, new leaf."

"I'll say. You're wearing clothes now," Angelus said, pointing out Demon-Mike's Best Pressed T-shirt and khakis. "I like you a lot better when I can't see your stalactites."

"Stalactites—plural?" Anya asked. She and Andrew exchanged a curious look. Anya had never been sure which realm of hell Demon-Mike came from, but she was doubly interested now.

Demon-Mike ignored them. "I look forward to fighting by your side tonight, Angelus. For Demondale. If we live, perhaps you will allow me to show my remorse for how I treated you in the past. Anything you want from Best Pressed Juicery, on me. As many add-ins and boosts as you want."

"That's a good deal," Anya informed Angelus. "A large pressed blood and entrails with vitamin D and protein powder comes out to fifteen-fifty."

"Before tip," Andrew added.

"I'll keep that in mind," Angelus said. "Thanks, Beast. We need strong fighters like you."

"Please"—Demon-Mike pressed his fist over his chest and bowed his horns to the vampire—"call me Mike."

A commotion drew Anya's focus away from the reconciliation. What appeared to be a solo human man was dragging a clear glass podium across the Bronze's stage. Anya thought that the human's black vest was vaguely familiar, but she couldn't place him.

"Who the hell is that?" Angelus asked, face transforming into a furious snarl. "I didn't authorize any entertainment tonight. It'll distract from the battle!"

"Maybe Drusilla requested it," Jonathan piped up. "She was upset about not getting to finish her set list earlier."

"Why would Drusilla want to perform in the middle of a fight against the slayer?" Angelus asked.

"To support the troops?" Andrew guessed.

"Because she's out of her mind?" Anya offered.

"Well, she's right over there," Jonathan said, pointing past a group of mosquito-centaurs.

Tailed by a group of jabbering chaos demons, Willow carried a swooning Drusilla. Enjoying the attention, Drusilla offered a royal wave to the demons she passed.

"Dru?" Spike shouldered past Bro'os the loan shark and his ugly-suited cronies. Not that he needed to bother. Neither Willow nor Drusilla seemed to notice Spike chasing them down until Willow came to a stop in front of Angelus.

"Oh, hello, Spike," Drusilla said vaguely. She motioned to the flaky pink skin on his forehead. "You look a bit peaky. When was the last time you ate someone?"

"*I* look peaky?" he asked with an incredulous laugh. "You know what, Dru? We're finished, you and me. I can't do this anymore. If we live through this, we go our separate ways."

Drusilla cocked her head at him. "Of course, my darling. I foresaw you breaking up with me weeks ago."

Spike buried his fists into his eyes for a moment. "And did you think about telling me?" he asked.

Stroking one of Spike's enviable cheekbones with the back of her hand, she giggled. "No, silly. You told me."

"And did you foresee her?" Spike asked, throwing a dirty look at Willow.

"She took me fully by surprise. Just one of the wonderful things about her." Drusilla rubbed her nose against Willow's temple. Both girls let their eyelids flutter, lost in the snuggle.

"Fine, whatever. Bye, Dru. Good-bye, rebound girl," Spike grumbled. He glared at Angelus. "I'm going to get a drink before the shit hits the fan."

The group watched him sulk through the crowd, pushing his way to the bar and cursing at anyone who came close.

"Why aren't you two guarding the flag?" Jonathan asked Dru and Willow in a loud whisper. His eyes darted around furtively, as though he was worried the slayer would burst into the room just in time to eavesdrop on him.

Willow raised her lack of eyebrows at Andrew and Jonathan. "Wow, you two are still alive? I'm impressed. I thought for sure Angelus would slit your throats the second we left you alone."

"Oh, my daddy Angelus would never," Drusilla said, reaching over to smooth Jonathan's messy hair. "I called dibs on this little monkey the moment I saw him. If anyone gets to eat him, it's me."

Jonathan wrenched out of Dru's lily-white grip. "No one is eating me!"

"He's right," Angelus said. "The first drop of blood to be spilled tonight belongs to that vest-wearing idiot. Nobody sets up in my club without my okay. This isn't an open mic."

"What vest-wearing idiot?" Willow asked, wheeling around to follow Angelus's glare. The heels of Drusilla's boots whirled around in a blur, like a sword swipe. Onstage, the guy in the vest was affixing a microphone to the podium he'd positioned. Willow whipped back to face the group. Andrew and Demon-Mike sprang out of the way of Dru's formidable footwear for a second time.

"Oh, him? That's Jeff," Willow said. When she realized that no one had any idea who she was talking about, she clarified. "The Mayor's secretary. You met him earlier. Big desk, phone headset? I wouldn't mind seeing his blood spilled. Officious little shit."

As she looked back at the man in the vest, the pieces of Anya's memory clicked together. She recalled the small man who sat behind the desk at City Hall, passing out campaign buttons and wielding crucifixes.

Angelus growled, his fangs glinting in the dim light. "What is he doing in my club? And how did he get a podium inside without anyone noticing?"

"I showed them in through the stage door," Drusilla said, batting her long lashes at her vampire-dad.

"And why did you do that, Drusilla?" Angelus asked through gritted fangs.

"Dru had a vision of your plan failing," Willow said.

"The sun rose, and the dust was choking," Drusilla said, giddily bending forward. She seemed to remember that she was supposed to be frail and wilted against Willow's shoulder. "It was horrible."

"So you decided to abandon your post at the temple?" Angelus asked balefully. "You left the Black Flame flag unprotected?"

"Of course not," Willow said. "Protecting the flag was a mission assigned to me by the Mayor, not your troop of Girl Scouts. The goddess agreed to take the flag back to hell for the night."

"She went to visit her lover, Twerfon, in his realm," Drusilla purred.

Anya gasped. "Glory is sleeping with the god of cubicles?" For once, she had something juicy to share at the Vengeance LLC water cooler, and most of her coworkers were dead. What a waste of good gossip.

"We brought you an evil actually powerful enough to lure the slayer here," Willow said, nodding toward the stage again.

Jeff had vacated the spotlight. The stage stood empty for just a moment before there was a burst of noise. Red, white, and blue streamers erupted. A floor-to-ceiling poster unraveled against the back wall, revealing a photograph of an avuncular face with smiling blue eyes framed by the words BRING HELL TO SACRAMENTO: RICHARD WILKINS FOR GOVERNOR OF CALIFORNIA!

With a shiver of excitement, Drusilla kicked off the applause. The rest of the demon-packed club was slow to join. Until the thunder of Demon-Mike's hands cracking together made it seem rude not to take part. The Mayor walked out of the wings, waving at the crowd with both hands.

"He thinks this is a campaign event to thank him for his help today," Willow shouted to the group.

"Did he help today?" Anya asked.

"He's about to."

FOURTEEN
Jonathan

"HELLO, PEOPLE OF DEMONDALE!" the Mayor called into the microphone. "Wow, what a turnout! It is so wonderful to see the true working class of our town brought together like this. Unwinding after a long, hard Tuesday. How about we keep that applause going for our gracious host, Mister Angelus?"

The Mayor shaded his eyes and peered into the crowd. A spotlight above the stage swung over the audience. The Bronze's owner glowered under the illumination, his vamp face on. Conceding to the applause break, Angelus raised a hand of acknowledgment and the spotlight whipped away from him.

Squinting into the rafters, Jonathan noticed that there wasn't anybody operating the follow-spot. It must have been controlled by magic. Whether the magic was the Mayor's or someone else's, Jonathan couldn't tell.

"Demonic small businesses like the Bronze are prospering under the sunshade," the Mayor said. "Now, I'm an optimistic person. I believe that we are entering an era of demonic prosperity. An era in which vampires can walk outside at any time of day. Unshackled by the sun. Empowered by a community of like-minded fiends from all over— above and below. A community of true diversity like I see in this room. Different species, different abilities, different hungers, coexisting. We are living the dream here in this fine city. And I mean to extend this utopia throughout the entirety of the great state of California."

A cheer went up, this one unprompted. The Mayor pretended not to enjoy it, pushing his hands down as he asked the crowd to settle.

"Imagine, not being confined to one town," he said, wagging his thumb. "Traveling to the beautiful wineries of Napa County and drinking blood rich with cabernet sauvignon. Walking through Yosemite National Park, beholding the glory of the falls—which are second only to the ice floes of hell's Pyrlantabuz. I know I'll never forget my first taste of San Francisco sourdough, dipped into a steamy bowl of clam chowder. The year was 1895, and I was seated beside a fellow by the name of Burmut, a thrall demon who came to the surface with nothing but the green slime on his back and a dream. A dream of belonging to this crazy world of ours."

Spike returned from the bar, a pint of blood in one hand and a beer in the other. He chugged the blood first, then washed it down with an equally large swig of beer.

Angelus leaned over to him, murmuring, "I'm proud of you for taking a stand against Dru. Truth be told, I never really liked the two of you together."

"That was never much of a secret, old man," Spike scoffed. "You went all 'not my daughter' the second she brought me home."

"You were a reckless prick, always getting into trouble." Angelus chuckled. "I liked your hair back then, though. You looked better before the bleach."

Spike licked away his blood mustache. "You look better without the ponytail. The slayer did you a favor."

"I'll let that slide. I know you're heartbroken."

"Hey, Angelus," Jonathan whispered. He forced himself to stand his ground and not flinch when the hulking vampire turned toward him. "Are there electrical sockets in here?"

"Of course," Angelus said. "What is this? The Dark Ages?"

"I want to charge my weapon so I can be ready when the time comes," Jonathan said. He didn't want a repeat of the powerlessness he'd faced in the Church of the Eternal Night catacombs. This time, he would be prepared to face the slayer.

Angelus pointed him vaguely in the direction of the far wall. Jonathan considered telling the others where he was going, but quickly realized that Willow and Drusilla would only care so that they could eat him later. Anya and Spike wouldn't care at all. Andrew and his boss Mike seemed genuinely wrapped up in the Mayor's story about his founding of Sunnydale and its original purpose as a harbor for demons.

"I always knew that there would be a day when our secret haven would become an open utopia," the Mayor was saying. "And, having brought that paradise to fruition, I am determined to see its expansion."

Jonathan slipped away. For once, he was grateful for his size. He could creep between demons without being noticed. Most of the assembled beings had no body heat, either on account of their status as walking corpses or reptilian cold-bloodedness. It reminded Jonathan of wending his way through the warehouse full of party-bots. Minus Warren and Andrew shouting in his ears.

In general, it was unusual for him to be anywhere not flanked by Warren and Andrew. The three of them had always operated as a unit, one never seen without the other two. At least, that's how it had been in high school.

Since the sunshade went up and the schools closed, it was only Jonathan who sat at home, waiting for the others to return so they could go buy groceries or see movie matinees. Andrew had his shifts at Best Pressed. Most mornings, he was out of the house before what would have been dawn if the sky weren't one dark stain. Warren used to spend Monday through Friday at his internship, fetching coffee for the Mayor and giving tours of City Hall to other politicians considering partnerships with hell.

Jonathan tried to imagine how Warren would have reacted to being in Demondale's number one vampire club, surrounded by every conceivable type of demon. Would his friend have been able to play it cool? Warren had such a flash-bang temper, as likely to laugh as he was to rage. Jonathan couldn't picture his friend anyplace where he'd be at the absolute bottom of the pecking order. Warren had devoted his entire life to trying to find ways to position himself above everyone else. First, by recruiting weaker friends. Then, by programming the party-bots to obey his every command. And finally, with his obsession with Ascending. Warren would literally have rather changed species than stay weak.

For the first time, Jonathan found himself pitying Warren. Not for his untimely demise, but for the life he'd led. Nineteen years of never being satisfied, never accepting himself as a fragile human nerd. Jonathan himself was just that. Human. Dorky. The absolute bottom of the Demondale food chain.

But, despite everyone's assumptions, he had survived an entire day of running with the big dogs. He'd kept up. And now here he was, at the final battle for existence. Not running away. Or cowering behind someone stronger than him. He was ready to fight.

Or, he would be, once he found a power outlet.

Skirting the crowd, he found his way to the far side of the club. Fingertips skimming the wall, he glided toward the back of the room, farther and farther from the stage that had captured most of the demons' interest. The corners of the club were dim. The dark paint on the walls seemed to eat the light coming from the glass lanterns swinging overhead. Jonathan squinted down the wall into the shadows. He could barely make out the outlet he needed to power up his shrink ray. Fishing the extension cord out of his bag stole his focus. He didn't realize until it was too late that the outlet happened to be right behind a group—*a flock? A swarm?*—of vampires. All of them wore floor-length leather jackets that made them look like extras in *The Matrix*.

Extension cord in hand, he inched toward the outlet. Willing his heart not to beat so loud, he crouched. A breath away from the nearest leather coat. The smell made him flash back to shoe shopping with his mother. Shoving his foot in the Brannock Device like there was going to be any change from the year before. Getting the same pair of black-and-white Vans for school and pinchy patent-leather oxfords for special occasions.

Distracted by the memory, he lost his balance. Right as he plugged the extension cord into the wall, his left arm brushed the hem of the leather jacket.

The vampire whirled around. The tail of his jacket smacked Jonathan's cheeks. It was a white male vamp, his pitch-black hair slicked back into a pompadour, shiny and frozen in place with gel.

"Oi! Mind the jacket, all right?" said the vampire. Face transformed into bumps, he pressed an affronted hand to his chest, right in the open V of his mostly unbuttoned silk shirt. His fingernails were painted black and chipped.

Out of reflex, Jonathan froze in fear. But the fear only lasted for a moment. The longer he stared into the vampire's yellow eyes, the more his fear melted into confusion.

"Oh my God!" he blurted, shooting to his feet. "Tucker!"

Andrew's undead older brother glanced back at his group of equally leather-clad friends. One of them was wearing the *Pulp Fiction* bondage suit. At least, Jonathan assumed it was in reference to *Pulp Fiction*.

"Watch yourself, peasant. The name's Rowan. Rowan the Merciless," Tucker said, in an imitation Cockney accent reminiscent of Dick Van Dyke's in *Mary Poppins*.

Surprise sent Jonathan staggering back a step. "Do you think British people go around calling people peasants? Like at a Renaissance fair?" he asked. "Wait. Rowan? Like Rowan Atkinson? You renamed yourself after *Mr. Bean*?"

"What? No!" Tucker said with a haughty laugh that verged on frenzied. He pulled Jonathan over to the side, whispering in a voice much closer to the one Jonathan remembered. "After *Blackadder*. Come on, man. You're making me look like an idiot here. I've got a new reputation to uphold. How'd you even recognize me?"

Jonathan started to answer and stopped. It was clear from Tucker's new look—the shoe-polish hair dye, the leather duster, the motorcycle boots—that he was trying to be an entirely new man on the other side of the grave. The same way that Willow the vampire didn't wear the same pink fuzzy sweaters as Willow Rosenberg, the nice girl from Temple Beth Torah. A new look seemed as crucial a part of the vampiric process as learning hand-to-hand combat. But Tucker still just looked like Tucker. Under the bumps and fangs and *Lost Boys* ensemble, he had the same sort of overeager puppy-dog face that was genetic to the Wells boys.

Not that Jonathan was going to say *that* to him. One wrong move around a vamp with something to prove would result in his gruesome death. Sort of like when Tucker was alive and would throw over the board when he was losing games of Catan. Only with fangs.

"I knew you for a long time, Tuck—I mean Rowan," he said, his throat tight. "We camped out at Comic-Con together. We saw a sneak peek of *Starship Troopers!*"

Tucker accepted this answer without question. He peered—rudely—over Jonathan's head, scanning the demons closest to them. "Where are the other two loser musketeers? Did Warren doctor you guys some red wristbands so you could score free drinks after we kill this slayer thing?"

"Um, no. Warren's dead," Jonathan said. He held up his blue wristband. "And my ID still says that I'm nineteen. I'm here to help take down the slayer. Andrew and I already faced her twice and she was—"

"Did Andrew get the bite?" Tucker said, suddenly more interested. "I told him to volunteer for the blood farm program at the Church of the Eternal Night. Being undead is the only way to survive in this town anymore. You heard what the Mayor was saying about expanding the sunshade all over California? There's not gonna be anyplace for blood bags like you. Sorry." He stopped himself with a haughty chuckle. "Blood bags is what we vampires call the living."

"I got it from context clues, thanks," Jonathan said. Tucker had been a pedantic jerk before he'd been sired—always correcting the Trio's Klingon pronunciation and second-guessing their academic decathlon team. Jonathan didn't know why he'd thought that death could have made Tucker less egotistical. "And the Church of the Eternal Night burned down today. Just a few hours ago. Andrew and I were there. So was the slayer. She killed the Master—"

"She what?" Tucker snarled. "No, no way. If something had happened to my sire, I'd *know*. I'd feel it! You're lying to me, you shit heel." Two hands shot out, gripping Jonathan by the shoulders and lifting him off the ground. Terrified, Jonathan couldn't even flail. His legs went slack. He thought about Ethan Rayne at the Metaphysical Boutique. The resignation in his face when Angelus's fangs had struck him. How no one could even think to help him as Angelus drained him in three quick gulps. The way his body had crumpled to the ground, a bloodless husk.

"You were always jealous of me," Tucker hissed, blowing cold air in Jonathan's face. One of his fangs loomed dangerously close to Jonathan's eye. "You and my brother were always looking for ways to outdo me, to scrub the records I'd set and make me look like a fool. But now I am stronger than you could ever dream of. I have found a freedom that you will never know."

Jonathan's fingers scrabbled for the flap of the messenger bag still hanging at his hip. He knew at any second, Tucker could strike him dead and no one would ever question it. He'd be cremated along with all the other poor human schmucks who overstayed their welcome under the sunshade. His parents, blending in among the conservatives of Orange County, would never know what had happened to him.

"And once I'm through with you, I'll take care of Andrew myself," Tucker continued, a ghoulish Joker smile elongating his mouth. "If he's too chickenshit to die, then I'll have to kill him myself. If someone hasn't already beaten me to it. That'll teach him not to listen to me."

Jonathan's hand found the plastic hilt at his side. Tucker's mouth swung down. Fangs fought to bite through turtleneck. Jonathan could feel the tips of Tucker's teeth scraping against his neck, caught behind the cotton dam of his collar. The moment of faltering was all the time Jonathan needed. Shaking the shrink ray out of the messenger bag, he pressed the barrel of the gun into Tucker's ribs.

"Stay the hell away from Andrew," he breathed.

And pulled the trigger.

Blue electricity radiographed Tucker's skeleton. Shock softened his face out of its vampire lines. The last things Jonathan saw were brown eyes nearly identical to Andrew's. Bracing for the explosion of goo and bones that had followed the last time he'd discharged the shrink ray, Jonathan screwed his face up. The hands holding him disappeared.

As he crashed to the floor, Jonathan's knees took the brunt of the fall. Hiding his chin in his shoulder, he begged himself not to cry. Not out of pain. Not out of relief.

Something bumped into one of his undoubtedly bruised legs. Sucking in a breath, he cracked open his eyelids, expecting to see one of Tucker's friends kicking him while he was down. Instead, he found something too big to be a bug and too skinny to be a rat. Smaller than a standard-size action figure. Larger than a Dungeons

& Dragons miniature. It raised tiny white fists into the air, shouting in a high-pitched voice presumably only dogs could properly hear.

Jonathan glanced over at the shrink ray and back. It had actually worked. Tucker was shrunk to a twelfth of his normal size. Jonathan shoved him into the inside pocket of his messenger bag.

"It's a good thing you don't need to breathe," Jonathan told Tiny Tucker, clipping the bag closed again.

Getting to his feet, Jonathan was taken aback by the sudden silence in the room. The Mayor had paused his speech. And all the demons had turned to look at the far wall.

To look at Jonathan.

A vampire unmistakably dressed like a cowboy pointed across the club. "Kill the slayer!" he shouted. "Drink his blood!"

"He killed Rowan the Merciless!" shouted the vampire in the bondage suit.

"No! I didn't!" Jonathan said, scrambling to pick up the shrink ray again. He cradled it to his chest, feeling the pulsing warmth of the recently discharged barrel. "He's alive! I mean, still undead! Just scaled down!"

"Let's kill him! I want my free drinks!" shouted another voice in the crowd.

"Hold on just a moment," the Mayor said. "I'll let you all get to your slaughter soiree. But first, I want to remind you all that any creature with proof of residence in another dimension is now eligible for voter registration. Just come on down to City Hall and ask my buddy Jeff here for an application. Make sure that you register before the primary, otherwise—"

Onstage, the air started to ripple. The giant campaign poster pulsated, as though something huge was trying to birth its way out of the Mayor's photograph. A portal ruptured the air, spitting out the familiar blond-haired form of the slayer. With a Willy Wonka somersault, she leaped to her feet, the Dowsing Rod of Vem clutched in one hand. The Marnoxon gem blazed green light, the brightest thing in the room.

"Wow," the slayer said, glancing out at the crowd. "You guys threw me a party?"

FIFTEEN
Jonathan

"*THAT'S* THE SLAYER!" Jonathan said, pointing toward the stage. He looked back at Tucker's vampire friends imploringly. "See how much more confident she is than me? You only get quips like that from the Chosen One."

The Mayor pushed himself back from the podium, his mouth continuing to smile even as his visage began to transform. Dark veins crept over his face and hands. His hair and eyes turned jet black and he began to levitate, casting a gigantic shadow onto the stage below.

"You shouldn't have come here, Slayer," he said, the microphone beneath him still amplifying his genial attitude.

"Because I'm interrupting your magic show?" the slayer asked, gazing up at him.

"Because I'm going to have to kill you in front of all these nice folks." The Mayor chuckled. "And then they won't hear a word I have to say about tax reform."

Thrusting his hands forward, the Mayor sent a hadouken of energy at the slayer. The invisible blast caught the girl in the gut, lifting her off her feet and sending her flying. Her head cracked against the campaign poster.

"Well"—the Mayor laughed, floating back down to his podium—"that was an exciting diversion, wasn't it?"

The crowd of demons cheered even louder than before. From the side of the stage, Jeff even got some of them chanting, "Wilkins for Governor! Wilkins for Governor!"

Until the slayer hoisted herself back to her feet and threw the hair out of her face. When she knocked the dowsing rod against the stage twice, another portal opened. She jumped in. A second later, swirling purple light emerged on the second floor.

"Someone get the gosh darn stone away from her!" the Mayor roared, pointing at the new portal.

"And give it to me!" Anya shouted, buried somewhere in the middle of the floor. "That gem is the property of Vengeance LLC!"

The slayer flipped over the railing of the balcony and jumped down. Landing with a thud on the bar top, she picked up a stray flyer and clucked her tongue.

"A drink promotion?" she scoffed. "In my day, demons wanted to fight me to prove something about the nature of good and evil. This makes the whole thing feel so cheap." A demon tried to grab her ankle, and she smashed down on its hand with the end of the dowsing rod. The demon fell back screeching, and the slayer looked around the room. "Okay, now can someone punch the jukebox or something? Because otherwise, the only thing anyone is going to hear is screams and dust until I find your off switch."

All hell broke loose.

Jonathan scoured the room for the blond point of Andrew's hair, but he could only see the masses of demons surging toward the bar. They climbed over one another as they tried to get to the slayer. Someone honored the Chosen One's request—Drusilla and the Dollies music pumped out of the speakers again. Jonathan couldn't make out many of the lyrics over the noise in the club, but he was pretty sure that the chorus included Drusilla screaming the word *anachronism*.

On top of the bar, the slayer used the Dowsing Rod of Vem to beat back a crush of yellow-and-orange-striped demons. The loose-skinned bartender took a paring knife to the shoulder. A terrifying mass of wailing tentacles burst out from beneath the flaps on his face. The slayer banged the tentacles away with the metal lid of the bar's ice bin until the demon fell back. A citrus zester plunged into the eye of an encroaching chaos demon. As he fell, his antlers cut down most of the demons in a three-foot radius of him. The slayer laughed and portaled away again.

A scuffle on the balcony made Jonathan look up. The green glow reflected on the ceiling told him exactly what was up there. The staircase became a deluge of bodies—those charging toward the slayer and those already in retreat.

As demons began raining down from the balcony, Jonathan hurried to wind as much of the shrink ray's extension cord around his arm as he could. Mentally, he cursed Warren for talking him out of making a wearable battery for the shrink ray. If he lived through the day, he was definitely going to go back to work on a backpack battery. It would have been way easier to lug around than this giant orange cord.

A shadow fell over Jonathan's face. He heard a shout increasing in volume before he clocked the vampire body about to drop on his head.

A hand pulled him out of the way. The vampire smashed to the floor exactly where Jonathan had been standing. Looking back at his rescuer, he was shocked to see the salt-and-pepper hair of the now-sole proprietor of the Metaphysical Boutique.

"Mister Ripper!" he cried.

"For God's sake, kid," the warlock said with a grimace. "It's Ripper. Just Ripper. You make me sound like a senior citizen with all that *Mister* bollocks. I'm only in my forties, you know."

So were Jonathan's parents, but that didn't seem like welcome information. Instead, he heaved the last of the extension cord's slack over his shoulder, one eye on the ceiling in case of additional falling bodies.

"What are you doing here?" he asked Ripper. "I thought you hated us. Not all of us. Angelus, for sure. And Spike, probably. Maybe Anya too. I guess—no, yeah, I do mean all of us."

"You are an inconvenient lot," Ripper agreed. "But this town is my home as much as it is yours. I'm here to protect it." He held up a horn with a twisted mouthpiece that Jonathan immediately recognized. "And if I ruin that twat Angelus's precious club while I'm at it, then all the better. Someone ought to get their money's worth out of this thing."

Ripper pressed the Ram's Horn horn to his mouth. His cheeks puffed with a huge inhalation and then deflated in a piercing shriek that sounded unlike any instrument Jonathan had ever heard. Ripper and Jonathan stood frozen for a moment, the only two people inert in the chaos.

From concrete floor to corrugated iron roof, the Bronze shuddered. In a room full of Californians, everyone knew the feeling of an impending earthquake. Some demons shunted themselves into doorframes or dove beneath the bar tables. But most just rode out the wave, hoping that today wasn't the day they broke off into the ocean.

Beneath the Mayor, the stage cracked apart. The podium and Jeff the secretary fell into the newly opened abyss. The Mayor levitated to save himself, although not even floating above the wreckage could save him from the inescapable stink that emanated from the fissure and filled the club. Sulfur and manure and wet fur.

And then out poured a stampede of horrible, hellish animals. Sheep, goats, cows, llamas, pigs, and—

"Bunnies!"

Anya's bloodcurdling scream drew Jonathan's focus. He could see her, climbing up on a pool table to escape a throng of giant rabbits that tore into anything that dared get close enough to them. The loan shark Bro'os let out an agonized scream as one of the bunnies chomped a hunk out of his leg.

Leaving Ripper cackling with delight, Jonathan ran as fast as he could, praying that he had enough extension cord to stay plugged into the wall. He dove out of the way of a midnight-blue cow with a shrieking bone bat impaled on its horns. A screaming alpaca unhinged its jaw so that it dropped open to its waist like a PEZ dispenser ready for loading.

The berserk bunnies loped and growled below the pool table Anya stood on, seemingly scenting her fear. The curved ax she'd been carrying before the battle lay on the floor, out of her reach. The bunnies tromped on it, unbothered by the blade. Twitching blue-gray muzzles were stained with blood of all colors. Jonathan tried not to think about the cartoon rabbits of his childhood nightmares. Not even when the bunnies bared their sharp buckteeth at him.

"Anya, get back!" he called, aiming the shrink ray low to the ground at the vicious fluffies.

Anya skittered backward on the pool table, her head striking a low-hanging pendant light. "Jonathan, don't die for me!" she shouted back, imploringly clasping her hands. "Your tiny body won't be enough to satiate them! Save yourself!"

"No!" Jonathan protested. "I owe you this!"

Anya dropped her hands with a shrug. "Yeah, okay, that's true."

A spray of blue lightning indiscriminately blasted and shrank the hell bunnies. Blue blood and black bones shot into the air, splattering against the bottom of the balcony platform and hailing down onto the nearby demons. The kickback from the shrink ray jolted Jonathan's arm, sending the beam of electricity in a dangerous arc. A passing Fyarl demon, still outfitted in his waiter's apron, jittered under the blast, his insides lit up in the moment before he shrank down to the size of a ballpoint pen.

"The Fyarls are on our side!" Anya screamed. "Your antidemon prejudice is not a good look right now!"

"It was an accident!" Jonathan said. Panicked, he dropped the shrink ray and lifted the small-scale waiter. He set him on the pool table in front of Anya.

"Shoot him again!" she demanded. "He can't earn a living wage that size!"

"Taking two blasts from the shrink ray will kill him!" Jonathan protested. "Or send him to the Quantum Zone. We're not really sure what happens if the gun manages to double-shrink someone. Mostly, it just explodes them on the second try."

Anya crouched and prodded the Fyarl's teensy horns with the pad of her finger.

"Then how do you unshrink someone?" she asked.

Jonathan shifted uncomfortably on his feet. "The embiggen ray is still being blueprinted. But all the bunnies are gone!"

"That's what truly matters," Anya said. She jumped down off the pool table and retrieved her ax, holding it close to her chest. Bending to put her face near the miniaturized Fyarl, she promised, "We'll come back for you when the technology is available! Unless we all die in here!"

The air on the dance floor started to shimmer, portending the opening of another portal. Demons crammed together to be the first in line to take on the slayer. When the portal appeared, it was empty. The crowd in front of it went still, none of them willing to set foot in the shimmering unknown.

"There's no need to push," the Mayor said, bobbing in the air and wagging a finger at the demons below. "We're all on the same team here. A kill for one of us is a kill for all of us."

The slayer popped out, grinning. An extension cord trailed behind her into the open portal. In her hands was a blue plastic blaster, smaller than Jonathan's shrink ray, but with a much larger fan attachment in the back.

The 1.0 freeze ray. The slayer must have stolen it out of the Trio's garage.

"Hey! That's ours!" Andrew yelled, popping up beside Jonathan. His Eagle Scout knife was in his hand, the stubby blade locked into place. He shook it at the slayer. "That hasn't been field-tested, missy!"

The slayer didn't hear him. She fired the freeze ray straight up, zapping the levitating Mayor. Instantly, he was encased in ice, like Han Solo frozen in see-through Carbonite. Encumbered and powerless, he fell through the air. The Glairy demon oozed across the floor in a hurry, stretching himself to catch the frozen Mayor in the safety of his gelatinous body.

The slayer continued to spray down all the demons near the edge of her portal: A Wellex demon. Half a dozen of the adorable pop-eyed genital renders. One of the loose goats from hell. A vampire wearing a brocade jacket and a cravat. All icebound.

"Oh my God, it works," Andrew said, incredulous.

"Too well," Jonathan said. Bile burned the back of his throat.

Jonathan had invented the freeze ray for self-defense. It was supposed to be something he could use to stop an attacker and run away. Like pepper spray with less risk from a change in the wind. Seeing it take down demons just trying to protect Demondale was awful.

"Cool your jets," the slayer said with a maniacal laugh as she continued to cold-shoot anyone who got too close. "Chill out!"

"Oh no," Andrew said, gripping Jonathan's arm. "She's discovered Mister Freeze puns! Someone has to stop her before she asks what killed the dinosaurs!"

"She's going to overload the gun," Jonathan said. Panic was making it hard for him to swallow. He didn't know what would happen to the freeze ray under pressure. It had a hellish ice crystal at its heart, the magic of which Jonathan only vaguely understood. It could burst.

Or implode. Or misfire. "It's specced for short bursts, not a continual blast!"

The slayer realized this a moment too late. The freeze ray's stream turned to thick white ice in midair. The blue plastic of the barrel iced over from tip to handle, covering the slayer's hand. Undeterred, she used the icicle sticking out of the muzzle to stab a Juggernaut demon in the eye. The demon cried out and punched the icicle, dislodging it from the barrel but not from his eye.

Grabbing the frozen shaft of the freeze ray, and with it the slayer's hand, Demon-Mike from Best Pressed plucked her out of the safety of her portal. The portal instantly closed, cutting the freeze ray's extension cord in half. Braced against Mike's arm, the girl backflipped, her heel striking him hard in the open mouth. Rearing back, he let go of her. The slayer bashed him in the face with the green gem, sending his manager's visor flying across the club. The end of the dowsing rod stabbed into the chest of the cowboy vampire in the black Stetson, dusting him.

The second cowboy vampire howled in despair. He reached out and caught the end of the dowsing rod before the slayer could stab him as well. The two of them tussled for control of the staff, the slayer holding on to the green gem with one hand and the crook of her ice-covered arm. Planting a foot on the vampire cowboy's hip, the slayer gave the gem one last mighty heave and staggered backward. The gem in her arms. The staff with the vampire.

"She can't control it without the staff," Anya said. "If she portals away, there won't be anything to bring her back here!"

"That's great!" Andrew said. "It means she can't end the world!"

"It means no more vengeance demons, ever," Anya said, breathing hard. "If she leaves with that gem, none of us will ever get our powers back!"

Anya took off running. Jonathan called after her, but the vengeance demon didn't look back. Hair streaming behind her, she dove into the crowd, inexpertly lashing out with her ax to get the demons out of her way. Seeing her coming, Angelus took a knee and ducked his head. Anya ran up his spine and jumped off, screaming "For Arashmaharr!" as she tackled the slayer to the ground. The force knocked the ax out of her hand, but she grabbed hold of the Marnoxon gem.

A churning purple portal opened beneath them and sucked them through the dance floor. Taking Anya and the slayer...who knew where?

THE SLAYER

THEY FALL STRAIGHT down, skydiving through endless space.

Without the dowsing rod to guide it, the green gem opens portals indiscriminately. The Slayer grips the top half of the gem until her knuckles ache. The girl who tackled her—Anya, one of the humans from the showdown at the Church of the Eternal Night—holds on to the bottom and watches the worlds blow by. How she manages to look at the fuzzy shapes whipping around them without getting carsick is beyond the Slayer. Her own insides revolt every time a new portal opens under them and they start falling anew.

"Where, exactly, did you want to go?" Anya asks over the noise of rushing air. Her voice is unnervingly calm, if a bit acerbic.

The Slayer spits a hunk of her own hair out of her mouth. "What do you mean?"

"To open the portal," Anya asks. How can she sound bored while they're spinning between realities? "You must have thought something at the gem to make it go."

The Slayer struggles to think back. She recalls the anxiety of being in the middle of an endless horde of demons, one hand fused to the freeze ray. The anxiety turning to horror when the gem popped off the top of the guiding staff. The dread when she saw the ax-wielding girl diving for her. The shock and pain of being grappled to the floor.

"I just thought *get me out of here*," she admits, chagrined. "The wizard-staff thingy was doing all the navigation before. I guess I panicked. Stupid, I know."

She can imagine the epic scolding she'd get from her Watcher if she told him she panicked during a fight. Giles would say something like, *A Chosen One choosing fear has chosen death.* But Anya doesn't seem to be as judgy as Giles.

"An entire club was trying to kill you. Seems like a good time to panic," Anya says. She ducks her face into her shoulder and scratches her nose against the sleeve of her T-shirt. "Would you mind if we stopped plummeting through nothingness now? I really need to sneeze, but I don't want to end up flying off into some loser dimension. I refuse to live in a world without shrimp."

"I'd love to stop falling," the Slayer says. "But I'm not controlling—"

Her stomach bungees into her esophagus as the world skids to a stop. Her feet land in grass. She staggers to stand still, woozier than the rainy day at Disneyland when she rode the teacups three times in a row. Only when she reaches out to steady herself against the rough bark of a palm tree does she realize where they've landed.

Arched open hallways. White stone steps leading to a second story under a red tile roof. The burble of a fountain, flouting the Southern California water-conservation drought rules. Overhead, cotton clouds stretch across the brilliant cornflower-blue sky. The Sunnydale High quad is empty. Peaceful. Tranquil.

"This is my school," she says, staring around. "I used to eat lunch right there."

She starts to gesture to her favorite bench but stops when she realizes that would mean releasing the green stone. Both she and Anya have their hands on it. Letting go of it now feels like a mistake.

"Is this . . ." The Slayer gulps. "Is this *my* Sunnydale?"

"How should I know?" Anya asks, tucking her chin back. "I picked a dimension at random. I don't know your exact coordinates of origin. I just thought you'd like somewhere sunny." She pauses to waggle her eyebrows. "Get it? Sunny? Sunnydale?"

"I got it," the Slayer says. She doesn't know what to make of this girl. Someone who protected the Black Flame flag and chased her into a portal can't be trustworthy. But then why hasn't Anya tried to attack her since they landed?

"Shall we sit down?" Anya offers, motioning toward the short tile fountain at the center of the quad. She wrinkles her nose and looks down at the Slayer's frozen right hand. "We can give you a chance to thaw out."

Is that the other girl's plan? Sit in the sun until the Slayer has the use of both of her hands again? Is she one of those people obsessed with a fair fight? People like that never understand that no fight is fair when the Chosen One is given the training and strength to take on much bigger foes. Anya must have seen the Slayer fight all the demons at the Bronze. It's not like she hasn't had fair warning as to the Slayer's fortitude.

They sit on the edge of the fountain, the green gem held between them. The Slayer doesn't know if she's ever been this close to the quad's water feature. It's the designated lunch spot of the popular kids. The rich and beautiful get the picturesque background. The rest fight for benches and low concrete walls. It's ridiculous to miss the politics of high school, but she does. She misses exchanging insults with Cordelia Chase and hiding from Principal Snyder and studying for classes she'll never use after graduation. The rules of high school make more sense than the affairs of hell.

"How did you get the gem to stop dropping us through portals?" she asks.

Anya continues to stare up at the sky, the sun streaming down onto her face. In the light, her hair is reddish blond, warm against her pale skin. "I'm a magic user. You aren't." She squints over at the Slayer. "Kinda dumb to steal a Creation gem without the power to control it."

"I didn't have a choice. I was stuck in literal Hell on Earth." The Slayer tugs the gem slightly closer to her. "Also known as your home."

Anya sighs. "Look, Slayer—"

"Buffy."

Anya frowns. "Is that slang in your dimension? Or an expletive?"

"It's my name. Buffy."

"No! Really?"

"Really, truly. Buffy Anne Summers. Says it on my birth certificate and everything."

"And that's what you want people to call you? Because I recently found out that sometimes nicknames are mean."

The Slayer shrugs. She's spent her entire life litigating her name with strangers. Her first-grade teacher was convinced that her *real* name had to be Elizabeth and only referred to her as such for the entire year. Although, looking back, the Slayer is pretty sure Mrs. Sullivan was a demon. The kind fueled by the tears of children. Why else would she read *Watership Down* to a roomful of six-year-olds? All those rabbit murders haunted her for life. She had to be the only person alive creeped out by bunnies.

"What I don't understand—other than why you wouldn't just go by your middle name. That's socially acceptable, isn't it? Anne the vampire slayer?" At the Slayer's blank stare, Anya lets the name thing go and continues, "Okay, then, what I *really* don't understand is why you went all the way to Arashmaharr. Another dimension, part actual, literal hell. Not Demondale's diet version. And you slaughtered all the vengeance demons who could have wished you back home."

"They wouldn't have!" the Slayer says. Anger makes her breath quicken. "Vengeance demons are liars."

"Vengeance demon is a title, not a species. That's like saying all ice-cream truck drivers are clowns."

"What? That doesn't make any sense—"

All at once the Slayer remembers that Anya screamed something before tackling her. *For Arashmaharr.*

The Slayer jerks back, fighting to keep hold of the gem while her other hand swings the freeze ray into Anya's face. The extension cord is torn in half, but she hopes Anya won't notice.

"You're one of them," she growls.

"Part-time," Anya readily admits. "I also work at a juice bar. But yes, vengeance has been my job for a long time. And even though you killed basically all of my coworkers, I don't want to fight you, Buffy Summers." Reaching out, Anya nudges the freeze ray away from her nose. "Especially not with a broken toy gun frozen to your hand. I just want to understand. Something brought you to Demondale. And something made you decide to go on an apocalypse spree. So, what was it? Bad breakup? A warlock's trick?"

"I've never met a warlock," the Slayer says.

"That's what they *want* you to think," Anya says.

The fountain burbles behind them. Unlike in the Slayer's home world, there are no empty chip bags floating in it. Painted fish swim on the tiles at the bottom. After a moment of hesitation, the Slayer plunges her frozen hand in, drowning the freeze ray. The water is so warm against the frost encasing her hand, she's surprised it doesn't steam. The splintering ice creaks and pops.

"My parents are divorced," she tells Anya.

Anya nods sagely. "And it was your fault that their marriage failed."

"What? No!" the Slayer exclaims. "I'm trying to set the scene for what happened, okay? Because my parents are divorced—due to problems that had *nothing* to do with me, thank you very much—I have to spend summers in Los Angeles with my dad. And while I was gone, this girl started hanging around with my friends. She's our age and just moved to town, so Willow and Xander sort of adopted her. The same way they'd adopted me when I was the new kid. I think Xander had a bit of a crush on her. Which was kind of nice, actually, because it distracted him from his crush on me and that is just *never* going to happen. Even if I weren't sort of with Angel—"

Anya groans, eyes rolling back in her head. "This recitation of your tangled love life is intolerable. You are all hormonal children who want to have sex with each other. I get it."

The Slayer shifts her weight, uncomfortable. She doesn't know anyone who speaks so directly. It's not unpleasant, just odd. "So, when the school year started, Xander and Willow bring the new girl to everything. And I mean *everything*. Not only study sessions and the movies or whatever. Like, the secret stuff. Researching baddies in the library and my Slayer training sessions with my Watcher and patrols of the cemetery for the newly risen. This girl is just *there*. Things were pretty quiet in town, so it wasn't terrible. But this girl kept asking when the real monsters are going to come out. And if I'm bored. All kinds of things that I should have realized were . . . well, not normal questions. I thought she was trying to alpha me. Prove she was even tougher than the Slayer. It happens when people find out about the whole Chosen One thing." Mortification creeps across her skin as she remembers what happened next, how easily she was outwitted. "One night, she's like, 'Don't you think you're strong enough to take down more than one monster a week?' And I stupidly said yes. I told her that I wished I could get all of the monsters of Sunnydale to come out and fight, just to be done with it instead of waiting for them to attack me one at a time."

"Tricking you into wishing for something you didn't want." Anya laughs. "A classic maneuver. What was the name this girl was going by?"

"Hallie."

"Pretty blue eyes? Curly hair?" Batting her lashes, Anya mimes spirals sprouting from her head.

The Slayer nods, inwardly cringing as she pictures Hallie the new girl sitting in this very quad. Flicking her perfect frizz-free curls over her shoulder. Sharing Willow's sliced apples. Laughing at Xander's terrible jokes. Supplanting the Slayer in her own life as the normal girl she could never be.

"Halfrek," Anya says with a chagrined half smile. "She's crafty, that one. She got the Vengeance LLC Employee of the Quarter-Millennium twice! The higher-ups adore her." Sobering, she considers the Slayer through narrowed eyes. "Does that mean she wasn't in Arashmaharr when you murdered everyone there?"

"I didn't kill anyone who wasn't a demon!" she protests, offended by the accusation.

"You say that like it's a good thing," Anya says. Her lips press together into a tight line. "The girl who cursed you was human, by the way. With a demon's job. Like me."

Abashed, the Slayer looks back at her hand in the fountain, crunching through the thin layer of remaining ice. As the freeze ray bobs to the surface, she wipes her damp fingers on the side of her pants. "I assume Hallie is still in my home dimension. Hanging out with my friends. Replacing me."

"Being trapped in a human teenager's life would be torment for an all-powerful demon," Anya says with a shudder. "Playing along for a month or two as part of a scheme might be fun. But staying there? It'd be like living at a Halloween party. Vengeance demons haven't had access to magic since you've been running around with the source of our power. Halfrek is stranded, unable to portal away. As miserable as you are."

"I doubt that." The Slayer snorts. "I've been away from home for so long and seen so much evil. Demondale made me question everything I thought I knew. I mean, who blocks out the actual sun? How is anyone supposed to maintain a healthy amount of vitamin D? Much less a decent tan." She sticks her arms out and examines her pale skin. "I'm so pasty, I can barely recognize myself."

"Sure, but on the bright side, there's almost no melanoma under the sunshade. I'm definitely getting a sunburn here," Anya says. She fans herself with her free hand, squinting in the sunlight. "Just because it isn't *your* perfect world doesn't mean it isn't somebody's."

The Slayer chews on the inside of her cheek, considering this. "When I found out that there were other places like Demondale, I had to stop them. I mean, I was chosen to stop them. It's my job to stand against the forces of darkness. And knowing there were endless evil realities? It was like finding out that all of my nightmares were true.

"I stole and bullied and tortured anyone—demon or human—that I thought could give me information about how to end an entire dimension. And I did it. Over and over and over again. I'd portal in, find the Black Flame flag, and destroy it." Her insides clench like her intestines are strangling each other. *Guilt,* she thinks. *This feeling is guilt.* She can't make herself look at Anya as she continues, "They were bad places. Evil, obviously. Colonies of hell. But I don't know that any of them were worse than Demondale."

"It's not like you gave any of them a chance to be better or worse," Anya says. "Did you take a tour of a new world before you smashed up its flag? Try to make new friends? Ask around to see if the demons had any community care programs?"

The Slayer shakes her head, her sinuses burning in shame.

"The problem is your assumption that all evil is the same kind of

283

evil," Anya says. "And maybe that works in your reality. But then you start portal-jumping and trying to be the Chosen One in dimensions that didn't choose you. Maybe they didn't need a Slayer, but could have used a great babysitter or barista or kickboxing instructor. Did you ever consider adapting?"

"I—" The Slayer looks away, gazing into the burbling fountain, where the broken freeze ray bobs in the water. "I didn't. You're right. I didn't try anything but slaying. Slaying is the only thing I know how to do. I mean, one day you're a cheerleader at the top of the pyramid, and the next you're having psychic dreams and being called to save the world. It isn't easy having a destiny. No one else seems to. It's just me, standing alone, wielding the strength and skill or whatever. The prophecy doesn't say anything about gray areas where demons and vampires can be friendly. Or neutral! It says that if I see a vampire, I slay it, no questions asked. Except..." The Slayer's breath hitches as her chest tightens. "At home, I have help. I have friends and a Watcher who make sure that I'm doing the right thing. They weren't chosen, but they care. And they try so hard. And they see things without slayer-vision, so they're better at seeing the parts that aren't all good or bad. It's so much harder to do my job without them. Because, really, I do my job *for* them. I want to protect *our* Sunnydale. Where it's actually sunny. Where it never rains, but the grass stays green without magic. Where my mom is." A tear slips down the Slayer's cheek as she looks Anya in the eye. Swallowing hard, she says, "If I could just go back to when Hallie asked me if I thought I could take on more monsters, I'd tell her that one monster a week is a gift. It means there's time to research and train and have a normal life. There's space to be more than just the Slayer. I wish I'd known that before. Then maybe I wouldn't have gotten stuck in Demondale."

The last thing Buffy sees is the vengeance demon's face transformed. Red veiny wrinkles. No eyebrows. A heart-shaped open sore on her nose. A smile of perfectly human teeth twinkling in the sunlight.

"Wish granted."

The world burns white. And Buffy is transported.

Home.

SIXTEEN
Anya

ANYA HAD PRESUMED she was going to return to a raucous victory party. Instead, when she portaled onto the overseer's balcony, the Bronze looked like a makeshift field hospital. Wounded demons were being tended to on top of pool tables. The Mayor remained encased in ice from the waist down, but a group of vampires was doing its best to melt him with a dozen saltshakers. The remaining cowboy vampire had herded the infernal livestock, blocking them inside the broken remains of the stage.

Standing behind the bar, Angelus stopped pouring drafts of blood and beer and looked up abruptly, as though sensing Anya. Maybe he could feel the ripple of the closing portal. Or smell her pithy blood. Either way, his eyes locked on to hers. She lifted the Marnoxon gem.

A smile appeared on his handsome face, smoothing the vampire bumps on his forehead and turning his eyes into dark pools.

Holding the gem over her head, she announced to the club at large, "The slayer is gone. For good."

Applause thundered through the club. Triumphant hoots and hollers reverberated through Anya's chest as she descended the stairs. She spotted Willow kissing Drusilla so passionately that it bent the clairvoyant girl backward, the tips of her hair brushing the bloodstained floor. The Mayor wiped his damp eyes with the back of his hand.

Demons of all sorts clapped Anya on the back and ruffled her hair as she made her way toward the bar to claim her free drink. One of the Miquot Clan offered their stool to her. She slid into it gratefully, pleased to once again be off her aching feet.

"What'll it be for the lady triumphant?" Angelus grinned at her. "Anything for the slayer killer."

"A pint of Black Frost, please," she said. The Marnoxon gem glowed cheerfully against the bar, casting green shadows onto the high-gloss wood. "What are you doing pulling pints, Angelus? Don't you have employees to do that for you?"

"Ah, Clem's getting a stab wound healed up by the warlock Ripper." He nodded down the bar to Spike, who was hunched over a mostly empty pint of something brown. "And my old buddy Spike decided to quit. Says he won't work in the same place as his ex."

"It's time for me to be my own man," Spike slurred, flailing a hand in Angelus's general direction. "A hundred years I gave her. Nearly a hundred and twenty! Our love was older than sliced bread. Coca-Cola. The Ferris wheel. A great endeavor has ended tonight!" Liquid sloshed over his hand as he slammed his pint onto the bar, proclaiming, "'Love or hate, to me alike, it deals eternal woe.'"

"He would have kept pouring drinks and quoting Milton, if I'd let him," Angelus confided to Anya as he set her beer in front of her. "But he was overserving everyone even before he got drunk. I'm already hemorrhaging money on this free-drinks thing. Way too many demons survived." He set his elbows down on the bar, leaning close enough that she could feel the wintry chill of his skin. "All so you could go and take down the slayer yourself."

"Everyone else made an excellent distraction," she said, blushing at the praise. She took a noisy slurp of beer foam. "And I couldn't have done it with your assist. Well, I could have, but it wouldn't have looked as cool."

"It did look very cool. Good thing I went to get the knife out of my boot, huh?" he asked with a wink.

She shoved his shoulder. "You were not! You were helping me."

"Maybe, maybe not," he said with a chuckle.

"Anya!"

Spinning around on her stool, she found Andrew and Jonathan running toward her with red eyes and dripping noses. Anya couldn't tell if they were having an emotional outburst or an allergic reaction to the livestock.

"Oh my God!" Andrew said, throwing his arms around her and sobbing into her shoulder. "We thought you were dead!"

Jonathan flung himself on her other side. "You were gone for so long!"

Anya held her hands in the air, unsure where to put them or how to escape. She couldn't remember the last time she had been hugged by one person, much less two. This could very well be her first encounter with the thing people called a "group hug." She wasn't sure she liked it. It had much less of a clear ending than a one-on-one embrace.

"Spike might have pretended not to see their wristbands," Angelus murmured behind her.

"Oh, you're drunk!" she said to the human boys with dawning comprehension. "I thought you were being emotional."

"We're both!" Jonathan sniffled. "I think."

Carefully sliding out of the hug, Anya stood behind her stool, just in case of additional outbursts.

"Anya," Andrew said, catching the mucus dripping off the end of his nose in his sleeve. "I was so scared that the slayer killed you before we got a chance to tell you that you were right."

"Thank you, I know." She paused, waiting for an elaboration that wasn't forthcoming. "About what?"

"About us," Andrew said. "Becoming friends."

Tears leaked down Jonathan's face, pooling under his chin and dripping into his turtleneck. "We were wrong to betray your trust before. With the—the—*you know.*"

"Money made of lies, yes," Anya said, unimpressed.

"We're really sorry," Andrew said.

"So sorry!" Jonathan wept.

"And we wanted to make it up to you, so I . . ." Fishing in his pockets, Andrew retrieved a small wad of folded bills and extended it to her.

Anya examined the money in her hands. Some of the dollars were crinkled and old-looking. Others crisp and still reeking of fresh ink and cotton. "How am I supposed to trust that this isn't another trick? That you didn't just run home and print off more fakes?"

"We didn't, we swear!" Jonathan said.

"I borrowed money from Mike when we were out flyering downtown," Andrew explained. "Human-Mike. It's not everything we owe you, but it's a start—"

"Human-Mike has less money?" she asked. Her heart swelled and her throat constricted, forcing her to take a breath before she could continue. "You impaired his ability to procure goods?"

"And services," Jonathan said.

Anya was shocked to find her vision blurring with tears. "This is the sweetest thing anyone has ever done for me," she choked, fanning the moisture in her eyes with the money wad. "You know how much I hate Human-Mike."

She threw her arms out, pulling the boys back into a group hug. A shorter one.

Wiping her tears away, Anya stepped back, tucking Human-Mike's money into her pocket. There would be plenty of time to ponder the ways that being short a couple of hundred dollars would impact the human Best Pressed manager's ability to maneuver in the world. But now there was work to do. Not juicery work.

It was time to set everything right.

She reached for her talisman necklace and called out, "Blessed be the name of D'Hoffryn!"

Preceded by his typical cannonade of lightning, D'Hoffryn arrived, his blue head carried in the arms of Vengeance LLC's receptionist. With a tremendous effort, Anya held back a groan of annoyance. The receptionist—a blond girl who had been human until very recently—had somehow survived the slayer's attack on the office, living to spend another day complaining that Arashmaharr didn't have a Starbucks. Even though it did have a Dunkin' Donuts, which, as far as Anya was concerned, was just as good.

"Oh, wow, Anyanka," the receptionist said, her heavy Valley girl accent pulling all of her words up at the end so that they all sounded like individual questions. "You got the gem *and* a new hair color? I'm living for that strawberry blond. Earth totally agrees with you, girl."

D'Hoffryn raised his hairless brow at Anya, silently prompting her to respond.

Anya didn't know why the Lower Being had such a soft spot for this girl, who had been mortal less than a year ago. It wasn't like the receptionist was even authorized to perform actual vengeance yet. She'd been hired just to answer incoming phone calls and emails, but then she'd cut one person's brake lines and was suddenly declared a "real up-and-comer," the darling of the office.

Through clenched teeth, Anya forced herself to say, "Thank you, Harmony."

"I am quite pleased to see that you have retrieved the Marnoxon gem for us, Anyanka," D'Hoffryn said. He rocked his head back and forth in Harmony's grasp; his stubby horns tapped her arm. "Harmony, up!" he commanded.

"Oops, sorry!" Harmony scrambled toward the bar. She simpered at Angelus, nodding at the bar next to the Marnoxon gem. "Could you be a sweetie and wipe this down for us?"

Eyes blazing, Angelus slapped a bar towel down and pushed it in a lazy circle before slopping it back into the bucket whence it came. Harmony, immune to all forms of hostility, cheerily thanked him and set D'Hoffryn's head on the damp wood.

"You may relinquish the Marnoxon to Harmony," D'Hoffryn told

Anya. Face twitching, he blew out of the corner of his mouth to stop Harmony from arranging his beard hair over the edge of the bar top. "She has been authorized to transport the gem back to its rightful place."

Unzipping a large quilted purse emblazoned with huge interlocked Cs, Harmony beamed. "I know how important the gem is to the mission statement. Especially since it was taken and no one could, like, defend themselves or go poof or anything. I'll take extra-super-good care of it. I swear on Chanel." She tittered and held the open purse out to Anya. "Don't you just love that show? I'm such a Carrie."

"I never have any idea what you're saying, Harmony," Anya said, reluctantly placing the gem at the bottom of the purse.

"Ha-ha, that's exactly what Miranda would say," Harmony said. With a flourish, she zipped the bag closed and slid the purse straps onto her shoulder.

Anya turned back to D'Hoffryn, wondering how his pointed ears didn't bleed all day listening to Harmony's inanities.

"Sir," she said stiffly. "I was able to grant the slayer's Wish to return her to her own timeline. Will the other dimensions she destroyed be able to be salvaged?"

"Unfortunately not," D'Hoffryn said. "Direct contact between Creation and Corruption creates nullity. We cannot invert that nothingness with more Creation. The majority of the worlds that existed beneath Hell's Own Herald this morning have now never been. We can only be grateful that ours was not among those erased."

"Right, of course, I'm delighted to get to keep existing," Anya said. "But does that mean all the damage done to Demondale today can't be undone? Are the Powers That Be going to time-lock us?"

"What's time-locking?" Jonathan asked in a whisper.

"I don't know," Andrew answered. "It sounds timey-wimey."

"Oh my gosh! The Trio of Losers!" Harmony squealed. She peered around Anya's shoulder. "Am I right? No. There's only two of you. I could have sworn I went to school with three nerds who looked just like you."

"You did," Jonathan said, shaking like a Chihuahua.

Andrew nodded. "I asked you to prom. You said no."

"Oh, I'm sorry," Harmony said. Her lower lip jutted out in an exaggerated pout. "That must have been really hard for you."

"Um, not really. I'm gay, so..."

"No way!" She slapped the air between them. "If I'd known that, I totally would have gone with you! I just didn't want to get pawed by some random creep."

D'Hoffryn coughed, silencing the human children. "It appears, from my inability to create a new body for myself, that we have been time-locked. I believe that the Powers That Be intend for us to remember what has come to pass here today."

"Either that or they really don't you want you to have hands, huh, Hoffy?" Harmony tittered. "Maybe you should have listened to me when I said you needed to take care of your nails."

"Maybe," D'Hoffryn intoned mirthlessly.

"So, I can't resurrect the third nerd in this trio?" Anya asked. Human-Mike's money was heavy in her pocket. Without a Wish to grant, she had no reason to charge Andrew and Jonathan.

D'Hoffryn's shaking head squeaked against the bar. "Any injury sustained in the battle against the slayer will stand." The Lower Being's mustache drooped. "Our fallen comrades in Arashmaharr will stay dead. And my head will remain apart from my body."

"Sorry, I don't want to interrupt," Andrew said, peeking out from behind Anya again. "But, Mister D'Hoffryn, would the, uh, Powers let you have a robotic body? Because we have, like, a ton of those sitting in a warehouse in Docktown. They're all female, though."

"Hmm. That could be acceptable," D'Hoffryn said. His lips pursed in thought. "Tell me, what kind of modifications could be made to this robotic form? My original form contained the ability to shoot lightning from my hands."

"Do you want the lightning to do anything special? Like freeze or shrink things?" Jonathan asked.

"No," D'Hoffryn said. "Just blow shit up."

Andrew grinned. "Oh, we can totally make the robot do that."

While the nerd boys talked technical specifics with D'Hoffryn, Anya returned to her beer. She was relieved to find that it was still cold. Angelus came out from behind the bar, a pint of blood in his hand. He sat down next to her.

"Seemed like a good time to take a break," he said.

"It's been a long day," Anya agreed. "Even for Demondale."

The two of them watched as Spike slid down the bar, cropping up at Harmony's side.

"Hello, pet," Spike said, his accent twice as thick as usual. "The name's Spike. What's yours?"

"Harmony Kendall," the receptionist said, extending her hand.

"Didn't she *just* say that she didn't want to be pawed by a random creep?" Angelus asked Anya.

"Harm. What a beautiful name," Spike said, sweeping his lips over Harmony's knuckles. "Lovely to meet you."

"Those cheekbones can get away with anything," Anya told Angelus as Spike ushered Harmony down to his empty end of the bar.

The blond girl giggled, asking if Spike was from "the real England," as though there were another option. Spike responded in so much British slang that Anya couldn't make out the words. She laughed into her drink. "He is going to regret that."

"Oh yeah," Angelus said. He took a swig from his pint and licked his bloodstained lips. "But it will be a new regret. That'll be good for him."

Anya considered her own regrets. She had very few. There were some Wishes she wouldn't grant twice—mostly the ones where she had created dimensions that were entirely too niche. Like the world without paper clips. Or the worlds created to save *one* TV show from cancellation. She also wasn't fond of any reality where animals could talk. Too noisy. If something could talk to you, it shouldn't also feel entitled to poop in the street.

But otherwise, Anya felt free. Today she had thwarted the end of her reality and saved her one chance at a full human life. Well, a half-human, half-demon life. Looking around the Bronze, she felt a similar warmth to the one Angelus's whiskey had given her. This was her community. Beside her: her friends. With all this solidarity, she almost understood why the slayer had lost her mind when she was disconnected from her own world. It was so much to live for. So much more than Anya had ever expected when she'd put in for her sabbatical.

She set down her beer and faced Angelus. "I know your mother-lover died earlier today."

His brows drew together. "Sire. Darla was my sire."

"Whatever. I'm not good with jargon." She folded her hands in her lap, willing her fingers to stop twiddling. "But would you want to make some new regrets? With me?" Afraid she was talking too fast, she clarified: "I'm talking about a date. Or sex. Or both. I'm told they can go together."

He chuckled, setting his pint on the bar. "I'd like that. Aud."

"I'd like that, too. Liam."

Silence built up between the two of them until they both shuddered and recoiled.

"Ugh, no," Anya said, unsettled.

"No way," Angelus agreed.

"Human names are not sexy." She stuck out her tongue and scraped off the residue of her mistake with her fingertips. "Let's stick with 'Anya' and 'Angelus.'"

The vampire bobbed his head in agreement. "Definitely."

Once Anya had regained her composure, she found Angelus watching her intently. She worried that he was going to change his mind. Now that he knew about the Aud human behind the demon Anyanka, maybe it was all he'd ever see.

One of his hands skimmed the side of her neck, coming to rest beneath her ear. Her breath caught. Heat rushed up her neck and cheeks.

"No biting," she reminded him.

His mouth curled into a smile against hers.

EPILOGUE
Jonathan

SWEEPING THE LIGHTER flame back and forth, Jonathan sanitized the sharp point of his Richard Wilkins campaign pin before he pricked his index finger. Hissing at the pain, he squeezed two drops of blood into the feeding cup.

After realizing how woozy regular blood loss made them, Jonathan and Andrew had agreed to take turns feeding the miniature Tucker. Then, after realizing how creepy it was to have a tiny vampire suck on their fingers, they had ordered a dollhouse tea set for Tuck to use.

Jonathan slid the tiny teacup over to Tucker. Tucker, as he always did, raised an itty-bitty middle finger in reply.

"I've told you," Jonathan said. "If you want people to believe that you're really British, you're going to have to do the V sign. It means 'up yours.'"

Tucker ignored him, seating himself at Janine Melnitz's desk to enjoy his lunch. The *Ghostbusters* firehouse had once been a pristine, unboxed display piece in the lair's living room. It had even survived the wreckage of the slayer fight that had dented the decorative Hylian Shield and destroyed the sliding glass door. But, a week into living together, Tucker and the miniaturized Fyarl waiter drew a line down the center of the Hoth playset they'd been sharing. Without a pen small enough for them, the line had been made out of the Fyarl's quick-hardening mucus, ruining the plastic floor of the ice planet. It had been the last straw for finicky Tucker, who spent an hour jabbering into Andrew's ear about needing his own space.

Andrew, thrilled to have his brother back in his life, no matter how small or surly, set the firehouse and Hoth at opposing ends of the kitchen table, with the USS *Enterprise*'s bridge and a Hot Wheels garage between them for entertainment. It was a growing neighborhood. Andrew had plans to expand into a Bowser castle and a Batcave. If he could win the eBay auctions for them.

"You two play nice," Jonathan warned Tucker and the Fyarl. "I'll be back later. And Andrew might even have a new expansion for you. He said he was going to stop into the toy store on his lunch break."

Jonathan prayed that he'd be able to crack the embiggening ray before the entire kitchen became a tiny amusement park for its two unwilling occupants. The longer they kept Tucker, the more likely it was that he'd try to attack them the second he was full size again. As it was, he'd exhausted himself trying to bite Jonathan's hand the first week.

Jonathan rushed out to the driveway. While Anya couldn't resurrect Warren without disrupting the time stream, she had granted Jonathan and Andrew's Wish to have the keys to their cargo van. The Death Star that Andrew had airbrushed onto the side shone in the porchlight.

Buckling himself into the driver's seat, Jonathan craned around to check the carpeted back seat. Boxes of Warren's things were stacked against the walls, awaiting donation. The Urn of Fernda sat nested inside a pile of long-collared button-down shirts, its screaming stopper peering over the top of the box.

"Glory insisted on a prettier vessel," the Mayor had told Jonathan and Andrew when he returned the urn to them. Along with another box of chocolates to thank them for their service to the community. "But, hey, you got a little prize in the bottom there! Like a toy in your cereal box, how about that?"

Warren's Raphael Ninja Turtle action figure had been lying at the bottom of the urn. The black flame hadn't burned it, but it had imbued it with an inverse sort of radiance. A dark aura surrounded it, pulsating with evil.

Jonathan and Andrew agreed to bury the toy in place of Warren's corpse. There wasn't room enough to bury a full body in the cemetery these days anyway. And who knew what kind of unholy powers would be contained within an action figure that had been steeped in hellfire? What if it passed its nastiness on to the miniaturized Tucker and the Fyarl? Or the other toys in the house? Jonathan had never been quite convinced that *Toy Story* wasn't a documentary. He wasn't going to risk all of his Jedi figurines being poisoned by the literal Dark Side.

Besides, Warren would have liked that his final resting place included a hum of disquieting power. It was a very Warren vibe.

Driving the van with his window down, Jonathan called out a greeting to the Glairy demon undulating in the grass at the park, slowly absorbing a screeching possum into himself. Two jogging chaos demons, their antlers streaming goo behind them, encouraged Jonathan to honk as he drove by and cheered as the van trumpeted "The Imperial March."

Demondale had become a friendlier place since the Battle at the Bronze. Those who had fought together smiled at each other instead of growling. Andrew said that Best Pressed was drawing lines full of demons offering to pay for one another's juices to show their gratitude. Tips had apparently tripled.

Jonathan did wonder if some of the increase in tips had something to do with Anya quitting. How she had convinced Ripper to hire her full-time, Jonathan would never know. She had even persuaded the warlock to change the name of the store.

Parking the van out front, Jonathan peered up at the new awning. It was just as gray as the last one, but it now read RIPPER'S MAGIC SHOP.

Anya scuttled out of the shop, shouting something over her shoulder before the door abruptly swung shut in her face—possibly by magic.

"Ripper and I are having a minor disagreement about paint," Anya announced as she jumped into the passenger seat, tucking a bulging plastic bag between her feet.

"He wants to keep the inside gray?" Jonathan asked.

"Only because it conceals his disgusting cigarette smoke staining the walls. Filthy warlock," Anya said. "But we'd be getting a lot more foot traffic if the interior was something you could see from the street. Imagine walking past and seeing a glimpse of perfect sky blue through the windows. Where else are you going to see sky blue in Demondale?"

"Glory's temple?" Jonathan guessed.

Anya scoffed, finally remembering to pull on her seat belt. "Then you'd have to deal with Glory," she said. With a jolt, she tapped the dashboard clock. "Let's go! We're going to be late."

Jonathan hid a smile as he put the van into gear. They had this same conversation whenever they carpooled together. Anya had yet to fully wrap her mind around how long it took to drive somewhere. Demondale was only ten square miles. Driving might not have been as instant as taking a magic portal, but it was certainly faster than walking or riding a horse.

"If we were late," Jonathan said as the Magic Shop shrank in the rearview mirror, "couldn't I just wish that we weren't?"

Anya fiddled with the radio dial, scanning past the news, the Spanish language channel, and the hits of the seventies, eighties, and today for the grainy classical station. She was old-fashioned that way. "You could. But then I could send you to a Wishverse where it's always a quarter to six."

"Who would pick you up from work?" Jonathan asked over the screech of violins. "Does your boyfriend have a car?"

"Ugh, no." She fell back against the seat with a groan. "Vampires love walking everywhere. For people without heartbeats, they certainly get their cardio in."

Jonathan was pretty sure that neither Anya nor Angelus knew *how* to drive, but he didn't mention it. He didn't really want to share the road with a thousand-year-old chaotic-neutral demon or her vainglorious lover. Immortals had less to be scared of behind the wheel. It had taken almost an entire month for Jonathan to convince Anya to wear a seat belt. She'd only given in when he'd explained how expensive it would be to have to replace the windshield if she flew through it.

Less than ten minutes later, the van cruised to a stop in the Bronze's parking lot. The barnyard stink of hay and excrement hung in the air like a fog. Despite Angelus's best efforts to block the sale, one of the cowboy vampires had purchased the warehouse next to the Bronze. Gorch Family Farms housed what was left of the hellish livestock that had been unleashed during the slayer's last stand. Its walls trembled with the shrieks and squeals of the infernal beasts.

"They're not the best neighbors," Anya told Jonathan as they hurried away from the smell. "But you can't argue with the product. Goat cheese just tastes better when it's hell-fresh."

"I'll take your word for it."

Jonathan flashed his ID to the bouncer, who barely looked at it before giving him a sharp-toothed grin.

"Human child!" the one-eyed Juggernaut demon exclaimed, all the veins in his neckless body jumping. Jonathan's hand and ID disappeared into the demon's massive hands as the Juggernaut gave him a welcoming shake. "I love this guy," he told Anya as Jonathan's teeth rattled in his skull. "Without him, I would not have experienced the fight of the century."

"The century is almost over," Anya told the demon flatly.

His snakelike smile only widened. "Imagine the bloodshed the new millennium will bring."

Flexing his hand to check that none of his bones had crumbled, Jonathan followed Anya into the club. On the rebuilt stage, Sweet, the new lounge-demon, was crooning. His oversize zoot suit was the same livid red as his skin. Unlike Drusilla and the Dollies, Sweet had no backing band. The jazzy piano and trumpet underscoring him played from nowhere—or everywhere—leaving him room to effortlessly tap-dance. The crowd on the dance floor swooned and sighed with his every movement.

Clem was pouring drinks behind the bar. Spotting Jonathan and Anya, the loose-skinned demon flapped a sharp-nailed hand in greeting,

"The usual?" he called.

"Two!" Anya called back. At Jonathan's questioning look, she sniffed. "What? It's happy hour. I'm not going to waste a deal."

"Do you even pay for your own drinks here?" Angelus asked, materializing out of the crowd. A leather sleeve glided around Anya's waist, drawing her close enough for him to kiss. "I heard you're sleeping with the owner."

"I've seen your books, lover, you really can't afford to comp all of my drinks," Anya said, booping the vampire's nose with her index finger. "You know how much Black Frost it takes to get me drunk."

"You could start drinking something with an alcohol content higher than a loaf of bread," Angelus said.

Anya blinked at him in confusion. "But hard liquor isn't part of the happy hour special."

"Jonathan!"

Grateful for the distraction, Jonathan spun around, spotting Andrew, Willow, and Drusilla seated at one of the tall bar tables. Squeezing between two passing Fyarl waiters and a knot of reptilian demons throwing darts at a caricature of the slayer, Jonathan made his way over.

A deep-fried "flower" sat in the middle of the table, alongside two pints of blood and a chocolate milkshake. A binder full of real estate flyers lay open between Andrew and Willow. When Jonathan climbed onto one of the empty stools, Drusilla was busy signing autographs for a cluster of fans, most of them vampires in Church of the Eternal Night T-shirts. It hadn't taken long for the church to rebuild. It had reopened under the leadership of some vampire named Kakistos, whom the Mayor swore was a real dyed-in-the-wool villain.

"Dude!" Andrew said. He tore off a deep-fried petal and held it out to Jonathan. "You have to try some of this bloomin' onion. Spike was not overselling it when he said it was the perfect food."

The deep-fried onion was, in fact, delicious. Softer than an onion ring with all the salty crunchiness of a Funyun. And even better with the tangy, spicy dipping sauce.

"Wow," Jonathan said, licking the salt from his fingers. "That's even better than the fish and chips we got last week!"

"The food here is far better than it needs to be," Anya said, claiming the last empty stool at the table. She reached for an onion petal and popped it into her mouth. "Who goes to a bar for quality food?"

"I have a reputation to uphold here," Angelus rumbled, standing behind Anya with his chin resting on top of her head. He had acclimated to his short hair, wearing it styled in a point. Not dissimilar to Andrew's.

"I boosted your reputation when I made this place famous for being the site of the slayer's defeat," Anya said, making a cross-eyed attempt to look up at Angelus. "You could serve flash-frozen garbage at a premium and the club would get the same amount of business."

"But then where would we get bloomin' onions?" Andrew asked.

"Maybe the chain restaurant the Bronze stole the recipe from?" Willow said with a mischievous flick of her eyebrows. It was odd to see the vampire girl using her human face. Even in her leather catsuit, she looked so much more like the Willow Rosenberg that Jonathan had grown up with. Until one of Drusilla's admirers got too close and Willow's face instantly transformed into a yellow-eyed snarl. "Leave now," she warned.

The fans instantly scattered. Drusilla swung around on her stool, lashes fluttering, her face the picture of innocence.

"They were only being friendly, my ginger darling," Dru said. She drew Willow's hand to her face and rubbed her cheek against it.

"We have friends right here," Willow said, her face smoothing once again.

"Oh!" Drusilla looked dreamily around the table. "So we do. My daddy Angelus and the undrinkable ones. Hello, friends. Have you seen the new home our Andrew has found us?"

For the last couple of weeks, Willow had been paying Andrew to run errands and help with her and Drusilla's ongoing house hunt. Andrew insisted he wasn't a true Renfield since he didn't have to eat bugs or stay on call for the vampires' every whim. It was just more research as to whether or not he actually wanted to be turned. Ever since he'd found out that Spike and Angelus had both been turned in their mid-twenties, Andrew was more open to the idea of getting older before receiving the bite.

"You've settled on a place, then?" Angelus asked.

"We think so," Andrew said. "It's been hard to find somewhere that combines Dru's love of haunted properties and Willow's hatred of anything colonial."

"With room for my dollies," Drusilla added.

"But this place looks promising." Andrew spun the real estate binder around so that everyone could see it. The flyer showed a slim

Victorian house near downtown. The inside seemed nice enough, with cozy rooms and multiple fireplaces and built-in bookcases that could surely house at least some of Drusilla's dolls. There was also, inexplicably, a set of prison cells in the basement. Complete with rusted metal bars and seatless toilets.

"Miss Edith will have to listen to me now," Drusilla said, humming with excitement. "Otherwise it's off to a 'pestilential prison with a lifelong lock.'"

"We still need to check it for termites," Willow said. "The Mayor said that he could try to clear them for us, but the spell requires multiple sacrifices to an Old One and bribing the housing inspector, which seems like more trouble than it's worth."

"Speaking of the Mayor," Anya said, helping herself to more of the bloomin' onion. "Jonathan, have you accepted his job offer yet?"

Jonathan choked on a mouthful of onion.

After giving back the empty urn, the Mayor had told Jonathan and Andrew that they had proven to be assets to Demondale. There would always be jobs open for them at City Hall. Especially since so many of his employees had died in skirmishes with the slayer. Andrew had declined immediately, citing his job at Best Pressed and pseudo-Renfielding for Willow and Drusilla. Jonathan had asked to sleep on it.

That was three weeks ago.

"You told me not to take it!" Jonathan said defensively.

"Anya!" Willow chastised.

"That was when I thought he was offering some unpaid garbage internship," Anya said, wagging an onion petal at Jonathan. Horseradish sauce dribbled onto the table. "Free labor is for fools. If you're going to get paid, you should definitely do it. Haven't you always wanted to be a powerful human like the people in your picture books?"

"Comic books," Andrew corrected, a hand covering his full mouth.

"Whatever," Anya said. Her unwavering focus remained leveled at Jonathan, even as a Fyarl arrived with her beers and two Shirley Temples. "What's more powerful than politics?"

Jonathan drew the Shirley Temples to his chest and fished the cherries out of both. "I don't know. It feels weird to take a job that should be Warren's when I, you know."

"Murdered him with your shrink ray?" Angelus offered.

Jonathan winced. "Yeah, that."

"You're going to have to let that go," Anya said. "It was an accident. And you tried to bring him back to life. The Powers That Be stopped you. Things happen."

"Besides," Andrew said, "if Warren's Ascension had actually worked, he wouldn't have kept working at City Hall. Would the Scorpion King answer emails and fetch coffee? I don't think so."

"The Mayor isn't going to wait on you forever," Willow said. "He already has a new Jeff, who is as obnoxious as the old Jeff. And somehow also named Jeff. You'll need to hurry if you want to get into City Hall before the election. Who knows who will replace the Mayor when he becomes governor?"

Even after a month of having more friends than just Andrew and Warren, Jonathan found that this much attention made his insides squirm. Five people all staring at him—half of them apex predators who could snap his neck as easily as give advice—activated his inner coward. He daydreamed about creating an invisibility ray so that he could disappear just long enough for everyone to lose interest.

But he'd miss them if they all gave up on him.

"I'll consider saying yes," he promised, taking a long pull from his drink. The bubbles tickled his nose. "I guess it would be nice to spend all day with full-size people instead of refereeing fights between Tucker and the Fyarl."

"The Fyarl's name is Gershman," Angelus said, helping himself to a bite of the bloomin' onion.

Andrew hushed him. "If we name him, it will be that much harder to give him back once we figure out how to make him full size."

"*If* we figure out how to make him full size," Jonathan muttered into his straw. So far the embiggening technology was twice as effective at exploding as the shrink ray. In that it embiggened its targets zero percent of the time but exploded them with 100-percent accuracy.

A stool screamed against the ground the next table over, drawing the group's attention. Even with the collar of his leather jacket flipped up, the bleached-blond hairdo was instantly recognizable. And not at all unexpected.

"Hello, Spike," Drusilla said, wiggling her fingers at her ex. A wrinkle appeared between her eyebrows as she spotted his companion. "And Spike's blond friend."

"It's Harmony," the girl said, loud and slow. With some difficulty due to her skintight pink minidress and the blended drink in her hand, she hoisted herself onto a stool. "We've met before, Drusilla."

"And we will meet again," Dru said wearily.

Spike chugged a pint so briskly that Jonathan couldn't even tell whether it had been beer or blood. Belching, he said, "Fancy meeting you lot here."

"It's Tuesday," Jonathan said. "We're always here on Tuesday."

"And you always run into us," Willow said pointedly.

Spike pretended not to hear her. He knocked on his table, making the pineapple slice on the lip of Harmony's drink wobble. "Me and Harm are out celebrating. My girl got a promotion at work today."

"It's true," Harmony tittered. "You are looking at a full-fledged vengeance demon!" She squealed, sticking out the green gem pendant she wore around her neck. It looked nearly identical to Anya's, although the silver—a thousand years newer—was untarnished. "Couldn't you just die?"

"It would be difficult. And yet I am tempted," Anya said, her face pinched in disgust. Angelus rubbed a consoling hand down her arm. Anya grasped his fingers like a lifeline. "I also have work news," she announced.

"Are you coming back to Arashmaharr?" Harmony asked, setting a scandalized hand to her chest. "Hoffy didn't tell me anything about it."

Anya's nostrils flared. "No, my other job. My earth job."

From the plastic bag she'd brought with her from the Magic Shop, she withdrew a gleaming purple conch shell, bigger than both of Jonathan's hands put together. It had a tightly coiled spire and wide-open mouth revealing polychromatic insides. Even in the Bronze's dim overhead lights, it had a pulsating inner glow. Jonathan thought he could hear the shell faintly singing, calling to him. Serenading him with a melody it felt like he had always known and never remembered. Drusilla shrilly trilled along with it.

"What's that?" Andrew asked, transfixed.

"It's the sister piece to the Ram's Horn horn," Anya said. "This is the Conch Clarion. We just got it in at the Magic Shop. It summons all the monsters from the waters of hell. Octopus-spiders. Krakens. Globsters. God only knows if it gives them the ability to breathe on land or if it just drops evil seafood on people."

"Like in *Watchmen* when Ozymandias teleports the squid," Jonathan whispered. Stroking the side of the conch, he shivered. It was smooth and cold, as though still underwater.

"Hey, watch it!"

Onstage, Sweet's music cut out. The red-faced demon was being shoved out of the way by a dark-haired girl in a tight black tank top and low-slung jeans. Beside her, a bespectacled man in a suit and tie had a crossbow leveled at the crowd.

"Nobody move," the man in the suit said in a quavering British accent.

Andrew snorted. "Get a load of this nerd."

"What are the chances that another Brit would move here?" Jonathan asked. "It's like every new person we meet is from the same island."

The dark-haired girl grabbed the microphone. Licking her red-painted lips, she bared her teeth in a bloodthirsty smile.

"Got wind there's a girl in this town, causing trouble. Calling herself the slayer." She paused, giving a raspy, self-assured laugh. "Which is funny, because that's my job."

"The slayer popped back to her own timeline a month ago," Sweet said. He held up his red palms as the nerd in the suit aimed his crossbow at him. "Who are you?"

"I'm Faith, the vampire slayer," the girl purred into the microphone. Jonathan felt the hair on the back of his neck stand on end.

The man in the suit leaned over, awkwardly squinting against the stage lights. "And I'm Wesley Wyndam-Pryce, her Watcher."

Questioning murmurs swept through the room. Could there be more than one slayer? Would lightning really strike the same club twice? All around the Bronze, demons reached for pool cues and darts that could be used as makeshift weapons. Every vampire face shifted to bumps and fangs. Anya's and Harmony's necklaces glowed phosphorescent green as their skin shriveled into vengeance-demon veininess. Andrew flicked open Tucker's Eagle Scout knife.

"Screw it," Jonathan said. Jumping off his stool, he scooped up the Conch Clarion and let loose a battle cry. "For Demondale!"

Bringing the shell to his mouth, he blew. Unleashing hell.

Again.

ACKNOWLEDGMENTS

This book would not have been possible without the work of so many people. All my thanks to:

The women in the *BtVS* writers room, who inspired me to become a writer. Marti Noxon, Jane Espenson, Rebecca Rand Kirshner, Tracey Forbes, Ashley Gable, Dana Reston, Elin Hampton, Thania St. John. The show owes its legacy to you.

Britt Rubiano and Cassidy Leyendecker, for making my Wish come true and geeking out with me through the process.

Laura Zats, my agent who I found many years ago by typing "Buffy the Vampire Slayer" and "literary agent" into the same Google search. Thanks for being my Giles ever since.

Dad, who introduced me to the Buffyverse.

Erin and Liz, who have very different opinions on the bunnies of *Watership Down*.

The cast members of *Buffy the Vampire Slayer*, but most especially Charisma Carpenter, Michelle Trachtenberg, Sarah Michelle Gellar, Alyson Hannigan, Eliza Dushku, Emma Caulfield, Amber Benson, Julie Benz, Juliet Landau, Kristine Sutherland, Clare Kramer, and Mercedes McNab.